JEWELS

Juniper Creek Book 1

Tracey Retallack

ISBN 978-1-0689424-1-9

This is a work of fiction. All characters, organizations, and events portrayed in this novel are either products of the author's imagination or are used in the author's imaginary land described within this book. In summary, it's fiction, people, enjoy.

Cover Design: Tracey Retallack

For Marc

Dear Mrs. Hughes

Enjoy the Story!

xo [illegible]

3-23-25

Jewels

Seven years ago ...

A DOZEN ROLEX WATCHES STOOD at attention in the display case. They were distinguished, elegant, and proof that anyone who wore one had 'made it'.

Each one cost more than Jul had spent on his old truck.

"Lovely selection, isn't it?"

Jul stepped away from the saleslady. "It is."

"Which one can I show you?"

He couldn't even afford to be standing there. "None at this time, but thank you. I'm waiting for my ..." Jul gestured towards Cara with his thumb.

The woman leaned closer. "Are you two shopping for rings?"

"No." He shook his head. "She's looking at bracelets today." Jul made a mental note to guide her away from the diamonds whenever she finally decided they could leave.

He glanced at his watch—which was not a Rolex—and confirmed that the store didn't close for another hour and a half. They could be there all night.

It already felt like they had been.

He paced back to Cara's side. She was too busy staring in the mirror to notice him. She held her wrist close to her cheek. It wasn't clear if she was looking at the bracelet or herself.

Jul crossed his arms and rocked his weight front and back. An unwanted noise popped from his mouth when his lips flinched.

"Look at that."

Cara was staring at him when he opened his eyes. He was in trouble. "Sorry, I didn't mean to—"

She cut him off. "The sparkle. Isn't this one gorgeous?"

Fake lights bounced off of the gold links the same way as the others she'd tried that night. He opened his mouth, but she spoke before he had to invent something positive to say.

"I love it. Can I get it?" She put on a smile and twined her free hand around his arm.

It was a mystery how he'd come to be in charge of her spending. "It's up to you, I guess."

The salesman took her to the cash register and packed the empty box in a bag. "Here you are, miss," he said.

"Thank you so very much." She winked at the man, then started for the door.

Jul followed. "Cara?"

A guard almost as tall as he was blocked his path to the exit. "Allow me to show you to the cash register, sir. That bracelet hasn't been paid for."

She'd done it again.

So had he.

He calculated the balance of his savings account while he settled her bill. It declined directly in proportion to the number of times they went out together. "Thanks for your help."

The salesman gave him a look.

He seriously thought Jul was trying to leave without paying? "I thought she'd already bought it."

The man pressed his lips together and nodded once. "Have a good evening, sir."

Jul departed quickly, willing the sweat on his brow to disappear.

Cara waited near a bench with her phone on her ear. She ended the call before he reached her. "People are going to think we're getting serious with all these gifts you've lavished on me."

Like he had a choice. "You didn't impress the security guard when you walked out."

"Looks like you made it work without getting arrested. You're a big boy." Cara pinched him through the argyle sweater she'd made him wear. "See? I told you the gym would help."

"Cara—"

She put a finger on his lips. "I have a surprise for you this weekend."

Buying another trinket had been surprising enough to carry him for a few days. "And what would that be?"

"Let's go to the car and I'll tell you all about it." She passed him the keys to her father's Porsche. "I've got us dinner reservations at Orthio Elafi, best Greek in the city. We have to celebrate our three-month anniversary. You didn't forget, did you?"

It hadn't even been on his radar. "People celebrate three months?"

"You should. You said it yourself—this is the longest relationship you've ever had."

As he popped open the microscopic trunk, Jul took a moment to reflect on his life's romantic history. It took all of ten seconds. Their relationship certainly wasn't what he imagined a romance to be. It certainly wasn't like anything he'd seen his friends live through.

He compressed himself into the driver's seat. "Where are we going?"

"Where *are* we going, Julian?"

He tried to remember the name of the restaurant. "I didn't know there'd be a quiz."

"I, for one, think we should go a little further." She flicked her tongue across her top lip. "It's time to get closer."

His pulse accelerated. "You know how I feel about this. And I still live at home so—"

"That's the surprise. I'm stealing you away for the weekend." She threw her arms around him.

"But we're going to Dar and Stel's for Thanksgiving dinner."

"I've already told you I'm not having dinner in a cramped garage. They'll understand when you cancel." She stroked his palm. "Think about it—me, you, king suite, river view ... not that we'll be staring out the window much." Her kisses stung his neck. "It's time, babe. Time we levelled up."

He leaned back as far as he could, which wasn't very far, but enough to get her attention.

"Julian?" The shoulder of her top slipped down, revealing her lace bra.

He tried not to look. "Your strap thing fell. Everything's showing."

A devilish smile spread over her lips. Cara dipped her fingertips into the edge of her blouse, floating them to her cleavage, then back up again. "There's more where this came from, babe. I've been shopping."

He didn't even know that was possible without his wallet nearby.

Jul picked a collar tip free from the edge of the sweater.

"You have to relax. Let nature take its course."

Nature or not, everything had become uncomfortable. The sweater, the seat he'd squeezed himself into, the constant pressure to buy her things or get him into bed. "I already said yes to Dar and Stel."

"It's time you said yes to me." She nipped his neck. "It'll feel so good, I promise—"

His head banged between the window and roof. He held her hands away. "I'm going to Dar and Stel's."

"Excuse me?" Her fingernails dug into his skin.

Hearing himself say the words sparked a fire inside. "I can't cancel on them. They're my best friends and they already bought the turkey. It's their housewarming too. We've been building that suite for months."

"It's a garage—"

"It's more than that." She never listened. She never tried to understand. "It's their home and ... and I'm ... going. They're my best friends."

"What about me?"

He didn't answer.

Her right eye twitched. "Julian Ariets, you're giving up a weekend with me to be with them?"

Was he really going to do that?

Blood rushed through his head, pounded through his body by his wildly beating heart.

"Yes. I'm going ... with them."

"You need to get it going with me." Cara snaked herself into him and pulled his hand onto her chest.

"No." Jul snapped away. "I'm not doing this anymore." He reached for the door handle. "I'm not going to a hotel, or buying you any more crap, or changing my hair, you hear me?" He fumbled to escape the vehicle. "I've got a perfectly good truck. Why are we driving this car?" He wrestled the sweater off of his body. It looped on the steering wheel when he chucked it. "And I'm done being your dress-up doll. It's over."

"Oh yeah? Well, I'm done dealing with *you*." She threw the sweater at his feet. " I'll find myself a real man who doesn't live with his parents—somebody with an actual car, not some shitty, dented farm truck. And you know what? I'll find him by the end of the week." She climbed out of the car. "Don't think you're anything special."

That was the problem. He wasn't.

"Mark my words, Julian, you'll be sorry. I swear you'll never kiss another woman without thinking of me." Cara shrieked as he walked away. "You'll never be able to forget me."

JULIA TRIED NOT to stare at the waiter while he lit the single candle. She didn't want to spoil the surprise for her cousin.

He set the plate between them, then lit a sparkler.

"What's this?" Amanda set a hand on her chest.

She hadn't seen it coming. Julia celebrated inside.

"Thanks and thank god you're not singing to me." Amanda touched her hands to her forehead. "And Jules, you're in trouble."

"Happy birthday, miss. Enjoy." The waiter left them.

"Chocolate and baklava?" Amanda squinted to read the syrup letters on the plate. "Happy thirty-seventh? You had to tell them my age?"

"They had to make the message food safe, I guess." Julia shrugged. "It's a wonderful milestone to celebrate," and it was one hundred percent up to her to lead the celebration. Her aunt and uncle hadn't even sent a card before they went to chase stars again.

"When you reach this age, I'll be sure to remind you that you said that. Though I guess by then I'll be in my fifties and have other things to worry about." She set the candle and sparkler on the side of the plate. "I adore baklava. Thank you so much for bringing me out for dinner. This has been a wonderful evening. And day, for that matter."

They'd spent the afternoon window-shopping downtown. "Next year, we'll actually buy something."

Amanda tapped her fork on the plate. "All you need to worry about is getting that career of yours going. Save spending for another time."

Honey melted on Julia's tongue, sweetening the moment. Her cousin took another taste, and she did the same.

A muffled ring sounded from the depths of Amanda's belongings. "Could be my parents." She dug through her bag.

It could be, but Julia doubted it. They were in Arizona waiting on some meteor shower. It wasn't her area of expertise—she avoided anything to do with star chasing—but she knew enough to be sure that they didn't need to go stateside. They could have seen the thing from any dark sky in Alberta.

She wondered why they'd leave their only child on her birthday.

She wondered a lot of things about them.

Amanda gasped when she saw the caller ID. "It's about the job."

"Why are they calling on a Sunday night? Answer it!"

"Amanda Sundboe speaking." She left the table to take the call.

Her cousin had dropped everything to help Julia after her parent's accident, and it was time for her to change focus. Amanda deserved to fulfill her life's dreams just as much as anyone, maybe more. She'd spent too long living bound by obligation.

Julia mumbled a quick prayer.

The minutes ticked by. She pushed the plate away to keep herself from finishing the entire dessert while her cousin was gone. Finally, Amanda appeared in the doorway. She was smiling.

It had to be good news.

"What? What did they say?"

"They offered me the Senior Travel Consultant position." Amanda rested her head in her hands. "If things work out, I could be a partner in a year."

"I'm so proud of you! That's exactly what you wanted." She was almost afraid to ask her next question. "Which location?"

Amanda held Julia's hands. "Jules, we need to talk."

She knew exactly what her cousin was going to say. "You're moving out." She'd always known, deep down, that it was coming.

But knowing wasn't the same as being ready.

Amanda took a deep breath. "I put feelers out—multiple feelers—when I decided to make this change." She kept a firm grip on Julia's fingers. "One place I applied for was Constellation Tours and Travel."

"The one in downtown Calgary." The commute would be way too long for her to want to stay at Julia's home.

"No, that's Cooper Touring." Amanda rubbed her temples before grasping Julia again. "Constellation is located ... it's overseas. It's in Sydney, Australia."

Julia didn't know if she'd made the noise aloud or thought it. She pulled her hands away. "Another Transit of Venus swinging through? Thought that only happened once in a lifetime." Her chin quivered when she spoke.

"No, but I know what you're thinking. Your parents—"

"Died there." The Matthews had gone over for three weeks to celebrate their anniversary years before. The trip should have ended with the Transit of Venus, a rare event where the planet was visible as it moved between the Earth and the Sun. A car accident ended it instead. "Didn't you get your fill of that place when we went to bring them home?"

Amanda's mouth opened and closed a few times as she scanned the table. "I'm not sure I can explain it. I'm not in search of some celestial event, I'll leave that to my parents. But Jules, ... it calls to me. I'm not sure I can put it into words. It's like I have unfinished business there."

"You have *no* business there. Bringing my parents home was enough." Julia pressed her hand against her lips as she bit them together. "I'm sorry. All I want is for you to be happy." Even if it hurt? "This is a shock."

Amanda nodded. "I know it is. I should have warned you, but honestly, I never thought I'd get the job. My application was decent, but it was a long shot that they'd even look at it, never mind choose me. Jules, I just ... I had to try. I've been thinking about Sydney since the moment we touched the ground there. I had to discover if the universe wanted me back on that side of the world." She scraped her fork through the words on the plate. "I feel like it's meant to be. Like I *have* to do this. Does that make any sense?"

It did, if it was someone else—anyone else. But it was her cousin, her best friend. "When are you leaving?"

"It's going to take a bit of time before it's official. I have to get my paperwork in order, sell some of my things ... pack."

Julia rolled the burned out sparkler between her fingertips. "How long are you going for?"

Amanda eased back in her chair. "The initial visa will be for five years. We'll see after that. I can apply for residency ..."

Julia held her tongue. The room blurred around her.

"I didn't say yes, yet. I don't have to let them know for a couple of days." She pressed her hand on the table. "Jules, if you need me, I won't go. I need to make sure that you are okay before anything's settled."

"You've been making sure of that for five years." The time had come for her to live her own life. Julia could understand it, logically. She just had to convince her heart that it was strong enough to keep going. "It's a big surprise. If you'd said you were moving to another province, it would be hard." Moving to Sydney was excruciating.

"Jules? Are you alright with this? Are you going to be okay? You're the priority." Amanda reached for her. She pulled her hands down, tucking them under her legs. "Of course, I'll be alright." Because she had to be, for Amanda's sake as much as for her own.

Chapter One

JULIAN ARIETS' PHONE BUZZED ON the café table. It was a message from Darvvin, his best friend.

At coffee. S is. I getting. There

Dar called it 'Newfinese texting'. The truth of it was that he'd never quite mastered the fine motor skills to hit the letters the right way.

Jul knew what his buddy was fishing for. He didn't bother to reply.

"Is dis yours?" A tiny girl set a key fob beside his cowboy hat.

He felt his pockets but knew it was his the second he saw it. He'd had his initials custom tooled on the back. "Thank you very much. How did you know it belonged to me?"

Her mother was close behind. "Even if it didn't have a King Ranch tag on it, I'd guess it was yours from the leather work alone." She smiled and pushed a stroller to the table near the window.

The little girl delayed, clasping her hands in front of her pink unicorn shirt. Her pigtails fluffed in the air as she twisted from side to side.

"If you hadn't brought this to me, how would I get home? Will you carry me all the way up the big hill?"

She giggled. "You too big."

"Livi? Come, eat."

The little girl waved and skipped to her mother.

Jul turned back to the dark screened laptop in front of him. He signed in and proofread his two-sentence proposal. "You'd think I'd have more by now," he muttered, rubbing a hand over his eyes. Chair legs scraped over the tile, distracting him again.

"Hey, cowboy. I finally have a break in the lineup." Savannah tossed a towel on the counter and then took a seat. "Doing anything fun this weekend? Camping maybe? One last long weekend before the summer is over."

He thought she wasn't working until later. If he'd seen her when he came in, he wouldn't have stayed. "Too busy for that." Jul pushed back his chair.

"Whatcha working on?"

"My business plan."

"That sounds *so* interesting!" She tipped her chin but kept her eyes on him. "It must be super exciting to be a successful businessman."

Little did she know, his business was imaginary at best. "Exciting, yes. And very, very busy. I really have to get this done."

Savannah made a pouty face that he was certain she thought was attractive. She looked more like a blushing bass fish. "You work too hard. And you know what they say, all work and no play makes Julian a dull boy." She scribbled 'Savannah' onto a slip of paper. Two hearts formed the colon she used to separate her name and number. "If you can fit me in, I'm—"

The bell on the service counter rang violently. “Anybody working around here?” A stumpy woman hollered, halting the din of café chatter completely.

Savannah scurried away, leaving Jul to give his head a shake. He had to try something different. There was no way he could keep going back there if she was getting brave enough to leave him her number.

✦✦✦

A FEW BLOCKS from the Coffee Stop, the guests had checked out early from the Wilbur Inn. The next group wasn’t scheduled to arrive until after four. It left a nice window of time to make preparations.

“But first, coffee.” Julia Matthews, the new owner, had at least an hour to escape before her chaotic weekend began.

“One last break.” She stepped off the curb and walked towards Main Street. “One last break before the last group of the summer.” One last group before she had to shut her business down for renovations. The Victorian manor had been well maintained through its hundred years, but the guest rooms desperately needed updating.

Better plumbing wouldn’t hurt, either.

Her phone rang as she turned the last corner towards the café. “Julia Matthews speaking.”

“This is Roberta from The Construction Firm.”

She’d never expected they’d confirm. “I’m so happy to hear from you. Thanks for the call. I can hardly wait for Tuesday.” She was itching for the work to begin. If she could get it done quickly, she’d be open before ski season started.

"Mr. Carson asked me to let you know there's been a … problem." She coughed. "He says he won't be able to do the work for you after all."

Julia stopped still in the middle of the sidewalk. "What's that?"

"Um, he's had … a conflict, and he's had to …" the woman stumbled over her words. "Look, I've refunded your deposit in full. I'm so sorry about this, Miss Matthews."

"But I booked it in June." Julia pushed her glasses into her hair. She just had to breathe.

✦✦✦

THE LITTLE GIRL at the next table giggled, and Jul couldn't help but smile. It was probably a routine outing for the family, but it looked like bliss from where he sat. The child waved when he did, then smushed a blueberry between her fingers. Behind her, movement caught his eye. A woman paused on the sidewalk.

He recognized her as soon as he saw the way she stood. He'd seen her often—throughout the summer, in fact, starting at Wildon's hardware in June. She hadn't noticed him then, and she'd never noticed him since, but he couldn't focus on anything else whenever their paths crossed. She was a picture, a portrait of everything he'd ever wanted, everything he'd ever dreamed.

Too bad he'd never had the nerve to say hello.

She stood still as she listened to the phone, glasses in her hair, lips slightly parted. Then she sucked in her bottom lip and bit it.

Jul got goosebumps. Her lips were a miracle and he took a moment to admire them again. The corners curved upwards, ready to stretch out the neat bow in the middle, seconds away from a smile. Her bottom lip was full, plumped like a bead of water waiting to drop off a wire just before it got too heavy. Jul regularly imagined what it would be like to kiss those lips. He dreamed of how exactly they would fit against his.

She said a couple of words and then took half a step to face the building.

Jul turned his back to the window. When he adjusted his computer screen, he could see her reflection instead of his own.

Whatever he had been doing the past few months—which wasn't much—clearly wasn't working. He cracked his neck and shook out his shoulders. It was time for action. As soon as she came in, he was going to make a move—he had to. Yes, he was going to get up, say hello and ask ...

What was it again? The words dissolved as he tried to remember them.

The phone dropped from her ear. She braced herself against the brick pillar between the windows. Her head fell onto her arm, and she grasped the chain around her neck.

Something was wrong. He'd never seen her like that. Jul knew he should go to her, find out what happened, and see if he could help.

He gripped the table instead. He needed to think things through a little longer. Why go through any of it if he wasn't *absolutely* sure?

Blood rushed back into his fingers when he set the table free. Jul took a last sip from his empty coffee cup and tossed it into the garbage can a few feet away. Just beyond, Savannah was crying to the new manager. She'd go out with him in a second if he asked. She was going to try to do just that, even though he hadn't. But that other woman—he had to make the move and say hello at least. Julian checked the spot where she'd been standing.

She wasn't there.

The bell over the door rang out, and she entered, marching straight for the order counter.

Jul slouched and lifted some papers in front of his eyes.

AT LEAST THERE wasn't a lineup when Julia got inside the café. That was a small blessing.

Heather Haynes, the new manager, welcomed her while the other girl shuffled away. "What can I get for you today?"

"Just a latte, please. As big as you make them."

"It's that kind of day, is it? To stay?"

There wasn't an empty table to be found. "I'd better take it to go. You're packed."

"You could squeeze in." Heather glanced over her right shoulder at the tables near the window. "I'm sure someone wouldn't mind sharing."

Julia considered it for a moment. A mother had her hands full with two small children at her favourite spot, so that was out. There was a single cowboy next to the counter, but he seemed engrossed in some kind of paperwork. She didn't want to interrupt. Besides, she had phone calls to make. "Just to go, thanks. I've got a crazy afternoon ahead of me."

While she waited, she opened the browser on her phone and searched for a list of contractors in Juniper Creek. There wasn't much of a selection. Julia closed it and started a text for Amanda, but there was no point in sending it. She'd be in bed on her side of the world for a few more hours.

JUL FANNED OUT the pages enough to make a split that he could see through. Twisting, he tried to see the woman's face again, but she moved so quickly that he couldn't quite get her in focus. He tried to follow her as she walked to the far counter.

"Peek-a-boo!" Tiny brown eyes peeped over his pages.

He jolted back, losing the papers to the floor.

"Olivia Armitage!" Her mother dropped her phone, her reach hindered by the baby in her arms. "I'm so sorry, sir."

"It's fine." Julian stooped to gather his paperwork. "She surprised me, that's all." The little girl had tears in her eyes. "You're very good at peek-a-boo, young lady."

She rubbed a chubby hand over her face and returned to the table. Her mother leaned close, quietly scolding the girl.

JULIA'S MIND CHURNED as she waited for her drink. "You don't happen to know any good contractors, do you? I'm fixing up the inn. It's beyond my capabilities or I'd just do it myself."

Heather shook her head. “I don’t, but whatever you do, I’d suggest staying away from Dale Carson.”

Julia crossed her arms over her chest and made a noise.

“Uh oh. You already know him?”

“Yeah, ‘Mr. Construction Firm’ just cancelled on me. They were supposed to start on Tuesday.” It made her want to scream. From the second she’d met him, she’d had her doubts. “As soon as I read his tagline, I should have called off the whole deal. ‘Excellence in Erection’. Can you believe that?”

“That’s terrible, but somehow it doesn’t surprise me.” Heather popped a lid on the paper cup. “Call Wes Wildon. He’ll know someone for sure.”

“I’ll give it a try. Thanks.” Julia took her coffee and tucked an extra five-dollar bill in the tip jar before she left.

SQUATTING DRAMATICALLY REDUCED Jul's line of sight. It only took a second for him to lose track of the woman. He eased back into his chair, eyes carefully fixed on the tabletop. After a breath, he got the nerve to glance around.

She was leaving the store when his eyes found her. The door jingled, and all he could do was watch as she rushed past the windows and out of his sight again.

“Dammit.” He shoved his papers away and kicked the chair under the table.

“Bye-bye.” The little girl waved.

His face warmed up, and he prayed she hadn’t heard him. “Bye for now. Have a good time with your mama and baby." Julian pulled his hat brim low and left as briskly as his boots would take him away.

Chapter Two

"DAR NEEDED MY TRUCK, SO I'll drive you home." Jul settled into the Brewer's minivan. "Said he needed to see a client."

"Right, that one." Stel adjusted the seatbelt over her baby belly. "He didn't get a chance to return the call before the long weekend."

"But it still is the long weekend." It was, for a few more hours anyway. "They might be gone until later."

She looked back at her boys. "Luke's already falling asleep. You're going to keep him awake if you don't settle yourself, Davey."

Jul watched his godson kick in his car seat. "You look like one of those bucking horses we saw."

"I wanna be a cowboy like you."

They crawled into the line of traffic leaving the rodeo grounds. "I never rode a bucking horse."

The boy's feet slowed. "A bull?"

"Never. I'm more of a farmer kind of cowboy." He might have wanted to stay on the farm if he'd had half the chance. He wasn't sure what he was anymore.

Jul glanced at the kids in the rearview mirror. If he'd done life differently, he'd be driving his brood, with his wife at his side. They'd spend the rest of the holiday Monday enjoying their home together and the next morning, he'd kiss them all goodbye before he went to work. But if—*when* that happened—he'd definitely be driving them in a truck, not a minivan.

"Jul, did you hear me?"

"Sorry, I was just thinking of something else." He turned down the radio.

"Mr. Lang left a message. He wants help with his apples." Stel slipped her phone back into her bag.

"Isn't it way too early? It's only September second."

"It is, but you know him, always in a hurry to get things done. I'm not sure him and Marg are doing so well this year. That's a big property for seniors to manage on their own." She leaned back. "Do you mind swinging by on the way home? It won't take too long to pick them if we do it together."

Stel was six months pregnant. "You're not picking apples. I'll go after I drop you off."

"That's a big ask. He's not even your neighbour."

Jul cracked his neck.

Stel fiddled with the buckle on her purse. "Well, he is now, I guess, but still."

"Dar would kill me if I let you pick apples. You don't want to be responsible for that, do you?"

She giggled. "Definitely not. Thank you. We're happy to have you alive, you know? Not just for the apples."

He sniffed in reply. Everything was uncertain, but being a part of the Brewer family again made up for some of it.

In a few minutes, they were out of Juniper Creek and a few minutes later, they pulled into the drive at the Brewer's acreage. Jul helped Stel unload her little crew.

"You can take the van over if you want," she offered.

"I'll just walk." It wasn't far to get to the road and Rowan Lang's place was next door. Fresh air might clear his head.

"There's a break in the bushes along the southwest side between our places, just before you get to the pond. The deer use the trail there. It'll be a bit faster if you really don't want to drive. Prettier too."

He decided to give it a try. The Brewer's land gently transitioned from trimmed to untamed. Closer to the caragana windbreak, the grasses grew long. A small path appeared between the bushes, and there the green was worn down to dust. On the other side, Lang's place was feral. Julian hadn't been over there often, but he could see the deterioration in the last few months. Their lawn grew wild, edges once carefully clipped blew ragged in the breeze. A watering can had blown under a rusted threshing machine along the side yard. Jul picked it up as he passed and brought it to the house. The open garage door revealed piles of clutter within. Mr. Lang waited for him on a stool inside.

"And there he is. Sent out the big guns today, eh?" Rowan Lang leaned hard on his cane as he stood.

"Nice to see you, Mr. Lang. No need to get up." He set the can down at the corner of the building. "Looks like this got away from you."

It looked like a lot had.

"Thanks, son. Didn't know where that went." The man eased back onto his stool. "Margaret gave me hell for calling Stel on a holiday. I forgot all about it."

"No trouble. We were coming home from the rodeo."

"That's a thing we haven't seen for a year or two." Mr. Lang stared at the cane in his hands. "Used to be fun to go down there. Now it's a bit of a chore how they've got everything set up. Ah well, now it's apple time. I've got two five-gallon pails. Hope that'll do it. Stel usually makes jelly with them. You going to carry these home?"

He hadn't thought about that. "If there are too many, I'll come back with the truck." The lawnmower was tipped on its side. A stream of plastic cord from the weed trimmer lay on the workbench, the plastic line flowed down to the floor below. "You two doing okay around here?"

"Fine, fine. Always need help with the apples, though." He shuffled to the end of the garage. "You passed the orchard on the way in."

Orchard was a strong word to describe the two forgotten trees at the end of the yard. A mess of overgrowth beside them was likely a garden. "Did you plant much this year?" Jul asked. The place was a jungle of weeds.

"Not much. Margaret wasn't feeling so good. Have to pull out what we've got in a bit."

There wasn't going to be much to harvest but plenty to dig under. "I can help you if you like."

Lang frowned and didn't comment.

Barely a blush had formed on the fruit. They needed a few more weeks. "You sure you want me to take these now? I could come back—"

"They've been falling off the tree. That's a sure sign they're ready."

It was a sure sign it had been windy, but Jul wasn't there to argue. He got straight to work.

He looked over the land as he picked from the trees. "You've sure got a great view from here." It was every bit as beautiful as what he could see from his balcony at Dar's guesthouse—maybe better. Lang's house was on higher ground. A herd of deer feasted near the shared pond, and further west, canola and oat fields rolled out from the fence line. The crops were changing to gold, a sharp contrast from the snowless mountains on the horizon.

"I've got a ladder for the high ones. It's set there alongside the house. Never got around to putting it back in the garage, but I guess that's good 'cause we need it today." The man halfheartedly started to walk towards the house.

Jul stopped him before the charade continued. "Let me get it." His boots clunked on the worn deck boards. They were practically crying for a new coat of stain. Jul lifted the ladder with a grunt and returned to Lang, enjoying the view once more.

Mr. Lang tapped a bucket. "I remember times when we filled five of these buckets per tree."

Jul wasn't sure that was accurate. "That would be a lot of work for Stel. She's a busy girl."

"When's that baby coming?"

"I think December." In a few months, Dar would be a dad again.

Jul would be a bachelor 'uncle' for the third time.

Mr. Lang whistled. "They're blessed, that's for sure."

Jul fumbled and knocked the bucket on its side. Mr. Lang helped restore the contents with his foot.

“Thanks.” Jul set up the ladder. “Do you think I could help get your yard cleaned up for winter? I noticed your deck could use a coat of stain. I could do that for you, too.”

“I’m sure you have your own life to run, son.” The man batted some low branches with his cane.

He had to sell his offer. “Actually, I’m still working on getting my company going. It’s taking longer than I expected. I seem to have too much time on my hands.” His eyes drifted over Mrs. Lang’s garden again. “I’m getting bored. Bored at the guesthouse while I, um, wait for a few things to come together.”

Mr. Lang jerked his chin towards Darvvin’s property. “Doesn’t he need your help?”

“Only here and there. And I’m sure you don’t have too much to do here ...” The more he looked, the more he realized the land desperately needed attention. “It would be doing me a favour. Give me something to do.”

“Doing you a favour, eh?” Rowan twisted his lips to the side. “Could do that, I guess. I’ll pay you ten—”

“No. I don’t need the money. Make a list of the yard work. I’ll stain that deck if you tell me what colour you want. I can even pick up the paint for you. What do you say?”

“I’ll have to think of some way to pay you back.” He reached out to shake Julian’s hand. “But if you need something to keep yourself busy, I’m happy to help you out.”

✦✦✦

JULIA WAS ALONE in the inn for the first time since she’d bought it. Her pulse was unpredictable—excitement and anxiety mingling together.

'Just like everything else right now,' she thought.

She ascended the grand staircase in time with the ticking of the grandfather clock. The rhythm grounded her. It was a heartbeat confirming that the space was still alive, despite being as empty as could be.

"It's only temporary."

Wainscoted walls absorbed her words like they were listening. The inn welcomed her still, exactly as it had when she bought the place. It welcomed her and waited to see where she would take it. The surrounding air was tight like the house was holding its breath. She was holding her breath too, waiting for the replacement contractor to return her call.

Julia let herself into the master suite. The Wilburs had named each of the guest rooms after a colour, and they labelled the master as 'the Blue Room'. It was no mystery how they'd come up with that title. The designer had used blue on every surface—draperies, wallpaper, and décor. A giant four-poster bed anchored the room. The oak was orange with age and battled the cobalt carpet below. A blue floral duvet usually dressed the bed, but the cleaner had already taken it away. Only a white mattress cover remained.

"I'll have to go shopping." She would get something new for the room, something toned down and elegant. Part of her wanted to go that minute, but there wasn't any rush. There were no more bookings.

"For now."

Julia slipped off her shoes, then slid herself to the middle of the mattress. After a moment's more contemplation, she stood and bounced.

The results were disappointing.

She tried again.

Two more hops in and the headboard shifted, thudding into the wall. Her feet sank into the pillow-top mattress and she jumped harder, but she couldn't get any air. Memory foam swallowed the force behind every move. As she steadied herself on the sponge-painted wall, she caught a glimpse of herself in the mirror.

She looked ridiculous.

Her phone rang, cutting her laughter short.

"Julia Matthews speaking."

"Are you panting?"

"Amanda." She fell to her knees. The caller was her cousin in Australia. "I'll turn on the video."

"Panting and in bed, yet you still answer my call." Amanda appeared, shaking her head. "I should let you get back to it—unless you're alone. Then maybe you should just stop."

Julia showed off the surrounding space. "I'm in the Blue Room. They say that Jean Ypres himself stayed here when the railroad came out west."

"John what?"

"Ypres." She repeated slowly, using her best French accent. "Jean Ypres and then they called the town Juniper Creek after him. Get it?"

"Your guests will love the history lesson. How was check out, by the way? Did you hear from the contractor?"

"Check out went fine. As for the contractor, I'm sure I'll hear in the morning. I'm going to get this figured out." She had to keep telling herself that. It kept the panic at bay. "I should have become a contractor myself. Then I know it would get done and done well."

"I don't doubt that you'll solve this problem, but even the best of us need a little help from time to time. You included. Let me know if I can do anything." Amanda propped her phone on the desk and leaned closer. "Are you going to open up your bookings while you wait? I guess you don't even know yet, do you?"

"No, the renovations are still up in the air, bookings are up in the air ... my life." She lay back and traced the swirled carvings on the headboard. "I'll know more when that Brewer fellow calls back. Can't blame him for not responding on the last long weekend of summer."

"Let me know when he does, even if it's the middle of the night, my time."

"Speaking of," Julia was sure it was still early in Sydney, "you can't be on lunch break yet. What's up?"

"Ah, I forgot to mention something when we chatted Saturday night." Amanda brushed the sleeve of her jacket and then folded her hands in front of her. "It's my parents—"

Julia's heart jumped. "No! What—"

"Everything's fine. Absolutely fine." She raised her hands. "I didn't mean to scare you. It's just that ... they're going through Juniper Creek today on their way back from Fairmont." Amanda sat tall. "They might call on you. They want to see you ... and the inn."

Julia felt like hanging up. She took a deep breath instead. "How do they even know where I live? There's only one person who could have told them, and I'm talking to her."

"Jules," Amanda moved close to the camera, "they ask about you all the time, you know. They do care."

"Why don't they just ask me?"

"Well … it's been a while since you talked, hasn't it?"

"Twelve years, three months, and four days." She shoved her feet back into her shoes and slammed the door behind her.

"Hold on, hold on," Amanda raised her voice. "They don't know what to say. They don't know how you'll react. They probably don't even know how they'll react. Look at me."

Julia crossed one arm over her, propping the phone so she could watch Amanda's face.

"They love you. They loved your parents. For mom to lose her sister, to lose both of your parents like that … it was a hard time for all of us—"

"But you stepped up, and they didn't, and we shouldn't have had to go through that alone. You had a life. You dealt with everything. They went on vacation." Time had blunted the edge of the loss, but it still hurt. Julia leaned on the handrail, overlooking the steps below. "Do they even have my number?"

Amanda cocked her head. "They might."

A knock and the doorbell sounded simultaneously.

"Doesn't matter because they're here." Julia hustled down the stairs. "Perfect timing. You can say hello too."

"I've got to run, Jules. Love you. Call me back."

"Amanda!" The screen darkened as Julia reached the front door but she didn't have time to worry about it. The silhouette of a single man appeared through the stained glass. By the time she'd unlocked the deadbolt, he was turning to leave. She didn't recognize him. The relief of it made her eyes water. "Good afternoon."

"Hello there." He grinned when he saw her. "I wasn't sure anyone was in."

Julia detected a faint Newfoundlander accent. He was slim built and a head taller than she was. His messy dark hair might have just come off of a pillow. "Sorry, I was upstairs. We're closed. Temporarily. Renovations."

"That's exactly why I'm here, miss." He passed her his card. "My wife said you'd called. I'm Darvvin Brewer, Brewer's Builders. Your place is amazing."

"I'm Julia Matthews."

"Julia?" He shook her hand. "Nice to meet you. Sorry, I didn't get a chance to call back. We had family business over the weekend. I was heading home from the rodeo this afternoon and thought I'd better stop in and meet you face-to-face. It seems you need some help."

"It seems like I do." The sniffle gave her away.

His cheery expression melted into pure pity. "I don't mean to pry, miss, but are you alright?"

It was the faintest trickle of a tear alongside her nose, but she knew he'd seen it. "I'm fine." She pulled herself together. "I've had a bit of an overwhelming weekend. My contractor cancelled last minute."

"Right. Carson." He didn't look surprised. "I'm finishing up a few projects over the next couple of weeks, but I bet we could start here and there around your house while we do all that. I could come by and see exactly what you're needing tomorrow? Wednesday? Make some kind of plan and give you an estimate."

"I'm available tomorrow whenever you are." Julia could hardly believe what she was hearing.

"See you at ten?" He tried typing into his phone, then gave up, and wrote on the back of her card instead. "Many thanks for this opportunity. This house is some fine." Darvvin Brewer lifted two fingers to his right temple and saluted her. "See you in the morning."

Julia locked the door behind him and leaned against the wood trim. It had taken three days, but she'd figured it out.

She had to call Amanda and tell her the good news.

She had to call and apologize.

✦✦✦

THE FIVE-GALLON pails bumped against Jul's legs as he returned to Brewer's acreage. When he got to the yard, his white truck was parked at the garage. Darvvin was home.

"Need help?" Dar took the bucket from his left hand. "Thanks for doing this."

"It was a good thing I went over. Their place is a mess. I'm going to help them get it ready for winter."

"You volunteered, or you were volun-told?"

"I offered. I've got time."

Dar shook his head while they carried the harvest to the house. They set the buckets inside the door.

"Daddy! Unca Jul!"

The four-year-old was the perfect crotch-height bulldozer. Jul caught him just in time.

"Let's go to the table, David. It's time for a feed." Dar kicked off his boots, and the men parted to wash up before joining the rest of the family.

Jul scrubbed the dirt from under his nails. His hands were getting callused again. There'd be more when he got going at Lang's. "That's a good thing," he mumbled. It would help Mr. Lang, but it would help him too—keep him busy, keep his mind off of things.

He slapped his face and went to the kitchen. Whatever was cooking smelled delicious, as always. The Brewer house was warm like a hug and he embraced the feeling.

Stel brought the water jug to the table. "How'd it go at Lang's?"

"You've got two pails of apples to deal with."

"And he got himself another unpaid job." Dar laughed.

Jul carried Luke to the table and latched the tray on his highchair. "You were right, Stel. They are having trouble keeping up. I've got time to help them put up their yard for winter."

She settled the stew pot in the middle of the table. "I knew Margaret was under the weather. I feel bad I didn't spend more time there."

"Don't even think of it. You've been busy creating life." As she passed, Dar patted his wife's belly. She bent down to kiss him.

Jul watched from the corner of his eye. He could see the adoration there, even after all the years they'd been together. He wanted that too, one day. Hell, he'd wanted it years before. He took a long drink of iced water and bowed his head for grace before the meal began.

"This is so good, love." Dar's smile started on the left side of his mouth. "I'll need the sustenance if we get that new client."

"Right! Tell us how it went." Stel set her hand on his arm. "She's letting you quote?"

Dar nodded. "Going to take a peek tomorrow, but it looks promising." He savoured a bite, glancing between his wife and best friend. "Sure to happen, even."

Jul tore open a bun and smeared an uneven layer of salty butter on both halves. There should have been more specifics. Something was up.

"Yes, b'y," Dar said to the table at large. "We're sure to be busy with this one. You're going to have a big estimate to write up, Jul. Might keep us busy all the way to the new year. Do you want to hear all the fine details?"

He didn't. He wanted to enjoy the meal and the distraction of the kids for a while and then head home. "What would they be?" He divided part of his bread into small bits and set them in front of Luke. "And why would I need to hear them?"

Dar took another bun from the bread basket, fixing it methodically before he replied. "I got a job with your lady today."

Julian replayed the words in his mind. He was sure the whole family could hear his heart beating. "You did what?"

"Yeah, Dar got a job with Savannah." Stel giggled.

The name brought him crashing down. "I'd rather be alone for the rest of my life."

“Could still happen if you don’t get off your arse and say hello to that woman one of these days.”

Jul rotated the bowl before him and tackled his meal from another angle. “I don’t know what you’re talking about.”

“You think it’s a secret?” Dar’s squint wrinkled his nose. “Not the woman who is interested in you, the one who isn’t—that girl you’ve been pining over all summer—“

“I haven’t been pining!”

“—the one you won’t go up and introduce yourself to, no matter how much you see her.” Dar pointed his fork in the air. “Wasn’t it twice you saw her that one day? She must not be very observant, because any other woman would have reported you by now.”

Butter melted into rivers on his bread, and he watched it flow over the edge to the plate below. The men had known each other for more than half their lives. Teasing was a given in their friendship, but the subject was a sore spot he didn’t want to touch.

“And her name’s Julia Matthews.” Dar set a business card on the table.

“Julia?”

“Jul-ya,” Davey chimed in.

“That’s quite the coincidence.” Stel pressed her hands together.

“Meant to be even.” Dar curled his smile and looked at his best friend.

Jul read her card. He let the words sink in.

“I felt bad for her. For sure she’d been crying when I got there—”

"Of course, she was crying." Stel wiped Davey's face. "All alone in her big house and then Carson cancels on her. Poor thing. She's got a business to run."

"And no one to share it with." Dar shoved Jul's shoulder. "She owns that old Victorian downtown—the Wilbur Inn. If she hires me, I can help her and you." Dar set his hand on the table between them. "I've been telling you all summer to come and work for me while you re-invent yourself. Work with me hands-on besides writing up estimates. You could become a partner, even. 'Brewer and Ariets' has a nice ring to it."

Jul ignored him.

"This is the perfect chance to meet her. You could see her every day, get to know her a little." Dar refilled his glass and raised a mock toast. "With real talking and less stalking."

"It's not that. At all!" Jul pushed his chair back. "I can't work for you. I'm helping Langs now. I've got my business to set up—"

"Yeah, and how much of that have you finished in the last five months?"

Julian had been working on it. He had a company name—Ariets Efficiency Solutions—and a logo. "It's coming along. I can't rush it."

"Uh-huh." Dar rolled his eyes. "Well, think about it. Work for me and you're guaranteed to see her daily. If not, you're destined to wander the town waiting on her to randomly appear. Your choice."

Jul had worked for Dar's father back in Newfoundland when they were teenagers. He'd liked it. He missed it. If his mother wouldn't have killed him, he would have ditched university to stay there. Life would have turned out completely different. Dar's offer was tempting, and he could see himself in that world again. Plus, there was a chance he'd run into that woman—Julia—on his way in and out of the place every single day. They couldn't help but make some connection.

"And there he goes again … this is exactly what happens when he sees her." Dar waved a hand in front of Jul's eyes. "So you will come and work for me? I could use a good man." He smirked. "Looks like she could too."

It never worked that way. Even if he did see her, it would be in passing, nothing more than a quick 'hello' as she rushed by. There would be no chance for deep conversations or getting to know her. "I'll keep it in mind, but not right now. Thanks for the offer."

Dar set his jaw and nodded once. "Suit yourself, then." Stew slopped over the side of his bowl. "But if you don't do something, I don't know how this is ever going to happen."

Julian had no idea, either.

Chapter Three

EVERY SATURDAY NIGHT, JULIA HAD a date. It was online, and it was with her cousin, but it had to count somehow. She gave herself an invisible check mark for staying socialized, no matter the circumstances. A glass of wine rested beside her iPad in the kitchen's dining nook. It was as good as things could be with her cousin living on the other side of the world.

The screen lit up and Amanda's smile glowed in the Sydney sunshine. “Good evening.”

“Good morning to you.”

“You're looking much better than you did last weekend. The new guy hasn't quit on you yet?”

“I kind of feel like I struck gold with him. He's fantastic. Of course, they're working on other projects. He couldn't jump right in, but he's going to start whatever he can over the next few weeks. Then this place will become their focus.” It wasn't what she'd planned, but it would work. “They're starting in the back three rooms. Once those are finished, they'll do the two big ones and the other small one at the front.”

“Won't that delay you even more?”

“It's supposed to be minimal. The big rooms only need bathrooms and major redecorating. I needed somewhere to keep the furniture from the other rooms during renos, anyway. I want to keep the main floor clear."

Amanda leaned on her hand. "Tell me about this Darwin fellow. He sounds like he's quite something."

"It's Darvvin, two v's. His dad messed up the paperwork or something when he was born. It was easier to keep it than the change it back to Darwin."

"That's a wealth of information, but not what I was wondering." Amanda had a grin on her face that Julia couldn't quite read. "Is he handsome? Single?"

"I'm sure his wife finds him attractive, and he has almost three children."

"Almost three?" Amanda sat back. "That's quite an achievement. But you like him, yes? He might have a brother. Maybe he'll bring some charming, burly worker through your door—"

Julia shook her head. "There has to be something more important to talk about than men."

"But I thought this was part of your grand plan—move into a new town, get into some new social circles ... offer up your new blood." When she didn't get a response, she went on. "Wouldn't it be nice to have some company? Not every single woman I know lives alone in a six thousand square foot house. That sounds lonely."

"It's called solitude. Reframe it."

"If you say so." Amanda shrugged. "Tell me what you've been up to. No guests, no work happening. What have you been doing with your days? Have you even left the place? You should go out ... meet someone nice." She took a drink. "Have babies."

"Says the woman who never settled down."

"Too late for babies for me, but if the right fellow even knew I existed, I could still settle down. I might be older, but I'm not expired, you know."

"Tell you what, I'll look if you look. Fair?" Julia raised her glass to the camera. "And I have been going out, for the record. I have church in the morning—"

"You wild thing, you."

"And," she'd done a lot of things the past week, "I've been crossing items off my list. All the things I haven't had time to do in forever."

"Your bucket list?"

It couldn't be called a bucket list. None of the things on it were important enough to hold in a bucket. "It's more like a basket list—sleeping in, staying up late, watching romcoms, reading." She'd never admit it to anyone, but she'd contemplated relocating to the blue suite until the renovations started. If she'd kept the bedding on-site, she would have slept there all week.

"Sounds like you're on vacation. Good place to relax, is it? A fine Victorian inn in a small town. What luck they weren't fully booked." Amanda smirked.

"Darvvin promised he'd get it done as fast as he can. I'll be opening in December, or early January at the latest."

Amanda relaxed into her seat. "I'm looking forward to you getting it going again. Aussies love a good Canadian vacation. My agency could put together a special excursion and keep your Wilbur Inn busy all year.

"That's another thing—I'm rebranding. 'The Wilbur Inn' sounds so dumpy. I need a new name for the place. Any ideas?"

"I'll program myself to dream about it." Amanda drained her mimosa and poured another. "If anything comes up, I'll be sure to let you know."

"So, when are you coming to see it? You could come for your birthday."

"It's been a while, hasn't it? Maybe in the new year. I could escort a tour group."

"It's long overdue. You haven't been back in seven years. Your parents didn't even call." Julia put her hand to her mouth. "Sorry—"

"Funny ducks, those two." Amanda was expressionless. "I hope you didn't wait around on them."

"No." Julia knew better than to do that. "I thought that chapter of my life was over."

"You thought you'd never see your aunt and uncle again?" Amanda squinted. "Well, my dear, it's in their mind to meet up with you. One day, they're going to show up. You might as well start thinking about what you'll say when they do."

Julia knew what she wanted to say—part of it, anyway. "They can call if they want to talk to me. You said you gave them my number."

"You blame them for stepping out of your life, but you didn't exactly try to keep connected, either."

Julia took a long drink while she censored her reply. "I didn't know I was supposed to. I was mourning my parents." She sipped again. "And I was only eighteen."

"And it was horrible. And you survived. We all did, thank God."

Julia stayed silent.

"I wish I could hug you."

She hated seeing the expression on Amanda's face. It made her feel like the most pathetic girl on the planet. "Tough to hug me when you live all the way over there, isn't it?" Julia looked at the table light above her. "I didn't mean to sound like that. It just ... it still hurts—losing my parents, then your parents vanished right after the funeral. Then you—" she stopped before she said something she would regret. "Never heard from them again. Why? And now I get to sit and wait for them to show up whenever they feel like it."

Amanda opened her mouth to speak but took a drink instead. She licked her lips. "You want to be in the driver's seat on this one? I can text you their number and you can make first contact. Though I'm sure you already have it jotted down somewhere. It's the very same one they've had for your entire life."

"I can't call—"

"I've heard the phone rings on their end, just like yours does. One of those new age, two-way phone lines that makes calls and receives them."

"I get it." She left the table and brought the entire bottle of red back with her. "Truce? One thing we can agree on is that you don't need to be in the middle of this, right?"

"Cheers to that." Amanda drank and looked out her window. "All that matters is that the work is starting on the inn and in no time at all, you'll be the most popular place around there."

"It will definitely be good to have everything figured out." Julia rubbed her eyes.

Amanda's brows creased again. "Really, Jules, is all well? Money's okay? You're okay? I didn't mean to stress you out with all this talk about my parents. I only wanted to warn you."

"It's totally stressing me out, but I'm okay." She guzzled from her glass. "I wasn't planning on putting myself through a big transition. I thought I could sweep in and take over and do what I do—solve the problems and make things better. I guess I wasn't thinking that owning a place like this is a perpetual work in progress. But it's all good." Julia finished her glass of wine but didn't refill it. "And don't worry about the money. What have I done in my life that cost anything other than this? Mom and Dad left me well taken care of. I'd budgeted for the renovations and closure before I planned it. I don't want the delay to go on for too long. I'm going to look into connecting with some businesses around here. Open the place up for small events, parties, teas, and that kind of thing. It will be a lucrative way to pass the time."

Amanda tilted her head. "Well, please let me know if you want to vent, or cry, or laugh, even. I like to give you a hard time sometimes, but I'm always here for you, you know."

That had always been true. "I would never doubt it. Thank you." She blew a kiss into the camera, then yawned. "I'm going to close up early tonight. I need to—"

"Breathe. Just breathe. All's well."

"All's well."

Amanda smiled. "Guess I should do something more with my day, too. Call me whenever you need me and I love you."

"Love you. Talk soon."

The screens went grey. Julia decided to shut the house down for the night. She'd developed a routine to ensure that every door and window were locked. It was almost a meditation.

Her footsteps echoed through the parlour when she made her way back to close a window. Rebecca, her cleaner, had covered the furniture with white sheets.

"Looks like icebergs." She shivered and hugged her arms close.

No one had entered the front door that day, but Julia checked it anyway. Her path took her around the perimeter of the front room, the furniture shrouded as that in the parlour. Every window remained shut tight, and it was a quick check. She proceeded to the dining room and secured the glass doors, then walked across the empty floor to the butler's pantry. There wasn't a table or chair in her way. She'd stacked every piece of furniture against the inside wall.

"I can hardly wait to dress this up again." Once everything settled, she could get things going.

Julia moved through the pantry and closed the pocket door behind her. In the kitchen, she tightened the locks on the windows and secured the back door. After gathering her iPad and a glass of water, she turned off the lights and went to her suite.

The clock ticked in the hall. It seemed louder than usual.

"It isn't," she said, dulling the din for an instant.

A memory waved over, transporting her back to the day of her parent's funeral. She'd walked into the family home that night, knowing they'd never be there again. It would be her and Amanda on their own. She'd hoped back then that her aunt and uncle would come around.

"And it's been years ... I'm not doing this." Julia pushed the sensation out of her head and heart. She'd made it through and come out on the other side—and there was no need to revisit that feeling ever again.

What she needed was some rest, she decided, and she settled into the snug seating area in her apartment. Two armchairs flanked a sofa and an ottoman fit between it and the fireplace. Stout windows crowned the tops of the built-in bookshelves on either side of the hearth. She turned on her speaker. Her favourite playlist was ready to go. It was a mix of fifties and sixties rat-pack-type tunes that her parents had liked. She played it almost every day. As she flicked on the gas fireplace, the music propped up the heavy silence around her. Julia reached for a lip gloss she'd left on the ottoman and swiped some on. The reflection was dim on her iPad screen, but she could see the sparkle. She wished she could show Amanda.

She wished she could show her parents.

Her mom would have said it was pretty. 'That colour really suits you,' she would have said.

She could hear her father's words like he was laughing in her ear. 'Slow down, Jula-belle,' he'd say. 'You're growing up too fast.'

Julia clutched the chain around her neck until the diamond pendant left an imprint on her thumb. She'd found it among her parents' belongings when she brought them home that last time and never took it off.

Peggy Lee sang 'I've Got the World on a String', nudging her to cheer up. That song usually worked. It usually made her feel unbeatable. At that moment, it sounded like a tease.

She scrolled through her phone. A quick online search reminded her of her aunt and uncle's phone number. Amanda had been right—she knew it by heart. She didn't bother to try it. Instead, Julia typed in another phone number she hadn't used in more than a decade. There was no use dialling. Nobody would answer, at least not the people her heart wanted to hear.

Sometimes she had the world on a string, but somehow she'd dropped it. Stress and circumstance had torn it from her fingers.

Sometimes she wanted to be called on. Sometimes she wanted someone to take an interest, to show they cared for her even if it couldn't fix the past. Somehow, her aunt and uncle hadn't even managed to make that small gesture for all those years.

"Sometimes a girl just needs her mom."

It didn't sound like her voice saying the words.

Julia stopped the music. She tossed the lip gloss back to where she'd found it and turned off the fireplace. The lights went out with a bang when she slapped her hand on the switch. Julia slammed the door behind her and went to bed.

Chapter Four

WORKING AT LANG'S THAT WEEK was a good distraction—it kept Jul busy and out of Dar's way.

Then Sunday came. There was no way to get out of the family trip to church.

Dar behaved himself throughout the service. No mention was made of the inn, or Julia. Jul almost believed his friend was letting it go and things would get back to normal.

When church was done and the family was back at the Brewer's van, Dar held the door for Stel. "Sit, love. Jul and I will get the kids."

Stel settled while the men loaded the boys in their seats. Jul had Luke, Dar wrangled David.

"Let Daddy get the buckle." A jingle sounded when Dar reached forward. "Oops, better get those. Can't lose the keys to Miss Julia's place." He was facing his son, but looking at Jul.

"Why did you bring them to church then?"

"Got to keep them safe, eh?" He patted his son on the tummy and shut the door.

Jul tried to ignore him.

From the driver's seat, Dar started chattering again. "Good thing we've almost got that dealership job done. I'm stretched for staff between that and starting at Julia's. Not to mention all that work I'm doing on her custom vanities. Do you think she'd come out and see them one of these days?"

Jul could feel Dar's eyes on him from the rearview mirror. He didn't look up.

"Yes, b'y. If only we had another good man on the job. That'd be a fine way to get things—"

"Dar," Stel squeezed his leg, "hush."

Thankfully, he listened to his wife. Jul didn't have to say anything until he declined Stel's dinner invitation when they got home. He retreated to his suite. All he wanted was some solitude, and he definitely didn't need to hear Dar chirping at him for the rest of the afternoon.

It looked like rain over the mountains, but there was sun to enjoy before that happened. Once he settled, Jul tuned his guitar and looked over the land from the balcony on the west end of his suite. Deer grazed a short distance away. A youngster wandered a few steps closer, flicking its big ears at the music as he strummed. "You've got it easy, buddy," he whispered. God and nature had everything figured out. Humanity was too variable.

A second later, the animal bolted, frightened by Julian's phone. It played 'The Imperial March'. He knew very well who it was, forcing a decision on whether he'd answer or not. "Hey, mom."

"I just thought I'd give you a call and see if you're still alive." A scratch sounded over the line. He could picture her holding the phone to her chest. "Allen, he's alive."

"That's that, then. Say hi to Dad and thanks for the call."

"Are you with Dar and Stel?"

"No. I'll give you their number and you can call—"

"You know I already have it. I almost tried there first. I wanted to talk to you for once. It's like you disappeared into a hole or something."

He hadn't called them much, but then nothing was changing in his life. "I don't have any updates for you."

"Well, maybe we have some for you."

"Are you changing provinces again?"

"Of course not. Goodness." Marlene clicked her tongue. "Have you given any thought to what you'll be doing for Christmas?"

"That's almost four months away."

"These things take planning." She cleared her throat. "Do you remember the Garrisons?"

They'd been the Ariets' neighbours when Jul was a boy. "Sort of."

"That's our news. They'll be here and we think you should come out for Christmas this year, too."

"That's not news—"

"You won't be traveling for work, will you? You're probably not working yet at all, because I'm sure you would have called. And I doubt you're seeing anyone." Disappointment tinged her tone. "You should have plenty of time to visit. The icing on the cake is that the Garrison's daughter is coming out for the entire month of December. Do you remember her? Patricia's her name." Marlene's voice deepened. "She's beautiful, Julian. Blonde. Very sweet. Recently divorced. Her husband—ex-husband—didn't want kids, but she always did."

Jul stopped listening. Even without the threat of one more awkward introduction, the invitation was a hard pass. He waited for her words to end and then let himself lie. "Can't make it. I've already promised Davey I'll be here. I couldn't disappoint him."

"That Cara woman isn't back in the picture, is she? Taking all your money again?"

He pulled the phone off of his ear and nearly ended the call.

His mother's voice continued. "You shut down every relationship you've ever had within weeks. I'll never understand why you let that one drag out."

He'd never understand either. "You know I'd never get involved with her again. I haven't talked to her since I broke it off. It's been years."

"Yet you still don't come and see your parents."

"That doesn't make sense—"

"I was telling your father how lucky we are to have each other since you and your sister abandoned us."

She was being ridiculous. "You moved away from here, remember?"

Marlene changed tactics. "Maybe all the Brewers would come out with you?"

"Stel will have a newborn. There's no way they'll do that."

"Well, think about it."

"Oh, look at the time." He stood like he was about to leave the house, gripping his guitar by the neck. "I've got a big presentation to finish tonight. Say hi to Dad for me." Jul held on for her final guilt trip.

"I hope we get to see you sometime soon."

Their conversations were always the same. Just once he'd like to have something to say besides 'no'. Something had to change—or he needed to build up a more solid bank of excuses.

Once he'd hung up, he put his guitar away. "No time like the present." His computer was out of power, but he set it up on the end of the island to charge. In a rare moment of inspiration months before, Julian had made a list of three potential clients. The sticky note he'd written them on was missing.

He crawled around the kitchen floor. "There you are." It had fallen under the fridge. The first company was as good as the next. Actually, it was better—it was smaller, and the owner didn't have a reputation for being intimidating.

He wrote the name on top of a blank sheet of paper.

"Ogilvie Ag and Farm Centre," he said, then he copied their phone number alongside it. He brainstormed with them in mind. In no time, he'd filled the page, listing everything he could think of that would benefit the company. As soon as his computer came back to life, his research began.

"There has to be a way to help this guy." It was a small operation—microscopic compared to some companies he'd worked with. But a business was a business. Some strategies applied no matter what a person was trying to sell.

"Workflow ... inventory ..."

There was always some way to make a company more efficient. It didn't take too long to patch together a plan that wasn't much different from the ones he'd used in years gone by. In no time, he had an outline. A few hours later, the proposal was complete.

By midnight, he read through it one last time. It wasn't perfect, but it was done and that was miles ahead of where he had been that morning.

Twelve hours later, he had an appointment set up with the owner of Ogilvie Ag. He'd printed his presentation and dropped his navy suit at the cleaners. The only thing left to do was wait for Thursday morning.

As Darvvin would say, it was a large day.

✦✦✦

MUSCLE MEMORY KICKED in when Jul wrapped the silk tie around his collar. If he thought about it for too long, he'd forget how to bind it. He hadn't worn one in months.

Frank Ogilvie had sounded interested when he'd called and it took little to convince the man to meet him. His breakthrough was coming—he could feel it. The past year had been a hurdle—a grand series of hurdles—but he was getting his act together. The meeting proved it. It was only a matter of time until he was back to some kind of direction in his life—some focus, some purpose, some path.

Julian left the house early. The drive to Ogilvie Ag gave him time to visualize the day. A celebratory lunch would be in order. He'd take Frank with him and build on the relationship even more. Maybe they'd splurge and go somewhere special.

"Myrtle's," he said to the steering wheel. It was an award-winning steakhouse on the edge of the city. The food and service had always impressed his clients in the past. It would surely impress Frank Ogilvie, too.

Frank welcomed him when he arrived at the dealership. They sat side by side in the small boardroom near the service bays. The man had taken over from his father, he explained, and was eager to make it bigger and better than ever before. He listened while Julian explained his work and how it would be of benefit. Then he went quiet while he reviewed the customized proposal.

Frank flicked his thumbnail through the paper when he finished and shook his head. "I like it, only it's too big. Too big for my operation."

"But your numbers suggest—"

"Do you have a program like half this size?" The proposal scuttled over the table when he tossed it down. "I don't think it's a fit. I'll give it some more thought, but it seems like too much for us. We're doing really well this year. Profits are projected to be bigger than they have been in a decade. I'm not sure the expense of your consultation will offset the gains, if you know what I mean."

Jul kept his poker face and nodded. "I get it. Keep that information package. If you can think of a specific category you want to focus on, let me know. I can adjust things." The men shook hands, and Jul drove away.

It should have been a launching point, but he was no further ahead than he had been before.

And he was stuck wearing a tie.

He tugged it loose. Ignoring the inclination to go home and modify his work, he took a drive instead. In minutes, he found himself in downtown Juniper Creek. Lang's old paint can was in the back of the truck. He stopped at Wildon's Hardware to get a fresh supply.

There was always the chance that he'd run into Julia there, too.

+++

TANZY PATAMORE WAS 'a design marvel', according to Darvvin Brewer. Julia browsed her portfolio online. It was outstanding. The woman was a master at balancing classic style with modern convenience.

"She'd be perfect for the job," Darvvin said, "But she's fully booked."

Julia called her anyway.

"I'm going to need to juggle my schedule a little, but I can't resist helping Darvvin out. He's bailed me out a few times," she told Julia. "Besides, I've always wanted to design a Victorian."

They met early in the week. The woman sketched as they went through the rooms.

"We'll remove the nineteen-eighties and add a little more of the eighteen-eighties. With better plumbing and lighting, of course. I'll have some ideas for you in the coming weeks."

Switching to Brewer Builders from The Construction Firm was turning out to be a very good thing.

By the end of the week, Darvvin and another man—Stanley Merren—started some demolition. She got up early that Thursday morning to welcome them before work began.

They started in the most hideous suite. It was cleverly called 'The Peach Room' by the former owners. Peach wallpaper wrapped the walls, enhancing the peach paint. A border of peach-printed tile surrounded the acrylic shower. Another row of the same edged the backsplash of the sink.

The idea that it would be smashed away nearly made Julia giddy. She tried to be patient, tried to stay busy, but by midmorning, she had to see what it looked like.

A sheet of plastic separated the back of the house from the front. Julia waited for the hammering to stop, then called through. "Darvvin? Is it safe to come in?"

A scuffle sounded, and then his friendly face peeked out. "Yes, c'mon through." He pulled back the plastic for her and followed her to the suite. "Don't mind the mess. We have to drag it out by the bin full and we haven't had the manpower to start that yet."

Stan stepped out of the bathroom, wiping his forehead with the back of his wrist. "Miss Matthews, you're not going to be too impressed. We hardly made a dent in it."

"I'm just excited things are happening." The acrylic panel on the rear shower wall was gone and the tile border lay shattered to bits on the floor. She could already envision how much better it was going to be.

Darvvin broke into her daydream.

"Nothing of note has come up yet, so that's good. We'll see when we pull up the bottom and that section around the fittings. Hopefully, we can get to that before the end of the day if there aren't any major interruptions."

She knew the second he said it that she was in the way. "Sorry, I only ... I wanted to take a look and then I'm going to the Coffee Stop. Do you two want anything? They have muffins if you want a bite. Something else?"

His mouth dropped. "Coffee Stop? Why yes, yes we do."

"I'm not sure I—" Stanley started to protest, but Darvvin cut him off.

"We would love coffee. And a muffin. Yes. Muffins and coffees. For both of us." He pulled his wallet out of his back pocket. "Black coffee, blueberry muffins, or whatever. Bran. They always have bran, and you know what they say about bran. Everybody needs bran, eh? From the Coffee Stop." He took out a twenty-dollar bill.

He was so enthusiastic, he must have been starving, poor man. "Keep your money. It's my treat. I'm so thankful you are here." She tapped her phone. "If you want something else, call me. I should be back in a half hour or so."

"Take your time, take your time. We're fine here until … whenever you get back. No need to rush." He'd started digging in his pockets. It looked like his hand was stuck.

"Okay then, see you shortly." She gathered her things, then left through the door in the back of her suite. The week had started with rain, but warmer temperatures had returned. Once she got to the front of the house, she pulled off her cardigan and draped it over her bag. A check of her phone proved nobody was looking for her. No one had even tried to book a room since the week before. She dropped the phone into the depths of her bag and ran across the street.

'*Should've come by earlier.*' It was close to lunchtime, and the place was filling fast. When she got in line, two people were ahead of her. There wasn't a seat to be found. The bell on the door rang in time with the constant flow of new customers coming in behind her.

"Hey, what can I get you?" Savannah, the bubbly granola girl, took her order.

Julia ordered three coffees and a half dozen muffins and took a spot at the side counter to wait.

+++

AT WILDON'S HARDWARE, the assistant manager hammered a paint can shut with a rubber mallet. "Do you need brushes or rollers?"

"I suppose." Jul made his selection and followed her to the checkout. His phone buzzed. He ignored it. "Thanks for all your help." The girl bagged his brushes while Julian's phone went off again. He paid and went out to his truck.

Another vibration from the phone got his attention. No one ever texted him during the day. He unlocked the screen.

> **Goat toe the coffeeshoetp**
>
> **Go trove Codessho**
>
> **Coffee was Ed to**
>
> **J L is**
>
> **Just his**
>
> **GO**

Then Darvvin called. Clattering demolition muffled the words, but Jul could still understand the message. "Where ya to?"

"Wildon's. I'm—"

"Lookin' for her there? Well, she's goin' to coffee. You need to get there quick. I called as soon as I heard the door close."

Jul had to park further away from the shop than he'd hoped. He almost ran as he turned the corner to Main Street, and Julia was already entering the café. He race-walked as normally as possible to get to the store in time, ending up third in line behind her. Sweat crept over his brow as he caught his breath. He'd never been so close to her.

He'd never tried to disguise a jog in dress shoes as a walk.

She moved to the side counter. As always, the whisper of a smile teased her lips. He sighed when he saw it. She took out some kind of lipstick and unscrewed the cap. A gloss-coated wand appeared. With a fluid sweep, she coloured her mouth, stroking the tip from side to side. She pulled her bottom lip in and pressed down on it with the upper, sliding them together, front and back. Her mouth opened and closed a few times before she was finished.

A little part of Jul's soul shivered.

Savannah took his order, all smiles and flirty eyelashes. "You clean up good. I haven't seen you in so long, I thought you moved, or something."

"Black coffee, please."

"Well, it's great to see you, even if it's only a minute. You look fantastic all dressed up." She tilted her head. "I kinda missed you, you know? You never called ..."

He stole a glance at Julia. She was nibbling her lip. "Coffee to go, please."

"No time for a visit? Busy man." Savannah winked and pulled a paper cup off the stack. "Anything else you'd like to take home with you?"

"Nope."

Jul watched the new manager hand a takeout tray and paper bag to Julia. She smiled, said thank you, and then she turned his way. The place was almost full. She'd have to walk right past him to get to the door.

He had nowhere to hide, nowhere to go without looking like he was avoiding her. When he drew a breath, his mouth dropped open. He'd fantasized about what he'd say so many times, the perfect words had to be ready to fall out.

It was time to make his move.

'GOOD THING I *got here when I did,*' Julia thought. The lineup stretched to the door. It would take some doing to navigate her way without crushing the muffins or spilling the drinks.

As she plotted her path, the man at the front of the line caught her attention. His navy suit had to be custom-made to fit him so well. There was no way he would have found anything for those shoulders off the rack.

Two steps later, her pace turned to a shuffle. She could make out his parted lips within his dark goatee as he stared at her. He appeared to have said something, but she hadn't heard him.

Brown eyes met blue.

A charge flowed through her. Electricity sparked down her neck, setting the fine hairs under her ponytail on end.

She felt the current run over her arms, through her core, and finally tingle to her toes. It buzzed through her. Her heart lifted higher and higher until it might float away.

He had to be looking at something else. Julia tried to see what he was so intent on, but there was nothing behind her but the coffee urns and kitchen door.

She felt the wave when she saw his eyes again—mountain shadow blue. Every other colour in the room faded beside them like they were hand-tinted on greyscale. They held her gaze. Their connection was unmistakable.

But he couldn't be—there was no way he could be looking at her like that—like he knew her.

Like he cared.

She definitely didn't know him. He wasn't the kind of man she'd ever be able to forget.

Another patron bumped her elbow. She let him go ahead and kept her gaze on the tall man in line.

She either had to stop or step forward.

She chose to move.

"Nice day, isn't it?" Her voice was a breath as she passed him.

ADRENALIN SLAMMED HIS system.

Jul's tie strangled him when he inhaled. He squeezed his palms closed to stop the tremor in his hands. Everything around him seemed white—white, and blank, and fuzzy, with only Julia clear in his sight.

His mouth opened wider still. "Haa ..."

The sound faded as he swivelled to watch her pass.

Her smile remained as she went to the door. She kept her eyes on him while she put on her sunglasses, then exited. The corner of the building blocked his view of her. As soon as she got to the window, she looked back, watching him until she disappeared.

Jul felt his pulse through his teeth. Flashes of light obscured his peripheral vision.

“I said your coffee is ready.” Savannah held his drink, standing much closer to him than she needed to be.

He took the cup from her hand. “I’m never coming back here again.”

Jul walked away.

Chapter Five

JULIA COULDN'T HAVE STOPPED IN the middle of the floor to talk to a man she didn't know, even if it seemed like he recognized her. She couldn't make out what he said when she passed. It sounded a lot like 'hi', or 'yeah'. Neither was enough to work with, so she kept walking. Her heart skipped when she saw him watching her as she left. His eyes followed until the brick wall blocked her view.

After Julia delivered the coffee to Darvvin and Stanley, she returned to see if he was still there. Nearly forty-five minutes had passed and he was gone.

Despite her disappointment, a hopeful thrill settled in. The feeling stayed with her that night, and throughout her visit to the Coffee Stop the next morning. She arrived well before lunch and lingered until two. By then, the crowd had come and gone and she knew the blue-eyed man would not appear. He probably wasn't from around there anyway, dressed up in a fine suit like that. The handsome stranger was probably just passing through.

"Probably heading back to his girlfriend in the city," she muttered.

Julia called it quits at the café. She packed up her belongings and brought her dishes to the counter.

Heather took them. "I hear you found a contractor."

"I did, Darvvin Brewer. I highly recommend him if you ever need any work done." Julia had been alone too much, that was it—too long alone, and in her head. She obviously didn't have enough going on if all she could think about was some man she'd never seen before and would probably never see again. "You must know him, right? You must know almost everyone who comes in and out of this place, don't you?"

Heather shrugged. "Most people. Why's that?"

"Oh," she wondered if her face was red, "I saw someone here yesterday. Tall, dark hair, suit and tie, and blue—" She stopped herself. Her tone was jumping around too much to sound nonchalant.

Heather smiled. "I think I know who you mean. He's been here before, usually sits right behind where you're standing." She pointed to the table alongside the counter. "You don't know him?"

"No ... I ..." Julia unzipped her purse, then zipped it closed again. "I thought I did. But I don't." She backed up a few steps.

Heather's eyes seemed to glimmer. "Ah, well, maybe you'll meet him one day. He used to come in here all the time, but he must be working out of town. Haven't seen him for a few weeks until yesterday." She picked up a pen. "I could give him your number next time—"

"No, it's all good." Julia glanced at her blank phone screen. "Oops, got to run. I'll see you soon."

Her mind was spinning. It fuelled her feet as she rushed home. What was she in a hurry for? She cancelled her weekly call with Amanda. There was no way she'd be able to talk to her cousin without mentioning the stranger. No, she didn't want to talk about him, but somehow, Julia knew she wouldn't be able to hold her tongue.

Plus there was the invitation to Brewer's that she didn't want to bring up.

Darvvin was building custom vanities for the suites and he invited her over to see them. 'Might as well stay for a feed, meet the family,' he'd said. Once she'd decoded it, she realized he was asking her to stay for dinner.

Big-city Amanda would never understand how it worked in a small town and Julia was in no mood to hear what she'd say about going to her contractor's home for dinner.

"I'll tell her everything next week when there's more to talk about," she resolved.

By then, she'd have more information about the new decor, the vanities, and stories to share from dinner. They'd found some damage under the shower floor—that would be a good topic for discussion. In a week's time, Julia might have forgotten about Mr. Blue-eyes completely and never think to speak of him at all.

She tried to ignore the little spark within, telling her otherwise.

✦✦✦

EARLY SUNDAY MORNING, Jul threw a coffee down his throat and ate a banana. He hoped it would keep him going for long enough to get through church. He looked forward to having the afternoon to himself.

'And catch up on some sleep.'

His thoughts drifted during the service, but he managed to keep his eyes open. After communion, Jul knelt to pray. He rested his head in his hands on the pew before him. When he looked up, he gasped. It was loud enough to get Dar's attention, but it was too late for him to see what caused it.

"Julia's here."

The Brewers helped him scan the room for her, even though Stel wasn't sure what she looked like. Dar rushed to the entryway as soon as the recessional ended, but he couldn't find her.

"Sorry friend," he said when he met them at the minivan, "if she was here, she's left now."

"*If* she was here? I think I'd know if it was her or not. I know her face like the back of my hand."

"I'm sure you're right about that." Dar smirked. "How come you saw her today but missed her all summer?"

He tried to remember exactly how it had happened. Jul had been praying—well, he'd said 'Dear God' because that was how it was supposed to start—but then drew a blank. His thoughts were all jumbled up when he sensed it.

Look up.

They weren't words he heard, or an image he saw as it passed through his heart. It was something that moved his whole system. It was like the blink that follows a loud noise or a reflex that moves a person before the mind can even process it.

When he heard the direction, he opened his eyes. 'The cross?' He wasn't sure who he was asking or who gave him the message in the first place.

Directly in his line of sight, Julia curtsied. She bowed her head and took the bread, then walked to her seat along the opposite side of the sanctuary.

Jul didn't understand it himself. There was no point trying to explain it. "I looked up and there she was."

"That's a miracle if I ever heard one."

He glared when Dar glanced at him in the rearview mirror.

"You have the most amazing timing. Like that first day you saw her at Wildon's. Like that day you saw her at coffee. And then … she talked to you. God above me!"

The memory of the moment in the café still made his heart pound.

"What was it you said back?" Dar huffed onto his sunglasses. "Something like that? Knocked her off her feet with that line, eh b'y?" He laughed.

"Dar, let it go." Stel grasped his forearm. "It's a wonderful thing that she goes to our church. Another sign of things meant to be."

"Men to be." Davey raised both of his hands in the air. "High five Unca Jul."

Jul reached for his godson's fingers and held tight.

The sound of tires rolling over pavement was the only noise in the van until Dar spoke. "I'm sorry. Just havin' some fun with ya. Don't mean a thing." Dar looked at him again. "You're coming over today, right?"

"We've missed seeing you lately." Stel turned as best as she could from the passenger seat. "We'd love some extra time with you."

If he breezed in at a quarter to five, he could leave by six thirty. He'd been getting so much practice ignoring Darvvin's jabs, it might even be bearable. "I'll come over for a bit."

"We miss you—your godson misses you." Stel knew which buttons to push. "Dinner's at five, but come early. You could even come right when we get home."

"I have a few things to work on—"

"Three then?"

He mumbled in agreement, then kept to himself for the rest of the drive. After they parked in Brewer's garage, he went to his house and changed.

It was easy enough to throw together a sandwich and eat while he scrolled through his phone. In a new browser window, he typed 'Julia Matthews' but paused. What if she'd be able to find out he looked her up? He hit the backspace button and replaced her name with 'The Wilbur Inn'. People searched for that all the time, so it had to be safe.

The site was formal and elegant, exactly what a patron would expect from a Victorian manor. A cropped photo of the building headed the page with a banner below.

'Closed for renovations until the new year. Watch here for more details and sign up for our newsletter.'

He navigated to the 'About Us' page. There was a short blurb about her, obviously written before the previous owners left. He read it aloud.

"It's our pleasure to pass the torch to Miss Julia Matthews, the new proprietress of the Wilbur Inn. She left the corporate world to take on this magnificent historical property. We wish her the very best as she cares for this beautiful merger of past and present in Juniper Creek."

There was another picture at the bottom of the screen, the manor with a trio standing on the front steps. It was badly lit and blurry, but he could tell Julia was the woman in the middle. Underneath was a link.

He risked the click.

The J.C. Journal had done a story about the sale of the Wilbur Inn. Somehow, he'd missed seeing it. The article included a picture of all three of them again. A single photo of Julia graced the bottom of the screen, likely a headshot from her previous career.

Jul scanned the article for any information he could find. She was thirty, and a lifelong Albertan. There was no mention of family. 'Miss Matthews recently left her role as Ener-AB's Director of Community Connections in Calgary. She's moved to Juniper Creek to pursue a dream venture—the ownership of the historic Wilbur Inn.'

"That's a major lifestyle change." It was kind of like what he was going through. But she was moving through it with strength and grace and he was drifting in the wind.

He zoomed in on her headshot.

"So pretty."

Sure, she'd finally noticed him, but it didn't help. Although he held the image of her beautiful face in his hands, they were still as far apart from each other as they could get.

Jul clunked his phone facedown on the counter and wrapped the last bit of his sandwich for later. He had to get his mind off of things. The best way to do that was to get moving. He loaded up the brushes and the fresh can of paint and wandered over to Lang's place. He had a deck to take care of.

+++

HER NERVES HAD kicked in before she left for Brewer's acreage, but she didn't have to worry. Stel made Julia feel at home from the very beginning of the visit.

"Your home is stunning. I don't think I'd stop looking at the scenery if I lived here." Julia stared at the mountain range in the distance. The Brewers had a spectacular view. They were also spectacular hosts.

Stel carried two glasses to the coffee table—one filled with water, the other with wine. "We're glad we can share it with you. Enjoy. This is the best seat in the house."

Davey wiggled on the sofa beside her. "Miss Jul-ya," he cried, and jumped to the floor.

"David. You know we don't jump off the furniture. Apologies, Julia." The boy ran off to join his little brother. "Lucky I've got one of each—chaos and calm. Davey's wild, Luke's my quiet one." She patted her belly. "This one somewhere in between?"

"Will you find out the gender?"

"No. We love the surprise." She lowered her voice. "But I think the midwife spilled the beans. She was talking about 'he'. Don't tell Dar."

"Midwife? Are you having the baby here?"

"That's the plan. David was born at the hospital, but Luke was born here. Being home was better. We have the same midwife as we did with Luke and we're healthy, so that's what we're going to try to do."

"Amazing." She couldn't imagine being as calm as Stel was about giving birth.

The Brewer's youngest boy, Luke, toddled close. He reached for Julia with chubby fingers.

"Do you want up?" She helped the boy onto her knees.

He wrapped his fingers in her hair.

"What a welcome." She had minimal experience with children, but it seemed to be going well.

"He's taken to you like a fish to water." Stel stroked her son's cheek.

The boy beamed, but didn't say a word.

"He's so quiet."

"He's slow to speak, but the doctor says not to worry. Davey does all the talking for him and then some." She shook his tiny foot. "You'll talk when you're ready, won't you?"

Darvvin came in with his phone pressed to his ear. "Julian's not answering."

"Julian?" Julia asked.

"Our friend. He's living in our guesthouse for a while. Coincidence, hey? Julia, Julian ..." Stel smiled and took a drink of water.

"He was supposed to be here at three." Darvvin pulled a roaster out of the oven and checked the contents within. "Gonna have to go over there if he's not here soon."

"He's coming for dinner?" Darvvin hadn't said anything about a friend joining them. It was enough of an adventure to be meeting his entire family without meeting their renter, too.

Julia bit her lip.

+++

THE LANGS WEREN'T around and Jul got the painting done without distraction. The sun was warm and he took the time to plant himself in a lounge chair while the paint dried. Clear mountains bordered the drying fields. He breathed it in. Soon everything would be golden. With any luck, the snow would wait until the crops were off to blanket the land. He stayed longer than he should have, enjoying the feeling of clarity for once. But as the sun neared the horizon, Jul knew he'd better head home. He was already late.

The phone flared up with missed calls and messages, three from the past forty minutes alone. Dar must have had some smart comment that he was dying to dish out.

He would have cancelled if the thought of letting Davey down didn't stop him. Jul dropped the device back on the counter and headed across the yard.

Before he could even cross the doorstep, Davey ran into him.

"Miss Jul-ya is here."

Darvvin scurried around the corner. "Where have you been? We asked you over for three."

"What's going on?"

"Miss Jul-ya's here." Davey danced around their feet.

"Don't be mad ... Julia wants to see those vanities, so we invited her for a feed too." Dar clasped his hands together. "Then you can meet her and get on with your life."

It felt like sand—like someone was drizzling cold sand over his head. The feeling spilled over his face and shoulders and sprinkled to his feet. "She's here? Right now?"

"Come see her." Davey leaned back, swinging off of Julian's leg.

He thought he was going to throw up. If he could have moved, he would have backed right out the door.

"You, my friend, are going to walk into that room and I'm going to introduce you and you're going to make friends with that woman and stop all this nonsense! You have to get your act together." Darvvin grabbed Julian by both shoulders. "You can do this."

Jul's feet rooted to the floor.

"Take Davey in with you. We're here for support. It's the best way." He lifted his boy into Julian's arms. "She loves the kids. And lighten up. Women like ... they like happy, light guys. Think 'happy' and 'fun'."

"I wanna be a airplane!"

"Put your arms out, David. Uncle Jul will fly you right in." Dar went ahead of them. "Come on, b'ys!"

Jul couldn't fall, not with his godson in his arms. He staggered forward as the boy sprayed airplane noises around them. They eased around the corner to the main room and he scanned the space. No one was sitting at the island or table. They weren't on the couch. For an instant, he thought it might be a joke, but then he saw her. She was on the floor at the window, all backlit with brightness and beauty.

Julian's socks slipped on the hardwood when he came to a halt.

Davey drooped over his shoulder. “Why you stopping?”

A STIR ERUPTED in the hall. When Julia looked up, a stranger was in their midst. He skidded to a standstill a quarter of the way into the room with Davey over his shoulder.

“Well, hello there.” Stel set Julia’s wine on the table. “I thought you said you’d be here early. We have other company tonight, too. Let me introduce you.”

Julia carried Luke and followed Stel’s lead towards the big cowboy.

“Jul, meet Julia Matthews. Dar is doing some work for her this fall. Julia, this is our best friend, Julian Ariets.” Stel pulled Davey from his arms and made space. “He lives in the garage.”

The man moved half a step closer as if shoved. “It’s a suite, actually. Above the garage.” He glanced back at Stel. “It’s not actually *in* the garage.”

He looked as uncomfortable as Julia felt. She threw on her business persona. It always worked. “Nice to meet you, Julian. Or is it Jul?”

He glanced at Stel before he replied. “Jul.”

“Jul.” Julia stepped closer when Stel lifted Luke away. “Our names are so similar. I guess it makes it easy to remember.”

He looked braced to run, but carefully took her hand. “Hi.” He looked past her, then back again. “Uh, yes. Hi. So nice to meet you. Julia. Funny we have the same kind of name, indeed.” He put his hands on his hips. “A real coincidence." He tucked them under his arms, and then returned them to his waist.

Blotches of red patched up his neck and over his jawline, all the way to his vivid blue eyes. Then everything clicked. Her knees almost buckled. "It's you. I saw you at the Coffee Stop on Thursday. You had a goatee, right?" His jawline was clean-shaven, his dark hair recently cut a little shorter, but the eyes ... "And you were wearing a suit." He looked like a rancher dressed in his patterned snap-up shirt and jeans. His belt buckle had to be bigger than her hand.

He stared back, eyes wide.

"Wasn't that you?" It had to be him. She'd never seen eyes like that before. At the café he'd looked at her like he knew her—like they shared some kind of secret. Face to face in the middle of Brewer's living room, he looked like she'd cornered him and was about to shoot.

He played with his collar. "Oh. Um." His eyes floated upwards, focused on nothing. "Ah yes. That was ... me." A rigid smile fell on his lips. "I shaved. And went to the barber." For an instant, he looked frantic, then he stared behind her. "You must have had all that coffee for Dar and the guys, hey Dar?" A laugh wheezed from his chest. "Lucky. All of you."

Darvvin moved between them. "Yes, it was much appreciated. Let's get you a drink, Jul. Excuse us for a moment." He steered his friend by the shoulders into the pantry beyond the kitchen.

IN THE SAFETY of the back room, Dar's fingers dug deep into Jul's arms. "What *are* you doing? Haven't you been thinking of what you'd say to her for months now? Just relax. Take a deep breath. Would it help to splash your face? Take a shot of whiskey?"

Whiskey sounded like the best idea, but that would only add to the disaster. "I need water."

Darvvin filled his order quickly, bringing the jug with him.

Jul drank it down like a man on the brink of death from dehydration.

"The evening *cannot* go like this." Dar got in his face. "We're gonna pull ourselves together and have a lovely evening with no pressure. There was nothing to do but meet her and that's already done."

The crisp water brought a little clarity. "She remembers me." He poured another and drained the glass to the bottom.

Dar massaged his shoulders like he was heading into the ring for the second round. "I know. Now let's show her 'nice and normal Julian' so she can attach that identity to you instead of whatever that was, shall we?" He slapped his friend on the back and fetched a large wine glass, filling it halfway with red. "Now, go back out there and relax. Be yourself. You're a good man. Show her."

Chapter Six

"WELL, THAT'S OUR JUL." Stel set Luke in the living room with his brother. She beckoned to Julia to join her. "You say you saw him at coffee the other day? Well, it's a day of coincidences, isn't it? You two were destined to meet." Her giggle filled the room.

"I can't believe it's him." She'd replayed his image over and over until it was burned into her memory.

It was better in her memory.

It didn't match the man she'd just met, almost like he didn't want to admit they'd seen each other before. The look in his eyes was nothing like it had been that day—that look that had stopped her dead in her tracks. Julia wondered how she could have imagined it was anything at all.

Stel had been saying something, but she'd missed it. "What's that?"

"David's named after Julian. He's Jul's godson. Julian David Ariets."

"Oh, that's lovely." Julia scanned the room, seeking something else to talk about. A series of family portraits on the far wall caught her eye. "These are lovely, too."

"Thank you." Stel stood beside her. "I took them. My company's called Shooting Star Photography, but it's on hold for a time." She patted her baby bump.

"Darvvin never mentioned it. Never had a chance, I guess." He hadn't mentioned a lot of things. His friend, for one. "I love this shot of you two. How did you get it?"

"Had to set the timer for it. It took about fifty tries to get a good one of Dar and me." Stel leaned on the back of the leather sofa. "The kid's pictures were fun to take. I'll have a large portfolio of children's portraits by the time I'm back in action."

A chair dragged over the floor. The men had returned. Darvvin joined the women, but Jul stayed behind. He sat at the island, scarcely turned their way.

Julia wandered to the bookcase, fixing her eyes on the photos within. "Is this your wedding party?" She lifted an eight-by-ten print. The man beside Darvvin was Jul, baby-faced, but she was certain it was him. "It's all of you. You've all known each other for that long?"

Darvvin stood next to her. "That we have. Stel and I grew up together. Julian and I met when we were fifteen, so what's that now? Nearly twenty years? He was our best man, weren't you Jul?"

The man nodded.

"You're from Newfoundland too?" Julia asked. Their conversation had been too limited to tell if he had an accent or not.

"No, he grew up here." Darvvin looked over her shoulder at the photo. "We met at Scout camp—a jamboree they call it. Hit it off and never looked back. Then he came and worked construction for my dad for a couple of summers."

Julia pulled the picture closer. The grinning man beside Stel looked so similar to Darvvin that they almost could have been twins. "Who's this? He looks fun."

Darvvin held one side of the frame. "That's Eddie, my younger brother by fifteen months. He's not a hard-looking fellow, is he? Loads of fun. You'll have to meet him sometime. He's single."

Stel grabbed her husband's hand. "I don't think he's single anymore, right? Plus, he lives out east."

"Oh right, right." Darvvin crossed his arms. "Not single anymore. And he lives on the rock, so it's not like he is even an option presently presenting himself. At present."

Stel turned Jul's way. "You and Eddie became quite close friends through the years, didn't you? You still stay in touch."

He answered slowly. "Um, yes. We are good friends. Too."

Julia examined Jul's image in the photo again. He wasn't frowning, but he didn't exactly look happy. "They took this picture before you smiled, Jul." It looked good anyway. He could have been modelling for a cologne commercial. She could imagine him on a magazine spread—eyes coloured blue on a black and white background.

"That was probably because of Annette. That girl beside him is my cousin. She was after him all night, but he avoided her like potholes." Stel giggled. "How'd you manage to escape her wiles?"

Jul cleared his throat.

"You didn't though, did ya?" Darvvin grinned. "Didn't she corner you in the coat closet after we left?"

"No. It wasn't like that. At all."

Jul's quick answer was the first thing he'd said that sounded like he was sure about it.

"Dar, we need to check on the meal." Stel pushed him towards the kitchen, then set a hand on Julia's arm. "Anything I can get for you?"

"No, thank you. I'm doing fine." She followed them, wineglass in hand. "Can I do anything to help?"

"Oh no, you're our guest. You and Jul." Stel waved a potholder towards their friend. "Enjoy. Visit."

There were only three stools at the counter, and he was sitting at the one on the end. If she sat in the seat on the other side, it would look like she was avoiding him. If she sat next to him—

She pulled out the chair beside him and settled in. As she sipped her merlot, she could feel him looking at her. He looked away the instant she lifted her head.

She felt a pull at her sleeve.

"This is Dino." Davey crawled the toy up her leg. "Mama says don't give him to Luke 'cause he's too little."

"David, leave Miss Julia to talk with Uncle Jul. Go see what Lukey's up to." Stel smiled at her guests.

Jul was gripping the bottom of his seat with one hand.

It was up to her to make conversation—he wasn't going to. "Amazing how I saw you at the café and now here. I can't get over it."

"Ah yeah. That is amazing." He let go of the chair and stuck his finger down his collar. A second later, he pulled a chain out of his shirt. "I got this."

Dar lifted his head, Stel stopped stirring, and the buzz of child chatter unexplainably silenced the minute he spoke. His voice was so loud, Julia would have dropped her glass if she'd been holding it.

"Um, I mean, Dar gave me this when he asked me to be his best man. We were talking about the wedding and all that. I just remembered—" He fumbled and tried to tuck it back in. "Never mind."

"What is it?" A large pendant dangled from the chain, but Julia couldn't quite make it out. She caught the object in her fingers before he could hide it away.

"You still wear that?" Darvvin poked his head between them. "That was my Grandpa Darwin's."

Julia squinted to read the dull silver. "A twenty-cent coin?"

"Yeah, they made them back when Newfoundland was its own country. Then the Newf twenty-cent piece got confused with Canadian quarters so they stopped."

Darvvin pinched the coin on one side while Julia did the same on the other. She felt the chain tighten and she let go.

Jul reached behind his head. "Let me undo it."

"It's here." Darvvin slid his fingers to the right of his collar and tore the chain off.

Jul rubbed his neck.

"The night I asked Jul to be my best man, I gave this to him." He grinned. "Looks like I made the right decision. Gramps never should have punched that hole in the top. This could've been worth something."

"Dar," Stel slapped a spatula on the counter, "let Julia see it. You still have the meat to cut."

"Right. Yes." He passed the coin to Julia and went to the oven.

Julia felt Jul's eyes on her as she examined it again. She gave him a gentle smile and cupped it in her palm. "It's wonderful. Would you like me to fasten it back?"

"No. No, thank you. I've got it." He let her drop it into his hand.

"It's so unique. What a gift." She smiled again, but he wasn't looking at her. The chain had left a red strip on his neck.

"I'm going to let the meat rest a minute." Darvvin wiped his hands. "Shall we go to see those vanities before we eat?"

"Good idea." Julia had almost forgotten that was the reason she was there. She nodded to Stel and then to Jul. "Duty calls."

He tipped his chin, took a swig from his glass, and didn't say a thing.

A FEW MINUTES later, Julia followed Darvvin to his workshop—the far bay in the garage where Jul also lived. She wished she'd worn flats instead of kitten heels. "I love Stel. She's amazing."

"That she is."

It was as good a time as any to find out more. "Your friend, Jul, he seems ... quiet." 'Quiet, awkward, and socially inept' was more like it, but she couldn't say any of that.

"He's a great guy, he really is. He just needs ... a little more confidence."

She had to ask. She might not get another chance. "Bad breakup?"

Darvvin sniffed. "Ha, no. Well, not lately anyway. He got laid off before Christmas. Moved here in the spring." The gravel crunched under their feet. "Jul just needs to—" he pressed his lips together, "—he just needs to take some action in his life. He's a bit stuck right now. Going around in circles, y'know? Starting fresh."

That was something she could relate to.

✦✦✦

STEL PATTED THE counter as soon as the door closed. "She likes you."

"I don't know about that." Jul rubbed his brow.

"She held onto that pendant forever."

She'd held it for long enough to warm it up, and it was warm enough for him to feel the heat from her hand while it settled back onto his skin, but the sensation had faded.

Stel chattered on. "*And* she sat right beside you. She could've left a seat between. And she remembered you from the coffee place."

"I was right in her way. She couldn't miss me."

"Relax. Rough start tonight, but she's wonderful. You have excellent taste."

If that was true, it was a newly developed skill. "I'll help the boys clean up for dinner." Jul took the children to the bathroom. Luke wanted to play in the sink and Davey doused his shirt with water and had to be changed. By the time they had finished, Julia and Darvvin had returned from the shop.

"Have you seen what your husband is making for the inn?" Julia was talking to Stel when Jul carried Luke to the table. "You do amazing work, Darvvin."

"I'm happy for the challenge." Dar set a bowl on the table. "Sit and enjoy. We've set you here, Julia."

"I wanna sit beside Miss Jul-ya." Davey hugged her arm until his mother pulled him away.

Julia smiled at the child, then at Jul. "Do you ever feel like you're in the kids' section?"

He hadn't expected her to say a thing. "Oh, right." Jul busied himself with the safety strap on Luke's highchair. "Let's get you settled, little man." It was difficult to find a place to look without staring at her. She was right in his line of sight. He observed the pattern on the tablecloth instead.

They prayed and passed the food.

"To good friends and good things to come." Dar toasted the table with his glass of water then winked at his friend when he set it down.

"Thank you for inviting me." Julia took the bread bowl from Stel. "I haven't eaten a meal like this in forever, or spent time with such great company."

"Do you go to church?" Stel jumped in. "Dar thought he might have seen you. We go to St. Francis."

Good old Stel. She always got to the bottom of things. Jul watched the scene unfold.

"You saw me there?" Julia asked. "I usually run in right before it starts and leave right after. I guess I should stay and be more social."

Stel beamed."Now you know us, so you should sit with us too."

"Sit with me," Davey cried.

"I'd love to join you. It's so good to make connections, get to know people." Julia sipped her wine. "Well, I guess you know all about me—"

Jul opened his mouth to deny it.

"—what's your line of work, Jul?"

"He helps me," Darvvin cut in. "Jul was the one who sent you the estimate, actually. And he's helping our neighbours. They're older and need some help with their yard. Jul came to their rescue. And he's starting his own consulting business. He does efficiency planning." He nudged Jul on the shoulder. "You could apply some of that to your own life too, you know."

Julian kept his face neutral. "I'm starting my business as soon as I get everything together. I've been out networking. Getting the business plan polished." He was sure he heard Dar snort.

"I used to do project management with Ener-AB before I bought the inn." Julia leaned forward. "I'd be happy to be a second set of eyes if you need someone to look at your plan when it's ready."

Dar pushed his face close to Jul. "When and if—"

"It's not ready." He gripped his cutlery and kicked at Dar's leg under the table. "Not quite."

"That's okay. Keep me in mind for when it is." She pushed food around her plate. "Many companies could benefit from better efficiency. I bet I could use your expertise once I get everything in order at my place. Is that something you would be interested in?"

Jul answered before Dar could interrupt. "I'm totally interested in you."

Darvvin's fork clattered on his plate.

"Your business, that is. Not you." His tone pitched higher. "Well, you, of course, but in a business way. In your business. Of course." Jul filled his mouth so it would stop talking. A wave of heat hit him, then heart palpitations. He wondered if he'd choke, pass out maybe, and then be out of his misery.

"I'll get us more water." Stel swished away to the sink. "Carry on. Don't mind me." She hummed over the hush that had fallen on the room.

Julia pressed the napkin on the corners of her lips. "So, Darvvin, can you narrow down how long the renovations will take based on what you've seen so far? Carson sure messed up my timeline."

"So did the damage we found in that bathroom."

Julia's forehead creased. "At least it didn't ruin the ceiling in the kitchen."

"Wes Wildon says he'll get your new fixtures here as soon as he can. I promise you, we're gonna get there." Dar looked over the faces around the table, resting on Jul for only an instant before he continued. "And since I know time is of the essence, I've gone out and found an extra man."

"You have?" Julia sat back.

"Ah yes, I worked with the guy years ago. He's left the hands-on part of the business now, but he knows your situation. He'd love to help you get going again just as much as I would. Does a good job at anything he tries. My dad didn't want to let him go back in the day."

Jul couldn't imagine who it was. He hadn't kept up with too many of the guys out east, but he thought Dar would have told him.

Even Stel looked confused. "What? That's really going to help."

"It's really going to help *you*, Julia. And did I mention he's modest too?" Dar shook Jul by the arm. "It's this one right here! Julian Ariets himself. He'll be working for me—for *you*, Julia—starting tomorrow morning. And we're so thankful he is."

Jul clenched his teeth and inhaled. The room spun around him.

"You'd do that?" Julia's voice was soft, disbelieving. "Even with everything else you've got going on?"

"I um—" He looked at Dar's smug smile and then back to Julia. She had her hand on her chest and was gently biting her lip. There was no way he could shatter the hope that rested on her by refusing.

"Of course he will. He's looking forward to the challenge, and he'd do anything to help, wouldn't you Jul?" Dar slapped his shoulder.

Her chin rippled for an instant, then she looked him in the eye. He felt the burst when they connected, like there was no one else in the room but the two of them.

"I'm so grateful that you'd take the time to do this. It was such a blow when the job got delayed, then the damage and—thank you, so much." She raised her glass in the air. "To new friends."

Jul set his mouth to 'smile' and clinked with everyone at the table—everyone except Darvvin.

Chapter Seven

"HI, I'M JULIAN ARIETS. I'm so happy to meet you." He walked closer, shoulders back, steps steady. "I live in the suite *above* the garage. It's a stand-alone home, actually, with double sinks in the ensuite."

Julia stood at the Brewer's stone-topped island as though she'd been waiting for him. Her chestnut hair flowed behind her even though they were indoors. "Jul." her exquisite lips spoke his name. "I remember you from the coffee place. I haven't stopped thinking about you."

He took both of her hands and lost himself in her eyes, which his keen observation skills had determined were brown. "There's a great view of the mountains here by the window."

"I couldn't possibly enjoy it alone."

"There's just enough room for two." He sat down and pulled her onto his legs, cradling her in his arms.

She dropped her head onto his shoulder and embraced him. "This is everything I've ever needed. You and me. Together at last."

It might have gone like that in a parallel universe, but it certainly didn't in the one Jul was stuck in.

Reality was such a disappointment.

He cut his thoughts back as they tried to remind him of the disastrous evening he'd had. He hoped she didn't notice his idiotic commentary. Dar had talked so much, that she might not have heard him at all.

But he knew that she had. It made his face hot. He threw on a T-shirt when he got home to cool down.

Late Sunday night, the text came through.

No b shuts at eight I'll child

Jibs starts st right I'll cry in

The phone rang seconds later. "Hey, the job starts at eight. I'll drive us. We'll leave about a quarter to."

"Thanks." Jul rubbed his face. "Thanks so much for today, too, by the way. You continue to amaze me, even after all these years."

"Imagine all the gas you'll be saving. No more driving around looking for her."

"I've never—"

"I bet you'll notice the difference in a week." Dar laughed. "She's amazing, eh? Stel loves her. She says no wonder you like her so much. And she thinks she's interested in you."

Stel's voice came on the line. "She would never have sat beside you or talked to you like that if she wasn't. And she wants to look at your plan. That's a sure sign."

He couldn't trust her assessment. If Stel and Julia hadn't clicked with each other like long-lost sisters, he was fairly certain she wouldn't be so optimistic. She was never that optimistic about anyone else he'd dated.

DAR HAD THE truck warming when Jul came down the next morning. It didn't help cheer him up.

"You look like a ray of sunshine."

Jul grunted, slamming the door behind him. "I can't believe you did this to me. Any of it."

"You know I'm going to pay you well, right?"

"You know it's not about the money. It's the principle of the thing. You used me to get what you want."

"What I want?" Dar drove out of the yard. "You wanted to meet her, you have. You want to see her again, you will. I think I'm a bit of a genie, actually. Your wish is my command."

"I wish I wasn't sitting with you right now. Can you make that come true?"

Dar slapped his friend on the chest. "Ah, but we've promised the lady. You don't want to let her down now, eh?"

"I don't even have work boots."

"You don't even have work clothes, by the looks of it." He tugged the cuff of Jul's check dress shirt. "Stay out of the danger zone this morning. Take my truck to Big West at lunch. Problem solved." He turned onto the highway. "I'd leave the Rolex at home next time if I were you."

"It's the Breitling."

Darvvin snorted.

Jul unfastened his watch and tucked it inside his jacket. "Everything's so easy for you, isn't it?"

Dar smirked. "Most things are only as hard as a person makes them for himself."

They drove in silence until they reached the Wilbur Inn. Julian had been past it before—once or twice—but it came as a surprise how grand the property was when they pulled into the parking lot.

"This place is enormous," he said. A round two-story tower anchored the southeast corner, nearest to the parking lot. A broad porch encircled the perimeter of the Queen Anne building. Fawn-coloured brick covered everything but the gables. Those were finished with wooden shingles. "This must have been the biggest house anywhere around these parts in its day." A banner hid the sign on the front lawn. 'Closed for renovations', it read, 'Opening soon'.

"Thank the western expansion of the railroad, or it would never be here. It's a beautiful home. Hope we can get it done quick for her sake." Dar parked the truck.

"This has to be a burden for her. Spending and not earning a dime."

"She budgeted for it, but the sooner the better. We've run into a few problems and we need to get supplies. Carson bought a load of materials but not what she really wanted so we're delayed with replacing that too. It's a big help that you'll be here, Jul. Honestly." Dar shut off the ignition. "And I'd really like to finish this by the end of November. The baby's supposed to be here early December and I wouldn't mind taking the month off to be with Stel."

Everything suddenly made sense. "So that's why I'm here."

"To help." The left side of Darvvin's mouth curved up. "It's about helping us all—Julia, my family, and yourself, too."

Jul shook his head.

"I know you're mad at me. Do it for her."

"That's the only reason I'm here." He took a breath as they approached the front doors. The aged oak had been carved by a skilled hand. Coloured glass panels on the top third of it looked like jewels in the light.

"She must not be up and about yet." Dar jingled a set of keys in Julian's face, then unlocked the deadbolt. "It's usually open."

They entered a grand hall. His heart was pounding, and he didn't notice much of his surroundings, just the bright orange sticky note on the newel post.

Dar got to it first. "I guess she's gone out early today. Maybe she went to the coffee shop." His grin faded when he saw Jul's face. "There's always a pot in the kitchen if you want one."

"Just show me what we're doing." Jul started up the stairs without him.

✦✦✦

NEWTON'S PRINT AND Signage was a short walk from the inn and only a few blocks from Main Street. It didn't open until nine. Julia sat in the café with her drink and checked the time. It was three minutes past eight. Darvvin would have arrived at the house by then.

Jul would be there, too.

She'd left well before she'd have to see them that morning and didn't want to spend any time pondering why. Julia held her coffee cup close to her mouth. Her hands smelled like vanilla soap. Not a trace of the spice and metal scent from Jul's pendant remained.

How could the guy she'd seen standing in line that day possibly be the same one she'd met the night before? Dressed-up Jul surely would have had something to say.

He'd looked ready to reveal it—ready to share the one thing that only he knew that would only be meaningful to her.

Cowboy Jul acted like an outlaw on the run.

Her eyes had been on Darvvin when he announced who his new crewman would be, but she wished she'd been watching Jul. By the time she looked at him, he was staring at the table, jaw clenched. Then she spoke, and he'd looked her in the eye for the first time all evening. If he heard the emotion she was trying to hide, he didn't show it. He smiled—or something just short of a smile, acknowledging that everything would be okay. Something about his expression convinced her he'd get things done, no matter what.

There wasn't a trace of pity for her situation, only assurance—exactly what she would have expected from the suited man she saw at the café. But after that, he didn't have much to say at all. It was as though Dressed-up Julian and Cowboy Jul were battling it out before her very eyes.

The man was a puzzle.

"A puzzle to solve," she mumbled into her mug.

"What's that?" Heather paused beside her.

"Oh, nothing." Julia pushed the visual of Jul Ariets out of her head. "I'm, ah, getting a group of local business owners together. Do you think the Coffee Stop would be interested in joining?'

Heather leaned on the next table. "Like a marketing group?"

"Something like that." She switched to the comfort of business mode. "I need to drum up some work while the renovations are being done. While I'm at it, I'd like to build a community between business owners around town. Help us help each other." Julia pulled a list from her purse. "I'd like to host bridal showers, baby showers, maybe Christmas dinners. I could have the Coffee Stop supply my baked goods when I host events at the inn. That would help me, and you too. I could recommend you to my guests. You could recommend me." The ideas were coming fast. "Maybe you could create a drink named after the inn or something."

"Like 'Wilbur tea'?"

Julia nodded. "Once I rebrand, it will sound prettier. I've made up a flier with some event ideas and another suggesting a local business group. I'm picking them up this morning when Newton's opens." She checked the clock. It was only eight twenty-one. "I'll drop one off sometime today."

"Sounds interesting. I'll run it by Donna."

"Great. And if you hear about anyone needing a venue for their shower or tea, do you mind passing my name along?"

"I'd be happy to." The bell over the door jingled. "I'll talk to you later."

'*One down, a whole town full to go.*' Julia still had plenty of time to check her messages. Amanda had left her a text the afternoon before. She'd missed it because she was at the Brewer's but had replied when she got home that night. Might as well tell Amanda about her invitation to Darvvin's home before their Saturday chat. It would give her cousin almost a week to get over it. Guaranteed, her reaction to that would be milder than what she'd have to say when she heard about Jul.

She wouldn't mention him at all, she decided. There really wasn't anything to tell.

Julia took out a pad and paper and listed all the businesses she could think of, then plotted her delivery path for her flier. With a few minutes to spare before the clock turned to nine, she left the café to pick up her order.

Chapter Eight

DAR PASSED JUL A SLEDGEHAMMER. “Ya getting sore?”

He was, but he was okay with it. He got a workout and stress relief all in one. He wasn’t going to tell Dar, but he enjoyed being back at work with him, not only for the distraction of sore muscles but the camaraderie. He’d forgotten how much that meant, somehow. And the immediate sense of accomplishment was addictive. In a swing, Jul could break away the ugly and poorly finished, then shovel it into a pail and throw it out for good. Out with the old, in with the new.

Dar put him in charge of demo and dumping, and so it went for most of the week. Stan had bad knees, so it made sense that Julian would be the one to cart the waste bins to the dumpster. He didn’t mind the heavy lifting a bit.

“You might get to see her, too, eh?” Dar suggested.

There was always that chance, but the week flew by and he never did. She kept to herself or went out almost every day. He wondered what she did and who she was seeing. All he knew for sure was that whenever she was home, she wasn’t coming to see him.

Friday morning was about the same. She hadn’t left before they arrived, but he saw her drive away before nine-thirty. Twenty minutes earlier, he’d been out in the yard.

Timing was not his friend.

Jul sighed and headed back to work. He was almost up the stairs when he heard the front door. Tradesmen came and went, but he hadn't met that one yet and as far as he knew, they weren't expecting anybody. "Can I help you?"

"This is quite the place. I've never been in here." The stranger let out a low whistle. "I was actually looking for Julia. Is she around?"

"No. She's gone out for a bit." For the first time, he was glad she wasn't there. "Can I take a message?"

"Sure." The man gave him his business card. "I'm Shane Harnes. I manage parks and open spaces for Juniper Creek."

"Jul Ariets. I'm a friend of Julia's." At least he hoped to be, one day. "And I'm working on the house."

"Is Brewer here?"

It shouldn't have been a surprise that he knew Darvvin too. Dar knew everyone. "Yes. Should I get him for you?"

"Nah, I'll find him. Is he up here?" Without waiting for an answer, Shane bolted up the stairs.

Jul was close behind him. "Um, if you'd wait—"

"Brewer? What the hell are you doing in here?"

Dar popped out of the corner bedroom. "Shane, what are you at?" They shook hands. "Good to see you."

"This is a good gig you've got here. Looks like you'll be busy for a while."

"Another month or two. You've met Jul?"

Jul watched from a few feet away.

"We met." Shane nodded. "I wanted to see Julia. It's business, but I guess it wouldn't hurt my eyes to take a look at her, either." He elbowed Darvvin, and they laughed.

Julian did not.

“She dropped off a brochure saying she’s putting on dinners and that this winter. I was thinking we’d try something new for the staff Christmas party. That’s if you don’t tear down the place before.”

Jul cleared his throat. “I can take your information and pass it along,” or drop it in the dumpster, burn it in a ditch. “Then you can be on your way.”

“Let’s head downstairs.” Dar led them to the check-in desk, where he found a paper and pen.

Jul snapped them out of his hands. “How many guests?”

“There are five full-time guys and their wives. About the same for seasonal, I guess. Then me. Twenty, twenty-five max.”

Jul diligently wrote the numbers down.

“Don’t tell me you’re going it alone?” Dar shoved Shane gently. “What about that girl from the dance?”

“Ah, flying solo for now.” Shane shook his head. “Is Julia single?”

Dar shot a look at his friend. “I believe she is.”

“Well, maybe she’d be my date?” Shane leaned on the counter. “She’s pretty sweet. If I’d been alone at that dance, who knows? She might be going with me, anyway.”

Dar clicked his tongue. “I’m sure I couldn’t comment on that.”

“Shouldn’t comment is more like it!” Shane elbowed him in the side.

The jar of paperclips tipped. Jul swept them together. “I’ll give her the message as soon as I see her.”

“Thanks. Do you have her number?”

Jul didn’t. “I’m sure she’ll call—”

"Her card's right over here." Dar offered one up to Shane without hesitation.

Jul's neck cracked when he twisted his head.

"Thanks for this Brewer." Shane read the words and waved the card against his fingers. "I'll call her—or maybe she'll call me first. We could arrange a private meeting to figure things out, just the two of us." He laughed again. "Gotta run. Nice to see you, Brewer. Julian, make sure she gets my card." He waved and made his exit.

Dar stared at the door for a moment before turning back to Jul. "I'd say you'd better up your game, my friend."

He inhaled, willing his heartbeat to slow. Nothing had happened. Thank God she wasn't even home. The guy was crude and … unsophisticated—and he was going grey. "I'd be really worried if he wasn't so much older than her."

"So much? Ten years, if that." He squeezed Julian's shoulder and headed upstairs. "Lucky he only came calling for business."

Jul tucked one of Julia's cards in his wallet.

✦✦✦

JUL'S NOTES REMAINED on the table where she'd left them. The script was perfectly formed, but so compact that it was tough to decipher. With a little concentration she could understand it.

Parks and Open Spaces
Christmas dinner
25 guests

Darvvin had tried to explain the situation, which was just weird. Jul had taken the message—why wasn't he telling her? He was nowhere to be seen.

She couldn't put a face to Shane Harnes' name, but the Wilbur's had introduced her to half the town the night of the rodeo dance. She might know the man when she saw him.

'*Save that for next week.*'

It had been too late to call him Friday by the time Darvvin gave her the message.

'*I'll have to do it Monday*,' she thought. And then her thoughts turned to Jul. She'd only seen him in passing all week. He'd been driving out behind her in Darvvin's truck one day. She waved in her rearview mirror and he opened his hand on the steering wheel. She counted it as a greeting, even if she wasn't sure it was.

Julia set up for her call late Saturday afternoon. She didn't have a thing to worry about, really. There was plenty of material to share without even a whisper about Jul.

Amanda was right on time. "So, how was this dinner party? With your *contractor*." She dragged the word out.

"It was great. Excellent company. Excellent meal. I met his whole family and his best friend." She jammed her fingernails into her palm. She wasn't planning to talk about him at all. "They have two little boys. Davey is four and Luke is two. Darvvin's wife, Stel, is amazing. Their baby is due in December. She thinks it's a boy but isn't going to tell Darvvin." Julia sipped. "They have a gorgeous acreage southwest of town. Their best friend lives in a suite over the garage. They've known him since they were teenagers. He was the best man at their wedding." She gulped down her wine to stop the ramble.

Her cousin sat tall. Julia could tell by the way she cocked her head that Amanda *knew*. It had only been thirty seconds, and she already knew something was up.

The floodgates opened. Julia told her everything—how she'd already seen Jul at the Coffee Stop and then how she'd gone to Darvvin's only to find out that his best friend in the world was the same man.

"Hold on a minute. He's Darvvin's best friend, he's named Julian, *and* he's the coffee shop guy? You have horseshoes up your—"

"It goes downhill from there." Thinking about it for the entire week had left Julia even more puzzled. "He wouldn't say more than two words to me unprompted. It was like pulling teeth to get anything out of him. I asked Darvvin about him when we were looking at the vanities. Jul was laid off last year and then moved to their place. I thought he might have gone through a big divorce or something, but Darvvin says he hasn't had a breakup for a while, whatever that means."

"You have a lot of information about a man who didn't really talk to you."

Her face heated up. "I was just trying to figure out why he had that 'deer in the headlights' look the whole time I was there."

Amanda set her glass down so hard that a crack sounded on the table. "They were totally setting you two up."

"No." The possibility had never crossed her mind. "I mean, he lives there, and he's over for dinner every night.

He probably felt uncomfortable with a stranger in the house." She replayed the evening in her memory. "There were some odd interactions a couple of times I guess, but—"

"It's a little too convenient to me. Two great singles make for an excellent matchmaking opportunity, in my humble opinion."

The man *had* seemed nervous or something. Then Stel shot down the comment Darvvin made about his brother. There were silences, uneasy laughter—"It *was* a setup!" Julia groaned. "Stel had me over twice last week. I wondered why she was asking me twenty questions. I thought she just wanted to get to know me."

"Questions about relationship status, by any chance?" Amanda smirked.

"I was asking about him. Asking if he was okay with working here with everything else he has going on. I'm not sure how it got on the subject of past relationships." She covered her eyes. "I feel like such an idiot."

"Why? I think it's a great compliment to both of you. They've known him forever and you for only a few weeks and they thought that you were good enough for him. You should be flattered." Amanda coiled her hair around her finger. "So, why is he single? Or did Stel only ask about you?"

Stel had offered up the information freely. "He had a disaster of a girlfriend a few years back. Stel thinks the girl traumatized him."

"Then you should be able to relate. You could be a caring shoulder for his beautiful blue eyes to cry on."

Julia tried to dismiss the visual. "Do you think he knew it was a setup?" She pictured him sitting on the other side of the room, as far from her as he could possibly be.

"Maybe he didn't know either and was surprised to see you, too. Could be, right? Do you think you'll see him at the café again? Did you manage to get anything out of him that you could follow up on?"

"Potentially. I offered to look at his business plan when he's ready." Her face was hot to the touch when she set it in her hands. "Oh, and he's working here."

"What?"

"With Darvvin. Helping him get the job done faster."

Amanda squinted. "How is it that you've neglected to share that little pearl of information all week? What else are you hiding?"

"I wasn't hiding anything. I didn't even know this was a thing to hide." She covered her eyes. "How am I going to get out of this?"

"You *want* to get out of this? Why? What happened when you saw him at your house this week?"

"I didn't."

Amanda's chair tipped back when she laughed. "Were you hiding from the man who you think they aren't trying to set you up with?"

"Of course not. I've been busy."

"Right." She dabbed the corner of her eye. "What's the worst that can happen? Julian's a dud? Then you're no further ahead or behind than you were to start with. Do what you normally do around the house, whatever that is. You've run into him twice without even trying. Who knows what could happen with him working in your home? But I guarantee Jules, if you sit alone in your room, nothing will."

Julia inhaled. She might as well tell Amanda the rest. "They've invited me to sit with them at church tomorrow and back for dinner."

Amanda stifled a laugh. "Well, roll with it. You like Stel, right? Build that friendship with her. Who cares about Mr. Gorgeous-businessman-cowboy?"

"Yeah, who cares about him?" She could buy into the friend angle at least. "I like Stel. I think we could become good friends." All she had to do was focus on that. She didn't even have to think about Julian, or his eyes, or the way he was so gentle with Dar's boys—or the way he looked like he wanted to run whenever he saw her. "Why isn't he into me?"

Amanda smiled tenderly. "Aw, give him a chance to get to know you. He's only seen you twice."

✦✦✦

THEY SAW JULIA'S 4runner in the church parking lot as soon as they arrived.

Stel knew all the details. "We're meeting in the gathering area." The two women were becoming fast friends. They'd spent two afternoons together at the acreage—while Jul was hard at work in town at her house.

"Miss Jul-ya." Davey ran to her side when they entered the building.

"Hi, Davey." She knelt to hug the boy.

Jul didn't know how she managed with her skirt and heels, but the motion was impossibly elegant..

“Good morning, Brewer family.” Julia reached for Luke’s hand while hugging Stel.

“We’re so excited to see you today.” Stel shifted Luke on her hip.

“And having you to the house.” Dar had his hand on David’s arm, preventing a runaway.

Jul watched from a few feet away. The Brewers had her surrounded and she was inaccessible, the sun in the middle of them all.

“Shall we take our seats? Dar likes to visit while people come in, so Jul and I leave him and get the kid set up in our row.” Stel looked for the big man. “Julian?”

He took a step closer.

“There you are.” She took Davey’s hand from Darvvin. “See you in a bit, hon.” They shared a kiss before she entered the sanctuary.

“Good morning.” Julia looked surprised to see him. “In all the fuss, I wasn’t even sure you were here.” She smoothed her hair over her shoulder.

He caught his breath. “How could I miss it?”

Her eyes scarcely squinted. “Of course. Can’t miss church.” She walked in front of him and they went to their seats. A few feet from Stel’s row, Julia slipped.

Jul caught her elbow. “You okay?”

She pressed her hands on her coat. “Yes, thanks. There must have been something on the floor.” She didn’t look at him when she sat down.

The boys sandwiched her between them, Davey on one side and Luke on the other.

Stel frowned at them. "If you need your space, please say so. They'll leave you be, won't you boys?"

Luke climbed onto Julia's knee and Davey cuddled beside her.

"Ah, I don't mind." She set an arm over each child and hugged them.

Jul watched from the aisle seat. He might not have been a part of their group at all, just another parishioner at the end of the row.

Julia read from a book that Stel had brought. Luke curled her hair around his hand as he listened. Even Davey was still for once. Jul wondered if anyone would even notice if he simply wandered away. If he'd driven himself, he could have made some excuse and gone home.

Luke looked at him as though he'd heard everything going on in Julian's mind. He wrapped his chubby hand around Jul's thumb, dispelling the thought.

Motion from the end of the row took his attention. Dar joined them, taking his place beside Stel. He caught Jul's eye and gave him a quick thumbs up. Stel pried the kids off of Julia in the minutes before the service started.

"I have to be quiet now." Davey held his lips closed with both hands.

Julia smiled at the boy, then turned to Julian. "Did you have a good week working at the house? It seems like things are really rolling now."

He stumbled over his words. "Oh. Yes. Fine. Good. I didn't see—"

The organ whined and drowned out everything he was trying to say.

"This is the day the Lord has made. Let us rejoice and be glad in it." The pastor's voice rang clear but it was the last phrase that Julian grasped that morning.

Sounds came into his ears, but they were incomprehensible as though they were another language. He dropped his chin and noticed her petite, polished shoes beside his wide, dusty boots. Julia Matthews was delicate and divine to see. She was smart and kind and standing by his side—close and yet so very far away.

A hymn began, and Jul started singing to himself. He closed his eyes as the sounds came from within, a kind of prayer that his soul knew but his conscience didn't. At the interlude, a soft touch on his shoulder took him out of the moment.

"You have an amazing voice." Julia's pretty brown eyes reflected the lights overhead as she stared up at him."Keep going. It's wonderful to hear."

His heart pounded some words out of his mouth instead of the song. "Oh, ah, thanks. I even sang at Dar and Stel's wedding."

"Be quiet at church." Davey's voice carried to the surrounding rows, entertaining the parishioners nearby.

Julia nodded to Davey and touched her finger to her lips before mouthing the word 'sorry' to Julian. The smile on her face made the room brighter still.

He let her go ahead of him for communion. It was powerful to kneel beside her for prayers when they'd returned to their seats. He tipped his head down and rested it on his hands so he could see her without being noticed.

Julia's eyes were closed, hands clasped beneath her chin, and her lips moved as she prayed.

Would she pray for him? Would he recognize his name on her mouth if she said it in silence?

He watched for as long as he dared while he said a prayer for her.

Another Sunday dinner with her was hours away. A thousand new words to say to her came into his mind and he tried to make a plan. He attempted to visualize how things would go. It had to be better than the week before.

Thankfully, the bar had been set pretty low.

+++

JULIA SENT A text message to Amanda shortly after she got home from dinner with the Brewer family.

Church went fine. Dinner was great.

Sleep well, princess.

There was nothing else to say. What was she supposed to do, write a novel about how Jul had an incredible voice and looked fantastic in his dress coat and jeans? The singing was one thing, but she'd expected him to look amazing and didn't need to go on about it. How could Julian Ariets look anything but spectacular?

She'd been hopeful at church. He seemed a little more relaxed when she said hello, and he was definitely more confident than she was after she slipped on the way to their seats. He'd steadied her almost before she knew she'd stumbled. It was hard to forget the comfort that his hand provided. Stability had been playing hide and seek in Julia's life for years.

"Teen girl crush," she whispered to the air as she replayed the rest of the night in her mind.

He'd seemed to enjoy dinner with the Brewers and the conversation that followed. Darvvin kept them laughing with stories about his brother, Eddie, and the summers that Jul had lived with them. All things considered, socializing was a huge success compared to the weekend before. Then, while they were having dessert and coffee in the living room, Jul disappeared down the hall. A while later, she noticed he hadn't returned. It had been more than twenty minutes, not that she was counting.

"Do you think your Uncle Jul is alright? He isn't here anymore." She asked Davey.

"Where'd he get to?" The sound of light switches clicking on and off accompanied Darvvin's search through the back of the house. "His boots are gone." He sent a text, then tried to phone, but got no answer. "I'm gonna go over—"

"It's been a long week. Maybe his mother called. She's been on him the last while," Stel reasoned. "He probably didn't want to disturb our conversation. One thing's for sure, Jul would never make a fuss over himself."

True as that might be, it was odd.

'I've got to figure him out,' Julia thought. She also had to ease the tension between them, especially since she was getting closer to the family. He was there first, but there was plenty of room for everyone.

'I'll have to connect with him more directly.' And she would—as soon as she figured out what that way was.

Julia pulled a blanket over her legs. Her gaze drifted to the stack of photo albums on the top row of the bookshelf. One was open in her arms before she knew it.

Golden memories of her family home stirred when she looked through the pages.

'*Brewers have a home.*' The inn was only a house—a temporary roof for people to sleep under until they went on with their lives. She longed for that feeling of home. It tore at her heart to look through the images of herself with her parents, but she kept going.

"We were so happy," she said.

A series of pictures of her mother and her aunt graced the next page. They'd looked happy, too.

Julia groaned and closed the book.

Dar and Stel had been together their whole lives. They had each other and their children, their acreage was stunning, and they even had their best friend living right there with them. Some people just had it figured out. In her life, she'd slated relationships like that for later.

"What if it is later?"

What if later had already passed her by?

She opened the album again and tried to peel her favourite snapshots from the adhesive backing. They were stuck so tight she couldn't free them without damage. Julia took pictures of them with her phone. Newton's printed photos and she was happy to give them her business.

"Better to have them on display than in a book." Decorating her space with happy memories would make it feel much more like home.

She couldn't shake the growing hope that someday, something else in her life might make it feel that way, too.

Chapter Nine

"YOU DIDN'T HAVE TO DISAPPEAR like that last night. One minute you're in the kitchen, next thing, you're gone." The scolding started even before Dar buckled his seatbelt Monday morning.

"You didn't have to go on about Ed." Jul shifted in the passenger seat. "He's not coming out here or something, is he?"

"Of course not. If you'd been listening, you'd have heard me say that he's seeing someone. Again. That's a worry of another kind." Dar turned up the heat. "And for your information, Julia noticed you left without saying goodbye before we did."

Guilt twinged his chest.

Dar continued. "Imagine the impression that made. You can't string two words together with the woman and then you vanish."

"I can't string two words together because you never let me say more than one at a time."

"Always an excuse, eh?" A patch of Dar's hair flapped with the breeze from the vent. He tried to pat it down. "Look, I'm having an issue in that back room we're working on. There's an old staircase between the rooms and we have to deal with it. You can tell her all about it, explain the whole thing. Alone."

"That's rich." Jul squeezed the grab handle. "You won't let me say a word at dinner, but you'll let me deliver bad news."

"There's no making you happy, is there?" Dar signalled his turn into town. "It's nothing too bad, you'll see. We just have to let her know."

Julia wasn't around when they arrived. They went upstairs. Dar explained the situation. "She'll probably want to take a look. Do you mind if I jump in then, being the one responsible and all that?"

"Fine."

"Great. Thanks." Dar shook his head. "You know where her suite is, right?"

"Suite?"

Dar dropped his shoulders and looked at the ceiling. "She lives in that room at the back of the house, right under us, actually. The door marked 'private'. Just knock. If she's not there, check the kitchen or the library."

Jul didn't know the place had a library.

"Main floor, the big room on your right as you come in. Head towards the back of the house. There's a set of pocket doors. If she's in there, they'll likely be open wide."

It would have been much easier if she had been waiting for them when they'd arrived.

"Do you want me to come and check on you in a few minutes?"

"No." Jul reviewed his message while he went down the stairs. With any luck, she'd be coming around the corner and he wouldn't have to knock.

She wasn't.

He could smell apples and coffee in the kitchen. A plate of muffins sat on a tray, but she wasn't there.

It would be easy enough to check if she was in the library before doing anything else. Jul wandered through the parlour. Even from the entryway, he could see that the pocket doors were closed tight.

He'd have to knock.

Once he returned to her door, Julian set himself up, feet solid on the floor. He took a deep breath and raised his hand.

✦✦✦

AMANDA TEXTED IN the middle of the night.

I can hardly wait to hear all of the juicy details ...

Julia tucked her phone away without replying.

Everything was ready for the day. Coffee was brewing, and she'd arranged a fresh batch of apple muffins on a plate. Darvvin and Jul had arrived a few minutes earlier and once they were settled, she'd activate her plan—invite them down for a bite, then pull Jul away for some advice.

'It's the perfect way to make him feel more comfortable,' she told herself.

She'd ask for his expertise and get him talking. They were both business people. Asking him to help her was completely acceptable. She'd help him in a heartbeat if he ever asked and she was betting he'd be happy to help her.

Julia brushed her mouth with gloss and did a quick hair check. She smacked her lips together twice before opening the door. The lights from the kitchen were blocked by an imposing form. She cried out moments before she realized who it was.

His hand banged on the trim. "Julia, I'm sorry. I didn't mean to scare you." Jul Ariets looked as shocked as she felt.

She breathed out a laugh. "It's alright. I wasn't expecting anyone to be there." Least of all Jul. Julia pushed her hair behind her ear and closed the door. "You must be after me."

"I am, um. I've been ..." He wiped his face and started again. "I mean, I was looking for you. For a message. I have one. For you. I was trying to find you, that is." Red blotches climbed up his neck. He tucked his thumbs in his belt loops and tried to smile.

"I ... we wondered what happened when you left last night. Were you under the weather?"

"A little. I just had to leave." He wiped his forehead. "I'm fine now. And I'm here and things are ... progressing. At the house—"

"That's great." She had to ask before she lost her nerve. "I'm glad I met up with you, actually. Do you have a second?"

"Sure." He glanced at his wrist but wasn't wearing a watch. "I'm ... what's up."

Julia tried to keep her voice steady. "I'm wondering about your consulting business. I need another perspective on a new booking system and I could use a second set of eyes. Would you be able to help me? I know you're busy."

His mouth opened, but he was silent for a second or two. "I don't have my computer here. With me. Working for Dar, so—"

"I don't want to interfere with your work here. I thought you could come by one evening this week if you have time.

Tonight? Tomorrow? I don't want to take you away from all the other things you have going on, but if you can squeeze me in—"

"I'll squeeze you—" His heel connected with a baseboard when he stepped back. "I mean that will work. Tonight?"

She'd imagined the conversation would be smoother than it was, but he sounded positive about their meet-up. It was a start. "If it's no trouble. We could always meet later this week, or next, whatever—"

"No." He almost shouted. "It's all good. I'm sure I can get a feel for you—some idea of how your business works if we meet tonight."

"Wonderful. Is seven a good time?"

"I will—I'll be here whenever you want."

"Perfect."

They stood a short distance apart as the clock ticked around them.

"You said you had a message for me?" Thank goodness he had, because she didn't have any idea what else to talk about.

"Um." Jul squeezed his hands tight. "I was coming to tell you we've run into a problem in that corner room. There's a staircase—"

His words were dulled by a storm of footsteps. "There you are." Darvvin stomped down the hallway towards them. "I came to see if you got lost." He tapped two fingers to his temple and saluted them. "Good morning, Julia. Sent him on a bit of a search mission for you. We have to let you know about a little challenge that popped up. Do you have time to look? We'll just show you."

“Oh, sure.” She followed Darvvin to the stairs.

Jul stayed put. When she looked back, he was exactly where they’d left him, staring at his boots.

Julia called to him from the bottom stair. “You’re joining us, right?”

The smile on his face wasn’t genuine, but it was there. “Yep, right behind you.”

AMANDA WAS GOING to have a field day when she heard everything that had been happening in Julia’s life.

‘*If she hears it.*’ Julia didn’t need to share everything—or *anything* for that matter. ‘*Besides, there’s nothing to share.*’

While she awaited Jul’s return that evening, she nibbled on cheese and crackers like a nervous mouse. Julia brewed a fresh pot of coffee and set out some cookies. Music played softly in the kitchen, a vital addition to the environment. It was important to have background noise in the event they ran out of things to say.

“That’s not going to happen.” She wouldn’t let it.

As the clock ticked closer to seven, Julia took a seat in the front window and watched the traffic go by. She scurried to the hall when she saw Jul's truck and waited just inside the front room to hear his footsteps on the verandah.

“Hello. Again.” She noticed the smell of fresh cologne as soon as she opened the door. He’d showered and shaved before he came over. Jul wore what looked to be new jeans and a new button-up shirt, dressed like he was going to church but without the sports coat. “Thanks for coming back. Here all day and then to come back …" She was trying to sound perky, and hoped she had.

"No problem. I didn't have much going on tonight. Quick dinner. I checked you out online." He cleared his throat. "Your website, I checked it. Then I drove here."

Julia rubbed the corner of her sweater between her finger and thumb. "Well, I appreciate it. We probably could have met on Sunday, too. I seem to have a standing invitation to dinner at the Brewer's place. I should have thought of that earlier, I guess. Saved you the trip."

He shook his head. "Do you really think the kids would have let go of you long enough for us to talk? Do you think Dar could stop telling stories for more than five minutes?"

It was the most natural thing she'd ever heard him say. She tried to keep her laugh natural sounding, too. "I guess you're right. This will definitely be less distracting." He followed her towards the back of the house. "I thought we could meet in the kitchen. I have the coffee on."

"Great space in here. I've only glanced in briefly." He set his bag on a stool at the end of the island.

Julia brought a pair of mugs to the counter. "This room and the library are my favourites. One thing I quickly learned from owning this place was that I don't need an enormous house. I could handle a library, a kitchen, and a really great master. That's one thing I'm lacking here."

His hair almost had a blue sheen in the bright lights. "They didn't leave it like the upstairs, did they?"

She nodded. "They did. That corner used to be a three-room servant's quarters back in the day. Somebody converted it into a small living room and bedroom with an ensuite. I'm not sure that happened thirty years ago, but they definitely decorated it back then." Julia set down her coffee. "Come and see it." She led him to her suite.

Julian scanned the room. "It's comfortable in here. I'm sure you could do a lot with a little paint." He brushed his hand over the joints between the floorboards. "At least they didn't ruin the wood."

"This room is alright, actually. It works, but take a look at this." Her bedroom door was open, and she led him through. "I'd love to know what you think we could do in here."

He tripped as he entered.

"You okay?"

"Fine. Just … the carpet."

"Isn't it something?" The floor was smothered with hunter-green. "And check this out." Julia opened the door to her ensuite. "I'm lucky to have it, but still."

He peeked his head inside the cramped three-piece bathroom. Hunter green and burgundy screened tile banded the inside of the shower. "The eighties hit this room hard."

She laughed. "It did. I wasn't too worried about it at first, but it's wearing a little now. And I wish I had a tub."

"Ask Dar about this. He'll put a guy on it."

"Maybe you?" She giggled.

Her comment won a little laugh from him. "You never know what Dar will get me to do. You could live in one of the other rooms while it gets done. The tile would be straightforward. Replace the sink, toilet, shower." He peeked back into her bedroom. "Might not be enough space for a tub, though."

"Barely enough here for my bed and tables."

"Yeah." His eyes roamed over the furniture. "I'm not sure he could enlarge the bathroom, but …" Jul's voice faded.

She could see his eyes jumping from place to place. "I have decent storage." Julia kept her tone light and gestured to the doors on the wall. "Thank goodness for that. There's quite a bit, considering the size."

He ran his fingers over her footboard then pulled back like he'd been burned. Jul walked out. "Definitely ask Dar to look at it. The timing is probably right to fix it up since you're closed."

"Spoken like a true efficiency planner." It hadn't been a good idea to show him her room. "I guess I shouldn't waste your time. Let's get to work."

They returned to the kitchen without speaking.

Jul set his bag on the counter. "Let me get this thing fired up."

Her notepad was ready beside it. "I can hardly wait to hear your ideas for my future."

Jul lost his grip on his belongings but caught the computer just before it slid off the counter. He didn't have the same luck with his bag. It tipped and a forest of paper fell to the floor. "Ah no." He scrambled to collect them.

Julia knelt to help. Some of the smaller notes had floated under the stools. She gathered them as fast as she could.

Jul swung towards her.

They collided and she fell to her side.

"Julia!" He leaned over her. "My god, are you alright?"

"I'm fine. We barely connected. It was just a surprise." The impact was more startling than anything. "I'm not hurt—"

"But I knocked you down. Let me see."

She pushed herself higher, but before she could sit up, Jul had her face in one palm, and the other hand tangled in her hair.

"Let me look." Julian examined her face, grazing his fingers along her hairline. He ran them down to her temple, over her eyebrows, and back up again.

"I just lost my balance. I'm fine." She felt like an idiot, but she wasn't hurt.

"Where did we connect?" Jul's fingertips skimmed her brows, then her cheeks.

"It's fine—" She was nudging away when she saw it.

Brown eyes met blue.

Earth met sky.

The world stopped.

It was right there in vivid blue.

Julian *cared.*

She hadn't been imagining it.

It *was* there.

Her fingers curled around his. "I'm fine. Completely fine." And she meant it with all her heart. It was impossible that an acquaintance could look at her that way, but he did. His expression was similar to what she'd seen at the café, but more intense—more sincere. A pulse went through her, but she didn't move. Neither did he. They kept close, kept their hands clasped together, eyes exchanging secrets. Their breath fell into sync.

Jul blinked and wrenched himself back. "I'd better help you up. Are you sure you're alright?"

Julia kept a hold on him as he moved. "I'm sure. Really." Still hand in hand, she accepted his strength when he helped her to her feet.

He let go as soon as she was steady. "I'm so sorry. I can't believe that happened."

"I can't either." Her heart was running. It felt meant to be, like destiny—like a collision course planned out for them before the beginning of time.

She gazed at him for a second more. The moment was vanishing as reality fell upon them. Her peripheral vision returned. His cologne scented the air as he made some space between them. Her hand missed his warmth and was getting cold, the other still clasped a paper. "There was this too. That's what I was reaching for when we ran into each other." She scanned the message when she offered it to him. The curving script read 'Savannah'. There were hearts—and a number.

Julia jerked her hand away. The paper fluttered to the floor like an ember.

"No!" Jul dropped again and swept all the pages together. He crammed them into his bag but crushed the offending scrap. "This shouldn't even be here. If there's one thing I don't need, it's that. I should have thrown it out the second I got it, but she was sitting right there. That girl from the coffee shop. She's a bit—" He looked around the room but didn't focus on anything. "Is your garbage under the sink?"

"Uh-huh." She couldn't say anything more without choking.

"That's the best place for this." He tossed the paper away and then washed his hands. "Now, where were we?"

Julia took a seat at the end of the island. "We were about to talk business." She let her hair fall around her face and drew a star on the pad in front of her. "The business of how to make things run smoother around here." She dug her fingernails into her thigh. It didn't diminish the sinking feeling in her heart.

Of course other women would be interested in him. It was naive to think anything else.

But it was clear that he wasn't interested in having a woman in his life at all.

Chapter Ten

DAR HAD THE TRUCK RUNNING when Jul joined him early Tuesday morning. "You got home late last night."

"Were you waiting up?"

"Davey heard you drive in."

"You let him stay up past seven-thirty? Amazing." Stel had the kid's schedule regimented like life depended on it. She never let the boys miss bedtime.

"Ah well," Dar grinned, "I'm sure you must've had a good night, anyway. Helped her out, helped yourself out?"

"It was fine, and it was strictly business."

"I hope you're lying, b'y. Things are dragging on."

It felt like a date—or at least something between a date and a client call. He was sure she'd changed her clothes and done her hair before he got there. The conversation had been going fine. It couldn't have been an everyday event for her to show off her bedroom. Then the phone number issue tipped things around—right over, upside-down. Julia went from hot to cold in a flash. Their visit flipped from summer warmth to a crisp walk on a frosty autumn morning—not entirely unpleasant, but you didn't want to be in it for too long, and you had to dress accordingly. For Julian, that probably meant a gag and something to secure his hands so he couldn't say or do anything stupid.

It was too late for that. She'd heard and seen it all.

Jul demolished the wall between the second and third room at the inn that morning. He dragged debris down to the dumpster and hauled materials up. There was ample time to let his mind wander.

"Think positive," Dar had told him.

He tried.

'At least Julia didn't get a concussion.'

That was the only glimmer of goodness the night offered. It was best to smash things for the day and try to forget it.

Mr. Lang phoned halfway through the drive home.

Dar listened carefully until the call ended. "You still helping Lang's?"

"He found some potatoes in the back corner of his garden. Wants help to bring them in."

"Need a hand?"

"No, I've got it," Jul replied. "Can't be too much there if he only just found them. And I'll eat at home tonight. I'm kind of tired."

"Suit yourself, but I'm happy to help. You don't have to do it all on your own."

But Jul needed some time alone. He needed to clear his head. He walked over to Lang's again. The wind accompanied him, pressing down the tall grass.

'Just like her pillow.'

The memory was as clear as if he was still standing at the foot of her bed. Her satin-covered pillow held the indent from where she lay her pretty head. He could just see her cuddled in with the covers up to her chin—or not.

He squeezed his eyes tight. No wonder he'd panicked and left the room. The image still made his pulse race.

The breeze toyed with the undergrowth, increasing in strength. With any luck, it would become a gust and the memory of the day before would blow away. He paused when he came to a group of deer grazing near the caraganas. They jogged away when he passed, a halfhearted motion that ended seconds later when he turned for the house.

Rowan Lang waited near the garden with a shovel in his hand. "Hey, young feller. Walking again, eh?" He laughed. "You're gonna want to drive when the rut gets going unless you want to fight."

Jul didn't understand what he meant. "Who will I be fighting?"

"The deer, a course. They'll be defending their space." He handed Julian the shovel and leaned on his cane with both hands. "Who knows? You might be a threat to some buck if you walk through his territory."

"This is their mating ground?"

"Doesn't look too romantic, but it is. Seen them out there the past few years. There's a buck around with a decent-sized rack. Wouldn't want to get in his way."

They wandered to the far side of the garden. Jul could make out the potato heaps under the dying leaves. He started to dig. "You must watch the wildlife all the time. I watch them too when I can."

"Yep. We've got a good view from the kitchen table. You'll see the buck scratching and rubbing his horns. When he finds his doe, he'll put himself in front of her, hoping she'll notice him. They'll wait for days sometimes if they have to, wait on the doe to get the hint."

Jul freed a pile of potatoes from the earth. "Do you have something to put these in?" He didn't wait for Mr. Lang's answer. A wheelbarrow lay half buried in the lilacs at the edge of the yard. It only took a minute to rescue the thing and load the harvest inside.

"I'm sure thankful you're here. Margaret is especially. She worries for me, you know?"

"Do you have any family close?" It was a wonder nobody was there to help them.

"Nah. One son is in Vancouver, the other's in Winnipeg. We do okay, though."

They *had* been doing fine, but things had changed.

The sun was setting by the time Jul finished. He rolled the barrow of potatoes to the garage slowly enough for the men to walk together. A bucket was portioned off for the Brewers, and Mr. Lang promised he'd put the rest into storage somewhere in their house.

Jul doubted that would happen. "I'll help you bring them in."

"No, you've done lots for tonight." Rowan waved his cane. "That should be the last of it unless you want to help me dig the whole garden under for the season."

There was little chance of that happening without Jul's help. "I'll get Darvvin's rototiller. We can do that later this week."

"Sounds like a plan. Have a good one and thanks again."

Jul said goodbye and started for home. With every step, the full five-gallon pail swung into his leg slowing his pace.

The deer hadn't wandered far since he'd passed them the first time. Julian stopped to watch them before he crossed to Brewer's yard. A fawn noticed him and took a few steps closer, curiosity stronger than fear.

"You want a potato?" He tossed one on the grass between them. It startled the animal and sent the group trotting away.

He should have known not to do that.

Hungry, he was hungry. As he left the herd, he regretted saying he'd eat at home. Toast wasn't going to cut it after such a long day. He envied the deer. "Grazing all day," he muttered. "Never say the wrong thing. Things just seem to work out." It was so simple for them. The buck found his doe and got close. That was it.

And he'd never have to explain another doe's number.

"You've got it way too easy." Jul shouted.

A doe flicked her ears, then went back to grazing.

"See what I mean?" Jul marched towards Dar's land, thoughts spinning in his head.

And then he froze.

Dust settled over his boots when he stopped in the middle of the path.

"The deer." In a flash of inspiration, Jul knew exactly what he had to do. A brilliant idea formed in his mind. Certainty warmed his chest as the thought evolved.

'The perfect solution was right there this whole time.'

He'd been overcomplicating his life when it could have been so simple.

He'd planned to go to Brewer's house but detoured when he saw the lights in the garage.

Dar was working in his shop. "You just finishing? That must have been a lot of potatoes—oh, it was. You brought some with you."

"I need to talk to you."

Dar tucked his pencil over his ear and crossed his arms. "You're quitting, aren't you?"

"What? No ... well, eventually, but that wasn't what I was going to say. I want to talk about ... it's this Julia thing." He was sure that Dar rolled his eyes. "I know you're frustrated with me, but I think I've come up with a plan."

"I look forward to hearing this." Darvvin pulled out a stool.

Jul almost wished he hadn't started the discussion. He walked to the window and gazed at the darkening day. After a long breath in and out, he began. "You know the white-tailed deer?"

Dar's eyes opened wide. "They haven't started talking to you, have they?"

"I watch them all the time." Jul shared his newfound expertise. "Did you know that a white-tail buck will spend hours—maybe even days—around a doe before they pair? To get her attention, to get her to notice him." He felt Dar's eyes on him as he paced.

"Right and then they mate and he leaves her and finds another one. It's the Eddie Brewer dating method. Not built for long-term anything."

"No, that's not what I mean. That's not what this is about." Jul breathed out a slow sigh. "I think I need to put myself in front of her. I need to get into her space so I can get her attention."

"What do you mean? You see her every day at her place … well, most days. Sometimes. And church. And here. I'm sure the Sunday feed is a regular thing now. Thanksgiving dinner this weekend—"

"No Dar-man. I need more than that." It was time for the reveal. He sat beside his friend. "I've given this a lot of thought—" Jul coughed lightly. "I'm going to ask her if I can move to the inn." He was expecting a big reaction, and the look on Dar's face didn't disappoint. "Just for a couple of months. Just during the rest of the renovations."

Darvvin looked up to the lights above them. His eyes moved side to side and his mouth repeatedly tensed and released. Eventually, he spoke. "You, Julian, and believe I mean this when I say it," he set his hand on Jul's shoulder, "you're bat shit crazy, my friend. You've lost it. buddy."

Jul opened his mouth to protest, but Dar continued.

"I love you like a brother. I love you more than I love most of my brothers. I love you like Eddie. I've known you for more than half my life and I would do anything for you—anything. But that's pure insanity. What are you going to say to her? 'Hey Julia, can I move in with you for two months to see if we can pair?'"

"Hear me out." The plan was so simple. He'd go over with Dar in the morning and ask if he could rent a room for a few months. "We can tell her that Stel is getting really tired with the baby coming."

"But Stel isn't getting tired. Well, no more than usual—"

"It just seems right." Jul felt bottomless certainty, and he hadn't felt that way in a long time. "It will help me connect with her in a way that I won't be able to do any other way."

Dar opened his arms wide and shook his head. “Couldn’t you just ask her out to dinner some night?”

“I could barely bring myself to knock on her door. I lose my words anytime I try to talk to her.”

“So, it’s easier to move yourself to her hotel and see where that takes you?”

“It sounds extreme, I know, but ... it’s exactly how it works in nature.” He wished Dar would stop being so doubtful. If it worked in the wild, it had to work for him. “The buck puts himself in front of the doe. It’s just going to be happening at an inn in my case. It will be good for me—for both of us—to see how we get along in daily life.”

Dar pointed his finger. “You want a wife without the hassle of the first date.”

“That’s not it and you know it.”

“That’s exactly what it sounds like.” Dar pressed his lips together and stared at his hands. “Tell me this, should a b’y stand ashore with the lifejacket while his best friend jumps into wild water? Makes no sense.” The room was silent. “You know, I would do anything to help you. I would, and I will. I just think you need to sleep on it for a couple of days.” He raked his hands through his messy hair. “I’ve never seen you like this about anyone. What was your longest relationship? That thing with Cara. Three months? Julia’s a great girl, but I doubt that you even know her well enough to appreciate it yet.” He turned his face towards Jul again. “What if you give it a week? Think it over.”

It wasn’t what he wanted to hear, but it was probably a good idea to sleep on it for a few days. There was a chance he was a little foggy.

"And you are coming back to work with me, right? I like it that you're there, y'know. Feels like the old days."

"Yeah, I'll keep working for you." Working with his hands had been good for his soul. "I can't promise I'll be there forever. I really do have to get my own business together."

"You have to get everything together." Dar shook his head. "Moving in with her ... you're some unpredictable, you are."

"Let's just hope this works."

Chapter Eleven

EVERYTHING SHOULD HAVE CHANGED IN that instant. The moment he got his 'great idea', everything should have clicked into place. Jul knew what he had to do—but things were exactly the same as before.

The week passed with no progress. Jul worked at the inn, ate with the Brewers, went to bed, and stared at the ceiling until he passed out. The cycle started over every morning. Julia did her thing, he did his, and he barely saw her.

Thursday night, they finished early. Davey hung off of Jul's leg after their usual embrace when he came in for dinner.

"Walk me in the hall." The boy balanced on Jul's feet and giggled.

That was always good for his heart to hear. Jul held the boy's hands and walked them around the corner.

Stel blocked their path. "What in the world did you say to Julia the other night? What exactly?" She looked strangely menacing with a ladle in her hand.

"I said a lot of things." Why would Stel care? "Better photos for her website. A yearly maintenance shutdown." They'd discussed how to make availability easier to search and shared ideas about efficient scheduling, but that was after the papers fell and he'd held her and—"The phone number?" He couldn't remember what he'd said word for word. "I didn't say anything. I just threw it out."

"Why are you carrying around some woman's phone number?"

"It was Savannah's. She gave it to me without me asking. I just lost it in my stuff—"

"Well now Julia thinks you don't want a relationship at all." Stel sagged. "I spent all afternoon with her, trying to let her know you are very much interested in a relationship someday. With *someone*. All the while trying not to sound like I was pushing you on her. Or her on you. Do you know how hard this is? Knowing your side and being her friend."

She had it all wrong. "I didn't say I didn't want a relationship. I said I didn't want Savannah."

Stel cracked a spoon on the edge of a saucepan. "Well, whatever you said, that's what she heard. I'm glad she told me so I could do some redirection." She shook her head. "Not that it seemed to work."

Dar dished out his two cents. "She seemed fine this morning. Didn't she?"

"I didn't see her today." Jul was wondering what would happen when he saw her next for longer than a minute. He'd seen her Tuesday morning, if he remembered right. She said hello but he hadn't seen her again that day and he hadn't seen her since. "She's been avoiding me." Jul sank into his chair. "I thought that was going to be the start of things, the best interaction we've had together." He wondered if Stel knew about their collision and that moment when they looked at each other. If she knew about that, she probably knew that he'd backed away, too. Warmth surged through him. “I don’t know how she got that impression out of what happened. Maybe it’s a sign.”

Dar nodded. “Maybe it is—“

“Darvvin Brody Brewer. If we don’t have something positive to say, we’re not saying it, remember?”

“That was positive. I was agreeing with him.“

Jul slumped in his seat. “It shouldn’t be this hard.”

Stel took the chair beside him. “If you’re being honest, you haven’t exactly been acting yourself, have you? It’s only a road bump. It’s probably a good thing she’s even got the concept of a relationship going in her mind. She’s even thinking about you getting involved with someone. Her wheels are turning for sure. I think it’s time to take action.” She clasped her hands. “I hope you don’t mind, but Dar told me about your idea—the move to the inn.“

The men looked at her, then at each other.

Darvvin raised his hands. “Sorry, I thought Stel would—“

She cut him off. “It’s time to ask Julia if you can stay there.”

Darvvin opened his mouth.

“I’m dead serious, Dar.”

“Move in?” Dar raised his voice. “At least she’s not going to think it’s because he’s stalking her.”

“Dar.” Stel shook her head.

“What? It’s true.“

She faced Jul. “Do you still think that’s the way to go? Or maybe you’ve come up with a different idea?” She held Julian’s hand. “I don’t want you to feel rushed, but you’re only going to be working there for another six weeks or so. I’m sure we’ll still see her—she’s becoming a good friend. But

I'm not sure that's going to help you if something doesn't change."

Moving to Julia's place had seemed like the only option when he came up with it, a sure solution to every obstacle in his way. They had connected, somehow. That had to have been real. She had to have felt it too. If only he'd done something more—but what did that even mean? 'Something' was a mystery, but he knew what nothing was—it was what he'd been doing every day.

He was practically an expert at *nothing*.

He'd made no extra effort. He'd taken no risks. Jul was going along with the daily routine. So much for being the 'buck'.

If he did nothing more, in a few weeks, he'd only be seeing her at church or the Brewer's for dinner. He had to put himself in front of her—that was the way to make it work. He still believed it.

"It actually gives me peace when I think about it. If she agrees to it, of course."

"True, she could always say no —" Dar silenced when Stel gently jabbed him in the ribs. "When then? When do we do it? And you're sure there isn't a simpler way?"

"There's no other way." Stel slapped both hands on her thighs. "You'll go tomorrow."

✦✦✦

JULIA WAS LATE making the coffee on Friday morning, and the crew would be there soon. She had to get going with her day, and she wanted to be back in her room before work began. Disappointment lingered from her evening with Jul. It was better if she didn't see him.

Somehow, she'd blurted the story to Stel—the number part anyway. The rest she kept close to her heart.

Stel assured her that he must have simply been embarrassed.

"And so he should have been." Holding onto another woman's number for some opportune time—

That wasn't it at all. If there had been a number in her things and he'd found it, she might have reacted the same way as him. "But I wouldn't have said I wasn't interested." Especially after they'd connected—they'd been so close that she could have kissed him. It was as though he'd rejected the potential that they'd be anything more than friends.

It wasn't true to think she didn't want to see him—she longed to see him, but there was no point.

Julia poured a coffee for herself and went back to her room.

Darvvin and Jul were waiting at her door.

"—think about it for a bit?" Darvvin was trying to whisper but missed.

She was too close to eavesdrop. They would have sensed her in a second. "Think about what?"

"Julia." Dar saluted.

Jul watched his boots.

"We have a bit of a problem and hope you can help."

"What happened?" It couldn't be a big problem based on how he was smiling.

His mouth started, and it took longer than it should have to get to the point. He—correction, *they*—were hoping

Julian could move in. "Stel needs to take it easy. This would really help."

Julia tried to make sense of it. "I saw Stel yesterday. Is she alright? She didn't say a thing."

"Oh, that Stel. She would never have said. But we've been talking about it for a bit." Dar nodded. "She's working so hard with the boys and with the baby coming in, um, in a few months. I thought she could use a bit of a break. Once we're done working here, I can be home for Stel and the baby and he can come back." He tapped the toe of Julian's boot. "Not that we're kicking you out, of course."

"Of course," Jul said to his feet.

In a way, it felt like fate. At the very least, opportunity was knocking. If there was one way to crack Jul's shell, having him under the same roof as her would do it.

Julia responded quickly, "Of course, he can stay—you are welcome to stay, Jul. I'm happy to help in any way I can."

She showed him the Blue room. Somehow it seemed perfect for him, master blue suite for the big man with blue eyes. As nice as it was, she knew the Blue room barely compared to his space at Dar's.

"No mountains here," she said. "You'll only have a street view. I'll show you the garden later, but I know that's not going to be the same. I hope it will be alright."

"Lots of other things to enjoy besides the view," he replied.

She wasn't sure what they would be, but he sounded optimistic. "I don't have any bedding. I sent it home with Rachel, my cleaner. She's gone for the long weekend." She checked the linen closet in case she was mistaken, but it was nearly empty. "I'll run to the city and get some sheets. I'm sure I have enough blankets—"

"No, I don't want you to go to any trouble over this. Whenever it works is ... fine."

Jul wasn't in a rush. No wonder. He was practically getting evicted. She couldn't let him feel like she didn't want him either—that she didn't want him at the inn. "You are welcome anytime. It's no trouble to pick up bedding, but if you'd rather wait, Rachel said she'd be back on Monday afternoon to get things set up. I guess that means you can move in on Tuesday morning at the latest."

"You'll both be at our place for Thanksgiving dinner on Monday, anyway. One last weekend at our place and then you can move in Tuesday before work." Dar clapped his hands together. "It's all settled."

Jul just nodded.

ON SATURDAY NIGHT, Julia stocked the table with an entire bottle of wine and a charcuterie board big enough to serve six. She wasn't very hungry and probably wouldn't be eating much of it. There was a pit in her stomach. She felt bad for Julian, and bad for having to tell her cousin everything that had been going on.

"What a waste." She attempted to make herself comfortable at the corner table. It was a waste to worry. Amanda lived on the other side of the world. She wouldn't even know what was happening in Julia's life if she wasn't told. "I don't have to say anything." It wasn't anyone else's business who stayed at her property, so she'd keep quiet, keep it to herself. As long as Julia could be strong—

The screen had barely come to light when she blurted out the news. "He's moving in."

"Hello to you too." Amanda drank the contents of her glass in one go. "I was going to give you trouble for missing my birthday, but I think this will be more interesting."

Julia set her head in her hands. "I'm so sorry. I can't believe I forgot." Amanda's birthday had fallen on the previous Tuesday. "My mind was on other things. Happy belated birthday."

Amanda nodded. "Thanks. Now, if we could start again, that would be fantastic."

Julia blew a breath through her lips. "Jul asked to rent a suite here for a while." That wasn't true. Darvvin had done all the talking. "And so I said yes." She lifted her chin, only to drop it for a drink seconds later.

"That makes no sense."

"Well ... Stel is getting tired with the boys and all that. They think if he lives here, it will take some of the pressure off until the baby is born."

Amanda's laughter was loud and long-lasting. "That's rich. He's moving in with you? Because of Stel? Aren't they having you for Thanksgiving dinner on Monday?" She wiped her eyes. "It's worse than a soap opera."

Julia waited while she pulled herself together. "I can't imagine how Jul felt when they told him they wanted him to leave." He was like a little kid getting passed between divorced parents.

"Sure," she muffled another laugh, "Take his side."

"I feel bad for him. They want him out and he can't even move in until Tuesday. Rachel is away for the weekend and I've got no bedding. I told him I could go to the city to buy some, but he didn't want me to go to any trouble."

"Shame you won't have him for a few days longer."

"I'm only helping some friends."

"Uh-huh." Amanda smirked. "There is never a shortage of news when I talk to you, that's for sure. They're really tightening the screws on this setup thing."

"I guess." Julia closed her eyes. In a perfect world, people would meet and fall for each other and nobody would have to interfere. There would be no setups, or awkwardness, or beds with no bedding. "I'll humour their little infatuation, but they're wasting their time. Once the baby's born, he can go back and figure out his life."

Amanda watched her for a moment. "You say that like you don't care."

"I do care. I care about the Brewers. I even care about Julian when it comes down to it. I wouldn't have wanted to tell my best friend to go live somewhere else, even if it was for a setup." Jul looked lost when Darvvin was going on about the move—lost or at a loss of some kind. She recognized it well. She'd felt like that too in life. "Anyway, he doesn't seem to be picking up any of their hints. He's made it clear that he's got other things on the go in his life that take priority over love."

"Oh?" Amanda sipped. "How would you know that?"

She wasn't planning to mention that either, but—"Jul was over here the other night. Helping me with the website and that. Actually, I'm not going to go into it. I can't."

"What happened?" Concern replaced the grin on Amanda's face.

She'd had a million miles of thoughts about the night. "We had this moment. Or maybe we didn't." It was easier to tell herself that the feeling that struck her when they were so close to each other was a beautiful fragment of her imagination. Except, deep down, she knew it wasn't. It felt as sure and solid as the seat she was sitting on. "I thought we connected. He'd dropped a bunch of papers and I was helping him pick them up when it happened."

"When what happened?"

She couldn't describe it. "It doesn't matter. I found a woman's phone number. He was embarrassed and threw it out, but made it clear that the last thing he needed was something like that." Julia could still feel her heart drop, just like the moment it happened. "Stel thinks he's a little gun-shy. She says he's always wanted someone, just not the girl who gave him her number ... that he's in a big transition time right now."

"You saw her recently? Don't you think the timing of this move is interesting?"

"I'm tired of thinking about any of it." She finished a cluster of grapes. "I'll go along with their scheme and try to make the best of it."

"Too bad, really. The timing seems out of sync." Amanda leaned forward. "Once everything settles, there's still hope."

"I'm not holding my breath."

Chapter Twelve

JUL HAD EVERYTHING PACKED BY Saturday night, a fact that he never planned to reveal to anyone. Early Tuesday morning, he piled his bags and guitar in the truck. As he was driving away, Dar ran out of the house, waving his arms.

"Stel has some food for you two and the boys want to say goodbye."

His little godson waved from the back door.

Julian shut off the ignition. "I didn't think they'd be up." He couldn't leave without a hug, even if he'd be seeing them on Sunday at the very latest.

"You had your mind on other things." Dar smirked. "She hugged you before she left last night. Do you think she'll be hugging on you when you get there this morning?"

Jul wasn't sure it could be called a hug. She'd embraced the Brewers one by one and already had her coat done up. Then Davey dragged her by the hand and said 'Hug Unca Jul too'. Julia put on a smile and stuck out her hand. They leaned close and patted each other on the back. It was enough to appease Davey, and then she left. "We'll see what happens."

"It was a grand feast, don't you think?"

"It was." As usual, they'd gone person to person before Thanksgiving dinner to say what each was most thankful for.

Julia's message choked him up.

'I can't actually remember a time in my life when I was invited to celebrate with friends. It's always been business associates who felt sorry for me,' she'd said. Her voice cracked and Stel hugged her. Dar comforted Stel and Davey took advantage of the moment to cuddle between them.

Jul and Luke maintained their positions in their seats, but Jul knew he should have gone to her, too. He wasn't strapped down like the two-year-old.

"Jul?" Dar shoved him gently.

He snapped out of the memory. "You guys had her surrounded during dinner. There was hardly any room for me at the table."

Darvvin laughed. "No room for you at the table, b'y, but at least there's room for you at the inn."

They went inside. Stel gave him the rundown on all the food she was sending, and they packed it to the door. Jul hugged the boys and promised he'd see them soon. After a quick embrace and 'good luck' wish from Stel, he left them.

"See you in a bit." Dar waved.

Jul tried to calm down as he drove. He'd left early and would arrive before Dar. That would be a good thing. It gave him another opportunity to talk to her uninterrupted. Nothing could go wrong. There were no incriminating phone numbers anywhere in his possession.

"Hello, Julia," he said to the steering wheel.

He sounded like a telemarketer.

"Hey, Julia." He cleared his throat. "Hi. Julia." He lowered his voice. "Hi there ... Well, hello. Good morning."

He'd have to save 'honey, I'm home' for later.

In his dreams, he could see it so clearly. The door would swing wide open before he even had to touch it. Julia would greet him with a big smile on her face, just like the night he'd gone over to help her.

But Jul had been working there long enough to know that it wouldn't go like that at all.

His nerves hit when he drove into the yard at the inn. He struggled to carry too many things to the porch at one time. A note with Julia's name on it was wedged in the sliver of space where the double doors met. He pocketed it, tucked the first load of his belongings inside the building, then returned to his truck for the bags of food.

The only thing that he and Julia had settled was a move in date. They'd spent no time at all figuring out any other important details like eating arrangements. It sent him into a panic when Stel had brought it up, but she told him not to worry. The stuff she sent would keep them going until they could make a plan.

He worried anyway.

The clock ticked hello as he rolled his suitcase to the desk at the bottom of the stairs. A set of keys lay under a piece of paper. 'Welcome!' it read in swirly letters.

"Good morning. Let me help you with some of that." Julia entered from the back hall. She was put together like a dream. "I was going to go out for some groceries quick, but I heard you drive in." She patted the countertop. "So I thought I'd wait and say hello."

"Stel did food." He pointed at the bags near the hall table.

Julia tilted her head to the side.

"I mean hello and, uh, Stel made extra food and had leftovers from last night. You know how she is. And I had milk and a few eggs from my place. Peanut butter." Julian took a breath. "I cleared out my fridge."

"Stel sent food? Isn't she supposed to be resting? That woman is amazing." Julia lifted a bag. "All of this?"

He nodded and picked up the rest.

"Let's get it in the fridge and then we'll put your things upstairs." They set the bags on the island. "Did she cook for you for a month?"

"Oh. No. That's for both of us. For you *and* me. She thought we could use some food, I guess."

"Food is totally her love language." Julia looked over the items. "I won't need to buy much at all. This will take care of us for days." She paused at a large bundle wrapped in tinfoil. "Is this an entire ham?"

"I completely don't expect you to feed me." No one would ever accuse Jul of being wise in the way of women, but he was certain that successful business owners didn't like being saddled with needy men.

"I can't have a guest here and not have eggs and milk in the fridge. I need to eat too, right? And this situation is a bit different than if you were a *regular* guest."

He liked the way she said the word, even if it didn't mean anything.

They finished unpacking, and she rinsed her hands. "Let's get your things up to your room."

He could almost hear what Dar would say if he walked in to see Julia carrying his bags up the stairs. "I can get everything."

"You have a guitar. You'll have to play it for me sometime. Here." She jingled the keys in the air. "Front door, kitchen door, and your room key, but I left it open for you."

He clipped them onto his keychain, then tucked the welcome note into his wallet. "Thanks. I'd better get these things put away before my boss shows up."

"Welcome to—" she hesitated, "I'm changing the name, so I guess I'll just say welcome for now. If you come up with any bright ideas for a new name, let me know." She fiddled with a stack of index cards, slapping them against the counter to square them up. "I should be around most of the day today, and you have my number if you need anything. Oh, and the coffee's on. Come and get a cup when you get settled if you have a minute. I still have to show you where everything is in the kitchen."

Jul planned to take some time to arrange things in his new room, but he ended up dropping his bags through the door and going back downstairs. The guys would arrive within half an hour, and he wanted to have a few minutes of quiet before the workday started.

He returned to the kitchen. Julia was polishing the marble counter near the stove. A strand of hair had fallen away from the rest and waved in time with her movements. Music played in the background. She didn't see him at first, giving him time to feel the moment. It was like he was watching something on stage.

"Hi again." She wiped her hair away with her wrist when she noticed him. "Coffee?" The pot was on the counter closest to them. "Cups are up here. There are travel mugs too if you want to take some upstairs with you for work." She set one down on the table. "Cream? Sugar?"

"Black is fine. Thanks." He poured himself a cup. "Can I get something for you?"

"I'm already working on one. Here." She slid a plate of muffins towards him. "Is the room okay? You were pretty quick."

"I just threw everything in the door. I can unpack tonight."

"You needed coffee. I get it." She sipped from her cup. "How about the comforter? I was hoping the grey would tone down the blue in there a little."

He hadn't even noticed it. "When did you pick that up?"

"I went to the city on Sunday after church."

"You shouldn't have—"

"Trust me, it's a million times better than the floral disaster that was in there." She leaned on her hand. "Do you like it?"

Julian jerked a cupboard open. "Where are the glasses? I think I need some water."

"Right here." She helped him. "It must be hard for you to leave the guesthouse. You had everything there, right? Kitchen and all that?"

"I did." He took a long drink of the cold water. "But things are going to work out fine here."

"It's only for a few weeks, and then they want you back."

He could have done without the reminder.

Julia's eyes smiled at him while she drank. She was chatty and clearly playing her innkeeper role, but it was a starting point. That was all he had to do, focus on that, make it through day by day. Keep putting himself in front of her—

"Muffins?" Dar stormed in, startling them both.

Jul wasn't sure if his friend was clueless or cruel.

"Good morning. Would you like one?" Julia offered him the tray.

"I don't mind if I do, thanks." He tore the top off of one. "We're going to make some good progress today, I'm sure of it. The peach room is practically done. It's not going to be peach anymore."

"I can hardly wait to see the final product." She turned to Jul. "Remind me to show you the before pictures of that suite with the draperies and everything. I don't think you were working here yet when it all came down. Think how my bathroom looks, but peach."

Darvvin was still chewing, but he couldn't help but talk. "You saw her bathroom? The one in her suite?" The words popped out as uncontrollably as the crumbs from his mouth.

Jul nodded.

"Hm." Dar dipped his chin and then finished his bite before proceeding. "Anyways, we're going to go on with the Sewing room enlargement, reconfigured just like we talked about, Julia. Then I can get to the bathrooms in the big rooms." He elbowed Julian. "So don't get too comfortable, my friend, because you're going to have to move one day soon."

✦✦✦

LATE TUESDAY MORNING, Julia called Stel to thank her for sending the food.

"It was the least I could do," her friend said. "Thanks for letting Jul stay and taking the load off of me here."

The woman sounded completely sincere, even if the evidence hinted there was more to the story.

Dar left before lunch, so it was only Jul and the rest of the men working until nearly five that day. Julia was already picking from the selection of item's Stel sent when Jul joined her for dinner.

He'd cleaned up and changed clothes.

It was a little like entertaining a normal guest. They made small talk and she filled him in on the history of the house. But where other guests let her serve them, he wouldn't. He seemed adamant about helping whenever he could. Jul didn't hesitate to clean up.

"Just leave me to it," he said. "I'm sure I can figure out where everything goes."

She wasn't going to do that, but appreciated his offer.

"I'm not abandoning you to do everything yourself." Julia stacked some leftovers in the fridge. "But thanks for helping."

"Anytime." He folded a tea towel over the oven door handle.

She might have been imagining, but he seemed to be settling in, a little at least. "Let me give you the grand tour, now that we have time." If she could keep him moving, there was a chance that conversation would flow, too. "I'm don't think that you've spent much time on the main floor. A walk-through might help you get your bearings."

"Lead the way."

She showed off the butler's pantry first. "I usually keep this stocked with snacks and drinks when I have guests. It's running a little low now, but you've got special access to the kitchen, so that shouldn't be a problem. Lots to eat in there."

"I don't think we'll run out of food," he half smiled and followed her through the dining room to the patio doors.

"I have a fire garden out here."

"Fire garden?" He squinted in the evening light.

She opened the door and let him through. "Fire pit. Sounds fancier to say garden." It sounded silly when she thought about it. "Anyway, this is a nice space no matter what you call it."

"It's a good setup." Jul took his time wandering around the stone pit in the middle. He took a seat on the bench and looked around.

Julia swept up some drying leaves instead of sitting beside him. He was quiet, lost in his thoughts.

Finally, he spoke. "It's nice out here. Reminds me of Dar's in a way. Better here, though. Don't tell him I said that."

She balanced the broom against the wall. "Hopefully, we'll get to use it sometime this fall. I need to brush up on my fire-making skills, so maybe you can show me. You said you two were Boy Scouts, right?"

"We were. I'd be happy to show you."

"Maybe this weekend sometime?"

"Ah, sure." He shoved his hands in his pockets, wandering the pathway opposite to where she stood.

"Want to come in and see the Front Room?" They entered through the dining room doors. "Make yourself at home. There's a big screen and a wood-burning fireplace, too." When she glanced back at him, a sheet of paper was in his hand.

"This was in the door this morning. I picked it up when I was bringing my bags in and then forgot about it. Just found it in my coat pocket."

"Oh?" It was an old envelope with her name on it. The handwriting seemed familiar. Someone had scrawled a note on the floral paper inside. She scanned it.

Julia covered her mouth. Her throat was desert dry.

"You okay?"

"Where did this come from?" She tightened her grip on the page to stop herself from shaking.

"It was in the door. Wedged between them. When I got here this morning."

"I have to make a call." Her hip connected with the side of the sofa when she rushed past. She jogged through the hall and struggled to get a grip on the doorknob to let herself through. When she was in her suite, Julia called Amanda.

Her cousin's voice sounded as the screen came to light. "Hope you have something good to—"

"Did you know about this?" Julia slapped the paper in her hand. "Your parents showed up. Did you know?"

Amanda's chin dropped, then she frowned. "You saw them?"

"They left a note sometime yesterday. Julian just gave it to me." She bound herself in her arms. "Why don't they leave me alone? It was fine that way. Things were fine."

"I had no idea they'd stop by. I thought after they didn't come the long weekend—"

"Yeah, me too." She read the note out loud. "Hi Julia, we were passing through Juniper Creek and wanted to see your place. It's beautiful. Talk soon, Auntie Wanda and Uncle Jesper. Hugs."

Neither of the girls said anything while the words settled.

"Hugs," Julia shouted. "Like they've always been in my life. Like they were just away for the weekend and it hasn't been twelve years." The rage pushed tears into her eyes. She wiped her nose. "Why? Why are they doing this?"

"I don't know. They're getting older, they're—"

"Messing up my life again. I don't want it. Maybe once upon a time I wanted them involved, but I don't need them now. I got over it." She threw the envelope on the floor and wiped her forehead.

"Jules ..."

"I'm so glad I wasn't here to answer." Thank God for the Brewers. If she'd been home—

"I didn't know they were going to stop by. They must have been coming back from BC. But you know they have it in their minds to see you. I told you—"

"Can't you tell *them*? Can't you tell them not to bother me? Why now when they never bothered with me then?"

"I haven't the slightest idea because I'm not my parents' keeper." Amanda cleared her throat. "I promise you, I have no control over what they do. If I did, you wouldn't be feeling like this about them because they would have helped us when your parents died."

She'd gone through hours of counselling and years had passed and somehow a piece of paper made everything fall apart again. It hadn't worked. Julia wasn't over it, not even close. "It shouldn't have happened like it did."

"None of it should have. We just have to learn to get through it."

"I don't think it works that way. I don't think 'getting through it' ever lasts." Julia crumpled onto the couch. Her eyes were blurry.

A moment later, she heard Amanda. "Are you still there? I can only see your ceiling."

She pulled the iPad on her knees.

"Jules," Amanda's voice was gentle. "I'm sorry this is upsetting to you"

Upsetting and impossible. "Look, I have to go. Poor Jul is waiting for me. I left him without an explanation."

"Julia—"

"I have to go. Talk later." She ended the call and switched her phone to silent.

'*I have to pull myself together.*' She looked a little worse for the outburst—a glance in the mirror proved it. Julia shook out her hair and wiped her eyeliner straight. After she touched up her lip gloss, she felt better about facing Jul. He didn't know her well at all. What would he think about the whole thing?

'*I'll explain that it was from someone I didn't want to hear from.*' That was completely true, and she could probably say it without getting emotional.

She opened her door to a darkened hall. He'd shut off the lights there and in the kitchen as well.

Jul had locked the front door and the French doors in the dining room and turned off every light on the main floor. The only noise came from gears clicking in the clock. He was nowhere to be found.

Her nose burned.

She had no messages on her phone. He hadn't even tried to contact her.

She sent him a quick note.

You must be exhausted.

Let me know if you need anything.

Good night.

The awareness lapped at her like a wave. She'd been expecting something, but it hadn't happened—and it wasn't going to. Julia wasn't sure what that something was, but finding herself alone in a dark house with Jul shut up one floor above her wasn't it.

She returned to her room and fell asleep waiting for his reply that never came.

Chapter Thirteen

JULIAN NEVER SHOULD HAVE ENTERTAINED such a stupid idea. If he could have gone back to Dar's that night, he would have. For a few minutes, Jul had his keys in his hands and was poised to leave with whatever he could grab. But what would the Brewers say about that?

What would Julia say?

Dar was right. He was insane, that's all there was to it. 'Bat shit crazy' summed it up.

Julia was a busy woman, and Jul quickly discovered that it was easy enough to go his way and let her go hers with little interaction. He had to have dinner with her, but the rest of his time was flexible and he flexed it as much as he could. Lang's place had never looked so good for all the hours he spent there Wednesday and Thursday night.

Despite the darkness, Jul's eyes popped open early Friday morning. He cursed softly and pulled the blanket up higher over his head, wishing he could sleep longer—or stay in bed all day. How was it that he was under her roof—as far away from her as he could be in the same house, mind you—and dread waking?

After dragging himself to the bathroom, he splashed his face. Water would help him wake up, but he wasn't sure what it was going to take to face the weekend ahead.

A knock sounded. He opened the door a crack.

It was Darvvin.

"That's how you answer? You look a wreck." Dar frowned. "What if I was Julia?"

"You're not Julia. Why would she even come to my door? It's not like I can order room service here."

"What on earth are you wearing? Have you heard of pants? And this," Dar pinched the sleeve of the ragged T-shirt, "it looks like it could crawl away on its own. Set it free, man, because that thing should be put out of its misery."

He'd had the shirt since he lived with his parents. It came with a case of beer and it was perfect for when he just woke, or it was Saturday, or if he was lazing around. Jul crossed his arms over his chest. "What do you need?"

"I heard things aren't going so well here. Seems you've been a bit of a recluse."

"I've been working with you every day. I've been helping at Lang's. Not to mention working on my company. What more do you want? "

"I'm sure you've been run ragged. You must have built a multimillion-dollar corporation by now for all the time you've spent on your 'business'. But really, what are you doing? You moved into her house so you could 'get in front of her' and you're never here?"

He was such a know-it-all. "You've got all the answers, don't you?"

"This is your answer, remember? You're the one who came up with this plan."

Jul slumped on the edge of his bed. "I don't know what to do to make this happen. I have no idea. All I can think of is to stand there in her space, but I can't just follow her around. That's creepy."

"I don't recommend that strategy at all, but it's basically what you came up with when you decided to move in, right?" Dar sat next to him. "You didn't think of anything you would try to do to impress her before you made this move? 'Standing there'—that was going to be your big thing?"

Julian leaned heavily on his legs. "I don't know what I thought. I guess I didn't think I'd have to plan it out. Things would happen on their own and she'd see I'm a good guy. Or something." It was a little fuzzy. "I mean, you and Stel. How did that work out?"

Dar smiled when he remembered. "We did lots of things. I took her for slushies and shopping. We went for walks and rode our bikes. We watched the ocean. I took her to the Harbour Hop—"

"Right, you were twelve."

"Thirteen, thank you very much." He leaned forward. "I just spent time with her. That's all you have to do. Listen to her. Stel had nothing to say at first. She was really nervous, but I kept listening. All that time we spent wandering around and talking—that was big. Suddenly, we were a couple."

"But that's dating. We aren't dating. I don't even know if she is at all interested in dating. How can I do any of that?" He scratched his fingers through his hair. "I found a note on the door the other day. I forgot about it and didn't give it to her until after dinner. She bolted when she saw it. Left to call somebody."

Dar paused as though he was waiting for more. When nothing came, he spoke. "You have quite the issue with papers in your possession and Julia's reaction to them, don't you? She's a businesswoman. She calls people from time to time. Bound to happen. You might even have to call people when you grow up and become a businessman someday."

Julian dragged his hand over his stubbly chin. There was one explanation he could think of. "Do you think she has someone else?" Shane Harnes came to his mind.

"We'd know by now—Stel would, for sure." Dar sniffed. "Good lord, you're jealous of nothing. Everything's arse backwards for you, isn't it? You've moved in before the first date." He stood up. "You want to date her eventually, right? Well, you'd better get creative if you want to put yourself out there in front of your 'doe', Mr. Buck." Dar kept preaching as he went to the door. "Get rid of that shirt. It's the worst thing I've ever seen. Put on some pants. Clean up your face. Asking Julia out for dinner wouldn't hurt the situation a bit. You're a great guy and I think she even likes you in spite of all this nutty behaviour you've been putting out there. Stel's sure she does." He raised two fingers of his right hand to his forehead and waved as he turned the doorknob. "I'm always here to listen if you need to talk."

"You're only here to tell me I'm crazy." Jul shut the door in Darvvin's face before he had to hear anything else.

He looked at himself in the bathroom mirror. The shirt was torn under the arms and had holes scattered over the bottom. A single thread held one seam along the neckline and the yellow stain on the chest proved he must have worn it at least once while eating hotdogs. He peeled it off. Maybe it was time to let go.

Darvvin knocked again.

That was someone else who needed to let things go. Julian bunched the T-shirt in his fist. "I get it, okay? I'm getting rid of the shirt. I'll be more *creative*." He chucked it at his friend and it bounced off his face.

It was a powerful statement. Jul perfectly executed the gesture. It said beyond a doubt that he 'got the message' and that he'd 'heard quite enough'.

The only issue was that the person knocking wasn't Darvvin at all.

Julia Matthews stood in his doorway with a stack of towels in her arms. Her hair was out of place where his T-shirt had connected.

Jul crossed his hands over his boxer shorts. He was sure he could see her eyes travel from his shoulders to his chest to his toes and back up again.

"New towels." She dropped them at his feet. "Rachel comes today—every Friday—at ten thirty to clean. I just wanted to let you know ... to see if you were okay." She cupped her hands around her eyes and rushed away. "You look okay to me."

Julian waited until she was out of sight before he moved.

Down the hall, Darvvin emerged from the plastic barrier wearing half a grin and pointing to his lower body. "Pants, b'y."

Jul swept the T-shirt and towels together. The door shook the entire top floor when it slammed behind him.

It wasn't working, not a single part of his plan—if you could call it that—and it was getting worse by the minute. He needed to talk to someone, someone who would have an impartial view of his problem and give him solid guidance, someone he could trust.

He dialled the number as soon as he found it.

"Jul?"

"Edward."

"All's good, yeah?"

"Yes. You act like I never call you."

"You don't ever call me."

Jul rubbed his brow as though he could rub the conviction away. "Everything's fine. More or less. I mean, the family's fine."

"I was worried when I saw your number. I'm just on a quick break—"

"I need some advice." Julian launched into a summary of everything that he'd been going through, every hope and frustration that had happened over the past few months. He tried to condense it. "So, what do you think?"

"You done talking already?"

Jul sensed the sarcasm but waited for Ed's reply.

"That was a lot of information. Let's see if I kept it all straight. You met a girl and moved into her house, but not in *with* her. Dar scammed you into working for him and there's something about deer that made you move. And now Dar thinks you've lost it and the girl saw you half-naked. Is that it?"

"Kind of, it's more like—"

"I'm not sure I see the problem here. If she saw you half naked, that should help, eh? Unless you've completely let yourself go the last couple of years—"

"Eddie!"

His friend laughed.

"It's not funny. It's a mess."

"Ah Jul, what's Dar been telling you?" Voices sounded in the background. "I'm at work and I really have to get back to it. I'll have to call you later, okay?"

Their talk ended with no enlightenment. Jul wondered why no one seemed to appreciate the seriousness of his situation.

There was nothing he could do but shower and get dressed—that was of primary importance. He told himself that he could get away with working upstairs for hours before he'd have to go down. It was a small consolation. At some point, he'd be running into Julia. That was inevitable.

Jul fastened an extra button on the top of his shirt before smacking some cologne on his face. It was time for work, and he hoped there was something big to break.

+++

JULIA PACKED HER laptop, a notebook, and pens and left the house. Rachel was coming and didn't need her looking over her shoulder. She had enough to keep her busy for the day. She'd scheduled a meeting with her designer, Tanzy. That would take an hour at least. After that, she planned to deliver the last of her promotional fliers.

"That will check the box on networking this week."

When she finished running around, Julia treated herself to a latte at the Coffee Stop. Her cup was still half full when Amanda called, but she didn't answer. She wanted to think, and there was no time to chat with her cousin.

And she didn't want to, anyway.

Julia tapped her pen on her lip. There had to be some way to make Jul feel more at home, to ease the poor start they'd had.

'*To make up for this morning.*' The memory still made her blush.

She pondered and wrote notes until it was four, until it was time to head back to the house. The town pretty much shut down at five. There was nowhere else to go unless she wanted to hang out at the Saloon.

Darvvin was finishing up when she came in. "See you Sunday. Have a good weekend. And Jul," he smiled at his friend as he walked out the door, "don't worry about coming out our way until Sunday feed. We're good. The Langs are doing fine. Take it easy. Settle in." He saluted as he closed the door.

She expected Jul to vanish upstairs until dinner, but he waited at the check-in desk. There was only one button open on his shirt. He looked like he was going to choke. It would have made her giggle if the entire scene at his door that morning hadn't been so embarrassing. She wondered how long it would take to get the picture of his bare torso out of her mind.

"I have to apologize. For that ... for throwing the shirt." Jul moved aside, careful to keep the desk between them. "I thought Dar was back. He'd been ... harassing me a few minutes before and I thought he came back. It had only been a minute."

"Harassing?"

He looked down. "He knows how to push my buttons."

"Please, don't worry. I'm sorry I didn't announce myself when I knocked this morning." Julia straightened her jacket and headed for the back of the house. "I had an idea today. Can I show you something?"

He nodded and followed her out the kitchen door towards the garage.

"This was the stable and coach-house. I'm going to have it made into a suite. Maybe an Airbnb type of thing." She led him up a flight of stairs in the back corner of the first bay.

The room was dry-walled, but the mud and taping hadn't been done and the floors were plain plywood. "It's not fancy, but it has heat and power. There's a powder room on the end there." The roofline pitched in on both sides, but there was a large area in the middle with high ceilings. Three dormer windows along the west brightened the space. There was another large window on the north wall.

"It's roomy for sure." Jul smoothed his hands over the joints between the sheets of drywall. "Did you want me to start working on it?"

"No, not at all." She wrapped her arms around herself as she wandered. "At the risk of you feeling like you are getting sent out to the garage again, I thought I'd offer this space to you. I don't think any of us realized how you would feel going from a completely contained apartment at Darvvin's to having to share with me here. We barely know each other. That has to be hard on you." It was the only way she could rationalize why he'd been missing in action for the past few days. "It's far from finished, but if you have anything you would like some extra room for, you can use this space. I don't want you to be stuck doing everything in your bedroom. I want you to feel comfortable." She faced him. "You don't have to leave every night. Consider the inn your home for the next little while."

His eyebrows rippled. "Um, thanks for this, but I'm not sure what I would do in here."

"Well, what *have* you been doing the last few days?" The words burst out of her mouth before she could smooth them out. "You play the guitar. I'm sure you could bring your music out here, your work, work out stuff if you want ..."

Half a grin touched his mouth. "Work out stuff?"

Her ears got warm. "I thought you probably had weights—maybe you go to the gym, but you could stay here if you have weights or whatever." Julia's chest tightened. "And your guitar. Wouldn't it be nice to play it up here? We can bring in whatever furniture or equipment you need."

He turned a slow circle in the room. "You know, that's a great idea. It will work well, actually."

"Well ... great. Figure out what you want and we'll bring it up. I have a few extra tables and chairs. A couple of lamps would help too. We can get you set up tomorrow, or tonight. Whatever. Think about it." She walked to the stairs.

"Maybe a desk and chair or two." Jul was almost jogging to keep up as they returned to the house.

"We'll make a list and get everything sorted out." The ball was in his court and she had to let it be. "You're probably starving. We need to think about supper." She opened the fridge, enjoying the cool air on her face. "We're almost out of the food Stel sent, but we could make some sandwiches. Have to think of something new tomorrow."

Jul closed the fridge door. "Why don't you let me get dinner tonight? My treat for you going to all the trouble." A breath passed through his lips before the words came. "For moving me in and setting me up in the garage."

She expected him to close the space between them and take her hand, but he didn't. Julia studied his expression. He wore blue plaid that matched his eyes. He was smiling and nearly looked calm, so she instantly knew that there was no way he meant what she hoped he did. "That would be nice." Julia opened the cupboard behind him, seeking a trio of fliers. "I'm up for anything here. The Greek place is fantastic, but they have pizza if that's not your thing."

A blink was his only hesitation, so she knew she'd called it right. "I love Greek food. Tell me what you want and I'll go pick it up."

Chapter Fourteen

IF SHE HAD BEEN ON speaking terms with Amanda, Julia would have called as soon as Jul drove off to pick up their dinner. There was no way he was actually asking her out—there couldn't be. He struggled to communicate on even the most basic level.

'How would he have coped on a date?'

She opened a bottle of wine and set up two glasses while her music played around her. Wine had never seemed to help him relax when they'd had it at Brewers, but she was sure it would help her.

They ate in the kitchen. He was pleasant, but had little to say. It was like pulling teeth to get anything out of him. Conversation was scarce during clean up.

In a final effort to smooth things over, she made a suggestion. "Would you like to hang out in the front room? I have another bottle of this red."

Jul checked his watch. "Ah, sure. That would be good." His smile flicked on and off his lips. "I'll get our glasses."

She carried the bottle and brought her speaker along. "Do you feel like starting a fire?"

The crystal clinked in his grasp, and his eyes opened wide.

"The fireplace. It's the only one in the house that's still wood-burning."

"Right." Jul piled wood on the grate.

She tried to hang back but watched over his shoulder. "I've never seen wood arranged like that."

"This is log cabin style. It helps keep the oxygen flowing. They've put in a gas starter?" He nudged the logs, then searched the outer edge of the hearth. "Are there any—"

Before he could finish, she presented a match. "They hang right here."

"Oh. Thanks." He struck it and turned on the gas. In a few minutes, flames were licking at the wood.

Julia took a seat on one end of the sofa. "It was installed before the Wilburs bought the house."

"Very convenient."

"Definitely." She watched him fuss. "I love a wood fire. Gas fireplaces are easy, but there's something about the atmosphere of this one."

"I'll say."

If all she was going to get was two-word replies, it was going to be a long night. She finished what was in her glass and refilled it, topping up Jul's drink at the same time.

He added another log and turned off the starter before he took a seat at the far end of the couch. Jul faced the fire squarely, feet flat on the floor, back stiff. He kissed his lips together, then looked at his knees. "I have to apologize for that note the other day. It fell when I was coming in and I shoved it in my pocket. With the move, I just forgot about it. I promise that won't happen again. I know you are a busy person and it was—"

"Don't worry about it." He'd been feeling guilty after all that time? "It was a note from someone who stopped in while I was at dinner ... my aunt and uncle. Took me by surprise. I haven't seen them for many years. Do you have any family nearby?"

"No. Dar is the only family I connect with and we're not even related—his family and his brother, Ed." He smiled at the fire before he drank. "I only have one sister. She's married to an American. Lives in Texas. We were never close and distance sealed the deal."

"That's too bad." He couldn't be further away from her while staying on the same piece of furniture. "I'm an only child. I always thought having a sibling would be so much better. What about your parents?"

"Retired. Moved to the Okanagan four years ago." Another mouthful passed through his lips before he licked them. "All of my family abandoned me. My aunts and uncles are scattered over Alberta and Saskatchewan. I have a few cousins, but I don't stay in touch." He stared straight ahead. "I'm not sure where I'd be without the Brewers."

Julia hugged her knees with one arm, nesting the glass between them and her chest. "I'm not sure either, even though it's been such a short time since I met them. Knowing them is a real blessing." He glanced at her and she wondered what the look was in his eyes. "So you moved there early this year?"

"In April. I needed a change. Sold my condo in the city and they invited me to stay there while I regrouped. While I regroup, I guess. I'm still figuring things out."

"Me too. We could start a support group." Julia raised her glass to him, but he didn't seem to see it. "That's exactly what I needed. A change. What happened in your life?" She angled towards him.

He turned slightly her way, pausing before he let himself share. "I thought I was getting my Christmas bonus, but they laid me off instead."

"That's terrible." She couldn't reveal that Stel had already mentioned it. "What did you do?"

"I was shocked. I'd been there ten years. That was a Friday afternoon, and I was ... lost. But by Sunday night, I was relieved. I had time to spend with Dar for the first time in years. Got to know David and Luke." He smiled into his wineglass.

"Did you get a package from work?"

"Yes, thank goodness. It was a pretty generous severance. I could've stayed in the city and done nothing for a few years if I wanted to, but that didn't make sense. I unloaded my condo before I even had to think about it. It was a nice place. Downtown Calgary, right beside the river."

"Could you see the mountains?"

"No. It faced the wrong way. And now I'm in Dar's suite and it's the best place I've ever been in." He emptied his glass. "Traded a Range Rover for my truck. Stopped wearing suits and ties. I'm even back in flannel." He lost a finger in his collar. "Life's good, I just ... I need to figure out work and I guess I shouldn't stay at Dar's forever."

Julia swirled the last of the wine in her glass. "I can't picture you living downtown." If she hadn't seen him in a suit that first day, she'd never believe it. "You seem to belong here, cowboy. It's like you're telling me about a different person."

“I guess I probably was.” He shrugged. “Dar and Stel helped me through it. I was at their place most of the time anyway and it made sense to live there, too. Do you know the history there? The suite over the garage was their first house when they moved to Alberta. Dar built it. I helped when I could. Once their big house was done—the one they're in now—they kept the suite up for guests from back home, but no one really comes out. I guess Ed does sometimes—” He stopped short and lifted his empty glass to drink again. “I'm going to get us more, if that's okay. Throw another log on the fire.”

“Yes, please.” Her gaze followed him when he poured. Yellow firelight flickered against the blue of his shirt. She'd wondered if his build was only an illusion beneath the fabric. Seeing his back and shoulders flex as he prodded the fire brought back the vivid memory of the morning. She shivered despite the heat in the room.

“What about you?” Jul replaced the poker on the stand and took his seat again. “I've been talking your ear off. Why did you need such a big change?”

“Turning thirty is a great motivator.” She shrugged, almost wishing she hadn't mentioned it. “I was tired. Stuck. Doing the same thing as I always had with little gratification. I made it to director.” He looked impressed, but she waved it off. “No, nothing to celebrate. It was empty. I thought it would be the end all and be all, but it ended up meaning nothing.”

He nodded. “I get it. You get to the top of the mountain and there's nothing to see.”

"Yeah." That was *exactly* how it had felt. "So I thought if I moved apartments—of course, mine was not nearly as nice as yours sounds like it was—if I moved apartments, or got a house, or moved out of the city, maybe that would help. When I saw this place, I fell in love." It was dark, and she told herself she didn't need to worry. He wouldn't be able to see her blush. "Everything was going fine until the renovation delay. I'm really glad Darvvin showed up. It's a lot to juggle."

He pressed his hand on the seat between them, splaying his fingers wide. "We're going to get this done as soon as we can. I can work on the weekends if you need me to. If it's getting tough financially—"

"No." She held her glass with both hands. "I couldn't possibly ask you to do that. You're already working here five days a week. Plus, you have your own goals to work on. Money's okay. I saved a bunch when I was working. What was I going to spend it on? Workaholic with no family." She took a breath. It felt safe to share her story. "And I got an inheritance when my parents passed away."

He shifted closer. "What?"

"Stel didn't tell you?"

"No. What happened?" His eyes were glossy in the light.

She wondered if hers were too.

"My parents were celebrating their twenty-fifth anniversary with a trip to Australia. They were amateur star chasers. My aunt and uncle pushed them into it. I don't think they would have cared otherwise. There was a 'once in a lifetime' celestial event happening—The Transit of Venus." His face was blank, so she explained. "It's where Venus is visible for a short time as it moves between us and the sun. One of the best places to see it was in Sydney, Australia. It was right before my high school graduation, but they were supposed to be back in time. Unfortunately, they were in a car accident while they were touring around. They didn't even get to see the transit."

He shook his head. "I'm so sorry."

Julia had said too much, but for some reason, she had to keep talking. "I'd just turned eighteen. My cousin Amanda rescued me, thank goodness. She's fourteen years older. Our mothers are sisters ... were sisters." She looked at his lips and the way his chin curved beneath them. A gold line of firelight traced his jaw. "Anyway, she stepped in to help me when no-one else seemed to think it was necessary. It was a hard time. My aunt and uncle never even came to my house when I got the call about my parents. They called Amanda instead." And now they were trying to elbow back into her life? "Thank God she came right over. She stayed with me ... went all the way to Australia with me to bring my parents home. My aunt and uncle carried on with their lives like nothing ever happened. I haven't talked to them since the funeral."

"That note—"

"It was from them. They have a sudden desire to reconnect. Now I'm at the mercy of whenever they decide to show up on my doorstep."

"When did Amanda move away?"

"Once I'd finished university. I got a decent job, and she felt like I was settled on a steady path—like I was ready, she said. It's almost been eight years. She said it called to her ... thought she belonged there." Julia drained her glass. It banged when it hit the table. "Australia may have got her, too, but it's not getting me. I guarantee I'll never going back there. Not even if something happened to her." Her nose burned, and she wrinkled it, blinking rapidly. It was terrible, and it was true. "Do you ever think there's a list over your life? Like a list of expectations that are imposed on you and somehow you have to answer for them whether you want those things or not." She grabbed the bottle and poured into both of their glasses. "What if you can't achieve them? Are you a failure? If key people aren't in your life anymore, does it even matter if you do anything?"

He didn't withdraw his gaze when she looked at him. "I have that list, too."

"You do?"

"Absolutely." He nodded slowly.

Julia edged closer. "My parents passed away before I graduated, so that never got scratched off my list. Nobody else could have stood in for them. Lord knows my aunt and uncle never would have tried." She gulped from her glass. "I got through university and it was the same thing. Amanda was there, but she left me right after. I've never married, or had kids, or bought a house—well, this one, but it's a business, not a home." She tapped her fingernails on the crystal. "Where does that leave me? What is the penalty for never crossing those things off your list? Regret? Failure? Insignificance?"

"I get it." His knee was almost touching her leg. "My mom gave up on me when I wasn't married by thirty. I think that's why they moved. She wanted me to have this fancy education and career. I jumped through every hoop she hung out for me and then I was still a disappointment because I didn't have a family. I worked eighty hours a week at that job she wanted me to have and I was gone for half the year. It was impossible." He sniffed. "They put our land up for sale before they even told me they wanted to move. And then I finally figured out that Dad wanted me to take over the farm. I had no idea, but by then, it was too late." Jul squeezed his eyes tight. "I should have just stayed in Newfoundland to work with Dar's family. That was what I wanted, not that anyone ever asked."

"Nobody ever asked me either. I've always done what I thought my parents might have wanted me to do." A rush coursed through her. He heard her. He understood. "It's all so unfair. How do the rules get changed when we don't even want to play the game? We don't even know we're playing! So many things in life will never be settled for either of us."

"You're right." Jul's voice was dark velvet. It cradled and cushioned her soul.

"So what do we do?" Her chin dropped, and she bit her bottom lip. "How do we get on with our lives when your parents left you and mine are gone? How do we deal with everyone ditching us until they feel like seeing us again?" Julia choked when she swallowed and rested her face on her arm to hide the tears. The clock in the hall ticked over the music and crackling wood. She wanted to curl up, curl away, douse the burning hurt inside.

And then she felt it.

Warmth and strength surrounded her. It was Julian. His arms engulfed her. He held her together. Her head fell onto his shoulder and she lifted her arm around his neck. Her tears flowed. Jul held her through every one of them.

"I'm sorry. I never let this out. It's been years. The note from my aunt—"

"Shh." His hand was in her hair, smoothing it down, and drawing her closer. "It makes sense to feel that way, no matter how long it's been." He rocked her softly from side to side as she calmed, as her tears diminished. "Your parents, your cousin ... you've overcome more than anyone should ever have to."

She didn't want to dwell on it anymore. The future was buzzing closer with every passing second—a future with someone in it other than herself. She and Jul—they fit together, two pieces of the same puzzle finally linked. Her nose dropped near the neckline of his shirt, still buttoned high, and she nuzzled into his skin. Julia inhaled the scent of him. She pressed in.

His posture tightened and he reached past her, then pulled back. She thought he was going to hold her hand, but she felt a tissue there instead.

He returned to his side of the sofa and planted his palms on his legs. "Are you okay?" His mouth dropped open again, but he said nothing else.

She dabbed her nose and eyes. "Of course I am. It's always been the expectation. I don't have many other options." Julia rubbed her thumb on the back of her pendant and fixed her gaze on the fireplace. It glowed vermillion, almost making the room seem darker than if it wasn't burning at all.

"Should I put another log on?"

Julia shook her head. “Don’t bother. I think it’s safe to let the fire extinguish itself.”

Chapter Fifteen

"CHILLY." Jul's words turned to fog as he spoke. The sun was working its way higher that morning, but it wasn't getting any warmer.

Julian had been seeking a good place to think but found himself humbled by creation instead. Somehow, that was exactly what he needed.

He'd driven west of Juniper Creek and parked at the side of a two-lane road. The Rocky Mountains spread out before him like curtains on a stage. It was a miracle, really. Every layer had once been flat ground. They jutted up out of the earth, kissing the sky. Bands of colour and texture bent upwards, higher than the trees. If that could happen, how hard could it be for a guy like him to find love?

"It shouldn't be this hard."

He'd wedged himself into the confines of the passenger seat with his guitar on his knees.

"It should have ended in a kiss," he sang to his own rambling melody.

Hours before, those hands had been around Julia. Those fingers had been in her hair instead of against wire. He'd caressed her curves instead of the cold contours of his guitar.

Julian lay his palm flat against the strings to stop the noise. The music didn't sound right.

A mere fourteen hours had passed since their evening together. The day before had been full of ups and downs, but the chance to spend time alone with her had been a wish only a week before. And then she started to cry. He was glad that he had gone to her. At first, he was positive she only let him hold her because she was upset, but he knew she calmed down soon after. The way she softened and pressed closer left no doubt in his mind.

Then came the disaster. She snuggled in—just like he'd always dreamed she would one day—and he simply set her aside.

"Unbelievable."

Julian closed his eyes and saw the replay again. Her pretty face creased and she flinched like she'd been smacked. Then it was over—totally over, dead-end over—like 'burning-a-bridge' over. It was reminiscent of the night she found the phone number, but worse. She left five minutes later and went to bed. That was that.

The memory of the scent of her hair was already starting to fade.

"Unforgivable."

He climbed into the crisp morning air and let the chill distract him. Playing his woes away wasn't going to work. Julian abandoned his musical ambitions and wrestled his guitar into the case. He picked up his laptop. He had to get going on his company—get a job, get a place to live—and get out of the rut he was stuck in.

A warning window flashed on his screen three minutes after logging in. The battery was almost out of power. He cursed to himself when he discovered that he hadn't brought a charger—not that he'd have anywhere to plug it in where he was.

There was one place he could go where he'd have the privacy to think, play his music, and charge his computer all at the same time.

Jul started the ignition and headed back east towards town.

HIS SPOT ON the apron at Brewer's garage was empty. He parked and unpacked his guitar and computer case. Dar wasn't home. That was probably a good thing. Jul let himself in. The heat was low, and the room offered him another round of cold. He switched on the fireplace and stood at the patio doors. The mountains were a distant band. He wondered where the deer were.

A spare charger was in easy reach. Jul wandered the rooms looking for other useful things he'd missed when he moved. He felt like an intruder rifling through another guy's belongings.

A text disrupted his distraction. It was Stel.

Davey wants to know if you'll come for lunch

That was a request he couldn't refuse. The boy had his face pressed on the storm door when Jul got halfway across the yard.

Davey hugged Jul's legs as tightly as he could. "I miss you Unca Jul."

Julian picked him up before he even took off his boots. "I miss you too. Good thing you invited me over." Part of him wished the child would ask him to move back. Nobody could blame him for honouring his godson's request.

"He's been waiting for you to come in since he saw you drive by." Stel had a row of bread slices spread out on the counter. "Dar's off to town. I'm sure he told me why, not quite sure I was listening." She giggled and put a coffee in his hand.

"Thanks. Do I ever need this today. That looks delicious."

"What? They don't feed you at the inn?"

He turned his back to her. "I had to leave early."

"Oh? What did you have going on early Saturday morning?"

He couldn't think of anything to say that made any sense.

"Everything okay?" She pulled a block of cheese from the fridge, then dug for a knife as she glanced towards her guest. "What happened?"

Jul stared outside.

"What's going on?"

He had to tell her. She was going to find out, anyway. "She ended up in my arms." He pulled out a chair and slumped down.

Stel faced him, eyes wide. "You should be much happier about that than you look."

It was hard to believe the sequence of events. "Do you want to hear the part where I asked her out to dinner and she ordered takeout instead? Or the part where she opened up about how her aunt and uncle are worming their way back in her life?" He stared at the light fixture over the table.

"Or maybe the part where she told me about her parents' car accident? It ended in tears."

Stel took his hand. "She was crying? What did you do?"

"I tried to make her feel better. I had my arms around her before I could even think about it."

"And?" Her grip on his hand tightened.

"And nothing." He remembered the horrible ending again. "When she relaxed a little, I got her a tissue and ... I don't know. She was on her side of the couch and I was on the other. And it was over."

Stel set her hand on his arm. "So nothing else happened."

"Nothing. I just had to get out of there this morning." Things should have been better when it was the two of them alone together. "I ... I froze. Shied away."

"What made you do that?"

He shrugged. It was better than admitting that some other woman's memory popped up the moment he felt Julia nestle close.

"What are you so afraid of? She let you hold her—"

"Oh, I don't know," he returned to the window. The mountains glowed bright against the band of grey clouds that hovered over the foothills. He searched them for answers, but they didn't reveal a thing. "Maybe she isn't interested in me and I'll make a fool of myself. Maybe she's not the person I think she is. Maybe that I'll fall in love and she won't."

Stel wandered closer. "I hate to say this, but I think you already have."

He felt her looking at him but didn't look back.

"You have to give it some time. She's only known you for a few weeks. You might have been in love with her for months now."

He couldn't argue with that. "I've ruined everything. I've got to be the man here, to take initiative, but I mess up every time." He groaned when he sat—so did the chair beneath him. "It could have been so much more." He pinched the bridge of his nose.

"How did you leave it?"

"She told me she was fine, and we wrapped things up then and there. Then she texted me before she fell asleep to apologize for crying, of all things."

Stel settled her hand on his arm. "It's a shame it ended like it did, but you did the right thing, holding onto her when she needed you. That's love in action. She won't forget it." She hugged him again. "I'm sure it's not as bad as you think it is. If she let you hold her, it can't be."

He wanted to believe her, but the hurt in Julia's eyes was a sharp memory. "I wish I could start from scratch. Everything I've done seems to have gone wrong. How did she misunderstand the Savannah thing? And the note from her aunt? And when I asked her to dinner?"

"You asked her out? Like you really said those words?"

"Yes. I'm sure of it." He couldn't recall the exact phrase. "I don't know."

"Look at it from her side. You do tend to ... back away unexpectedly." Stel traced her finger over the tabletop. "She told me that you were missing in action last week. I know Dar gave you a hard time, and I'm sorry about that. But it's something that she was worried enough for you that she brought it up to me. If she was even slightly unsure if you meant to take her out to dinner or order in, don't you think she would have picked the safer option? Better that than to be stuck at a sit-down dinner that the guy didn't even mean to invite you to." She sat back. "You have to stop this vanishing act you pull whenever you feel unsure. Even the best relationships have times of uncertainty. You'll be running forever if you don't figure out a way to deal with that." She went back to the counter.

Jul brought the boys to their seats, just like he always did. At least some things stayed the same.

"You know what?" She poured him a tall glass of water. "I think you can start fresh and this is what you are going to do. Buy her a flower arrangement—don't get a bouquet and make her cut them all. Get one that's done up already. Then you're going to take them to her and re-introduce yourself. It will be charming and it's the closest you can get to a fresh start."

"Then she'll know I'm crazy for sure."

"She'll love that. If you feel this bad, you've got to try something." Stel reached for his hand. "Or maybe this is the point where you decide to let her go. You can't live like this, Jul. You need to make up your mind. Are you going to give up on Julia, or are you going to make this happen?"

"I not giving her up."

Stel pressed her lips together and tilted her head, looking pleased and worried for him all at once. "Well then, you have to face things head-on, right? None of the success you've ever had in your life has come from running the other way."

+++

THE SOFA IN the bay window was Julia's perch for most of the day. It was a home base to land on when she was done pacing, second-guessing, and dinner-prep. The upholstery was just uncomfortable enough to remind her to stay in the moment and not fall asleep after the unsettled night she'd had. It was also the best place to see the traffic go by and wait for a certain white King Ranch to drive in.

"It should have ended in a kiss," she whispered to the room. She considered calling Amanda, but she'd already canceled their weekly call. Amanda didn't understand anyway, so she didn't need to waste her time. Besides, she didn't know what she would say. 'Hey Amanda, how's your day? Me? Oh, I just fell in love. No one has ever held me that way or looked at me like Jul does. I felt safe.'

"For the very first time."

But then he pushed her away. There was no point in starting a story that didn't have an ending, and Julia wasn't willing to believe that what had happened was the end.

"Stel," she whispered to the window. If only she knew Stel a little better and Stel knew Jul a little less, it would certainly help her figure things out. Maybe he was shy. There had to be some explanation for the mixed signals she was getting.

And what was wrong with her? She could have kissed him as easily as he could have kissed her. Maybe if she had, he wouldn't have left so early without saying goodbye. His stuff was still in his room, so she knew he'd be back, eventually.

She gritted her teeth, unsure of what was most annoying—that he hadn't said goodbye or that she'd expected he would. He was a guest at her inn. No one else she'd hosted had ever been expected to check in and let her know what they were doing.

But she'd never cared about any other guest.

Julia was stuck, she knew it—stuck humouring her new friends in their feeble attempt to make a match. There was no way out without causing hard feelings. If Jul was the one who wanted out, how could the Brewers argue? If he stayed, Julia had to find a way to cope, and that meant setting some solid boundaries. The last thing she needed was the torment of him being under her roof when she'd inadvertently developed feelings and he didn't care.

She waited, and stewed, and hoped with each glint of chrome that peeked through the bushes that he'd drive in. If he wasn't back by five, she was going to text Stel for answers.

She had to make sure he was alright. It was the least she could do.

He came in just after four-thirty.

Julia dragged the drop cloth back over the sofa and scurried to the kitchen before he saw her. There was so much she wanted to say and a few lines she absolutely had to make him hear. She took a deep breath, held it, and then breathed out, counting to ten. The door opened and something bumped the floor and then it closed again. Julia forced herself to walk close, measured steps. She put on her innkeeper's smile.

Jul's computer bag and guitar case sat against the wall. The door opened again and all she could see were the flowers.

"Ah, hi." He peeked over the plastic, holding the bouquet between them like a shield. "These are for you."

She'd planned her spiel all afternoon. There was probably enough to say to keep him listening for an hour. Every word faded at the sight of his offering. Colour burst through the sheer sheet covering the blooms. He set them on the round table near the check-in. Julia tore the bag open, revealing a glowing arrangement of mums, asters, and roses—orange roses. She traced the edge of the petals.

He shifted from foot to foot and cleared his throat.

The orange was vibrant against the other burgundy and mauve blooms. It was enormous and must have cost him—well, she had no idea how much, but she knew flowers weren't cheap.

"Um, I want to apologize."

She caught his eye, awaiting his explanation for dropping her like a hot coal the night before.

"I'm sorry about upsetting you last night. I don't want you to think I was prying or anything. I didn't mean to bring anything up that would make you feel bad." His face was tense, but his hands were open, palms facing her, pleading.

It wasn't what she'd expected, but then, neither were the flowers. "No one has ever given me flowers."

He squinted. "No one?"

She shook her head and bent forward to smell the roses. When she saw him again, he'd moved closer.

He extended his right hand. "I'd like a fresh start. What do you say? Hi ... hello, I'm Julian Ariets. I don't have a career or a home right now, but I'm a really good guy. Honest."

He was cutting down every boundary she'd worked up while he was gone and she was sure he didn't even know it. It brought a smile to her lips. "I'm glad to meet you. My name is Julia Matthews. I own a nonfunctional business and live in the old servant's quarters. And I'm a decent enough girl. Honest."

"I can handle decent." His shoulders loosened, and a smile appeared. They shook hands until it seemed too long, and then he withdrew and dug his finger in his collar.

"Thank you for that. And for the flowers. Yesterday was ..." It was something she'd never forget. "I've had a lot on my mind the last few weeks. Pent-up stress got to me, definitely too much wine." She carried the bouquet past him towards the kitchen. "I've made us dinner. Care to join me, or did you already eat?" If he'd already eaten—it didn't matter, actually. The flowers won him a lot of brownie points.

"I'd love to. It smells amazing in here. What's the occasion?"

"Well, we just met." She placed the arrangement in the middle of the island. "I'm not letting these things out of my sight." Julia turned her music down and tied an apron over her clothes.

"Is this Sinatra?" He asked.

"Yes, one of my favourite songs. Corcovado, Quiet Nights of Quiet Stars. Do you know it?"

"No, and I thought I knew them all. Strangers in the Night, I've Got You Under My Skin." He knocked the salt shaker over and scrambled to brush up the mess. "You've been busy today."

"I'm glad you came back for dinner. This would have been too much food for me to eat alone." She pulled out a tub of flour. "I guess the leftovers would have held me for a few days. It's roast beef. Care to cut it?"

"Of course." His blank face gave him away—he hadn't expected the request. To his credit, he took up the carving knife and fork and started to saw at their dinner with miniature strokes. The blade stopped partway down.

"The cord is still on." She clipped it for him and worked on the gravy while he continued.

He stopped again a few centimetres from the bottom.

"Two cords."

Shortly, a platter of freshly cut beef was on the table with a steaming gravy boat beside it. Julia set the roast vegetables to one side. She served water to drink—safer than wine—and took one last moment to smell the roses before joining him to eat.

"Thanks for making such a great meal." Jul dug in like he hadn't eaten all day.

Maybe he hadn't.

Julia wasn't going to ask. It was his business, none of hers. She poured a generous ladle of gravy over the food on her plate. "Roast beef is one of the easiest meals out there. Just a lot of chopping, but there's nothing wrong with that." She passed the butter bowl. "Other than throwing this together this afternoon, I had a relaxing day. Watched some television. Read for a while." Then she said it, despite her resolve. "What did you end up doing today?"

He seemed to chew for longer than he needed to. "I, ah, took a long drive west. Have you been out that way?"

"No." Why would she? There was nothing out west but the highway until you reached Banff. "What was happening out there?"

"Mountains. It's beautiful out there. I thought I could clear my head." He reached for his water. "I really have to get my business going."

Her mouth smiled, but she wasn't sure her eyes did. "In your truck?"

Water dribbled on his chin. He hid it with his hand. "Just wanted to think about things."

"You could have stayed here and we could have chopped vegetables together. That's a nice meditation. Lots of opportunity to think." She hoped her tone was light like nothing mattered in the slightest.

Jul carried on as if all was well. "Then I went to Dar's to get a few things I left there. I had lunch with the kids."

"Hm." She bit her lips together while she nodded. "You should have taken some coffee with you this morning. I wouldn't have made it past nine without a cup."

"I didn't want to disturb you."

"You wouldn't have. I was awake when you drove away." She'd stubbed her toe while trying to get to the window when she heard his truck. It was still throbbing.

"Oh, I didn't—"

"I'm sorry I missed seeing you before you left. I thought it might be a bit weird between us this morning. I wanted to make sure things were alright."

"Everything's fine." He dragged a chunk of potato through the pool of gravy on his plate. "And this is delicious. I'm sure you don't cook like this for guests."

"I don't." Julia might have been overtired, or slightly hungover, or—maybe she had enough of the elephant in the room. "But you aren't a usual guest, right? We've covered that. Our situation here is *completely* different." She stared past him out the window. She'd planned out exactly what she was going to say, exactly what her terms were going to be. It was time to find out where he stood. "I can tell that it's tough for you to be here. I know you'd rather be at Brewer's. When I heard you leave this morning, I didn't think it was a good idea for you to stay here at all."

"What?" He set his utensils down.

"I bet no one even asked you before you got shuffled over here, did they? They just told you to go."

"It's not like that." He pressed his hands flat on either side of his plate. "I'm happy to help them and ... I like it here."

He was trying so hard to put on a happy face. She bit her lip before she replied. "It's kind of you to say that, but you don't have to. I know it's nothing personal. You don't even know me. You've lost your entire home in exchange for a small room in a house with a stranger. Even with the garage space, it's not enough. I'm sure you never dreamed you'd be stuck with a roommate at your stage in life." She scraped her plate with the knife, and then set it back down. "I want to make this experience as easy for you as possible. We get along fine, right? We'll have to make the best of it." She searched his eyes for some hint of what he was thinking. "I'm fine with you being here, really I am, but what do you want? Do you want to stay here? If not, we need to talk to Dar and Stel. I'm sure they'd understand if you just want to go back."

"I want to stay, I swear to you." He tried to stand, but there wasn't quite enough space. The entire table tipped before he sat back. He grasped the edge. "I *do* want to be here."

Jul almost looked afraid of what she'd say next. He'd sounded sincere. She kept her tone soft. "Okay, if you want to be here, I'm happy to have you. Take all the time you need to get your business ready. We can look at it later this week. That will help you feel better about things, I'm sure." So much for her ultimatum. "And don't worry. The time will pass quickly and before you know it, you'll be back at your own place."

But the flowers had changed everything, and she wasn't sure she'd ever want him to go.

Chapter Sixteen

"THAT SHOULD DO IT." The men wrestled Dar's custom vanity into the northeast bathroom at the inn. "Now that's a thing of beauty."

Jul agreed. Dar made it from an antique sewing machine table, a perfect nod to the original sewing room-turned-guest suite. "Looks great. I'll get Julia. We can show her how it looks installed."

Dar shook his head. "She's out at our place. She'll have to see it tonight."

Again. She was out there again while Jul was one floor above the pillow she slept on.

His phone rang, and it was Ed, finally returning his call from the Friday before. He wasn't going to answer in front of Darvvin. "I've got to take this downstairs."

"Right." Dar made a face. "Building your empire."

Jul tried to ignore him. "Hi." He hurried to the library and shut the pocket door behind him. "Why are you calling me so early? And in the middle of the week."

"Guess it's afternoon there. Got your text about the disaster Friday night. And the one Saturday. And Sunday. What's happening with the woman now?"

It was on his tongue to say 'nothing' but he didn't. "Fine. Things are fine. We've settled into a kind of routine. You know, coffee and breakfast, dinner after work, dessert at the TV. She let me drive her to church on Sunday. We went to your brother's after."

"You're sure livin' large—I thought you'd have much better news for me after the naked story."

Their new daily schedule left a lot to be desired, and that was after starting fresh.

It didn't feel very fresh.

"She still thinks your brother forced me to move out and I'm suffering here."

"Isn't that what you told her? That you needed to move because of Stel?"

"No. Well, not in so many words. But she'll never figure out that I'm interested if she thinks I don't even want to be here."

"Imagine that. You hide out for a few days, then drive away without a trace, and she thinks you're not interested."

"Yeah, I know." Julian rubbed his hand over his eyes. "I don't know how to work things out from here."

"I'd try to stay at the house, for starters." Ed snorted. "Did you ever think of just having fun with her? That's my new strategy. Just have fun. Life's too short, right? Have a good time together for a bit and that's all you can do. Most relationships aren't going to last anyway, so enjoy the time you get, and then on to the next. If you find out she just wants to be friends, then it's even easier to move on."

Somehow, that sounded worse than if Jul never got to know her at all. "You're not helping me."

"Spend time with her. Do things with her that you think she'd enjoy. Something besides church."

He wasn't sure what those things would be. "Remember Cara? That girl I dated a few years ago. I did everything to make her happy, anything she wanted—"

"Not *everything*, as I recall." Ed was probably laughing at him. "I don't mean for you to let the girl walk all over you."

His shame over the relationship was within easy recall. "That was the biggest mistake."

"Don't sweat it Jul. Pull up your pants and carry on." He laughed at his own joke. "Help her with the work she's dealing with. That place is perfect. Tons of work there, tons of chances for a big strong 'buck' to come in and show her she can't live without him."

"She's not a damsel in distress."

"Well, you need to try something. You probably can't just stand half-naked in front of her and expect her to fall for you that way. Or maybe you can. You're actually the only guy I know who'd get away with that." Ed sipped something and took a breath. "No more hiding out. Help her. Take some control of the situation. Throw her a compliment or two. And have some fun for god's sake. Make her laugh. It nearly always works. Dar always makes Stel laugh."

She probably would have laughed at him in his underwear. He could certainly laugh with her at his own expense. He'd made enough mistakes.

Ed was still talking. "Lighten up. If it's meant to happen, it will. You can't make her want you any more than a buck can make a doe want him. It works, or it doesn't. Then on to the next."

He didn't want to hear that philosophy. "I guess ..."

"Ah, Julian." Ed clicked his tongue. "I've got to run, but I'm looking forward to hearing all about how you make it work. Bait the hook, cast the line, and reel her in. That's all you need to do. We'll talk again next week? You'd better have something good to tell me."

He hoped he would. "I guess it must be dinner time there."

"Yeah, I'm taking Lauren out tonight."

"On a Wednesday? You work tomorrow, don't you? I thought you'd be in bed early."

"There's still a chance for that. She's some fine, I tell ya." Another laugh erupted before Ed caught his breath. "Talk soon. Good luck."

The call had been about as helpful as talking with Darvvin, from a different angle, for sure, but lacking any useful advice. Jul jammed the phone in his back pocket. When he got to the top of the stairs, he heard a familiar voice coming from behind the plastic dust barrier.

Shane Harnes was back.

✦✦✦

FLOWERS CHANGED EVERYTHING.

Guaranteed Stel had been involved in the bouquet somehow, but the look on her face when Julia showed her the pictures proved she'd never seen them before. Even if she told him outright to get them, Jul had been the one to pick them out, and he'd been the one to give them to her, hand to hand. He could have just had them delivered, and his extra effort counted. It counted quite a bit.

No man had ever given her flowers. What a gift to get from someone who didn't even know she loved him.

"I guess he likes you, well, likes being there," Stel said. "Getting settled. I'm happy to hear things are going well."

'Well' was a bit of a stretch. Things were alright. He hadn't left the house without her since the Saturday before and could almost have a complete conversation without faltering.

Stel refilled their cups. "Do you have plans for his birthday?"

"He's never mentioned it." Should he have?

"It's November sixth. He probably didn't tell you because he doesn't want to make a fuss."

Julia wasn't so sure. Maybe it hurt that the Brewers had forced him out. Maybe he didn't want to share something so personal with her. Whatever his reasoning, it was only two weeks away. "That's coming up quick."

"We usually have him over if he's around, but I'm afraid that's out this year." Stel patted her baby bump.

"I could have a party for him at the inn. Lots of room to spread out." Julia's mouth moved before she'd given it any thought. "We could have a hotdog roast or something. The little boys would like that."

Stel looked pleased. "The big boys, too. Would you mind? That would be wonderful. Then next year, when things aren't so wild around here, we can host you two."

Julia nodded and then changed the subject. It was a relief when Luke woke up shortly after and Davey's quiet time was done. She said goodbye and Stel sent her off with a hug and a tinfoil roaster full of chicken and vegetables. The smell of dinner to come perfumed her drive home.

Jul's vehicle was the only one left when she got back. Julia set the roaster in the oven to keep warm.

She had a calendar tucked beside the coffee machine. She opened it on the counter.

"I've dropped the ball."

Halloween was only eight days away. Hilda Wilbur had given Julia specific decorating guidelines when they were teaching her the business. She should have had the inn decorated from top to bottom since Thanksgiving.

Julia flipped to November. "Two weeks exactly."

"What's in two weeks?"

Jul took her by surprise, but she hid the shiver. "Your birthday."

He read the calendar. "Stel told you."

"Why didn't you tell me? I think that's a legal requirement at any inn. Tell the innkeeper if you will be there for any special occasions. Thank goodness someone is looking out for you." She wrote 'Jul's Birthday' in bold Sharpie in the middle of the square and made a little drawing underneath.

He squinted at her artwork. "Exploding cake?"

"Cake and fireworks."

"It's very nice."

She could tell he was trying not to laugh. "Since there was no way Stel could do a party for you this year, we're having it here."

"What if I'm not having a party?"

"Is it a big number?"

"Thirty-five." He sighed.

"Big enough to celebrate, not big enough to have a breakdown. Party it is."

"But—"

"I've already invited the Brewers. You'll have to give me the names of your other friends, too."

"Just the Brewers. And you."

He'd opened the oven door by the time she looked up. "It's settled then. I'll get working on the details."

"Did you make dinner already? How—"

"Stel made it. So we have nothing to do for a bit. I have to decorate for fall and Halloween. I'll get started on that while we wait."

"I'll help you."

"You don't have to, but I might need a bit of a hand getting everything down the ladder." His fingers rested on a stack of papers. "Maybe we should work on that after we go through your proposal."

"Ready and waiting." He slapped the pages against his hand. "I wasn't sure you remembered."

"Of course I did." If she hadn't seen the papers, she might not have.

"Here's another thing to add to your list." He pulled a card out of his flannel shirt pocket. "This guy showed up looking for you again."

It belonged to Shane Harnes. "I totally forgot to call him. Was he upset?"

"Dar explained you've been tied up around here and had the voicemail disabled. If he's mad at anyone, it's me for not giving you the first message."

"He shouldn't be blaming you. You told him that Darvvin mentioned it, right?" She reached for her phone. "I'd better call him now."

Jul set his hand on her wrist. "I'm sure it's too late tonight. He was on his way home from work." An instant later, he'd let go.

"I guess it will have to wait for tomorrow." Julia smoothed a strand of her hair. "Darvvin said we met at the rodeo dance, but I can't picture him."

"Oh, well ... he's short—shorter than me. Smaller build. Kind of skinny." Jul looked at the ceiling as he shared. "He has white stubble—he's going grey. Definitely an older guy."

The description didn't help. "Is he a senior?"

"Um," Julian shifted from foot to foot and jammed his hands in his pockets. "Close. Mid-forties at least—probably older."

She couldn't help but laugh. "I thought you meant he was way older. You won't want someone to describe you like that in ten years."

"I'm happy to be there when you meet with him."

She could imagine him standing behind her like a bodyguard. "Thanks, but I'll just call him in the morning. Easy to arrange things between that and email. You don't even have to meet face to face nowadays."

"That is a great benefit of technology. Very efficient." He crossed his arms.

"Speaking of efficiency, let's look at this, shall we?" Her phone rang as she pulled out a stool. It was Amanda. She shut off the ringer and set it aside.

"You're not answering?"

"It's my cousin. I'll talk to her later."

Jul sat beside her. "Not much has changed with it since I met that Ag dealer."

"Oh?" She fanned the pages. "I'll take a quick read-through." Julia did her best to block him out and looked over the proposal, trying to imagine she was the one hiring him. After the first pass, she flipped it over and started again.

He coughed.

She saw his mouth twitch.

Julia clicked a pen and rushed the second read. He looked so uneasy, she needed to let him off the hook. "It's great. I'd hire you in a second. I'm not sure there's much advice I can give you. You must have been working on it for a while now." She glanced at the pages. "It's very thorough."

"It's been coming along for a bit."

She opened the document again. "There are a couple of little things. You might want to rephrase this section." She circled the paragraph in question. "And there are a few typos here ... and here."

His shoulders relaxed. "Thanks for looking it over. That's a big help."

"Who are you marketing this to first?" After he shrugged, she went on. "You must have someone in mind if you've been working on it for this long."

Julian looked up again. "Dawson Fire and Safety?"

"You're not asking my permission, are you?"

"No." He stared at the pages. "I'm not sure I should call them yet. I wanted to be in a better position before I approached them."

"It will probably never get easier, so why don't you just jump in? I think that's a great place to start. I've even heard of them and I've only been in town a few months. When are you calling?"

"Tomorrow?"

"Why don't you phone now?" She gave him a gentle nudge. "They'll have voicemail, plus they'll be expecting your follow-up later tomorrow." Julia pushed back her chair. "I'm going to start digging around upstairs. We have a little time before dinner." She dared to touch his arm as she passed. "Come and see me when you're done."

Chapter Seventeen

AMANDA ACCEPTED JULIA'S EXCUSE FOR missing their weekly call with minimal pushback. She didn't even complain about the two-word text replies through the beginning of the week. Then Julia completely ignored her last three messages. That had been a mistake. On Friday afternoon, Julia's phone lit up with a a semi-threatening text.

You either lost your phone or you're avoiding me. I'll be calling Darvvin Brewer if you don't reply.

"That could be disastrous." Julia went to her room to make the call. She took a moment to smell one of her orange roses a second before she called.

When they connected, Amanda posed like she was conducting an interrogation. "There she is. I was about to call the RCMP and do a welfare check."

"At least you didn't send your parents over to knock."

Amanda whistled. "Touché. You're still mad about that, I gather."

"Have you talked to them?"

"No. Have you?"

"Are they planning on stopping in?"

"You know them. No one can predict a thing they do, but I doubt they'll be doing the drive to Fairmont again this late in the year." Amanda crossed her arms. "You can stop blaming me. I'm in the middle here."

The whole situation gave her a stomachache. "Sorry. I'm only—"

"You sound stressed."

"Everything's fine." Julia knocked the iPad flat when she reached for it. The bouquet came into full view.

"Where did the flowers come from?"

"Can't a girl buy herself flowers?" Julia snapped the device into her hands and strutted to the parlour. "I'm in the middle of decorating here. Getting ready for Halloween and I'm way behind. I should probably go."

"Are we talking tomorrow night? We missed last week, and I never heard—"

"Sure. I should have the decorating done. I'll show you then." She heard footsteps and pulled her iPad close as Jul came in. "Oh, looks like they need me. I'll text you tomorrow if it's going to work. Bye." She ended the call before Amanda could say anything else.

Jul put his hands up. "I didn't mean to disturb you. I didn't know you were on a call."

"It was only my cousin. She knows I'm busy around here."

He didn't look like he believed her. "We wrapped early today. I came to see if you need any help."

Boxes lined one side of the parlour. Julia was using the area in front of the window to sort the masses of fall decorations the Wilburs had left for her. Thank goodness Jul had been there to help. It was one thing to haul the cartons down the ladder, and another to carry them to the main floor. "Nope. I think I've got it under control."

He surveyed the mess. "I'm sure you do, but I've got nothing going on. I can help you."

Jul didn't have to do anything, and her focus broke apart. Every time she saw him, he made her heart pound. It was annoying. She wasn't the kind of girl who went weak in the knees at the sight of a handsome man who said all the right things.

But then, he wasn't really that guy either. He hardly ever said the right things. It was almost a happy accident when he did.

"Alright." She shoved a box to the side and searched for her list. "I have to get the garland put up so I can add the final touches. I've sourced some wheat sheaves and they're holding pumpkins for me at Co-op."

"So you want me to pick them up?"

"Oh no, not at all. I set up a tarp in the back of my 4runner. I can do it."

"I have a truck. Once you own a truck, you haul things. You don't make people mess up the carpet in their SUVs."

Julia stopped herself from refusing. "Okay. If you don't mind and you have nothing better to do on a Saturday morning—on your day off, might I remind you—would you mind picking them up for me? The pumpkins are in town, but the wheat is at a farm west of here. Kel Fennel's place. Do you know him? You probably passed it last Saturday when you were out there."

His chin jerked up, then he shook it off. "I'm sure I can do that for you. Just tell me where and when." Julian stood beside the piles of greenery along the floor. “We’re putting this up now?”

“No, I’ll set it up while you’re out tomorrow.”

“Or we can do it now.” He scooped up a mass of pine garland. “Where do you want these?”

Even if she said no, she was sure he’d insist. “Along the railing out front.”

The swags were easy to attach to the handrails, even easier because he was there. They developed a system once the first ones were tied. Jul wired the garland to the railing. Julia attached sprays of fall berries and artificial flowers where they met. They had most of it done in an hour.

“This is fantastic.” She viewed the deck from the front driveway. “We’ll definitely finish decorating tomorrow. Even if we did nothing else, it looks fall-ish.”

Julian watched her from the deck. He wore a smile she couldn’t quite read. “And you thought you were way behind.”

“I guess I was wrong. Luckily I found wheat and pumpkins. They will be a nice finishing touch for Halloween.” She met up with him at the top of the steps. “What are you dressing up as?”

“What for?”

“Halloween.”

“Um, this.” He brushed his hands over his plaid shirt and denim. “Maybe newer jeans. Nobody will see me anyway.”

There was no way she was going to let him hide out in his room on Halloween. “But I’m dressing up and I could use the help handing out candy and counting kids. Stel showed me their pumpkin costumes. They’re coming to trick or treat. What would Davey think if you didn’t dress up?”

"How about a cowboy?"

She tried to imagine him as anything else. "You're a cowboy every day. How about the Lone Ranger? Similar, but not exactly the same."

"No. Do you actually think I'd look good wearing white pants tucked into my boots? I don't even own white pants—and I'm not buying any either." He went back into the house.

Julia followed. "No, not that one. There was that newer movie a few years ago. That Lone Ranger wore darker colours. I know you have a suit jacket. You must have a vest, too." She searched for a picture on her phone.

"Does that mean you'll be Tonto?"

She laughed. "No. I'm going to be a Victorian lady. I rented a dress from a boutique in the city. Victorian house, so I have to fit in with the ambiance."

He passed the phone back to her. "Well, I don't have a mask or a white hat either."

"That's a weak excuse. We can find a mask anywhere. And what colour is your hat? I'm sure it would work."

"I only have my straw one in the truck. The rest are at Dar's. I guess I'll have to head out to the acreage and look." He checked his watch. "If I left now—"

"Things are pretty much at a standstill here until we get that stuff tomorrow. Why don't I go with you? I have some toys for the kids that I forgot when I went the other day."

Half a smile showed on his face. "I guess I'll go get my keys."

+++

JUL HADN'T THOUGHT it through. If he had, he would have made an excuse to go another time. At the very least, he should have cleared the visit with Stel before they left. She could have distracted Julia while he assessed the condition of his place before she saw it. He couldn't remember what kind of mess he'd left it in the Saturday before. But Jul hadn't done any of those things, so he drove to Brewer's with sweat threatening his back and armpits.

They parked in his standard spot. Julia climbed out before he even had his door open. "Must feel good to be back on your home turf for a bit."

"Kind of." It wasn't home. It was temporary—temporary like everything else in his life. He had to look on the bright side. It was the first chance to be alone with her in a place that was more like his than anywhere else they'd been together. They'd only ever been at her house or under the watchful eye of Darvvin at his.

He unlocked the door and let her go up the stairs first.

She made a beeline for the patio doors. "How did you ever move away from this?"

It was cool that afternoon and mist hovered over the pond at the edge of the property. A herd of deer grazed off to the south and behind them, the mountains stretched along the horizon.

"It seemed to be the only thing that made sense at the time."

"Right. They kicked you out." She dropped her chin and pulled her jacket close. "Sorry. I know Stel is ... it's only for a short time."

He stared at Julia while she stared at the land, all his favourite things in one picture. He turned on the fireplace to ease the goosebumps on his skin. "This will help a little. I guess we won't be here long."

She walked away from him, eyes fixed outside. "I've wanted to see this place for a while now."

"You have?" He'd wanted to see her in it since the first day he saw her.

"Oh, yes." She wandered into the kitchen. "I want to get some inspiration for the suite over my garage. Dar said he'd have to clear it with his friend before I could." Her grin proved she was oblivious to his disappointment. "And now you've brought me here yourself. He did a great job in here." She opened a drawer and watched as it eased shut. "Don't worry. I'm not going to kick you out to the garage at my place. You'll be safely back here before that project even starts, I bet."

Maybe she wasn't going to kick him out, but he felt like he'd been kicked, anyway. "I'll be right back." He needed some space and he left her briefly in the main room. Jul scanned the bathroom and bedroom for anything he'd left on the floor. A clean house might impress her—nothing else seemed to.

"Are you going to give me the grand tour?" She called.

"It will be short, but sweet." Julian faced the hallway. "Storage on the left, bathroom on the right, bedroom straight ahead."

Julia peeked into the bathroom first. "I'm so jealous. You have a tub." Her hand landed on his arm as they stood close in the small space. "I didn't think there would be room for a tub in a place this size."

"There's this great inn I'm staying at and I have a tub there too. You should talk to the owner."

"Would you put in a good word for me?"

He thought he saw her wink, but that couldn't be right. "I'm not sure what she thinks of me. It might not help you much." Jul backed out of the room.

Julia walked past his kingsize bed and stepped half a pace into the walk-in closet. "I guess with a closet like this, it's fashion show time. What've you got in there?" She took a seat on the end of his bed.

It was a good thing he could escape to the confines of the closet. The sight of her sitting there was almost too much. She'd worn tight denim again, and it showed off the shape of her legs in the best way—and she was on his bed.

Jul took sanctuary in the walk-in. He rested his forehead on a shelf and inhaled.

"Did you find your white hat and pants yet?" The bed creaked beneath her when she called out.

She seemed completely unaware of how she looked sitting there and had absolutely no idea at all how he felt about her. He was at a loss. "What am I supposed to be looking for again?"

"Grey hat? Black hat? You must have a black hat. Isn't that standard issue for every cowboy?"

He thought he heard her giggle. "Only the outlaws." Jul selected the two hats closest to him, pulling the black one low over his eyes. It was a bad idea. All he could see were her legs until he tilted it up.

Her mouth opened. She slid her hands over her thighs.

She hated it.

"No good?" Jul dropped it on the bed beside her and flipped a dark grey one in its place.

"No, it's great. Really good. They're both really good. Either one. You could make either one work." She carried the black hat close to her chest and walked a wide loop around him. Julia paused at the window. "Jacket? Vest? Shirt? I'm sure I've seen you in black pants, right?"

"You don't ask for much, do you?" He tossed the grey hat on the bed and returned to the closet. A white shirt hung underneath his grey sports coat and vest. He changed into them. "This could use a wash." Jul jerked the cuffs down from the coat sleeves.

She'd moved to the side of the bed. Her hands were on the mattress and her knees pressed tight together, feet wide, almost like a little kid. Jul's black hat was on her head, but it had slipped over her eyes. Julia lifted her chin as he got closer and tipped back the brim. Despite the fit, the look suited her perfectly. He wondered how he'd never imagined her dressed like that. It was a picture he'd never forget.

"You look great. We need to get you a hat of your own. Something that fits." He knelt, angling it so he could see her face better. Her hair waved down her back, providing a graceful frame for the gentle jawline he'd studied for so long. "There's a western store in town. They have anything you could ever want. Maybe you should be ..." Fresh gloss glimmered from her mouth, sending a charge through his system. She sucked in her bottom lip and nibbled at it. Every word he had vanished. He felt her breath on his face when she exhaled an instant later.

Jul lifted the hat away. A band of hair dropped in front of her eyes, but she didn't move. He took it between two fingers and pulled the strand over to the side, drawing through to the bottom of the lock. His hand tingled when he caressed her skin. Her cheek was silk in his grasp.

Jul leaned forward.

Julia wet her lips.

The door banged beneath them. "Julian, what're you doing here?" Footsteps stormed closer. Darvvin had let himself in. "This isn't a run, is it? Because if it is, God above me—"

"No!" Julia bolted, nearly knocking him to the floor.

Jul caught himself and rushed out behind her.

"—if you ran again, you're a lost cause, b'y—oh goodness, Julia. You're here too." Dar got to the top of the stairs the moment they scrambled into the kitchen. "Did I interrupt something?"

They didn't look at each other as they replied simultaneously.

"Oh no, nothing."

"Nothing, no."

Julia spread her palms flat on the countertop. Red speckled her skin.

Jul knew that had to be happening to him, too. The back of his neck tingled. He dug his finger along his collar.

"We're figuring out Jul's costume for Halloween." Julia tapped an irregular rhythm on the marble.

"Oh? Good. I just ..." Dar's eyes darted between them. "I just wondered what he ran over here for. Thought I'd come up and say hello."

The air was tight, holding back any words.

Julia spoke up. "Your washroom is around the corner, right?"

Jul cleared his throat. "Yes, it's—"

"I shut off the water when Jul left, sorry about that. I didn't think you'd be back here." Dar gestured to the stairs. "Why don't you go to the house and see Stel and the kids? They'd love to see you."

Jul clenched his jaw.

"Or maybe you two have more to do here? Actually, I'll go." Darvvin stepped back.

"No. We were just finishing up and then I was going to pop in and say hello. I have something to give the boys." She looked at Jul for the first time since they'd come out of his room. Her eyes widened for a split second, but she didn't show any other emotion. "We found what we were after, right?"

They'd found it and Dar blasted it away. He rubbed a hand over the back of his head."Yeah, more or less. I'll change and be right there."

Julia scurried towards the stairs.

Darvvin followed close behind her.

She raised her hand to him. "I can find my way, thanks." She looked back at Jul from the top of the stairs. "Don't forget those hats. Bring both."

The men watched while she left them. Jul felt the blood rushing through his ears until the door shut below them.

"I'm so sorry." Dar's arms opened wide. "I had no idea you brought her here. You should have warned me."

"Who barges in like that? Anything could have happened. Anything could have been happening." Jul had to slow his heart down and catch his breath. "What if I'd been running around naked?"

"I'm so sorry. I should've knocked. Though I guess that would've thrown everything off anyways."

Jul pressed his fingers against his forehead and paced.

"I guess you weren't running around naked. No one could get dressed that quick." Dar grinned, as though all was forgiven. "So, what *did* happen?"

"None of your business." It rubbed him raw, but he shut his mouth before he said something he'd regret. He had to get away. The bedroom door slammed behind him and he collected his thoughts and things.

DARVVIN WAS STILL lurking in the living room when Jul was finished changing. He raised his hands. "I'm gonna say it again, I'm sorry I interrupted—"

"Don't bother. I don't want to hear it." He jogged down the stairs and out the door, pausing only to drop his hats and clothes in the back of his truck.

Darvvin followed. "It's all good, you know? You're gonna be fine."

"I'm getting Julia and we're leaving." Jul marched to the Brewer's house.

Davey jumped him when he got inside. "Miss Jul-ya's here."

He lifted the boy and hugged him close. "Is she—" but Jul stopped. The kid wouldn't know if she was okay or not, and besides, Darvvin was listening to every word he said.

He followed the boy into the living room.

"Nice to have a surprise visit from you two." Stel smiled at him from the counter. She couldn't possibly know what had happened. "Why don't you stay for dinner? We've got loads of food, right hun?"

Darvvin didn't miss a beat. "Loads."

Stel was staring, and Dar was leering, and Davey was hanging off his leg. Luke toddled closer with every passing second, but Julia was nowhere to be seen. "I ... ah ..." And then he saw Stel's face brighten as she looked towards the hall. Julia walked in, likely from the bathroom. She wore a smile on her pretty mouth, but her eyes weren't convincing.

"We were asking if you two can stay for a feed." Dar took the floor. "Might as well—"

He saw the quiver in her bottom lip underneath the smile. "We would love to, but we still have some things to settle. Before we go, you have to tell them about the meeting you've set up, Jul."

Hearing his name on her lips would have been better if she'd looked at him when she said it, but she didn't.

"For your company? Had you out estimating with me all morning and you never breathed a word?" Dar took a chair beside him. "With who?"

Darvvin didn't deserve to hear about him, or his business, or his Julia, but it provided a good distraction. "Dawson Fire and Safety. Meeting in a couple of weeks for a look."

Dar slapped him on the back. “He’s got his fingers in a couple of pies, that one. He’d be good to land.”

A soft touch pressed onto Jul’s knee. David was beside him again. “Look what Miss Jul-ya gived me.”

“What have you got there?” He took the stuffed animal from his godson, then dropped it just as fast.

It was a white-tailed deer.

“I’ve got to go.” The hallway was clear and Jul went to the back door as fast as he could without running. He was in his truck and backing out when his brain caught up to him, reminding him that he’d brought Julia along.

She was just starting across the yard.

He heaved over the seat and opened the passenger door.

She climbed inside. “Are you alright?”

“Yep.” When he heard her seatbelt click, he put the truck in gear and rolled onto the road. Jul turned the radio up a little higher when they reached the highway. She was looking at him. He could feel her eyes. The air was thick, suffocating.

There were a million things to say—a million ways to try to clear the way between them, but nowhere to start. If she’d say something, get the ball rolling, let him know she wanted to talk about it—

But she didn’t say anything and he didn’t either and before long, they were parked at the inn.

He piled his clothes in his arms.

“I’ll get your hats,” Julia said.

“Thanks.”

She let them in through the front doors. "I'm kind of tired. I'm going to call it a night." She placed his hats on the stack he carried. "So goodnight."

She delayed. Julia was waiting for him to do something—to say something.

So he did. "Sleep well."

She pushed her chin forward and nodded slowly. "You too." Then she spun away from him and went to her door.

Jul was three steps up when he stopped. He couldn't leave things like that. She was still in the hall when he got to the main floor. "Wait."

The tension on her face faded. "What is it?"

He cleared his throat. "We're getting you that hat. I'll take you next week."

She pulled her arms tight around her. "No need for that. I'll take myself." With a turn on her heel, she left him and shut the door hard between them.

The stairs jeered as he went to his room, creaking with every step.

Jul sighed.

It was as good as over.

Chapter Eighteen

IT WAS MIDNIGHT BLACK IN Julia's room, but the clock showed six forty-five. An entire night had passed and he'd said nothing.

'Unbelievable.'

She pulled the blankets up to her ears, trying to block the certainty that she could have said something too. She could have asked him about the toy deer, and why he left her standing there, and how Darvvin interrupted and about—

"That kiss," she whispered.

She liked to imagine that Jul's steps were a little heavier than usual when he climbed the stairs.

"Good."

He clearly didn't care what had happened. It would be better if he went back to Brewers and left her alone.

She jerked upright and kicked off the covers. The rod fell off the bracket when she ripped open the curtain.

Jul's truck was in the same spot they'd left it the night before.

A sigh escaped her. He wasn't gone, but he would be leaving in less than an hour to pick up the supplies—if he still wanted to. It was a good thing the tarp was still in her SUV, in case she was going to have to go instead.

Actually, that was preferable. She would do it herself. She could be halfway out to the Fennel farm before he even got up.

It didn't work out that way.

By the time she was ready, Jul was in the kitchen with a coffee beside him.

"Did you sleep alright?" She didn't look at him while she poured for herself.

"It was fine." His cup banged on the counter. "I didn't get the address of that farmer's place. Did you send it yet?"

"You're still planning to go?"

He gave her a look. "Yes."

"I'll send it now. They said you can come anytime after eight. Co-op said nine or later."

Jul glanced at his watch. "I guess I can get going then."

"You're not eating?"

"Had toast." He pulled on a jean jacket. "You need anything else?"

When she replayed their conversation to herself in the middle of the night, Julia thought of what she should have said. She should have demanded an explanation, forced a conversation about what happened, but in the moment, the words weren't there.

"No. I've got everything under control," she said.

He pulled a straw hat on his head. "Text me if anything comes up." And then he walked away, unaware that his last glance at her made her knees feel like jelly.

The man could pull off a cowboy hat like no one else she'd ever seen.

Julia burned her tongue on the coffee. She set it aside. It was the perfect day to skip breakfast—she didn't feel like eating anyway.

"There's still so much to do," she muttered.

The parlour was cluttered with materials. She set out a few baskets and trinkets in the hall, knowing that they'd do nothing but collect dust. There was no point putting everything out, not until work was done and there were guests to see it.

Julia sorted the boxes and started a pile of empties at the bottom of the stairs. Jul would certainly carry them upstairs for her when he got back.

"I'm not waiting for him. I can do it myself," she declared. Her efforts were fuelled by sheer stubbornness. The climb to the attic was a challenge even with empty boxes.

Julia went back for a few more. At the bottom of the stairs, she heard the floor creak. A shadow passed across the hall.

Someone was in the house.

She tiptoed towards the room. From her position, she could see through the bow window. An unfamiliar vehicle was parked in Jul's usual spot.

The 'visitor' had gone towards the library—she heard the footsteps. Julia crept towards the other side of the entry to see better. A man came around the corner and almost knocked her down.

Julia jumped back with a cry.

"I'm sorry to startle you." He reached for her but stopped and raised his hands. "I ... The door was open."

"I usually have it locked these days. I'm closed for renovations for a few months. How can I help you?" She felt for her phone in her back pocket.

"I'm Shane Harnes."

"What can I do for you?"

His brow wrinkled, then he smiled. "I've been by a couple of times to arrange a dinner. We met in the summer. The Wilburs introduced us."

"Mr. Harnes, of course." She'd forgotten to phone him. "You've been patiently awaiting my call. I have to apologize. I did get your messages." No wonder Jul's description didn't help her. It didn't fit the man at all. His sharp haircut and athletic build would easily pass for late thirties.

"Please, call me Shane." He had thick black lashes. His eyes were as dark as Jul's were blue.

"Julia." She shook his hand.

He smiled. "I should have called first. I was going by and saw the lights."

"I'm glad you stopped in. Pardon the mess. I'm decorating for fall. Jul's out picking up a few things so we can finish."

"Jul?"

"You met him, I think." Heat crept up her neck. "He's staying here for a while. Just during renovations until he gets settled." It was a long story, and she didn't know why she'd even brought him up. "Anyways, you and I need to talk about your event, don't we? Can I get you a coffee?"

Warm smiles had worn handsome creases around his eyes. He was a nice-looking man. "I'd love one." He followed her to the kitchen, and she poured him a cup before they moved into the dining room. "I've lived in Juniper Creek my whole life, but I've never been in here. It's a beautiful place."

She unstacked two chairs and lifted the corner of a drop cloth off of a table. "Thank you. I fell in love as soon as I saw it."

He pulled his chair so close they were nearly knee to knee. "That's when you know it's meant to be, right? When it hits you the moment you see it."

"True." The memory of seeing Jul at the cafe flashed through her mind. She pressed her nails into her palm. The sooner Julian Ariets left her alone, the better. She didn't need him invading her thoughts, especially when she was having a simple conversation with a client. "So, for your party … we'll have dinner in this room. Imagine this all set up for Christmas. It will be lovely."

"I'm sure it will be. Everything in this place is beautiful." Shane smiled again. "And I trust you. You're the expert."

An expert who forgot to return her client's call. "This is the first event of this kind I'll be hosting, but I appreciate your vote of confidence."

He briefly set his hand on her arm. "I have a good feeling about this."

"Me too." Julia took a moment to appreciate his attentive grin. "Do you have a date in mind?"

Shane shook his head. "No. I'm single for now."

She opened the calendar to December and pretended she hadn't heard him.

"A day for the party, right." He closed his eyes and smiled. "I was thinking early December."

"December seventh or fourteenth would work. Twenty to twenty-five guests, right?" He confirmed with a nod. "We'll set up two tables of six … eight if we can. I'll have doubles arranged around the perimeter of the room. And I'll make sure you get the nicest spot. In fact, we can set it aside right now."

He looked off to the side. "That's alright. Just put me at a middle table. I'm sure we can make a change if I find that special someone."

"We can." She wrote 'Shane with group' on her page and then a new title, 'menu'. "Would you like a buffet or a plated meal?"

He blinked and clasped his hands. "Oh, ah, probably buffet. You never know what people like or don't like, I guess."

"And I'm sure you'd like to serve alcohol. I'll look into licensing for the night." She scribbled on her page. "I'll need your budget, too. You have my card, right?"

"I do, but only the inn number. Could I get your cell?"

"Of course." She hadn't given out her personal number in years, except when she gave it to Jul, but then she'd practically forced him to take it. "Do you want me to text it to you?"

"Please." He set his business card on the table. "I'll add my home number here and my personal email, just in case. Call or text me, anytime if you need anything."

"The most pressing item is the date because I'm sure the caterers are getting booked up." She gathered her notes and cracked them on the table. "That's everything I need for now. Unless you have questions for me?"

"No, I guess that's all." He followed her to the hall.

"Thanks for your patience. This is going to be a great event for your crew. I apologize for the delay."

"Don't worry about it. I can see you've got a lot on your plate. The place looks great. Will you be giving out candy on Halloween?"

Julia searched out the stapler at the check-in desk. "Yes. It will be good for community building. And besides, who doesn't love candy?"

"Everybody loves the sweet stuff." He flashed her a million-dollar smile and scanned the room. "Maybe I'll bring my niece and nephew over. They would love to see this—oh, Julian. Hello."

Her head shot up. Jul stood at the door, a mighty cowboy with a pumpkin wedged under his arm.

"Shane." He stretched his mouth into a near smile. "Nice of you to drop in. You interrupted Julia's project? And lived to tell the tale?"

She'd heard him laugh many times. It had never sounded like that before.

Shane pushed his hands deep in his pockets and smiled at the floor. "I guess she went easy on me, hey?" Then he took her hand between both of his in a firm grip. "It was great to see you again, Julia. I'll be in touch with that information and don't hesitate to call me if you need anything else."

"I'll talk to you early next week." She shook Shane's hand one last time.

The wreath on the door rattled when it closed.

Jul stayed stock still except for a twitch on his lips.

"Did it go okay today?"

He lifted the pumpkin. "I think I got everything."

"Awesome. I'll help you unload, and then we can finish up. Get the rest of these boxes put away." Julia took another look in the parlour. "I have a date tonight, after all."

"He asked you out?" Jul's voice rumbled.

"What?" He had to be joking, but his face was icy serious. "No. He was here to talk about his party. I forgot to call him back. Again. I'm lucky he's giving me another chance." She got pumpkin skin under her nails when she grabbed it from his arms. "I have that call with my cousin, of course. I try to do it every Saturday. Last week was just ... different."

"Right." He dropped his head and backed a step away. "Well, I have a date with Ed."

"Perfect." She went back to her piles in the parlour, pleased with herself when she didn't turn back as the front door slammed shut.

✦✦✦

"IT COULD BE a magazine spread." Amanda gushed when she saw the inn adorned for fall.

"You should see it in person. The camera doesn't do it justice." Julia walked a slow trail along the drive-through at the front of the house, scanning it with her camera.

"You must have been working on it for days."

Jul came out of the front door with his phone to his ear. "Excuse me. Didn't know you were out here."

"Or did you have some help? Is that your houseguest? Gorgeous—"

She shouted over her cousin's voice. "I'm showing off the house to Amanda."

Jul stopped at the top of the steps. "I'm going to the—what's that? Fine. Ed wants to say hello." He turned on the speaker. "Say hello, Ed."

"Hello, Ed." The man laughed. "And hello, ladies."

Julia hoped Amanda would behave. "Did you hear all that? Darvvin's brother Ed is on Jul's phone."

"And Julian too, I hope."

"Of course." She joined him at the top of the stairs, ready to press the power button if Amanda said something embarrassing. A flip of the camera framed them on the screen.

"Julian, how nice to meet you, finally." Amanda raised her mimosa to him. "Jules has told me so much about you."

"Oh, um. Nice to meet you too. I'm talking to my friend Edward ... Ed in Newfoundland. And here's Julia's cousin Amanda from Australia."

"Shame I can't see ya. He should've put you on camera, but I'll take what I can get. Nice to meet you both. Ed Brewer."

"Hi, Ed. I'm Julia. I've seen your picture at Stel's. Your brother's a great guy."

"Not you too." He groaned. "Imagine hearing that every day of your life and now from the other side of the country."

"Even I know he's great and I'm halfway around the world." Amanda winked. "Nice to meet you both. Hopefully, we can all meet in person one of these days."

"Well, I really should show you the entryway." Julia focused the camera on the side of the house.

"Yeah, um, I have to get my wallet and then I'm heading to the garage. I'll stay out of your hair until after."

"Then you'll finally be getting in her hair?" Ed laughed while Jul struggled to shut off the speaker. He stamped out of hearing range.

Julia slammed the door behind her.

"He's absolutely getting relationship advice from his friend," Amanda declared.

"For someone who's been single for more years than I've been alive, you're quite the expert."

"Ouch." Amanda drained her glass. "At the very least, they've been talking about you. 'Getting in your hair'. Ed never would have said that otherwise." She nodded to herself. "My god, Jules. He's so handsome and I'm sure he's even better in real life."

"Shh. I don't even know where he is." Julia dipped her head to see under the kitchen blind. He was walking through the garage door. "We're making things work until he goes back to Darvvin's. End of story." She had been telling herself that all day.

"He helped you decorate, right? You eat together. Your friends are trying to set you two up. It's only a matter of time." She smirked. "Even if he wasn't as nice as he sounds like he is, couldn't you be happy just staring at him all day?"

Julia pressed her finger to her ear. "What's that? You're breaking up. Something's wrong with the signal—"

"You wouldn't dream of cutting me off if I wasn't right." Amanda squinted. "Something happened, didn't it? You're not avoiding me simply because you're mad about my parents."

"I'm very mad about your parents. Mostly at them, but I'm mad at you too." Julia filled a glass of her own. "You should have told them to stay away."

"Don't change the subject. That's another dead giveaway. What have the two of you been getting up to in that big house all alone?"

"Nothing in this house." She saw Jul through the loft window. He was pacing.

"In another?" Amanda jumped at the comment. "Do tell."

"There's nothing to tell." If the kiss had happened, that would be something to share. If he'd even breathed a word of it once, she'd talk about it all night. The lack of follow-up proved that it didn't matter to him a bit. Life went on. It wasn't quite the same, but it was clear that no-one had to worry about what may or may not have happened at his place. "I've got nothing to tell you. Nothing at all."

Amanda was still and stoic until Julia spoke again.

"Five weeks and I get my house back to myself. Let me tell you about this party I'm planning ..."

Chapter Nineteen

REACHING OUT TO EDDIE HAD been pointless.

Ed called him some name that Jul couldn't quite remember, though 'stunned' and 'arse' was somewhere in the title. Other than that, the advice he got was nothing new.

Yes, Jul had to get off his arse, yes he had to let her know how he was feeling and yes, he had to talk to her about what happened at his place.

But how was he supposed to do any of that?

Everybody knew what Jul *should* do but nobody could explain exactly how he should go about it.

Julia went to bed before he had a chance to talk to her again Saturday night and it never really felt like the right moment the next morning during their drive to church.

Or that afternoon.

Or the next day.

She hadn't mentioned it either, so what did that mean?

At least her attitude towards him had improved. Saturday morning, she was icy, but by Thursday, she was amicable enough.

Thank goodness for that because it was Halloween and they had to spend all night together.

Jul wasn't looking forward to it. Not only did he have to navigate the evening with Julia, but the Brewers were coming over, and strangers, and he had to dress up.

Jul buttoned up his white dress shirt. "This is ridiculous." He pulled on his vest and then the jacket. His hat and mask lay side by side on the dresser. Jul set the hat on his head. The mask would have to wait. The last thing he needed was a fall down the stairs because he couldn't see out of the thing.

JULIA WAS ALREADY in the kitchen when he got there and Jul saw her before she saw him. He held onto the moment and watched her.

She was decked out in a floor-length caramel-coloured dress. It glinted gold on the island faucet as she dug through a utensil drawer. Her hair was pulled back from the sides of her face and she'd wrapped it in a little bundle on the back of her head. The rest fell over her bare shoulders. That was a sight to behold—she normally kept covered in button-up blouses.

She took his breath away. Again.

Julia lifted a pair of tongs. "All ready? You look wonderful." Her eyes flowed over him, hat to face to shoulders and beyond.

He flashed back to the day she'd seen him half-naked in the hall. Jul scratched his neck. "Ready, I guess."

"Did you try on the mask?"

Jul lifted it to his eyes and then pulled it down. "Do I really have to wear it?"

"You really do." She took it from him, brushing his hand. "Stel did a knockout job on that thing."

"At least it doesn't cut into my eye sockets anymore." Something was hanging off her back. "You've got a—"

"Ribbon. It's a single woman's trick for pulling up the zipper, but I dropped it and couldn't quite reach with these sleeves. I thought the tongs would help."

Thin bands of sheer fabric grazed the top of her arms. They couldn't be called sleeves. "So you'd rather get dressed with a kitchen tool than ask me to help?"

She pressed her lips in a kind of smile. "No, I ... go ahead." Julia pulled her hair over her right shoulder. Her crystal earring invited further attention.

Jul slipped the ribbon from the zipper's pull and set it beside the tongs on the counter. "How did you even get this in here?"

"I put it in before I got dressed."

He zipped the dress and backed away. "That took me two seconds. You can always ask me, you know?"

"Thanks." She rearranged her hair. "The guy from the paper will be here any minute now. I should have had a new name figured out, new branding—"

"A name will come. Tell him you're changing it. He can write a follow-up."

She didn't seem to be listening. Julia rifled through the cupboard over the coffeepot. "I wanted to touch up my lipstick. I need to put this on." A beaded choker clicked in her grasp.

"Again, I'm right here. Lone Ranger to the rescue."

At first, she looked like she'd refuse. Then she laughed, but it was weak—a watered-down version of what he loved to hear. She dropped the necklace into his waiting hands and held her hair high.

Loose strands tickled his skin, vines luring him to lose his fingers in it. He fastened the metal ends of the velvet ribbon. A gold teardrop weighed down the chain. He held the clasp for long enough to watch it roll side to side, moving with her breath. "There. All done."

She swiped her palms over the bodice of her gown. "Ready to go."

A heat wave fell over him, and he pulled at the ends of his collar. She was breathtaking, and they were together and they were alone and it was probably way too forward, but he had to tell her. "You look—"

The knock came before the words escaped.

"He's here." Julia pulled Jul with her to the front door.

✦✦✦

"NICE TO MEET you. I'm Zach Riley." The J.C. Journal had sent their novice reporter.

"Thanks for showcasing the inn." Julia smiled through her disappointment. "Where would you like to start?"

"How about a few shots from the street?"

She'd left the banner over the official Wilbur Inn sign. "I'll be renaming the place, so if you could block out the sign, that would be great."

The young man squinted into his viewfinder. "Alright. How about one of you on the grass here?"

"Sure." Julia rubbed the chill off of her arms.

"If you could relax, it would look ... better. Be natural."

She was sure she looked like a department store mannequin.

"Let's try a few next to the house."

The door opened when she reached the verandah.

Jul appeared with a granny square afghan in his hands. "Here. You're going to freeze." He pulled the multi-coloured mess over her shoulders.

The blanket was the least attractive thing he could have found in the entire house. It was worse than ugly, but the sentiment behind his gesture almost made her cry. "Thank you so much." She hugged him loosely before Zach interrupted.

"Can I get the two of you in front of your pumpkin display?" The reporter scooted them near the urn at the left of the door.

Jul took a step away, but she grabbed his hand. "You did as much as I did, plus all the hauling."

He grunted and kissed his lips together for an instant before standing behind her.

Julia let the blanket fall off her shoulders.

"Closer now. Could you please put your arms around each other?"

It was on the tip of her tongue to say no, but then she felt the heat from Jul's hand hovering over her waist. She took half a step closer to him, tucking her arm behind his back.

The reporter checked his light meter and then peered into the viewfinder. "Could you turn towards him a little more?"

Julia did as she was told. She inhaled, savouring the scent of Jul's cologne as she got closer to him.

"Did you photograph the JC high school graduation, by any chance?" Jul asked.

The young man smiled. "I certainly did. You must have seen the coverage in the paper." His camera clicked.

Julia covered her mouth and elbowed Jul.

"Do you want my coat?"

"No, I'm trying not to laugh," she whispered.

"You're trying not to freeze to death." He lifted the blanket over her shoulders again.

"I don't want that to show up in the pictures." She let the afghan drop but then she felt warmer still. Jul's arm fell snugly over her shoulders, pulling her close.

A truck turned into the driveway before the shutter clicked again. The Brewers had arrived.

Jul scuffed his feet. "You're still going to be cold. Why don't I—"

Zach offered more direction before he could finish. "Could you put your other hand on his chest, miss? Now tilt your head a little towards him."

She could feel the pendant under his shirt. Jul's heart was beating like he'd been running and he was holding his breath.

"That should do it." The camera beeped as the reporter scanned through the images. "And to confirm, you're Matthew and Julia Ariets?"

Jul dropped his arm, and she lifted the blanket over her shoulders again. "No, it's Julia Matthews and Julian Ariets."

“Ah, got it.” The reporter scribbled something new. “This will be out next Thursday. Have a good night, folks.”

“Those shots are going to be gorgeous.” Stel carried Luke on her hip. Dar and Davey followed. “You two make a handsome couple. And what a cozy wrap you’re wearing.”

Julia opened her arms wide to show it off. “Isn’t it? The Lone Ranger brought it for me.”

Davey’s pumpkin costume billowed around him when he jumped through the door. “Are you the Alone Ranger, Unca Jul?”

Darvvin howled. “Yes, my son. Uncle Jul is the Alone Ranger.”

Jul made a hasty departure to the kitchen.

THE BREWERS STAYED for longer than they’d originally planned. Julia was glad to have them, and glad to have Stel there, for sure. She kept the atmosphere light, and her boys were a constant stream of entertainment while they waited for people to knock.

“You look like you’re having more fun than the kids coming to the door,” Stel said.

“I’ve never given out candy before. I’ve missed out.” Julia set the treat bowl on the hall table.

“Even when you were younger?”

When she was younger, one of her parents would take her through the neighbourhood and the other would be on candy detail at home. The best years were the ones she’d gone around with Amanda at her aunt and uncle’s place.

Julia pushed the memory away. “I used to shut off the lights and ignore the doorbell.” She grabbed another bag of candy, tearing the corner too hard. It spilled all over the floor. "Oops. That was a little overenthusiastic."

"Let's help Miss Julia clean this up." Stel put her little boys to work, and they had the mess tidied in minutes.

Another group of children came to the door. Davey helped fill their bags.

"That was another group of five. Do you think there are this many people every year?" Julia swished her way to the check-in desk where Jul and Darvvin kept count. They'd hardly interacted with the women all night. Jul hadn't, anyway. Darvvin always had a kiss for Stel. "How many visitors have we had so far?"

"A hundred and sixty-four."

Jul had the numbers written in his immaculate, compact script.

"That's a lot," she said. His eyes were invisible in the mask, hiding any reaction to her presence.

Stel clapped her hands. "Well, little ones, we'd better head out. I'm sure the trick-or-treaters will slow down soon. Time to say bye-bye."

Davey ran away and circled the sofa.

Darvvin went after his son. "Thanks so much for the night. Keep us posted on how it goes."

"We will. There probably won't be too many more little ghouls out there." Julia helped with Luke's coat. She passed a diaper bag to Stel.

Darvvin said something to Jul and shook his hand as the women embraced.

"We'll see you at church on Sunday." Stel blew a kiss as the final flurry of action buzzed through the room.

And then it was quiet again, but for the clock ticking at them.

Julia sighed. She should have played music. Without the Brewers, it was way too quiet. The speaker was still in her room and she couldn't run off to get it.

Jul maintained his position at the check-in and she wondered if he was re-counting. It was a good thing that he had a 'job' so he would stay. Maybe, just maybe, they'd actually start talking about something important, like the weekend before.

Like the future.

Julia tilted her chin from side to side and stretched, wishing her neck would crack.

It didn't.

That was what they needed, something to crack open their ... *his* unwillingness to let her in. There had to be some way she could break through without scaring him away—some way that made him think it was his idea.

She reapplied her lip gloss. The tube made a cracking sound on the table when she dropped it.

Jul cleared his throat.

She wished she could read his expression, but there wasn't a chance of that happening with the mask and low lighting around him. "All decked out like that in a black hat. It's like we're having a showdown."

"Oh?" He dropped his head a few seconds later, and that was it.

Julia didn't understand why he still struggled to talk to her. She'd have to drag it out—get him to say something more. She opened her mouth, willing something profound to come out of it, but closed it before the wrong thing did. It was frustrating.

He was beyond frustrating.

She grabbed a miniature chocolate bar, wound up, and threw it at him as hard as she could.

It bounced off of his shoulder. "What the?"

"Don't you like that kind? Try these." She took one in each hand and flung them, then carried the bowl closer, throwing handfuls rapid fire.

"What are you doing?" Jul gathered a few bars and shot them back.

He had good aim and a hard throw, hitting her head and shoulders. A few bounced off the bodice of the gown. Julia raised her arms. "Okay, I surrender."

He sniffed and looked back at his tally sheet.

She still had a single bar in her hand and Jul was completely unprepared. She threw it as hard as she could.

It pelted him in the neck.

"Hey!"

Julia bent double with laughter. "That was the last one, I promise. I couldn't resist. That felt good." Her eyeliner was running. She ran her index finger along the outer corner of her eyes. Jul crossed his arms, but he was smiling. "You've got to admit, this has been fun."

"I'm not sure I should admit anything. But maybe." He leaned on the counter and smiled. "Yes."

"'Maybe yes' is good enough for me." Julia checked her face in the mirror and touched up her lips again. "Don't worry, Mr. Lone Ranger. We're almost done. Things have to be winding down soon."

"I'm sure I wasn't allowed to be out this late."

"You weren't allowed or didn't want to stay out?"

A knock sounded and voices cried out. "Halloween Apples."

"Here we go again." Julia swapped her lip gloss for the candy bowl and opened the door. She recognized the visitor right away. "Shane, Happy Halloween." He was dressed as a vampire and had spared no detail. A pale layer of makeup covered his skin. With his slicked-back hair and dark eyes, the effect was striking. "Great costume."

"Oh, thanks. I had a bit of fun with it." Two children stood beside him. "Allow me to introduce my nephew, Logan, and my niece, Emma. This lovely lady is Julia Matthews. You look absolutely gorgeous." Shane told her. "Let me see that dress." He took the candy bowl from her and held her hand while she stepped back. "Beautiful."

Before she knew it, he had her in a spin. Julia's skirts rustled around her legs threatening to bind them. "I'm going to fall over."

"Don't vorry. If you do, I vill catch you." A pair of plastic fangs caught the light as the motion was cut short.

Strong arms surrounded her, and the twirl slowed to nothing. Jul caught the candy bowl as it fell from Shane's grasp. "Hello there."

"Oh, hey man. I didn't see you." Shane flinched and moved towards the children.

Jul's eyes were invisible when he nodded to Julia. She nodded back, unsure of exactly what she was agreeing to.

After a beat, he positioned himself half a step in front of her. "Are you kids getting lots of candy tonight?"

"We already got two bags. We were gonna quit, but Uncle Shane said we should come here." The boy's smile revealed a missing front tooth. "This house is cool. No wonder he wanted to see it so bad."

"Did he?" Jul crouched down and gave a handful of candy to each child. "There are a few things worth seeing here, aren't there?" He added more to their bags. "I've got a joke for you. What did the skeleton say to the vampire and the vacuum?"

The little girl looked at her brother, and the boy shrugged.

"You both suck."

They giggled.

Julia did too. She couldn't help it. A rush hit her chest, and it wasn't from spinning.

"I hope you've had a great Halloween. I know this has been my favourite one ever." Jul resumed his position between them.

Shane's smile flattened out to nothing and his makeup couldn't hide the flood of red rushing up his neck. "Well, I think it's time to call it. School tomorrow for them, work for me."

"We're going to shut things down here, too," Julia pressed her hands together. "By the way, I have the final menu sorted. I'll email it tomorrow."

"Perfect." He glanced at Jul, then back at her. "Will the caterer let us do some kind of tasting thing? I mean, since he's new ..."

It was an odd request. "I'll ask and let you know."

The floor creaked when Jul stepped to the side.

"I'll be waiting." Shane pulled her into a half hug. "Thank you so much, Julia."

"Have a great night." She waited in the vestibule. Once their footsteps had faded, she switched off the outdoor lights and locked the door. After taking half a second to breathe, she returned to the hall.

Jul hadn't moved.

She whisked past him. "I didn't think he'd show up tonight."

"He said he was going to, didn't he?" Jul folded his arms across his chest. "You're still doing that party for him?"

"We've been talking about it all week." Her heels clacked the wood floor when she crossed to the front room.

"That explains the first names."

"Yes, the results of building rapport. You know how business goes, right?" She turned off the lamps in the bay window. "FYI, his party is on December seventh. If you're still here, you'll have to work around it. You could go to Darvvin's, or the garage, I guess." The curtains scraped on the rod when she closed them.

"I want to help you."

His words were scarcely audible. For sure, he hadn't thought about it before he said it. It was too committal.

He cleared his throat when she came back into the hall. "I said I want to help you. If you'll let me."

"I heard you." Jul was such a puzzle, standing there, waiting on her, but taking no initiative. "And I'd like to have your help." Julia approached him. Half of his face was blocked by the mask, the rest obscured by shadow. "All night you've wanted to get rid of that thing and now you've been wearing it for fun for the last twenty minutes." She tentatively raised her arms and untied the knot he'd made in the back. He tensed up, but the fabric slipped apart easily. Julia looked into the eyes she'd missed seeing all night. There had to be a solution in there somewhere. "You made an excellent Lone Ranger."

His chest rose and fell when he replied. "You are stunning, Julia." He looked to the side and pinched the bridge of his nose. "That is, you're a stunning Victorian lady. Not to say that you're not—"

He was sinking, and she had to throw out a lifeline. "I know what you meant." She was too close, too soon. She retreated. "I guess we'd better call it a night." Another step took her that much further away. "Change out of these crazy outfits." She swayed as she walked back a few more paces. The golden skirt whirled around her. "It's still early, though. Wine? We'll have to set up in my suite so people won't see the lights and come knocking—if that's alright with you." Three more moves had her in the pass-through, a few feet from her door.

He took two steps towards her. "I'll be down in a bit."

"Alright." The silky fabric of her dress whispered as it followed her away.

"Julia?"

She turned back like she'd been in a spin. "What is it?"

"You using those tongs again, or do you want me to help with the zipper?"

She knew it had to be too dark for him to see the goosebumps that came over her. Julia moved her hair out of the way.

"I'll get this too." He started with the choker.

The beads skimmed her skin when he passed it down to her.

"You're shivering." He whispered as he slipped his fingers between the top of the gown and her back. He held the fabric taut and took the pull down. Jul exhaled.

She let her head drop forward when she felt his breath. The tingle sprinkled down to her toes.

"You're cold." His voice got louder and he backed away. "You should go and—you can reach that, right?"

"It will work. Thanks." She flicked her hair back into place, glancing over her shoulder as she walked away. "See you in a few? The door's open when you're ready."

Chapter Twenty

IT WAS PROBABLY ANOTHER ATTEMPT at getting information, but Dar decided to promote Jul from 'grunt' to ... well, it was anyone's guess what the official title was. Dar brought him along for a few estimates and let him look at the fall and winter workflow.

"You can quote a project on-site as well as I can, maybe better because you know the paper side," Dar told him. "Go on a couple of visits with me and then you can fill in when I'm tied up. It wouldn't hurt if you could smooth out some of the scheduling, either."

Jul was going to object, but it was along his line of work. And anyway, what did it matter? It proved that Dar realized he was good at more than heavy lifting. Plus, he wouldn't be doing it for very long. Everything would change once he got in with Dawson and got his act together.

If that happened.

"When that happens."

He balanced a log on the stump beside the rack. With minimal force, the dry chunk broke in two. He split each piece again. Jul had chopped enough wood that afternoon to last them multiple birthday celebrations.

"Jul?" Julia's voice was music to his ears, even if it sounded like he was in trouble. "Remember that part where you quit work early to chop wood and then had a shower so you wouldn't be all sweaty for your party?" She leaned out far enough for him to see her. "Yet here I find you mysteriously working again. There's probably a rule somewhere against the birthday boy chopping wood for his own party, especially after he's showered."

"I was stacking—"

"I heard the axe."

"Kindling."

"Sure." Julia pressed her hands onto her denim-covered hips. She'd gone to Big West alone, just like she'd threatened to. It bugged him, but she was a sight to behold dressed head to toe in Western gear.

His phone rang, and Ed's number appeared. "I'll be in as soon as I get this."

"I'll be listening for telltale chopping."

Jul answered as the door closed behind her. "You calling to see if I got the gift you sent me?"

"If I could give you the perfect gift, it'd be that girl all wrapped up in a bow in case you don't go get her yourself. But I can't, so let me sing to you instead."

He let the song go on for a few painful seconds. "That's good now, thanks."

"I wish you every good thing, that all your wishes come to be. By the way, what's going on with that other guy?"

"Thanks for bringing him up." Jul had good news to report on that front. "He wanted to do some kind of food tasting, but she shut him down. Told him he could see the caterer on the weekend if he wanted. Without her."

"I thought you had real news. You've got to jump in if you're gonna beat him to the catch, eh? Anything new happen between you two since your Halloween disaster? You should thank your lucky stars she's even talking to you. Would you talk to a woman who didn't show up if you invited her for drinks in your bedroom?"

Ed had his story all wrong, as usual. "It wasn't her bedroom, and I *did* show up. She was already asleep." When he finally got the nerve to go down, she'd nodded off on the sofa. He watched her sleep for as long as he dared. "I covered her up with a blanket."

"You got it backwards again. You're supposed to use the blanket for both of you. Curl up *with* her."

He'd imagined that scenario a million times but—"I'm not quite there yet."

"I bet that other guy would have."

"Don't even say it."

"Well, happy birthday anyway and when you blow out your candles, make a wish for a pair of balls for yourself." Ed laughed. "What's happening tonight?"

"Your brother and family are coming over. Hot dog roast, cake. Birthday party stuff."

"If she's still having a party for you, things can't be too bad—even if they don't seem too good either."

Jul closed his eyes. "You're too kind."

"Ah, you know I love ya. And good luck with your big Dawson meeting tomorrow."

"I should know by lunchtime if that one's a dead end."

"Imagine if it goes right. Your next year might be your best year."

"Here's hoping." He saw Julia through the glass door again. "I have to run. Thanks for the call. I'll keep you posted."

"Talk soon."

Julia held a sheet of paper in one hand and hot dog forks in the other. She brought them down to the fire pit.

"How are those new boots?"

"Getting used to them. They're pretty comfortable." She lifted the leg of her jeans and flashed the stitching. He would have picked the same ones for her, snip-toe boots in wine red. "How are things going out here? Can I cross this off my list?"

"Everything's ready to go."

"That's it then." Julia folded a page in half. "We're officially ready. I'm just going to check out the snacks one more time."

He followed her to the kitchen. Bowls and beverages crowded the island. "It looks like you invited a hundred people."

"I had to have a decent selection. It's your party. It has to be perfect."

"Stop worrying. I already think it's the best thing anyone has ever done for me."

"I want it to be good. You deserve that, you know?" She moved a bowl and rearranged the plates, then checked the time. "Brewers will be here shortly. Shall we have an early birthday toast?"

Jul cracked a beer and filled her glass with Merlot. They tapped their drinks together.

"Happy birthday." She set her glass alongside a vein in the marble and bit her lip. "I have a little something for you. I'll give it to you before they get here."

"That wasn't part of the deal. You weren't even supposed to go to all the trouble of a party."

"It's just a little thing." After a moment of rummaging in the cupboard, Julia set a small box in his hand.

It looked exactly like it could hold a ring. "What on earth could this be?"

Her head tilted to the side, and she hugged her left arm across her body. She looked adorable, twisting side to side with a smile on that lip she was nibbling.

That was gift enough for him.

"Open it." She bounced when she said it.

He tore his eyes away and pulled the ribbon off the paper. Inside was a red leatherette box. He lifted the lid and a silver coin popped up from the black velvet lining. "What's this?" He had no words, but Julia had many.

"Do you like it?" She hurried to his side. "It's fine silver, and it has the year on it here." Her brightly polished fingernail pointed the number out. "It's uncirculated."

Jul looked closer. The surface held the images of a pair of white-tailed deer—a buck and a doe side by side, leaping over a fallen tree.

"It's a twenty-dollar coin. I was going to have it drilled so you could wear it, but how many coins do you need around your neck, right?" A breath came out when she smiled. "Plus, I know how much you like deer. Darvvin said that you love them."

A tag set behind it read 'Mates'.

Julian looked at her, then the coin, and then back at her again. “You have no idea what this means to me.” He wished he could tell her why it was so special. He wished he could put it into words. Jul pulled her close.

She put her arms around him, and her cheek settled on his shoulder. “So, you do like it?” Her laugh faded when he hugged her tighter.

Jul’s heart stretched thin like an overfilled balloon, stretched to its limits like it might burst. “I love … it.” She was the object of all his desire. He wanted her. He wanted to love her and for her to love him—the longing pulsed within him, down in his core. There were so many things he needed to say to her.

“Our hearts are beating at exactly the same time.”

He opened his mouth, wishing the right words would fall out. Nothing came, but they stayed together, breath and beings synchronized. For a fraction of a second, he felt connected, like they both knew exactly what the other meant. The feeling couldn’t be put into words, but it didn’t need to be.

A heartbeat later, it was gone.

“They’ll be here soon.” Julia dropped her chin. “I should have waited.”

The moment was slipping away like snowflakes melting in his hand. “Before they get here I—”

They’d been expecting it, but the bang on the front door made them jump.

“Unca Jul?”

Dar’s cheery voice called out. “We hear there’s a birthday boy around somewhere. Hello?”

Julia started for the door, but Jul took her hand. "Thank you."

She paused and smiled. "You're most welcome. We'll have time to talk later."

And then a whirlwind hit. It almost felt like the moment had never happened—another scene he wasn't even sure was real. There was no time to think about it in great detail. Commotion followed the Brewers whenever they arrived, and it followed Davey especially. Dar and Julian were close behind him when he ran to the kitchen.

He reached his little hands up to the counter, eyeing a jug of lemonade Julia had prepared. "I wanna drink."

"We have to wait until Miss Julia is ready, but you can take these to her now." Jul passed Davey a bag of chips and the boy left the room at a run.

"Isn't it something that we can all be here together to celebrate?" Dar squeezed Jul's shoulder. "Having a good birthday? I remember my first birthday with Stel—"

"You know what, maybe we should bring all this out now." Jul wasn't interested in sharing. "You grab the tray for the kids."

Dar set a hand on his chest. "Seriously, what's happening with you two?"

"You get a gold star for that effort to pry into my life. At least you were being direct." Dar had exercised massive restraint the past couple of weeks, but wouldn't be able to hold back forever.

"Don't be like that." He almost looked hurt. "We're best friends, and I miss your updates."

If he'd shown up twenty minutes later, there might have been some update to share. "You miss the entertainment. You think I'm nuts."

"Of course I think you're nuts. Doesn't matter though because it looks like whatever you're doing is working. What was happening when we got here?"

Jul hid his head in the fridge. "I don't know what you're talking about."

Dar pushed the door closed. "I expected to be picking up little pieces of your broken heart by now, but something's happening. I'm only a guy and I can see it. You should hear Stel go on. I don't know what was happening at the guest house the other day—and no, I'm not even going to ask."

Jul could tell it was his way of asking.

"Then Halloween night you were so close. Then tonight. I can see something's changed. I miss hearing about it."

Their entire talk needed some redirection. "This is a tough birthday for me. I'm closer to forty now than I am to thirty—"

"So am I—"

"I'm alone—"

"You're not alone. We're here." His eyes went wide. "She's here."

"You know what I mean."

"You're much closer to being with her than you were a month ago. Probably even closer than when you were at your suite that day." He followed Julian to the pantry. "No-one can change the past. Spend your energy on the future. Imagine where you'll be this time next year." He raised his eyebrows. "She likes you. A lot. And there's a lot about you to like. I'm *really* sorry I interrupted the other day. She looks at you all the time, Stel says. Haven't you caught her? Stel says she was in the bathroom for a good five minutes after 'whatever it was' happened at the suite. I bet she even got you something special for your birthday."

Jul couldn't stop himself from glancing at the box.

"She already gave it to you? That is yours, right? There's not a ring I didn't notice?" Dar's chin dropped. "No."

"No." Jul had to laugh. "No, it wasn't a ring, yes, it was for me and … never mind what it was."

Dar looked pained. "If there's ever a ring, tell me in advance. Please?"

"If there's ever a ring? You'll be the first to know, I promise." At the rate he was going, it would take another thirty-five years to get there. "I guess you're right. Things have changed a little. But we do nothing out of the ordinary. We talk about nothing."

"How are you going to get to know her otherwise? That's exactly how it was for Stel and me. What do you think we talk about now? It's not all world issues and your love life." Jul gave him a look, and he laughed. "We just made up. I shouldn't be like that."

Davey popped his head through the butler's pantry door. "Miss Jul-ya says come light her fire, Unca Jul."

Darvvin grinned. "Get on that b'y. The time's exactly right."

✦✦✦

AFTER DINING, DRINKING, and minimal cleanup, the big moment arrived. Julia and the Brewers lifted their voices in song as she brought out a cake with two candles. Julia made a wish while Jul blew them out—she wished she knew what he was wishing for. She also wished she'd had more time with him alone. It was amazing that the Brewer family had shown up ten minutes early. Not that ten minutes would have been enough time to hear him out. It had been a bad choice to give him his gift when their guests were about to arrive.

Jul momentarily vanished after dessert. He returned with his cowboy hat, the black one he'd worn at Halloween. He'd also brought his guitar and had something hidden behind his back. "Can't have a fire without a song or two, can we?"

"It's your birthday. Shouldn't you be enjoying it?" Dar poked at the fire.

"This is how I enjoy it." As he passed Julia, he set a felt cattleman hat on her head.

"What's all that? Now I feel underdressed."

"Dar-man, you knew you were coming to a fire with us, right? What did you expect?"

Julia smoothed her hair and re-set the hat while he tuned his guitar. Stel sat beside her.

"That looks great. Did Jul get it for you?"

"No. I went by myself." If she could do it over, she would have let Jul take her.

"You got the entire outfit on your own? You two look like a match, all dressed the same."

Jul thought so, too. He'd told her as much.

"Has he played for you yet?" Stel asked.

"Not yet. I'm not sure how we've missed the chance to be out here." She glanced at him across the fire pit and he looked ... content. Jul was completely at home and relaxed at the fire. They should have been out there daily. "We'll have to take advantage of it while the weather holds." Even if the only result of the experience was to give him a chance to unwind, it would be worth it.

He started his set with a few country classics, then the men tried to teach Davey some tunes from their scouting days.

"What was the one we used to sing on our way home from work?" Jul grinned while he played random notes.

"I know the one you mean, but I don't think it's a good one for little ears." Dar laughed.

"Yeah, right." The music faded. Jul took a breath. "Um ... here's a new one I've been working on." He drew the music out of the strings, and the song emerged.

Julia recognized the song better than any she'd heard that night.

He was playing Corcovado.

She couldn't look at him, or focus on the words, or acknowledge anyone around them. Stel was staring at her—she could feel it, but she pretended she didn't notice. Julia bit her lip and pressed her nails into her thighs.

The song went on, beautiful as ever—but better. She hung onto every phrase, trying to capture the sounds in her memory. As she sang the lyrics in her mind, she noticed something different.

Jul changed the word 'sea' to 'trees'.

It was nothing, but it was everything all at once. Julia stared at the flames, hoping the flickers would burn up any outward signs of what it all meant to her. She wanted the moment to last forever but longed for it to end. Hearing the words come from Jul's lips was—

"Some shocking good!" Darvvin led the applause. "That one's new? It's great."

Jul nodded. "Thanks." He looked at the guitar, then at Julia.

She flashed a grin before she looked down.

Jul sighed and patted the body of the guitar. "Maybe you all know this one."

A few notes in, Stel shimmied close to Darvvin. "Ah, Jul, we'll never forget."

"Really? I had to do the intro over and over at your wedding before you'd even start dancing, remember?" He laughed and played the introduction again.

It was easily recognizable, the song 'Can't Help Falling in Love'.

Darvvin pulled Stel to his side. Luke cuddled in.

Davey snuggled up to his uncle Jul. "Is this a kissing song?"

Julian kept playing while he answered. "I guess it could be. You'd better ask your dad later." He looked at his audience while he sang the last verse.

The chill of empty air surrounded Julia, but the fire was warm. She leaned in. Jul's eyes touched hers through the flame light. A shock pulsed through her, more intense than the moment she'd first seen him at the Coffee Stop. Julia wasn't strong enough to keep looking at him. She let her gaze fall into the flames. After a moment's rest, she lifted her eyes once more, instantly connecting with him.

He'd never stopped looking at her.

Chapter Twenty-One

JULIAN'S BIRTHDAY JUSTIFIED THE RAREST of all events—late bedtime for the Brewer children. It was late by their standards, anyway. Stel herded the family to the door at seven-thirty.

Jul brought them their coats. "That was the best birthday I've ever had. Thanks for being here."

Stel hugged him. "Thank your lovely Julia. It was her master plan."

Luke rubbed his eyes and wiped his face on his mother's shoulder.

Davey rolled on the floor between the walls at the parlour entrance.

"We wish we could stay longer, but I bet you're both happy we're not with the kids acting up. Dar, get David please."

Dar pulled the boy into his arms. "That was a time, friends. Happy birthday to you." His voice was quiet in Jul's ear. "It's all going to work out. If I don't see you before you head to Dawson tomorrow, good luck."

Jul nodded. "I'll let you know how it goes."

He followed them out with Julia by his side, and then they were alone again. The clock ticked in time with the country mix Julia played in the background. It was loud enough to hide his heart's heavy beat.

She broke the silence. “That was fun, but we still have lots of time. What would you like to do?”

“Want to go back to the fire? I threw another log on it before we said goodbye.” It was the best way he could think of to get back on track—back to where they were before the Brewers showed up.

“Let me get a bottle of wine.”

He watched her walk to the kitchen while he switched off the hall lights. A car honked in the driveway and he returned to the vestibule.

“They probably forgot something.” Jul stepped outside. Another vehicle had pulled in as Dar was heading out. The drivers had their windows down and were talking.

He recognized the Jeep. It was Shane Harnes.

Jul cracked his neck and called to Julia. “It’s for you.”

“What?” She stepped onto the porch beside him. Her shoulders dropped. “This is the biggest problem I have with this place. Anyone can interrupt—anytime, day or night.” She rushed to the desk and rifled through her files. “I’ll tell him to take the summary and call me tomorrow.”

Jul stared at the floor. The night was crumbling as the minutes passed. “Just see him. Maybe he’ll be quick.”

“I’m so sorry about this.”

“It’s not your fault.” He cracked the door open before he had to hear the knock. “What brings you here so late on a Wednesday night?”

Shane recited the words as if he’d rehearsed them. “I was, ah, coming home from a meeting. I saw the lights and thought I’d stop in. Easier than emails back and forth, right?" His face was clean-shaven and his hair was perfectly styled. Cologne invaded the surrounding air.

Jul blocked the doorway. "You must live close. You seem to pass by often."

The man set his jaw. "Is Julia here?"

"Hi, Shane. I'm at the desk," she called out. "I have your information ready. Shall we take a quick look?"

Jul stepped back to let Shane pass, then slammed the door. "I'm going to take care of the fire. I'll be right there if you need me. I'll grab my phone." He took the long way around to the kitchen to get the device. Julia's gift was right beside it. He tucked the coin into his wallet. Her welcome note from that first day he'd moved in was in there, too. Almost a month had passed, but little had changed.

That wasn't true.

"A lot has."

She'd given him the most amazing gift he'd ever received, they were living under the same roof, and she was with some other man instead of with him.

Jul took a last look at Julia on his way through the dining room. Shane stood against the counter while she flipped through papers.

At least there was a desk between them.

"It's her business," he muttered. No matter how much he didn't trust the guy, he couldn't interfere with her work.

Jul poked at the fading fire with a sharp stick. The coals glowed, but he was getting cold. It wouldn't take long for the fire to burn out completely. He wondered if there was any point in adding more wood. She might finish with Shane in minutes or it could take an hour. Either way, it wouldn't be a late night—she had stuff to do in the morning, and he had a meeting with Dawson. His pulse jumped when he remembered, but he let it go. That was the least of his worries. He knew that material backward and forward. Plus, he'd finished the proposal early, so he'd have time to focus on other things the night of his birthday.

That certainly hadn't paid off.

Jul stabbed at the coals like he was trying to murder them. The phone in his pocket buzzed, saving the last cinders from destruction.

It was his mother.

"Hi, Mom."

"I've called you five times already. Why aren't you answering? You missed your birth minute call." She clicked her tongue. "I was worried, so I had to call Darvvin and he told me you've moved in with some woman. What's going on?" She pronounced each word with sharp articulation. "Not a hint about it to your own mother."

He imagined what he'd say to his dear friend if Dar was still there. "Sorry. We were having a party. I left my phone in the kitchen—"

"That's no excuse for withholding that other tidbit of information. Who is she? How long have you been living with her?"

The fire was almost out. Julian dumped a bucket of water over it and stirred up the ashes one last time. "Hang on, I'm going inside."

JULIA STOPPED TO listen when she heard the dining room door open. Jul stomped over the hardwood. He cradled the phone between his shoulder and cheek while he scrawled out a note.

It read 'my mom'.

He added some words, then handed her the page and raised his hand in a kind of wave. 'Thank you. See you in the am', it said.

While she read it, she heard a constant chatter coming from the phone on his ear.

Her heart fell as he climbed the stairs. If she could get rid of Shane quickly, she might have the nerve to knock on Jul's door. There was so much more to say.

"How many rooms are upstairs, other than yours?" Shane asked once Jul was out of sight.

"Six, including the one Julian's in. But I don't live upstairs. I have an apartment on the main floor." She pointed down the darkened hall behind them.

"Must be bustling when you're fully booked." He leaned his elbow on the counter. "That hat looks great on you, by the way. You're one of those lucky people who can pull off any look."

She lifted her head enough to see him past the brim. "Oh, thanks." The file folder contained all the information she needed—she just had to sort it. "Here is the request I sent to the caterers. You liked Delicious Divine, right?"

"The owner seemed a bit overconfident, but the food was good. It was a shame you couldn't join me. Oh, and I made a few other requests. Did he send them to you?"

"No." They were pressed for time without making more changes. "I'll contact him in the morning and let you know right away. We have to get this ball rolling." She could still hear Jul's footsteps overhead. "So I guess the food's in the air, but let's confirm the rest. I have your party booked for December seventh starting at five-thirty. Dinner at seven."

"It's going to be great. Sounds like the entire staff will be there."

"That's an excellent turnout. The liquor license is a go. I have your deposit." She smacked her papers against the surface, then closed them into the folder. "I'll let you know what I hear from the caterer. I'm sure that will get settled tomorrow."

Julia expected him to thank her and head out, but Shane looked around the hall. "How are you planning to set everything up?"

She shouldn't have let him in. "Well, nothing's set in stone, but I thought the buffet could be in the hall here. We'll have the bar in the parlour." She led him towards the door. The sooner she answered his questions, the sooner he'd leave. "People are also welcome to mingle for cocktails in here and across the hall."

"It will be nice to spread out around here. Lots of conversation space." He had his hands in his pockets and sauntered through the front room. "Nice furnishings." He fluffed a throw pillow and tested out the sofa. After another look around the room, he moved to the cabinet over the fire. "Is there a television in here?"

"Yes. If there's a game and enough interest, we can have that on too. Are you sure dinner and mingling will be enough? I can look into some entertainment."

"Mingling will be fine. It's a tight crew. They socialize together most of the time, anyway."

"I'm glad to hear it." She walked towards the door once more, but he diverted his course into the dining room.

"How will you be decorating for Christmas?"

"It's my first Christmas here, but there is a tree for every room. Garland for the fireplaces. Lots of mini lights. White table cloths, centrepieces. All the bells and whistles."

He drifted past the stacked chairs, then around the perimeter of the space. "I really appreciate all the trouble you're going to."

"It will be lovely." She backed out of the room and was relieved when he followed. Safely behind the desk, Julia flipped open the folder again. "That's about it for me. Was there anything else before you go?"

His dark eyes smiled, sparking in the light. "I'm impressed. It looks like you have everything figured out here." Shane leaned as close as he could. "I just have one more question ..."

+++

"DON'T YOU TELL me to hang on. I want to know what's going on with you, Julian. I wondered why you hadn't called me for so long." Marlene went on a rant.

Jul paced from the fire to the sofa in the corner of his room without saying a word. He flopped down on it and focused on the street below. Eventually, her tirade slowed enough for him to get a word in. “Mom … Mother? Are you done?”

“I’m not done until you tell me what’s going on. I don’t know what’s got into you.”

“You have to give me a chance to talk if you want to know what is happening.”

That was the wrong thing to say. His mother started to cry.

“Oh, Mom …” he rubbed his face. “First of all, I am not ‘living with a woman’. I’m renting a suite at her inn. Her name is Julia Matthews. She’s—”

How could he describe her? She was everything to him, the most incredible woman he’d ever met.

Julia was the love of his life, and she didn’t even know it.

He couldn’t say any of that. “She’s the owner of this building. Dar’s renovating her place, and I’m helping him. She lives downstairs in a private apartment. It worked out better for me to be here than at the Brewers for a bit with the baby and all.”

“Is she single? Divorced? How old is she?”

“Single. Never married. Thirty years old.”

“And she owns this place you’re living in?” She didn’t wait for the answer. “Is she after your money? I hope you haven’t given her any money.”

He sighed and returned to the window. Shane’s jeep was visible in the parking spot below. Jul fought the temptation to throw his phone at it and smash both his problems away at once. “She has plenty of her own money.”

“She’s not another Cara, is she? For all the relationships you shut down, it’s a wonder to me you let that one go on—”

He'd never live that down. "She's nothing like that. She's wonderful—"

"Are you two dating?"

"Why would you think that?" She hadn't given him a chance to say anything. It was a mystery how she'd come to that conclusion.

"Well, you're living with a successful, available, and, as you said, 'wonderful' young woman. Why wouldn't you be dating her? You're living there, anyway." She took a quick breath. "Did you ask, and she said no? She's crazy to let you go. I want to see what she looks like. Is she on Facebook?"

"I'll send you a picture. Stel took some tonight." He was tired and tired of being grilled. "Look Mom, she's an amazing person. You'd love her. I'd be lucky to have someone half as good as her." His mother would find out eventually, if—*when* he made something happen. "I don't know where things are going, but I've never felt like this about anyone in my entire life."

"So you aren't just a guest at her hotel." She sniffed a knowing sniffle. "My darling, I know exactly what's happening here. A mother knows. You're in love." Muffled words followed as she called to his dad. "Allen, Julian's in love."

Chapter Twenty-Two

JUL LOOSENED HIS TIE A fraction. There was no need to choke himself—not that early in the day. Kick himself, maybe. His mother had kept talking for way too long the night before. By the time he went back downstairs, all the lights were out. He should have gone to Julia's door. He should have pounded on it until she had no choice but to let him in.

But he hadn't. He'd crept upstairs and gone to bed.

He sighed and gave himself the once over in the mirror. He looked professional, if nothing else. "Playing the role." Image hadn't impressed his other prospect back in September, but Dawson was a different breed. Jul had to look the part.

When he got downstairs, he found that Julia's door was open again. That meant they would have coffee there. Good. He had so much he needed to say to her.

She was talking to herself when he entered. "Weird." Julia tossed her phone on the ottoman.

He rapped on the doorframe as he passed through. "What's weird?"

"Good morning. It's Amanda. She's going to her business partner's wedding this weekend." She poured a cup of coffee. "I thought she had a thing for him. Kinda thought they'd end up together someday. They've been best friends since she moved there and this is the first I've heard about him even seeing anyone else." Julia set the coffee in his hand and smiled. "You look ready to conquer the world."

"I'm not sure about that." He straightened his jacket. "Can we ... I have to talk to you." His mother knew from their single-sided conversation how he felt. He wondered how Julia herself seemed to have no clue.

"Of course we can." She patted the seat next to her.

Jul took his time to settle, shifting, and repositioning for too long. She probably knew he was stalling. A newspaper caught his eye. "That picture."

"It turned out great." She set it in his hand.

A shot of the inn from Halloween covered the front page.

"And check out page nine." She flipped to a photo of a couple.

It was the two of them, posed together at the front door. Julia looked gorgeous in her dress. Her smile—she looked genuinely happy. He couldn't complain about his image either, but then how could he look anything but elated to have her in his arms?

"What do you think?" She shimmied closer, settling her hand on his shoulder.

A rush of warmth pulsed through his face. He focused on the picture again and read the caption below. "'Julian and Julia Matthews-Ariets share a warm embrace at the Wilbur Inn.'" What if she was an Ariets? Her name looked good beside his—as good as she did. His hand trembled, and he put the paper down. "I knew he'd get our names wrong."

"It's a great picture, wrong names or not."

She sounded annoyed, which was confirmed when he saw her frown.

"Oh yeah, it's great, it's ... I wish it were a bit clearer."

"Some clarity would be nice, wouldn't it?"

He could feel her eyes on him, but he kept his on the paper.

"I've emailed the Journal. Hopefully, they'll send me the file and I can have it printed. I'd like to put one in the hall—if that's alright with you."

"Sure. I'd like a copy too." Jul took the phone from his inside pocket and snapped a shot. "My mother wants to see us—to see this place and ..." To the average viewer, they looked like a couple. Everyone in town would think they were by the end of the day. "This might not be the best picture to send, I guess. She doesn't really know what to think about our situation here."

"Why's that?" Julia pushed her back into the corner of the couch. "Didn't you explain why you moved in?"

"She didn't know I'd moved here until last night." He took a long breath. "I missed my 'birth minute call', so she called Dar. He told her I'd moved here. Now I'm in trouble with her, and he's in trouble with me next time I see him."

"You hadn't told her?"

"Well, I haven't called them for a while." He drank. "You know how it is."

"No, I don't." Julia's tone was cool. When he looked at her, she was staring at a family photo.

"That came out all wrong." He closed his eyes. "If you knew what she's like ... My mother isn't—she completely got the wrong idea, that's all."

"Which wrong idea is that?" She'd curled her legs up between them like she was ready to kick if the need arose.

"Oh, you know, single guy living with a single woman, that whole thing." He scratched behind his ear. "I made it clear that it wasn't—it isn't like that. At all."

She was glaring.

Jul studied the fire. It looked more welcoming than she did.

"Right. She's getting mixed messages from this 'situation' we are in. I can completely understand that." She took a breath. "What did she say about your meeting today?"

He'd never even had a chance to tell her—she didn't stop long enough to listen. "She doesn't know about it. I'll email her if there's anything to tell." From the corner of his eye, it almost looked like Julia was shaking her head. He had to get the conversation back on track. "I have to tell you something." Jul turned towards her.

She put her feet back on the floor. "What?"

He had to tell her everything—how he'd fallen for her that first day he saw her ... how he'd fallen for her every time he'd seen her since. But the timing was terrible. He'd be leaving for the meeting in less than an hour. It would have to wait. "I have so much to say, but for now, I just have to tell you ..."

She pushed forward and parted her lips.

"I'm really grateful to you for encouraging me. I couldn't have set up this appointment with Dawson without you."

Julia sat back and nodded. Her cheek pulled in like she was biting it. "It's the least I could do for a friend. Help you get the ball rolling before you leave in a few weeks."

Julia had no concept of where he wanted things to go, or how much it hurt him to hear her talk about him leaving. If his mother hadn't ruined his entire evening the night before, things could have been different. Jul never should have answered his phone. He wouldn't have even had it if Shane hadn't shown up.

Shane was at the root of the problem.

Shane was the problem.

Jul smacked his cup down. "Did you get that party all sorted out? I saw him leave."

"You were watching?"

"No. I ... I couldn't help but see him drive away. I was pacing while I listened to my mother." His tie felt crooked again. He tugged it straight. "He was here late."

"Since you were occupied, I took the time to show him around the main floor. I'm not sure how twenty people are going to stay entertained for the evening, but he doesn't seem too worried about it."

Shane wouldn't worry about anyone else as long as he got to see Julia. "He's probably focused on something else."

She crossed her arms tightly. "Like what?"

If she couldn't see it, there was no point in spelling it out. "I don't know. I guess it's a big event. Lots of things to consider." He yanked down his shirt cuffs as he stood. "I'd better eat something. Thanks for the coffee."

"Uh-huh. Good luck."

He'd half expected her to follow him to the kitchen—that was how it usually worked, but she didn't. Julia stayed on the sofa and didn't even look at him when he went towards the door.

He heard her voice as his foot crossed the threshold.

"What if he'd called you?"

If Shane had called him, he would have lost the guy's number as fast as he could burn it. "He wouldn't have."

Julia eased towards him. "Just imagine for a second. If they'd called you way back in September before you were ready."

It clicked. She was talking about Dawson. "They had no idea about me."

"If Dawson called you and wanted you, even if you weren't quite ready, even if you felt less than confident. Would you have jumped in?"

That was a no-brainer. "Of course. I wouldn't have wanted to miss a chance like that. It might be once in a—"

"Once in a lifetime. Yes. It is."

She looked dejected. He didn't get it.

"Be direct with them, Jul. Make sure they know you want to be there and work towards their future with them. They need to know exactly where you are coming from. If you do that, you can't help but win them over. They'll absolutely love you." She tipped her head to the side. "You're the answer they didn't even know they needed. I'm sure of it."

She sounded more sure than he'd ever felt.

The morning should have gone differently, just like the last few months should have. His eyes roamed the room as he made his wishes, then settled on her. Julia looked unhappy and worried and ... gorgeous. She could make a sweatshirt look like high fashion. And those jeans. They fit like they'd been sewn around her, each rhinestone positioned on her hips as though they'd been precision placed to set off her curves.

She never wore pants like that. As far as he knew, she only had one pair of western jeans—the ones she'd worn on his birthday, the ones she'd bought without him. "Those aren't the jeans from Big West."

Her brows wrinkled then she smoothed her hands over her hips. "They are. I got a second pair, but I thought these were too flashy for last night."

"They're not. You wear them well." Nothing could ever outshine her, not even if she were encrusted head to toe with—"Jewels."

Her chin dropped. "No-one ever calls me that. Only Amanda."

"No," he put his hands on her shoulders, "I mean like ... gemstones. Jewels. A new name for the inn. Like Julia's, but not so diner-y." She looked blank, so he continued. "The inn. Jewels Inn. It belongs to you and there's stained glass and it's elegant and—"

"That's ... that might work." Her eyes were open wide, but she wasn't seeing him. "It's perfect, actually. Jewels. I can almost picture it on the sign out front."

She wasn't smiling, but she wasn't mad—at least not at that moment. "I guess I'd better go. Leave you to it."

Before he got too far away, Julia caught him in a loose hug. "I wish you all the luck in the world today. Please let me know how it goes."

"I will." He breathed in the scent of her hair, hoping it would fortify him. "Things are going to come together now."

"They'd better."

She pulled away, and he sensed it was time to go. Jul skipped breakfast. Leaving early would give him some time to think.

✦✦✦

HE DROVE OUT of town and down the highway. When he saw a herd of deer, Jul did a U-turn and headed back. He arrived at Dawson Fire and Safety a few minutes early, with time enough to review his notes.

'Be direct,' Julia had told him, and that was exactly what he was going to do. Jul held his head high when he approached reception. "I'm here to meet with Mr. Dawson."

"Welcome, Mr. Ariets." The woman smiled and led him to the boardroom, and the meeting began.

It was a good sign when he'd had the floor for longer than fifteen minutes. If Jul's offer hadn't shown potential, Dawson would have already shown him the door. The man didn't play around.

"Okay, you've got my attention." James Dawson reclined in his leather chair. "But how much of an increase are we talking about? I'm sure you've done your research."

He'd said it in such a way as to suggest that Jul hadn't. He was about to find out.

"Your primary industry is safety supply, but you've dipped your toes in several others, I see." Jul bought some time by reading through the list in his hands. "For example Pawsh Treatoria. What does that involve?"

"It's a dog treat business. My wife runs it out of the corner of the main warehouse."

"Is it working logistically?"

"Well ..." he rubbed his forehead. "All the shipments run through there. I admit we could smooth that out a little."

Jul nodded. "I get it. After a short analysis, I will streamline your warehouse usage."

James Dawson shrugged.

"But that's only the tip of the iceberg. I've discovered one of the most common culprits in poor workflow and less profit is a disconnect between policy and procedure. Your employees might not know the best practices to follow in their roles. Sometimes, they know, but they don't follow procedure. This often happens as companies grow. New employees come in, training is incomplete, so they do things the way everyone else does, unaware that it slows down productivity."

"Which in turn ..."

Jul rubbed his fingertips together. "It costs you money."

The man nodded and traced the butt end of a pen over his paper.

"You've grown rapidly and your team has grown along with it. What did I read? You've increased staffing by—"

"Thirty-five percent."

"Imagine if each one of those people were doing their job more efficiently. Even if half of them aren't following procedure to the letter—"

"I've got a problem."

"You're right." Jul nodded and lowered his voice. "Everyone knows you are the best around. No-one deals with safety like you. I can help you pull more out of what you have going on now and smooth the rails for everything you've got coming up."

"How do I know you can do all that?"

"Mr. Dawson, a man like you would never waste a minute of your valuable time if you hadn't done some background check on me."

The man smiled.

Jul looked him right in the eye. His voice was steady as he spoke the words Julia had given him that morning. "I want to work with you. I want to work towards your future success. And you know I can do this for you. You wouldn't be here listening to me if you didn't."

Dawson laughed and tossed his pen on the desk. "Sometimes a guy's gotta jump, hey?" He stood and tugged Jul's hand and arm. "Alright, Ariets, let's get these wheels turning. See if we can work something out."

FORTY-FIVE MINUTES later, Jul was back in his truck with his briefcase on the seat beside him. Inside, a framework dictated by James Dawson himself awaited their follow-up meeting the next Wednesday morning.

Jul smiled and smacked the steering wheel, then sent two messages—one to Julia and one to Dar.

Everything was still in the air, but he chose to trust his gut. It was worth celebrating, and he knew exactly who he wanted to celebrate with. He loosened his tie and started the engine.

Jul checked his phone as soon as he parked at the inn. Julia hadn't replied. After a quick search, he dialled a new number.

A woman answered, "Myrtle's Chophouse. How may I help you?"

His stomach growled, delaying him for only a second before he made his request. "I'd like to make a reservation. I'm hoping you have a spot for two tonight. Around six?"

And just like that, dinner was booked. He only had to wait a little longer to make sure he had someone to sit with at the table.

A bang sounded next to him. Dar knocked on the window, his smiling face so close that it almost touched the glass.

Jul smiled back. It looked like Dar had been waiting for him.

"God above me, I'm so happy for you. So happy for you and so sad for myself. Losing my best man. Guess you won't want to partner with me now, will ya?" He slapped Jul's shoulder. "I'm taking you out for lunch."

"I appreciate it, I'm starving." His stomach groaned again. "I haven't ironed out all the details yet with Dawson. Follow up meeting next Wednesday. Plus, it's only going to be a three-month contract, if it pans out." But he couldn't stop the feeling of satisfaction that grew the more he thought about it.

"*When* it pans out." They walked to Dar's truck side by side. "Three months to start, but they'll love ya and rave about you to everyone they know and you'll be the most wanted man out there." He winked. "Maybe you already are? What happened after we left last night?"

"You're lucky I'm still talking to you." Jul said it like he was joking, but there wasn't anything funny about the evening. "Between my mother calling me and your 'friend' showing up, things were pretty much over as soon as you left."

"But you got Dawson. That's something."

He'd nearly got Dawson, and that helped, but he was still playing the waiting game.

"I'm sorry about spilling everything to your mum. She was on me the second I said hello." Dar continued as they left the yard, "And Shane, well that was bad timing, but hopefully he's got his party figured and that's that."

"You know it's more than that. He was all dressed up. Couldn't you smell him?" The memory of the cologne cloud made him want to choke.

Dar took an extra loop around the block. "All these excuses are making me wonder ... you're not thinking about a big mistake you may have made once, are you? Is that what's slowing you down?" He parked down a side street, but they were so close to the inn that they could have walked. "It's not going to happen again, you know. She's the furthest thing away from being another Cara."

There was no point in denying it.

Dar met up with him on the sidewalk. "Cara was wrong when she said those things, y'know? She was mad. You're probably the first guy who ever put her in her place. I'm positive you're the first guy who didn't fall between the sheets with her."

"She started seeing somebody in our office the next week." Just like she'd said she would. She'd spewed off many predictions in those last moments. Jul stopped still. "What if she was right? What if I'll always think of her?"

"Don't even go there." Dar was firm. "If you'd loved her, maybe she'd stick in your mind forever, but she was nothing. An expensive nothing is still nothing."

Meeting her had been costly, but not only in the way Dar meant.

"Doesn't matter, I guess." Jul started walking. "Not after today."

"Sounds like Mr. Buck has something in mind. You finally going to get off your arse?"

Jul kept his dinner plans to himself. "You never know."

They entered the building before Jul clued into where they were. "The Coffee Stop?"

"Yeah, where'd you think we were coming?"

He didn't get to answer before he heard the screech. Someone body-slammed him an instant later. Jul's reflexes kicked in and he caught the person as she wrapped herself around him.

"Julian, you're back! I've missed you." Savannah aimed for his lips but hit his shoulder when he backed away.

"Stop. I'm not interested!" He thought he'd whispered, but the weight of every patron's eyes pressed upon him.

Savannah put her hand over her mouth and ran to the back room.

He didn't mean to hurt her. "You don't have to ..." Jul almost collided with a table. "Excuse me, I—" He lost his voice the second he recognized the couple sitting there.

It was Shane Harnes and a woman—Julia.

Jul felt blood rush through his head. He made fists in both hands, shoulders straining against his jacket. "I didn't expect to see you two here."

"Looks like Savannah didn't expect to see you, either." Shane's eyes fixed on his and he smirked. A challenge sparked inside.

The noise sounded from deep in Jul's throat, a growl that came out on his breath when he leaned on their table. He lowered his head. "Dar brought me, or I wouldn't be here."

Shane's chair scuffed the wall when he sat back. Julia's face was blank.

"Jul—" A hand touched his shoulder.

His vision cleared enough to recognize Dar's presence. "It's all good. Good to run into familiar faces. Lunchtime?"

"We're just finishing up." Julia arranged their cups with the empty dishes in the centre of the table. "Here's that final menu." She passed Shane a sheet of paper and tucked the rest into her bag.

The page creased when Shane jammed it in his pocket. "I've got to get back to work. Thanks." He nodded to Julia, ignoring Jul and Dar entirely, and marched to the door.

The whole café seemed to exhale.

Julia collected her things. "I've got to go, too. See you two later." She was gone before Jul had caught his breath.

"Your nostrils are flaring like you just ran a race." Dar followed him outside. "You sure got him to leave in a hurry."

It had been such a blur it felt like he'd been running the whole time. "She was out with him. Out to lunch." Ed had warned him. He hadn't acted quickly enough.

"*You're* out to lunch. You heard them. They were working out that party—"

"You know it's more than that. You know he's interested in her. You've known it since day one. Why can't you admit—"

"Why can't you admit you have to *do* something?" Dar spun him around. "You're threatened by Shane and you're still making no progress? That's some—"

"I was at Dawson's this morning. There was no time to 'make progress.'"

"It's always something, eh? Shane, or your mother, or your empire." Dar grabbed him by both shoulders. "What's it gonna take to get you off your arse—"

"Enough." Julian yanked his arm away from Dar's grasp and shoved him back. "Dammit Darvvin, stop!"

"Jul?" The man's face drooped.

"No more Brewer Builders for me. I quit, you hear me?"

"You can't quit. Come on now—"

"I've got other things to worry about—bigger things, better things."

"Dawson—"

"Never mind Dawson. Never mind any of it. Stay out of my way and I'll stay out of yours. And stay out of my business." Jul's shirt stuck to the sheet of sweat on his back.

"Julian—"

"What does it matter to you, anyway? What does *any* of my life matter to you?" Jul marched across the street towards the inn.

Darvvin didn't follow, which was a relief.

It just didn't quite feel like it in the moment.

Chapter Twenty-Three

JULIA PULLED A SWEATER OVER her head. November's chill bit the air outside.

The temperature inside wasn't very pleasant either.

There was nothing to apologize for. She was in business and providing a service. There was nothing to stop her from meeting a male client at an offsite location, especially when the water was shut down at the house. But even though that was true, Julia couldn't help but feel guilty, like she'd been caught red-handed.

Jul had been, too. There was no way Savannah would have thrown herself at him if there wasn't something more going on between them. The evidence had been there all along. Her number had been in his bag, she'd tried to kiss him when she jumped into his arms, and then he'd vanished again. Julia had only seen him in passing since the incident, which was a good sign of guilt.

"No wonder. She was all over him," Julia said to her reflection, but she didn't believe her rationale. Jul pushed Savannah away before he even saw her sitting with Shane. The whole restaurant heard him say he wasn't interested.

It was tough to decide what looked worse, but Julia was innocent. Did that mean he was, too?

"Whatever." She didn't want to think about it. She pressed her pendant into her thumb. "I'll be too busy anyway."

She had to meet with the graphic designer. Her photos were ready at Newton's. She had to make a trip to the city, but before that, Stel invited her over for tea. That was suspicious, but at least it would get her out of the house. Her day would be full enough without thinking about anything else.

The morning wasn't flowing like it usually did. Julia hadn't brought coffee in or turned on the television. Her door was still closed. There was no point in opening it if Jul didn't show up.

But what if he did?

Procrastination decided for her in the end. The knock came before she did anything at all.

"Can I come in?" Jul held a coffee in each hand.

"Of course. Good morning." She worked hard not to stutter. "I got a late start today." She moved aside to let him through.

He gave her a cup and then sat in the chair to the left of the fire.

"Thanks for the coffee." Julia sipped to buy herself some time. His rigid posture promised a serious discussion.

"I need to tell you I've ... retired from Brewer's Builders. But I want you to know that it won't affect the work around here too much. I'm going to make sure things get done as promised. We're in the home stretch with the first four rooms. The other two will be easy enough to finish. You're only refitting the bathrooms in there, right?"

"Yes. And decor."

"Plumbing should be done early next week in the first four rooms, then we'll figure out the other two. If my contract comes through, I'll be starting at Dawson's in the next few weeks." He talked to his hands. "I promise I won't leave you in a lurch."

He had a misplaced sense of responsibility. The renovations weren't his problem. "I've always known your goal was to get your business going. Working here was always temporary."

"Right." Jul's lips flinched. "Anyway, I'll be working on the Dawson file today, but I'll catch up on the house tonight and through the weekend. Do what I can to keep things moving now that they're a man down."

"But what about Darvvin?"

"Let's just say we don't see things eye to eye. It's better if I keep my distance for a few days." He drank his first mouthful of coffee since he'd sat down but didn't even swallow before he stood to go.

She wanted him to stay. "I'm meeting with the graphic designer today. Branding change to Jewels Bed and Breakfast Boutique. I love that name."

He frowned. "You still want to use it?"

"Of course I do. Thanks for suggesting it."

"You're welcome."

The atmosphere pressed at them like it required more from their encounter.

Jul walked towards the door, diffusing it. "I guess I'll get to work. See you later."

"Wait. I have to tell you about yesterday." She hadn't planned on mentioning it, but it came out anyway. "I hadn't seen your message. I'd been driving when it came, and then—"

Jul paused at the sound of her voice and glanced over his shoulder. "I know. You were out for lunch."

"It was a meeting. I had to get the menu changes sorted out for Shane's party. The water was off here. It made sense to meet there on his lunch break." He wasn't looking at her, but she was sure he was listening. "I'm so happy the meeting went well for you. I would have replied to you if I had seen it. You should know that by now."

"You don't have to explain. It's none of my business what you do or who you do it with." Jul's voice was calm and clear, but his eyes held a storm.

Her mouth opened and closed twice before anything came out. "Okay then. The same thing goes for you."

He caught her eyes, trapping them like rushing water and pulling them in. "I swear I haven't even driven past the café since September. I don't know why she keeps on like that." Jul took one step closer. "But I guess you said it yourself. We're just friends hanging in until I can go back to Brewers." He waved his hand in the air and turned to go. "I'll be in and out all day. Text me if you need anything."

She closed the door behind him.

Amanda was still unavailable and would have been asleep even if she was home. Stel was off-limits. But Julia needed to talk to someone. If she didn't, she might explode.

A FEW HOURS later, she found herself at Brewer's kitchen table. Stel had arranged a full plate of banana bread beside a bowl of butter. Coffee was ready and waiting. Julia topped hers with cream while Stel ushered her little boys into the living room.

"They don't get to watch television too much, so that should keep them entertained while we have a visit." Stel kissed each child on the head before she sat. "I feel like I haven't had the chance to see you."

"I guess we haven't." Their Sunday visits had been brief, and at Jul's party, there was little time to talk one-on-one. "It feels like it's been weeks, but it's only been a couple of days."

"You've got a new name for the inn. Jul's getting on with his career. Exciting things are happening in such a short time."

Julia could do without the excitement and settle on building some roots. "I met with my designer this morning. She's working on a new logo for the inn."

"It's a perfect name. How in the world did Jul come up with that?"

It hadn't even taken five minutes for Stel to bring him up. "I'm not sure exactly. He hasn't quite been himself the last couple of days."

"A lot has happened."

Stel probably knew exactly what was going on. "The guys might be fighting. Jul was upset about Darvvin telling his mother he was staying at the inn."

Stel bit into a slice and nodded.

"I can't believe he didn't tell her himself." That was another issue. Was it so bad to live at the inn that he had to hide it?

"Trust me, I wouldn't have told her either." She giggled. "She loves him, but she's a tough cookie. Tough on him for sure. So he got hammered on by his mum, then stressed about work, and then he and Dar had words yesterday afternoon. Did he tell you he quit?"

"He said retired." But it meant the same thing, more or less. "Do you know what it was about?"

Stel looked past her. "I know they saw you at lunch and there was a scene with Savannah. Dar was a bit fuzzy with the details."

She could have said the same about Stel.

"So, nothing really happened after we left you on Wednesday night?"

"No. Shane wanted to talk about his party. Jul's mom called, and he left to talk to her, and that was that." Julia took a bite of the bread. The butter melted into her tongue, truth serum willing it to let go. "Jul said no-one has ever had a party for him. That can't be true."

"We've had him often, and his mother used to do a dinner—until they moved." Stel looked her right in the eye. "But no one special to him like you has ever done anything for him, so this year was a big deal."

Julia wondered if the woman was speculating, but hearing it made her flutter inside all the same. "He's special to me too, but—" Walking the path between her friendship with Stel and her growing connection to Jul was getting too complicated. She took a chance. "It's two steps forward, three steps back with us."

Stel reached for her hand. "I wondered if you two were getting closer."

"We are. But then, we aren't." There was no point in holding back. "I thought everything would change after Halloween. The picture helps remind me that it was real." She'd had a copy of their photo printed for Stel. It was at the end of the table. "Sometimes it's like I'm making everything up in my head. I mean, Wednesday night, he was laughing and singing. Then yesterday, he was all business." She blinked away the memory. "And then there was the thing at the Coffee Stop."

Stel pressed her lips closed and nodded.

"He said it was nothing." It was terrible to see another woman's hands on him, but what bothered her most was that he'd said that he and Julia were only friends.

"I'm sure it was nothing. That girl has always had her eyes on him, but I swear he's never been interested. He only ever went to the Coffee Stop because of you."

That made no sense. "Me? I've only ever seen him there one other time."

Stel bit her lips together. "I shouldn't have said. I'm losing my mind. Mommy brain." She caressed her belly. "You're not imagining anything. I can see it too. Jul's ... struggling. He had that bad experience a few years ago and still doesn't trust his judgment, at least with matters of the heart. But I know he wouldn't even be there if he didn't have some hope that things would work with you."

Julia focused on the task lights over the kitchen. "She must have done a number on him." The woman hurt Jul so badly that it was hurting Julia too—and hurting their future. "It doesn't seem fair."

"Cara was his first serious relationship. It was like he came back to consciousness when he broke it off with her. That scared him. I think he vowed he'd never let anything like that happen again." She squeezed Julia's arm. "So he's being very careful with you."

"Too careful."

Stel hugged her and smoothed her hair. "Keep the faith. I've seen the way he looks at you, and how you are together and heard the way you talk to each other. Something's going to give. He just has to take the leap. Hopefully, you'll still be there when he does."

Julia wasn't planning on being anywhere else.

SHE NOTICED JUL'S truck when she passed through the driveway at the inn. It hadn't moved all day.

A light glowed from the room over the garage. The crew was still in the house and Jul was staying out of their way.

Julia went inside and busied herself in her room. After the workers left for the day, she heard Jul come in. Construction noises started upstairs shortly after.

She planned on leaving him alone, but when he hadn't come back down by six-thirty, she changed her mind. It was only good manners to offer him dinner. She had something to give him anyway.

He was working in the middle room on the east side of the house. Jul's head was down at the miter saw and trim offcuts covered the surrounding floor. He set a board against the guide and turned on the blade. A thin layer of dust covered the hair that had fallen over his forehead. When the saw stopped, he wiped his safety glasses on his shirtsleeve, then evaluated the cut he'd made.

"You hungry?"

"Hi." His eyes went wide when he saw her, much like they had when he'd seen her with Shane. "What time is it?"

"Past dinner time. I warmed up leftovers." They had plenty. No one had much of an appetite the day before.

Jul gestured to the scraps on the floor. "I want to get this done before I'm tied up with other things."

"I'll put a plate in the oven for you."

"Thanks. I really appreciate it." He measured the freshly cut piece and shook his head.

"Trouble?"

"I measured wrong again. I'm going to have to buy another batch of trim if I'm not careful."

"You probably need a break."

"I'll just finish up."

"Alright." She remembered her other reason for the interruption. "I have something for you." Julia passed him a flat box.

Jul tucked a pencil over his ear and opened it. A black frame slid out of the end. "Our Halloween picture."

She watched him breathe and release.

"I can't believe you got this together already."

"Newton's is pretty quick with printing." She'd gone to the city for the frame once she'd finished at Stel's. "Where do you think you'll put it?"

"My nightstand." His response was quicker than she expected. "Did you get one for the hall?"

"I did. If you ever decide to come downstairs again, you can take a look." It won a little smile from him. "I got one for myself, too. You'll have to come and see it. Maybe for coffee in the morning."

He slid the frame back into its package. "I'm going to help at the Lang's place tomorrow. I'll be out for most of the day."

She couldn't think of a thing to say to smooth things over. Julia had to let it go. "Okay then. I'll leave that plate warming for you whenever you're ready. I guess we'll catch up later." She patted the door and left him.

"Julia?" He stepped into the hall before she'd even made it to the top step. "I appreciate everything you've done for me during my stay. You've gone above and beyond."

"So have you." She bit her lip. Somehow, it felt like part of him had already moved on.

Chapter Twenty-Four

MR. Lang promised he'd be 'up and at 'em' by eight.

That was a long time to wait for a guy who was awake at five.

Jul made coffee and swallowed down dry toast before there was any sign that Julia had woken for the day. After he filled a travel mug, he headed out to Lang's place. On the way, he pulled over to call Ed. At least it wasn't too early for that.

Ed didn't even say hello. "I'm working. You've got two minutes."

"You won't believe what happened this time."

"You sound so desperate, I'll give you five."

Jul covered the story quickly, pausing just before the terrible finale. "And there she was, sitting right beside him." Ed laughed so loud, he had to pull the phone away from his ear. "It's not funny."

"It's not. It's hilarious. Now you're mad at her, and she's mad at you, and you're back going nowhere. Ya got me drove."

He waited for Ed to quiet down. "Thanks for nothing. I'm hanging up."

"Hey, you're the one asking me and I think you're being—"

"An arse, yeah I've heard that before, thanks. If you come up with anything that would actually help me, I welcome a call."

"Julian, listen."

The laughter had stopped, so he did.

"You two are in exactly the same boat. Sure, she was sitting with him, but that other girl jumped you right in front of her, and she knows you kept that phone number. Neither of you's looking so good. Don't ya think?"

"No." It wasn't close to being even. "She was *out* with him. In public."

"Well, I don't know how things work in Alberta, but out here girls who give you their number and then jump on ya look more serious than a pair sitting together. If I were you, I'd be wondering what she thought and try to figure out how to fix it."

It was impossible. "I've got to go. I'm helping a neighbour. I'll call you tonight."

"I've got to get back to it, too. The guys are going to love to hear this." Ed laughed.

"Don't—"

"Talk soon, Jul."

The timing was wrong, all wrong. He'd been hours away from asking her to dinner—not even hours. It could have happened in a minute if she'd been home or had called him back. Cancelling the dinner reservation hit him hard.

Finding her door closed to him Friday morning hit harder.

Jul dodged the idea that he'd left early to avoid seeing that happen again.

He drove the rest of the way to Lang's, barely glancing at Dar's place as he passed. Mr. Lang hobbled from his front door as Jul parked his truck.

"Young feller. Haven't seen you around much lately. I thought you said you were a bachelor, but I heard you took up with a young lady in town. That'll keep you busy."

"It's not that. I'm working at that old Wilbur Inn with Darvvin. Just staying on site until we can get a handle on things." He could stay completely detached if he let himself believe that story—detached and unaffected. "How are things going around here?" The yard looked good.

"Not much different from when we saw you last." They made their way into the garage. "You should see the buck roaming around. He's got a lady in his sights already. She's letting him get close now, so it's all but done. Maybe they'll make an appearance while you're here today."

"I've missed watching them." It looked like no-one had used the place since Jul had tidied the garage a month prior. Everything still seemed in order. "What are we working on today?"

Mr. Lang took a seat on his old stool. "Margaret's sister broke a hip. She's staying there for a while—in the city. This getting old thing, it's not for babies."

"You're all alone?" The thought of the man by himself was a concern. "I'm a phone call away. Darvvin too." Dar was a jerk, but he'd always be there for a neighbour.

"I appreciate it, son, but we can't be dragging you out for every little thing. We're not getting any younger. The work on the place isn't getting any easier. We need something smaller. Something close to Marg's sister and niece. The writing's on the wall." He took a long breath. "It's time to think about moving on."

Moving on? That could only mean—"You're selling?"

"Yep. That's where we're at. The realtor's coming to take pictures tomorrow. I want to put a bit of a shine on the place before he does." He tapped Jul's foot with his cane. "You ain't interested in some land by any chance, are you? Might be a good homestead to grow your future on."

Lang might as well have swept Jul's feet out from under him. Their place was the perfect place to raise a family. He'd longed for something exactly like it. If Dawson was a sure thing, maybe. Sometime in the future, yes, once he had some stability and Julia was—

"I hate to say it, but the timing's not quite right." Julian's voice said.

"That's a shame, but I figured as much." Lang groaned as he stood. "Let's get this place fancied up. No time to lose."

JUL HAD LEFT the place tidy the month before but he did another once over. They got the yard tractor going. Jul hauled a pair of trailers to the front near the gate, then parked the tractor and mower beside them. Mr. Lang duct-taped 'for sale' signs on each one.

When they were done, the men stood side by side and looked at the property. New snow iced the mountains white. The fields wore golden stubble. It was a stunning view. Jul tried to commit it to his memory.

“Looks good, son. Lunch?” Rowan urged Jul towards the house. “I’ve got a bachelor’s special waiting. Fried egg and bologna sandwiches.”

“I couldn’t refuse.” He let Mr. Lang set the pace as they strolled.

“If you don’t want my land, at least let me know if you want some of the stuff on it. You get first pick, you’ve helped me out so much.”

He’d never said he didn’t want it. “I’ll keep my ears open if I hear of anyone who does. And let me know if anything else comes up. I’m likely starting a new contract in the next few weeks, but until then, I’m flexible.”

“High roller, you, eh?” The man smiled. “Soon you’ll be back living in the city and it will seem like this was all a dream.”

“Moving back to the city has never been my plan.”

“Oh? What is?”

Jul didn’t want to go into it. “I ... I’m getting used to living out here again. Slower pace—”

“Slower? You’re already tied up in town and helping me here. Nah,” Rowan held open the door, “You’ll find your footing again and move on.”

He was wrong.

Mr. Lang invited him into the open kitchen and living room on the main floor. Whoever had designed the house had to have built it around the mountain view. The windows framed the vision. Jul couldn’t imagine letting go of something like that. “You sure you want to sell? You sure that’s the only option?”

Mr. Lang shrugged and took out a carton of eggs.

"It's a huge move to make." Everything would change for them if they left. The thought of it made Jul's pulse rise.

"Well, we can do it now or ... what? Wait for something to happen here that forces a move? I'd rather take things into my own hands. Make my own moves. Own my options while I still can." He tore the plastic off a stack of bologna. "It's not perfect. We love the place. It's almost Christmas, and Marg loves Christmas out here. But things aren't working anymore. Can't get swept away by time and circumstance."

Jul felt like it bothered him more than Mr. Lang. "How can you know it's the right decision?"

"Because that's life, son. If you wait to know it's one hundred percent right, if you wait for the perfect moment, you might wait forever." Bologna sizzled in the frying pan. "Life's about doing the best you can do with what you've got right now. That's what we've always done. It's all we know. We'll be fine, son. Don't worry."

AS HE DROVE home that afternoon, Jul's mind reeled with Lang's news.

'Dar probably knew this was happening and didn't even tell me.'

At least Jul had found out they were selling before it was gone—not that it made much of a difference. There was nothing he could do to change the situation. Lang had made up his mind.

Julia was in her suite when he got in. He cleaned up and downed another bottle of water before heading to work on the second floor. As he climbed the stairs, he called Ed back, hoping that his friend would have something helpful to say.

A woman answered. “Eddie’s phone, not Eddie speaking.”

There was a rustle, then giggles, then muffled words before Ed came on the line. “You like my new answering service?”

Jul was sure he heard kissing. “I guess it’s not a good time.”

“I’ll call ya back.” More liquid noises came through the sound piece. “Give me a half hour.”

The woman squealed.

“Never mind.” Jul hung up. He slid down the wall to the unswept floor below.

A tap sounded on the doorframe. “Couldn’t get through?” Julia held a beer in one hand and a juice glass filled with wine in the other.

“I did but I wish I hadn’t. Ed’s got company tonight.”

She sat beside him. “I brought you a drink. Sounds like you could use it.”

“You’re going to get covered in dust. Whoever worked here last didn’t clean up very well when he finished.”

“That’s okay. These aren’t my good jeans.”

They weren’t the sparkling ones he’d been thinking of for two days. “No call with Amanda tonight?”

“She’s at that wedding. Haven’t heard a peep from her.” Julia stretched out her legs. “And no Ed for you, since he’s ... busy.”

“He said to give him half an hour.”

“He sounds like a real charmer.” She laughed.

It was the best thing Jul had heard in days.

"Ed's not a bad guy, honestly. A little lost maybe, but then who isn't?"

Julia tapped her glass against his can. "Isn't that the truth?"

They sat in a comfortable silence.

Jul's mind flooded with all the things he wanted to say. He settled for sharing his most recent news. "Langs are selling their place."

"No." She rested her head against the wall. "The Brewers are going to be so sad."

"The Langs have lived there since before Darvvin even bought their land. They're the only neighbours they've known. Hopefully, someone decent will move in. I helped him tidy up before they take pictures tomorrow."

"Is that what's weighing you down tonight?" When he looked her way, she continued. "I mean, you seem disappointed or something. And yet, everything is coming together for you. The work here is winding down, and you've practically got Dawson. And Stel's due in three weeks so you can go back to your normal life. Everything's going to plan."

Almost everything.

He felt her eyes on him as he stared at the light above. "I'm going to miss this."

"The inn? You're welcome here anytime, you know. I'll have a grand opening and of course, I'll invite you. Actually, I *expect* you to be here. But I'm sure it will be good to get back into your own space. We've done well living around each other but—"

She didn't get it. They had a fundamental problem understanding each other. No wonder it wasn't working. "I'm excited about Dawson. I've been working towards that since—"

"Since that first day I saw you."

He slurped from the can.

Julia watched him. "So what's wrong?"

"This job. I wasn't planning on liking this work anymore. I haven't done construction for years." Dirt embedded the cracks around his fingernails. He'd worked calluses into his skin. "Is it insane that I like working with my hands? Love it even. And somehow over the years, I forgot. I mean, I loved the work when I was with Brewers for those two summers. How do you forget something like that?"

She let her head rest against the wall. "I understand exactly what you mean. I noticed this place because it was so charming. At that moment in my life, enjoying the building was enough. When the Wilburs were teaching me the business, the hospitality aspect struck a chord with me. While I was growing up, my mother hosted gatherings all the time and I helped." She smiled as she talked. "We loved throwing parties together. Here, I get to take care of people all the time—well, I will, soon. I don't know how I ever lost that memory."

He knew how. Losing her parents had taken all that away from her. "I guess you found exactly where you needed to be when you saw this place was for sale. You were destined to be here. But me ..." His days working construction were numbered.

"It's like you're at a crossroads?"

That was exactly it. There was a chance he'd already travelled too far on one path without even noticing.

"But does it have to be one or the other?"

"I'm not sure how I can swing both. Dawson's going to be a huge job. At least for three months." The beer cooled his throat. He was glad she'd brought it.

"It's good to have a time limit. If you like him and the work, maybe you can extend your contract, but if he stinks as a client, you can say you have another job lined up and bow out."

She had a point.

"Really. Try it for three months. If you don't get more work or don't like it, I'm sure Darvvin will always have a place for you. That's never going to change." She set her glass on her leg. "You have to start somewhere. Have to pick a direction."

Julia was right. She'd been right about a lot of things. "Mr. Lang said I'd be back in the city in no time, back to the same life I had before the layoff." He'd meant it as praise, but it felt like a curse. "I had a good life before, but this, this is so much better."

"Sitting in sawdust on a Saturday night is better than your river view condo?"

"Yes." It absolutely was. "And not only this. Dar and me ... but I've totally messed that up."

"You guys had words."

He'd shoved him. He'd put his hands on his best friend. "We've known each other for a long time. I hope we can reconcile." He shouldn't have let things get to him that day. "We were closer than we've been in years. And the boys. I remember Davey and Luke as babies and then they'd grown up so much when I finally got my head out of my—" He smiled at the floor. "Mr. Lang is wrong. I won't lose touch with them."

She leaned towards him, bracing herself on her hand. "It will take some effort, but if they are important, you won't let that connection go."

"They are important." Jul reached out before he let himself reconsider. "So are you."

A blush rose on her cheeks, but she didn't pull back. In an instant, her fingers wrapped around his.

His voice was soft. "I won't lose touch with you either. I promise."

Julia wiggled closer. "It's like we're stuck in each other's worlds now, isn't it?"

"Stuck?"

"You know what I mean." She bumped her ear against his shoulder and stayed close.

Her body warmed him. He hadn't even realized that he was cold. "I called my mother. Told her about the job."

"What did she say?"

Her words rang through his head like he was hearing them again. "'Thank goodness you're finally putting your degree to good use.'"

"Is that what she sounds like?" Julia's laughter was a little less stable than before. "I'm sure she's very proud of you."

He hoped so. His mother had plied him with a series of questions about Julia, too. She'd seen their photo. "I guess she approves. For now."

"Good for you. I'm sure it wasn't easy to call since ... well, you said she wasn't happy about you living here."

"I'm never completely sure about what she is or isn't happy about. The job situation was a win. Calling her was a great suggestion." Whatever Julia had put in her hair wafted towards him with every movement. "Your advice for Dawson was a win, too. Everything you said worked. I was direct. I said I wanted to move forward with them and he seemed impressed. I think that sealed the deal." He tightened his grasp on her hand. "Thank you for that."

She seemed flustered. "Well, I ..."

"I know, it was the least you could do for a—"

"You're more than a friend to me. I hope you know that. I'm sorry if you've ever felt like anything less." She was shaking. It was hardly noticeable, but it was there.

After a final squeeze to her hand, he let it go. "Thank you for the drink. I'd better get back to it."

"Ah, right." She pulled her hair back and collected their empties. "Don't work on this for too long. You'll wear yourself out."

He brushed the dust off his pants when he stood. "I won't. Church tomorrow?"

"Wouldn't miss it."

Chapter Twenty-Five

JULIA STUDIED THE PHOTO OF her parents. In the framed picture, her mother's arm was over her father's shoulder, and he was holding her hand. There was no doubt how close they were. Even a stranger would have seen the love through their body language alone.

Julia set it back on the table beside the picture of herself and Jul.

'Friends.'

The word sometimes had a bad reputation, but it was the keystone to every relationship. "Mom and Dad were best friends."

She'd almost talked herself out of bringing Jul a drink the night before. It turned out to be one of the best times they'd spent together. Somehow, sitting with him in the dusty room upstairs was just right.

"Like *old* friends," Julia said to herself as she buttoned her cardigan, but that wasn't the right definition. "More than friends, old or new." Chatting with Jul felt natural, like something they'd always done and something they'd definitely do again.

And he'd held her hand.

He held it again on the drive to church. It was brief, but it had happened. Everything that had been building between them had blown apart on Thursday afternoon. By

Saturday night, she started to believe that things were coming back together.

Jul offered to help her box up the fall decor and unpack the Christmas trimmings. She was going to decline but ended up agreeing. It was the perfect chance to be around him without any interruptions. She wondered what other goodness the day would bring.

When they got home from church, they parted ways to change clothes and freshen up. It wasn't long before she was outside again. Her first task was modifying the garland along the front rail. Anything Halloween-themed had to come down and Julia removed the autumn-coloured sprays. There had to be sparkling Christmas ones to replace them somewhere in storage.

Back inside, she could see that Jul had been busy. Boxes lined the hall, and he'd started stacking more in the parlour.

"You got all this done already?"

"Most of these are empties." He pointed to the surrounding cartons. "I put the Christmas ones in the other room. They're the red and green Rubbermaid tubs. I hope that means Christmas."

"Thanks. This really gives me a jump on things." She set her items down on a carton. The boxes were arranged like a cardboard wall. "Did you ever build a fort when you were little? This looks professional."

He half laughed. "On a haystack for a few summers."

"Haystack?"

They packed the fall decor away.

"There was a haystack near the east corral on our farm. We weren't supposed to go on it, but if we climbed up the back, Mom couldn't see us." He took a wreath from her and tucked it along the side of an oversized box. "It was like a tower. We'd push the bales to the edge to make a space in the middle. We couldn't stand up, only crawl. If we stood and Mom saw us, that would be the end of it."

"You and your sister?"

"Her name is Kelly. We got along when we were smaller. It was the teenage years that took a toll on her personality." They filled a box to the top, and he taped it down. "What about you?"

"No haystacks for this city girl." She wrapped the autumn bows in paper. "Mom would let me pull apart the living room every now and then. I'd use the cushions from the couch and drape blankets over them. Make a little hideaway." The memory was warm and yellow when she thought of it. "Mom would make us hot chocolate and crawl inside with me. Sometimes, we'd drink out of my tea set. Those were good days." She blinked hard. The season was making her too sentimental.

He gave her arm a quick squeeze. "Are you thinking of pulling apart the front room? We have enough drop cloths. I bet we could make a pretty decent fort."

He was joking, but she wished she had the nerve to hold him to it. "I'll save that idea for later."

There wasn't much left to package and once they finished, Jul hauled the boxes back to storage. Julia moved into the parlour to make sense of the Christmas items. The Wilburs had everything sorted by room—at least one tree and a variety of ornaments for each. She divided them into piles.

"You have a lot of decorations." Jul crossed his arms while he looked over the filled floor.

"We probably won't use most of this. I'm going to keep things fairly simple this year. Minimal decorations on the tables and that. With all the dust around here, that will be too much of a pain to deal with."

"Are we decorating trees today?"

"You'd decorate a tree before Remembrance Day?"

Jul raised his brows. "No?"

"No." She unwound a string of clear mini-lights. "But tomorrow afternoon is free game. When I was growing up, we always put up our little tree on Remembrance Day evening. Family tradition, but I haven't done that in years. When Amanda lived with me, we waited until the first weekend of Advent."

"I guess we'd better get everything ready for tomorrow night. We have a busy day—Remembrance Day service, Brewer's, decorating. We should skip that middle step. We're pretty busy."

The invitation to Brewer's had gone over like a lead balloon. "Sorry, I jumped the gun on lunch plans tomorrow. Stel said that Luke's been waking her up the last few nights. I blurted out that we'd bring over Chinese food before I even thought about it. I thought you were going to patch things up with Darvvin before church this morning."

"Dar was too busy talking to everyone else to say anything to me." Jul kissed his lips together. "But I'll go with you. Dar's the only one being a jerk, and Stel needs us."

Julia muted her laugh. "Okay, if you're sure."

"I'm sure." Jul pushed a box with his toe. "Let's get everything moved into the rooms they belong in. Then what shall we do?"

She peeled the tape off a carton of ornaments, then shut it again. "Do you think it counts as decorating if we set up my tree today, but don't put the ornaments on until tomorrow?"

He smiled. "That's called being efficient. Let's do it."

✦✦✦

JUL NOTICED A new photo in Julia's suite—an image of her parents. It nestled right next to their couple shot from Halloween. The positioning had to be significant.

She made sure the two photos stayed out when she packed a few things to make space for the tree. They moved the chair and repurposed a side table from one of the upstairs bedrooms. It made a perfect stand for her four-foot Christmas tree. Julia banished Jul to the couch while she strung the lights.

"Coloured bulbs?"

"Is there any other option?" She wrapped the tree from top to bottom. "White lights are fine for the other trees in this place, but the coloured lights feel extra special. Reminds me of our tree when I was growing up."

"We had colourful lights too—those big bulbs. Dad always did our lights." If his father put a single one astray, his mother made him reset the entire string. "You have your family's decorations, too?"

"I do." She nodded towards two boxes against the wall. "But there are too many for this tiny tree. I'll have to add them to one of the other trees on the main floor. Did you decorate your apartment when you lived downtown?"

"Not really." He had a ceramic tree. It was stuck in storage.

"When Amanda left, I almost didn't bother either. That year, I waited until the weekend before Christmas to do anything. But this year, neither of us is alone so we can enjoy it ... together for now." She brushed her hair from her eyes. "Thanks for suggesting we do this. It's like a new tradition. I'm turning over a new leaf."

"Or a new tree branch." He crawled under the table and reached for the extension cord. "Ready? Three, two, one."

The colours on the small tree warmed the room. Julia clasped her hands below her chin. "It's gorgeous."

"It is." A pink glow illuminated her beautiful features. Jul drank it in.

"Imagine when we get it decorated. But that will have to wait until we get back from Stel's tomorrow." She looked at her clock. "You're not going to run upstairs to work on the trim, are you?"

That was the last thing on his mind. "I can relax a little tonight. It's Sunday, after all."

"I don't play Christmas music until after Remembrance Day, but we could listen to the usual stuff. Or mix my list with the one from your birthday."

"A mix of country and the Rat Pack?" As much as he liked country, her music would sound just right. "That's alright. Just play that quiet mix you like."

She turned off the lamps, leaving only the fire and tree to light the space. A minute later, the music began. Julia sat beside him and covered their legs with a blanket.

"Dare I ask what you and Darvvin were fighting about?"

His chest tightened. Jul shook his head. "It was nothing. Nothing worth mentioning."

"It must have been something. I've never seen you two like this. Church was ... tense. And I can tell you aren't very happy about going over there tomorrow."

He didn't want to say too much. "That stuff with my mother ... work stuff. I mean ... he's such a know-it-all. He's so worried about my life."

"He cares." She wriggled on the sofa. "You two are just like brothers. I think you fight more than Davey and Luke."

"Well, Luke can't talk, so that probably eliminates most of it."

She laughed.

"It will all work out." They went back too far for it not to. "Maybe the two of us will go to his shop after lunch. Hash things out."

"Go before lunch. It will be a happier experience for all of us if you do it that way."

Julia wore a little grin on her face. He fell for her once more. "You're right. Again."

"Oh, I like the sounds of that. No one ever says I'm right and I've heard you say it two days in a row." She pulled the blanket off her legs. "I'll get us a drink."

"Stay." He took her arm before she got up. "I don't need a drink. Let's just sit. Enjoy this time."

Her eyes were glossy brown, reflecting the colours from the tree. She sucked in her bottom lip for an instant before she took her place beside him.

Jul put his arm over her shoulders while she smoothed the blanket. A song he didn't know was playing—something about dreams coming true, but the words were indistinct. Julia's fragrance surrounded them and he hugged her tighter, breathing it in. When he looked at her again, she was watching him, her pretty brown eyes full of questions. He hoped he saw anticipation there, too. He'd anticipated a connection with her for so long—she had to have seen it. It couldn't be a surprise for them to end up in a—

Jul got closer. Her lips smoothed together, providing the perfect target for his. He let his fingers glide over her cheek. Her brown eyes were bottomless in the gentle light. He let himself fall ...

A flash in his mind's eye yanked him to a stop—Cara's image.

Jul's throat tightened, and an itch jabbed at him, just below his ear. He hesitated, trying to block the memory as he clawed at his skin. His original motion went off course. Jul's mouth landed on Julia's forehead instead of her lips. Time paused with the kiss, allowing him the grace to savour the mild connection, but it wasn't enough. It wasn't what he'd intended.

His hand was in her hair and she tensed up, then lifted her chin. Jul tore himself away and faced the fire. Julia's profile was visible from the corner of his eye. There was no hint of what she might be thinking.

The music played on around them.

She shifted her weight on the seat.

He'd got it all wrong again, and she was going to leave.

He heard her swallow, then she rolled her shoulders back. After another breath, Julia leaned into the cushions and put her hand on his leg.

She stayed. Julia stayed with him.

He set his arm around her, and she put her head against his chest. Jul's hand found a perfect rest on her hip.

She pulled the blanket higher, sealing them in place. Her warmth rose and worked through him, like a healing force, like water on dry roots. If he could just let himself concentrate on her, all would be well. How could anything go wrong with Julia as close to him as she'd ever been, the flames flickering and the colours on the tree?

Eventually, those other memories from mistakes long before had to be pushed away for good—pushed away by fresh memories—by worthy ones.

Chapter Twenty-Six

JUL SET A STEAMING CUP of coffee on the kitchen table when he heard Julia's door.

She looked surprised. "This is great. Thank you."

"You're welcome. We have to go in about half an hour." Again, he'd been up before her, early enough to make a call without her hearing. After he left a message, he busied himself with breakfast preparations.

"My apologies for passing out on you last night. It was just so cozy." She was focused on her cup.

"I don't mind at all." Nobody had ever fallen asleep on him—though nobody had ever really had the chance. "You must have been exhausted."

"I guess."

He wanted her to say that she wasn't tired—that it was more than that. He wanted to hear her say she'd felt safe and happy—that it was one of the best evenings of her life.

She talked about their morning to come instead. "We'll walk to the service today, right?"

"It's almost too close to drive," he replied. She wore a camel-coloured suit that fit her just right. "The temperature's dropping this morning. I'm sure they'll keep it short, but you'd—we'd better bundle up."

She smiled. "Okay. I'll find a heavy scarf. Better gloves."

They finished breakfast and layered up, then walked the few blocks to the cenotaph.

Julia straightened the poppies on their coats when they arrived. She took a small packet from her pocket. It was a bundle of tissues. "Warning. I might not make it through without using these." Her smile wrinkled her nose.

There might have been tears building up even then. They should have stayed home. They could have watched a service on TV, side by side with the tree and togetherness.

The crowd pushed them closer as the ceremony began. He held Julia's arm while she dabbed her eyes during the speeches. As the dignitaries placed wreaths upon the monument, Jul saw a familiar face—Shane Harnes. He stood with the children he'd brought at Halloween and another couple. The man nodded to him, then carefully avoided making eye contact again. Jul braced himself for a confrontation, but he didn't have to worry. Even Harnes wasn't tactless enough to make a move on such a solemn occasion. As soon as the event was over, his group went the other way.

A man stopped them as he and Julia passed the entrance to the Legion.

"Hello there, young buck."

"Mr. Lang." Jul shook his hand. "Let me introduce you to Julia Matthews. She's the new owner of the Wilbur Inn. Julia, this is Mr. Lang, the Brewer's neighbour."

She smiled beautifully as she greeted the man. "It's wonderful to meet you. I've heard so much about you."

"Pleasure to meet you." He returned his cane to his right hand. "I never had a chance to call you back. I was getting dressed up for this when the phone rang."

"Don't mention it." And Jul really meant what he said. "Let's talk about it some other time. I'll call you later this week ... tomorrow." He raised his hand, hoping Lang would get the hint and let him go.

"Alright. It's best I get inside anyway, getting cold out here and busy in there." He nodded to Julia. "Nice to meet you, miss. Oh, and if you get a chance, the realtor says the listing is 'live'. I guess that might mean more to you than me, but he says you can look it up. Get more information there."

"Great. Thanks, and we'll see you later." He adjusted his scarf and started down the sidewalk.

Julia caught his hand. "What was that all about?"

"He just wanted me to check out his property listing. I'll have to look at it later." His pace quickened. "I bet the temperature has dropped five degrees since we got here. Are you warm enough?"

"I'm alright. We'll warm up quickly enough walking this fast."

He slowed down. "It will be good to get home."

She tucked her hand into his. "It will."

They walked towards the inn with matching strides when they found their rhythm. At the edge of the property, the trees rustled.

"Breeze is coming up. Good thing we're almost there." Jul pushed his hands deeper into his pockets, pulling Julia closer at the same time. She'd slowed down.

"We've got an entourage. Look."

They stopped on the sidewalk and watched a doe jog across the parking lot. A buck followed.

"That's so neat," Julia whispered. "I've seen deer wander through the garden before, but never a male. Wilburs said they've seen them fight it out this time of year. I didn't believe them."

Jul couldn't breathe, never mind find anything to say.

The doe flicked her tail and strolled towards the back of the house. The buck stretched his neck and trotted behind her.

They waited until the pair had run off through the backyard.

"There they go. Off to find some privacy ... maybe get to know each other better." She pulled out of Jul's grasp and started for the house. "And we should get inside. You coming?" Her hair swished over her shoulder when she glanced back at him.

Jul took a breath and hurried behind her.

✦✦✦

"HAVE YOU LOOKED outside lately?"

Julia hadn't, but she'd heard the wind against the house. She peeked out of the window from her suite, then went to get a better view through the door. Snow was already accumulating in the garden. "Stel said the weather was turning when she cancelled."

"Good thing we stayed home." Jul stood beside her, hands on his hips.

Julia glanced at his smiling face. "You could pretend you're a little sorry our plans changed. Poor Stel sounds exhausted. She said Luke is teething and Davey's turned wild. I can't even imagine what that means."

"I feel sorry for Stel, for a few reasons." He grinned.

Julia memorized his smile again and her heart fluttered. Forehead kisses counted, even if it wasn't what she'd expected. There was nothing showy or forced or fake about the connection from the night before. That move was one hundred percent Julian.

She had to steer them back there—get back to that place where possibility could carry them further. Fate had stepped in to provide that opportunity. They were home together, and there wasn't anywhere else they needed to be.

"At least we got some things done around here," she said. "Do you like the tree?"

"It's beautiful."

When she looked at him, he was looking at her. "Thanks. And you said you'd never decorated like this before. Now we have two trees up."

"The one in the library was a good trial piece. Trial by fire."

She'd left him to set it up on his own while she started the one in her suite. There were only a couple of ornaments she'd go back and reposition when he wasn't around. "It looks amazing. You can have it on when you work there. The rest of them will have to wait until closer to the seventh. No point turning them into dust balls." No point in mentioning Shane's name, either. Julia didn't want anything to upset their day.

A gritty blast hit the windows.

"Let's shut off the tree in the library. I'm not planning to go back in there today unless you need to."

"No. I'm not finishing Dawson's plan until tomorrow."

They walked to the parlour together. Julia unplugged the Christmas lights while Jul looked out the front window. The house creaked around them.

"That wind is picking up." Jul pulled the drape aside. "Look at this." A small drift had already accumulated along the front steps. The wind shoved snow in a whirl. "It's a good thing we didn't go out to Brewer's place today. We might have been stuck there."

Julia could picture it easily—the two of them together watching the snowfall from his patio at Darvvin's. "Might not have been so bad."

He dropped the curtain and followed her to the kitchen.

"Why don't you put your truck in the garage? It's going to get buried if you don't."

"Are you trying to get rid of me?" Jul reached for his jacket.

"I'd never do that." She felt inspired. "I have a surprise when you get back inside."

"I'll be quick." He tried to block the snow that forced past when he went outside.

It was time—Julia could feel it. The atmosphere practically buzzed with energy. She took a moment to go to her suite and shut off her phone. After applying a swipe of lip gloss, she rescued a well-loved burgundy box from the bottom shelf of her bookcase and brought it to the kitchen.

Jul returned a couple of minutes later. "Visibility's down to nothing. It's getting colder by the minute."

“Come and warm up.” She set a saucepan on the front burner and measured out milk in two mugs. Most of it ended up in the pan, but she mixed cocoa and sugar into what remained.

Jul watched intently.

“I have to heat it slowly. You don’t want skin on it.”

“Skin?”

“If you heat milk too much.” She dunked the back of her finger in the pot. “Not quite there yet.”

He leaned against the island and watched.

“Do you like hot chocolate?” The spoon dropped from her hand when she saw his expression. “We can have wine if you want—“

“No, I love it. I’ve just never seen it made like that.”

“It’s a family secret.” She gave him a wink that he didn’t seem to see. “But you’re practically family to me, so I guess it’s safe to share.” Julia dipped her knuckle in the milk, testing it once more, then stirred. “This will be ready soon. Do you want to watch something? The TV is better in the front room, but it’s so cozy in the suite with the fire and the tree. I only wish it had bigger windows. It’s always nice to watch a storm.”

He drummed his palms on the counter. “Wait here.”

Clatters came from the dining room. She could distinguish the sound of Jul’s footsteps on the hardwood, but wasn’t sure what else was making the noise. As Julia took the hot milk from the stove, he returned.

“Come with me.” Jul led her to the dining room. Directly in front of the glass doors, he’d set up a small settee. Beside it, he’d brought in a round side table. A string of multicoloured lights glimmered along the base of the French doors.

It was lovely, and it was all Jul.

"The couch is from the side wall in the front room. The table is from the hall." He rubbed the back of his neck. "Maybe this wasn't such a good idea—"

"It's a wonderful idea. How did you get this thing in here?" She looked at him and then back at the seat. "Easy for you, I guess. It's perfect. And those lights."

"They were extras."

She didn't know they had any.

The wind blasted the house and snow fell so thick that nothing beyond the side yard was visible. Inside was a haven—lights and warmth and Jul. "This will be the perfect place to see everything. I love watching the snow." Julia shivered. "We should get a blanket. Can you grab that one from my room?" There were a few more touches she wanted to add.

By the time he returned, music played, and she'd lit a trio of candles.

"Oh ... this is—"

"It's not a fire, but it's the best we can do." Julia rushed back to the kitchen. "I'll get the cocoa together. Be right there."

The sofa squealed when he sat down.

She filled the mugs with hot chocolate, then carefully arranged the contents of the burgundy box—a child's tea set. She set down the tray and squeezed beside him.

Little beads of moisture clung to his hairline. “Hey, I could get a different couch or something. This one is pretty small.“

“I don’t mind if you don’t.” She set her hand on his leg. “Are you uncomfortable? We can go to my room if you like.”

“No.” He shifted in the seat. “It will be alright once we get settled.”

The sofa cried again when Julia reached for their drinks. She lifted a miniature teapot so he could see it.

Jul’s face softened with recognition. “Is this the one you told me about? From your blanket forts with your mom?”

“Yes. It’s silly, but after we talked about it the other day, I wanted to show you. We can have our first sips out of the cups and then use the big mugs.”

The teacup disappeared in his hand as he studied it. “Ladybugs.”

“Ladybug picnic.” The bittersweetness of the memory fell away as she shared it with him.

Jul raised his cup. “To …?”

“To good things, and good memories to come.”

It was like drinking a warm chocolate shooter.

“These seemed so much bigger when I was ten.” Julia laughed when she set the pair on the tray. “Here, an adult-sized cocoa.”

The drink left a thin chocolate moustache on his lip. “Delicious. It doesn’t get much better than this.”

“I’m glad you like it. Store-bought cocoa doesn’t cut it after you’ve tasted homemade.”

“But I mean everything around us.” He took a full breath. “Could it be better?”

"Not much." His arm around her would improve the situation—or to get that kiss she'd been craving. A gust screamed outside, mirroring her frustrations. "Good thing we have the music to drown that out a little." She tapped her fingers on her cup. Someone had to say something of importance. Someone had to get things moving. "We've been together so much the last few days, but I never got to tell you—thank you for learning Corcovado. It means a lot that you sang it on your birthday. You have a wonderful voice."

He smiled at the cup in his hands. "Thanks. It's a good song."

"The song says 'sea', but you sang 'trees', didn't you?" If she let him know she'd heard him, perhaps he'd open up.

"It just makes more sense living where we do to say trees."

"It does for sure." She sipped her chocolate. "Stel was a wreck when you did their song."

"That's how she is, right? You should have seen her at their wedding. And before their wedding, and when she watches sad movies." He shrugged. "She probably even gets emotional when flour goes on sale."

Julia laughed louder than she should have. "Those two are so in tune with each other. They have a great relationship." The cup touched her lips again, but she didn't drink before she took it away. "I've had only one significant relationship in my entire life."

"Oh?" Jul leaned away from her.

"He wanted control. He almost seemed to want my things more than me. I was still living in my parent's house back then. He thought he had it made—instant homeownership if we got closer, access to a car. I think he'd already started planning where he'd put his TV and video games if I'd let him move in." Julia sniffed. "Then there was his little problem with honesty."

"Problem?"

"He was quite the storyteller. I was never sure what was true and what was some kind of coverup for his scheming."

Jul ran his hand over his face.

"But I stopped it. I ended it before it went any further. Before I got in too deep." She stared at the lights. "And now, here we are."

Ice pelted the window. It was quiet for way too long.

Jul shifted like he was about to stand, but sat back again. "I ... yeah, well me too." He silenced anything else that may have been on its way out with his cup to his lips.

Julia bit her tongue until he finally lowered his mug. He pressed the back of his hand to his mouth, then looked at her.

"I had one big one too. Big for me, not in the grand scheme of things. It was a long time ago." He made a fist. "She was controlling, too. Manipulative. Biggest mistake I've ever made and I'm not sure how I even got myself into that situation." He held the cup tight with both hands. "Everyone saw it but me. Everyone."

He was still hurting. "You loved her."

"Oh, no." Jul opened his eyes as wide as they could go. "No. Absolutely not. There was nothing there to love, and she only loved herself." He put the cup down and took Julia's hand. "I thought I liked how assertive she was, but it turned out she was just pushy. She wanted things her way or ... I have no one to blame but myself, I guess. I let her walk all over me. I tried to do whatever she wanted." His voice was dry. "Ultimately, she wanted something I wouldn't give her. That was the breaking point. When it was over, Dar said he'd seen it all along—said she was using me. All that time, I thought I was being caring, that I was something special to her, but really I was nothing. I was just someone to use to get what she wanted."

The ache came up in her chest, right over her heart. "She shouldn't have treated you like that."

"I'd like to have a talk with that guy you were going with. He shouldn't have treated you like that. That's unacceptable. Especially after all you've gone through." Jul put his arm around her. "It's not right."

His strength surrounded her. She let it sink in. "But we survived, right? We got out of it. We didn't settle."

"For three months, I let her get away with almost anything she wanted." He shook his head.

"But not for a year. I put up with it for more than a year." Julia covered her eyes. "I can't believe I did that to myself." It seemed like another lifetime.

"I'm sure you did the best you could back then."

Memory kicked in. "It was a ... challenge. Amanda was leaving me for Australia. I was alone. But then I learned that alone is better than settling—better alone than unhappy and putting up with lies."

"Mr. Lang said you have to do what you can and do the best you can with it. He told me that on Saturday and I've been thinking about it ever since. It makes sense to me, but it's hard to do. I don't know—"

"To me too." She twisted to see him in the flame and flare of mini lights. "I'm glad you got out of your bad situation. I'm glad I got out of mine. It's made us strong. Funny how we're both in similar positions. Both of us are over thirty, both have very little success in the relationship department. Neither of us wants to be controlled." She twined her fingers in his. "Maybe that's why you and I get along so well. We don't want to be controlled, so we don't try to control each other."

"I'd never try to control you. To push you to do something—" Jul stroked the back of her hands.

He held her so tenderly. She trusted his touch. She trusted him. Julia opened up. "I think fate brought us together—like we were meant to be. We saw each other at the café and then I found out you were Dar's best friend. It seems like we were destined to meet. Divinely orchestrated."

His eyes closed when he dropped his head back. A breath escaped his lips. "It's not quite like that." He shook his head. "Julia, I can't mess this up."

"You can't mess it up because we will do this together. I'm here, too. I'm part of this." He didn't back away when she moved to him. Julia let herself go, let herself get carried away with the surge she found in his eyes.

He hesitated for only an instant before his lips stroked hers. She let him lead the way. There was no need to rush. A wave turned over in her chest. She put her hands around his neck and drew him closer.

Then he pulled away. Breathy words came to her ears. "I have to tell you about the summer."

She pressed her mouth to his again. "Next summer?"

"No, last. I have to explain—"

A series of thuds sounded from the back of the house, then a ring like an alarm clock going off.

They jolted apart.

"That's the back doorbell." Julia stood.

The knocking continued.

Her heart had been running at full speed, but the noise made her panic. Julia rushed ahead of him. "Who could it be?"

He held her back. "Let me get it."

The sheer-covered window framed the shadow of a couple.

Jul unlocked the door. "Can I help you?"

"Jules!"

"Pardon?"

A woman pushed past him and bound Julia in a bear hug. "Thank goodness you're home. We've been stranded."

The man stomped in behind her. "And you must be Julian." He shook Jul's hand. "Forgive us for the interruption. We were driving back from BC and got caught up in the storm. I'm Jesper Sundboe."

Tears burned her eyes and nose. Julia shoved the woman away. "And this one's Wanda. They're Amanda's parents."

Chapter Twenty-Seven

"I BET YOUR UNCLE WOULD have helped me—"

"No. I can do this. You shouldn't even be involved." Julia bashed her hip into the mattress as they slid it down the hall. "The nerve of them showing up."

"You need to stop for a minute. Breathe."

Jul's tone stopped her in her tracks. Tears blurred the sight of him.

He leaned the mattress against the wall. "Let's lift it instead of dragging it. Okay? It will be faster. Better for the mattress. Easier on you."

"Fine." She grabbed hold of the piping and they carried it back to the old sewing room suite. "I'm sorry you have to give up your room."

"It's the best solution. We know the plumbing works in there. They can't even get to the bed in the red room."

The Red suite had become a storage room until the renovations were finished. It seemed like a good idea when they'd done it, but Julia regretted it. "I should have put everything in a shipping container. Then what would they do?"

They dropped the mattress onto the box spring.

Jul hugged her. "I'll give my old room the once over before they go in."

"I don't care what it's like." She kneed the mattress straight. "You can shower in my suite in the morning. I'll be busy making them breakfast, anyway. I have to call Amanda. She had to know about this." She dropped the mattress pad on the bed, then dialled.

Jul left her alone.

"Well, hello—"

Amanda's cheery voice amplified her anger. "Your parents showed up at my door and introduced themselves to Julian. Funny how they knew all about him."

"But it's—"

"Blizzard. Snowed in on the way home from BC. Thanks for the warning."

"I swear I had no idea they'd even gone to Fairmont this weekend. Jules, you just need to calm down—"

"Never in the history of ever has being told to calm down actually worked for anybody." She raised her voice. "They knew Julian's name. What have you been telling them?" The phone fell from between her shoulder and ear as she stretched the sheet corner over the end of the bed. "Things were fine without our worlds overlapping. Do you know Jul and I were just—" she stopped herself short. "I'm putting your parents in his room. It should be ready now and they can go to bed. Then it's up and out in the morning as soon as the roads are clear."

There was a tap on the doorframe and Wanda Sundboe looked in on her. Twelve years had carved deeper lines around her eyes and mouth, but other than that, she looked exactly the same—the same as she ever had, the same as

Amanda, the same as the face that looked back at Julia from the mirror every day.

"Say hello to your mother." Julia pressed the phone into her aunt's hand as she passed her. "It's your lovely daughter." She jogged down the stairs, away from the call and the woman who looked so much like her own mother, it almost crushed her.

Jul was carrying their bags when she met him on the landing. "Blue room's ready."

She nodded.

"Are you okay?"

"I'm going to be in about twelve hours. Eight if we're lucky." She barely looked at him as she passed.

Her uncle was resting in the kitchen. "My dear, we're so sorry to surprise you. We had nowhere else to go."

She washed her hands at the far sink. He wasn't the enemy. Wanda always ruled the roost. "Good thing you made it this far. It's bad out there."

"We heard rumours about snow in the mountains, but nothing like this." His pale eyes were weary. "You know we'd never just barge in on you. Wanda's been wanting to reconnect but, we never meant to—"

"We've set up the big room for you. It's all yours."

"We appreciate it more than you know." He looked at his hands. "We seem to have ruined your evening with your young man, too."

It was almost laughable—laughable in the way that things were so bad she had to laugh or she'd spend all her time crying. "We're not—" She cut herself short when her aunt sauntered in.

"Here's your phone. I thought you were finished with Amanda, so I said goodbye for all of us." Wanda set the device down and let Jesper put his arm around her. "I think we could all use some sleep."

"Good idea." Julia switched off the light over the range. "You're in the blue room. Top of the stairs, down the hall to the right."

"I showed them where it is." Jul entered from the hall. "Is there anything else I can do for you?"

"You've done more than enough, thank you. And thanks again for letting us stay." Wanda took Jesper's hand. "Good night."

The two departed.

Julia turned off every light in the kitchen except the ones over the table.

"I got the lights in the dining room. Moved the sofa back." Jul shifted his weight, then went to her side.

"Amazing how things can change in an instant, isn't it? One second all is well, the next, everything falls apart." She dumped the cold cocoa in the sink and washed it away. The mugs cracked together when she shoved them in the dishwasher. Julia swept up the tea set next.

Jul held her hands still. "That needs special care. Let me do it."

She bit her lip.

"We'll get through this, I promise."

She tried to believe him.

Footsteps closed in on them, then a muted cough. Wanda emerged from the dark.

"Pardon me. I just wanted to get a glass of water."

"The glasses are in here." Jul opened the cupboard while Julia escaped to the far side of the island.

Wanda filled two and started to walk away, but didn't make it far. "I'm wondering if I could talk to Julia. Just for a minute."

Jul raised his eyebrows.

"Why not? Better late than never, right?" Julia parked herself at the corner table with her back against the wall.

"Alright." He tipped his chin. "I'm heading up to bed. See you in the morning."

She wished he would stay, but she knew he couldn't. Jul waited until she nodded at him, then vanished.

Wanda watched him go, then took a seat across from her niece. She offered Julia one of the glasses.

Julia pushed it away. "You know a lot about my life for someone who hasn't even talked to me in twelve years."

The woman stared at the table.

She'd expected some pushback, some snappy retort. "At least this place was a convenient crash pad for you on the way home. That sure paid off."

There was no response.

"If Amanda hadn't swept in and saved me back then, I wouldn't be talking to her either. She left me too." Julia pressed her index finger into the tabletop. "You aren't allowed a piece of my life simply because you suddenly want it." It felt good to say it. It felt better than she'd ever fantasized it would. "You didn't even come over when the authorities called. You didn't even take us to the airport when we were going to get my parents' bodies."

Her aunt didn't appear to have heard a word she said.

Julia raised her voice. "What kind of person isn't there for their family? For their own daughter? It was hard on Amanda too, you know?"

Wanda turned the glass in her hands.

"The last time I saw you was at the funeral. Then you show up at my door tonight and expect me to be happy to see you? Well, I'm not. I never wanted to see you again."

Wanda lifted her head.

"It took years to stop waiting for you to contact me, to make some gesture, some indication that you ever cared about me—that you'd ever cared about my parents." She leaned back and crossed her arms. "You should have kept running away from me. It was better that way."

"I have to stop running away." Her voice was low and steady. "Jules, we're getting older. I have to face up to—"

"It was wrong for Amanda to tell you where I was, and wrong for you to find me, and so very wrong for you to show up on my doorstep tonight. And then you had the nerve to knock in the hope I would help you. Unbelievable."

Wanda whispered, "But you did."

"My mother would have expected nothing less." Julia pounded the table, accenting every word.

Her features distorted, and a whimper came from somewhere inside. "The day your mother died, I lost a piece of myself—"

"It always was about what you lost, wasn't it?" She spit when she said it.

"I lost my sister." Wanda dropped her head. "My sister and my very best friend. We'd grown up together. We were going to be old ladies together. You'd understand if you weren't an—"

"Only child? All alone in this world." Her aunt shuddered, and she knew she was being heard. "An orphaned, only child with an aunt and uncle and cousin who abandoned her, too. You were the only family I had left. How is it possible that you have better things to do in life than to stick around with me?"

Wanda dropped her face into her hands and sobbed. "It was all my fault."

"I'll say," Julia agreed. "You could have stayed in touch. You could have at least tried. You didn't even know if I was alright."

"Yes ... that too. But I mean their trip. The reason they're gone. It was ... because of me." She wiped her face on the sleeve of her robe and reached over the table.

Julia pulled her hands away and stuffed them under her legs. "What are you talking about?"

Wanda swallowed and took a few breaths. "We were supposed to go on that trip with them, your uncle Jesper and me. We had to cancel, but I urged your parents to go without us. It was the transit of Venus. It was their anniversary—"

"It was the last thing they ever did. And they never even got to see that ... thing."

"I know." Wanda sobbed. "Your mom called me a month before the trip. She had a bad feeling about leaving, she said. The timing was all wrong with your graduation coming up. She didn't want to go." Wanda's eyes moved but focused on nothing as she stared past Julia. "She said she had a premonition that something bad would happen if they went. I told her she was—" Her words got lost as she wept.

"She was what? Tell me."

The woman dragged a tissue over her face. "I told her she was being ridiculous. She had to go to Australia, I said. It was the trip of a lifetime." She looked at the ice-laced window and pressed a tissue to her mouth. "It was all my fault. I should have listened to her and supported her. Look what happened ... I couldn't face you." Then Wanda broke down. She pressed her face into her hands and sagged forward.

Julia couldn't hear her breathe. She watched the collapse, aware that somewhere inside she'd craved that kind of pain for her aunt. It was like watching a movie. She waited for the satisfaction to come, but it didn't. It should have given her the resolution she'd expected, but seeing her aunt suffer only drained her more. Wanda's agony was another layer of hurt, a reminder of the many times she'd lived through that same feeling.

Shame poured over her. Julia was all too familiar with the posture. In those moments, she would have given anything to be free of the feeling. There was something that she could give to her aunt that no one had ever given her.

Instincts kicked in. One moment she sat rigid on her side of the table, the next, she was holding her aunt through the tears.

"Believe me when I say I'm sorry."

"I do." Julia stroked her aunt's hair. "You've been holding that guilt for all these years?"

Wanda twisted the tissue on her nose. "Yes. I never should have—"

"Stop." The word was soft, but the woman silenced. "I've wondered my whole life why that happened to them. They were good people, and I needed them and they were gone far too early."

"It was me, my fault. I wish I would have listened to her."

"Aunt Wanda, it wasn't you." She whispered and tightened her arms. "You didn't cause their accident and you couldn't have stopped it, even if you were there. Amanda and I might both be alone if you'd gone with them. You were meant to go on, for some reason. They weren't." The words were as much for herself as for her aunt. "We'll never know why. We just have to accept it."

She hugged Julia around the waist. "You wear her necklace?" Wanda sat up and pulled a chain from the collar of her robe. "I have one, too." The same gold cross with the same off-centre diamond dangled from it.

"She'd been wearing it ... on the trip." It was with her mother's personal effects, a tangible survivor of the crash. "I never take it off."

Her aunt closed her eyes. "I had these made for us in two thousand and four. The cross represents the sun. Venus is the diamond. The Transit of Venus comes in pairs. Our family went to the first one, but your family couldn't make it. We promised each other we'd wear them in twenty-twelve when we saw it together."

Ticks from the clock in the hall accompanied their tears.

"Ah Jules, can we ever get past this?"

Mercy was but a breath away. "I think we should try."

Aunt and niece rocked together, weepy and listening to the wind outside.

Wanda pushed back Julia's hair. "You look just like your mother."

"So do you." She breathed carefully, trying to keep her tears contained.

"She lingers in everything you do, everything you are, Jules. There was no one warmer, or kinder, or more hospitable than your mom. No wonder you own an inn." Wanda kissed Julia's cheek. "She would be so proud of you. She is. I know it." Her gentle fingers wiped a tear that trailed down Julia's skin.

If she closed her eyes, it was easy to believe it was her mother's hand.

Chapter Twenty-Eight

JUL REACHED FOR HIS WALLET and took out the coin Julia had given him for his birthday.

"I've never even thanked her."

So much water had gone under the bridge since that day. He wrapped the metal tight in his hand. Julia was one of a kind. She was turning out to be—"Everything."

Fingerprints clouded the surface of the coin. He rubbed it back to a shine on the thigh of his flannel pants. The words around the edge caught on his fingernail as he dragged it over.

"Mates."

Their picture from the paper rested on his nightstand beside the clock—exactly like it had in the blue room. Jul held it close. "I've got to tell her."

But there was work to do before they'd get the chance. Her aunt and uncle were still there.

The night before, he'd stayed at the bottom of the stairs, far enough away that he wasn't eavesdropping on her and her aunt, but close enough to hear if Julia needed him. She hadn't and that was a good thing. The sun rose on a new beginning. She and her aunt were on the road to reconciliation, proof that although things could fall apart in an instant, things could come together just as fast.

Wanda and Jesper were already up when he got downstairs. Coffee steamed from the pot and Julia was making pancakes. In the pantry, he managed a quick check to see how she was feeling.

"I'm doing really well, actually."

And he believed her. She had this ... lightness about her that he hadn't seen. He wanted to hold her, to kiss her, and find out all about it, but that would have to wait.

After breakfast, her aunt and uncle got ready to leave. They wanted to get an early start. Jul started their Lexus, grateful to hear it fire up on the first try. He unplugged the block heater and passed the key fob to Jesper. "You sure you want to venture out on those roads? Looks like a chinook is coming. Might be better later."

"We have all-wheel drive. Should be alright now that we can see the road. Thanks for digging us out." He shook Jul's hand. "Take care of our girl."

"I promise I will."

Jesper nodded. They watched the women share a final hug, then he opened the car door for Wanda.

"Take care, you two," she called. "We'll have you over in the next few weeks. Thanks for saving us last night."

"Let me know when you get home." Julia blew a kiss and waved.

Jul met up with her on the verandah. They watched together until the car was out of sight.

"At least the wind blew some of the snow away. They'd never be able to get out of our yard if it hadn't."

He put his arm around her shoulders. "I guess the guys will be here soon—at least the diehards will. They won't be able to get up the steps if I don't clear it."

"Maybe they'll cancel. Darvvin texted a while ago to say that their road was blocked. He's put the blade on his truck. Once it's cleared up, he said he'll be down here to dig the rest of the driveway out."

"You could actually read all that?"

"Maybe Stel wrote it."

"Glad he let you know, at least." It irked him. He wanted an apology, but he was beginning to realize that he owed one to Dar and not the other way around.

"Let's go in where it's warmer." She pulled him by the hand.

It was hard to resist, but he wanted to have everything done and eliminate the possibility of any interruptions. "I have to dig this out. The snow blew in from the northeast."

"I can help—"

"Go inside and relax. I won't be too long." When she'd gone, he picked up the shovel. He hadn't even made it past the dumpster before Dar drove in. Jul started to dig.

Darvvin didn't delay. "How's it going' eh? Heard you had guests, and it's not even open. I'd better get a move on so Julia can get her business going. Too bad my best man up and quit."

Jul dug up a pack of snow.

"You two have a nice night together?"

It had been the best night—that kiss was for sure. "Until her family showed up."

Dar smirked. "So, things are going well, or going nowhere?"

"We're doing just fine." He pulled his jacket sleeve over the cuff of his glove. It was none of Dar's business. "I had to make space for her aunt and uncle to stay, so I moved into that back room, the old sewing room."

Dar heaved a pile to the side of the stairs. "You moved rooms? I was going to ask you when you were moving back to my place."

Jul stomped on the shovel while Dar stared at him.

"So, when are you moving back to my place again?"

"What makes you think I am?"

"What would make me think you're not?" He laughed. "Some of the unexplained events this last while? The fact you two haven't been hanging off each other for weeks makes me think this 'brave buck' thing hasn't really paid off. Not the way you wanted to at least." Dar shoved his toque a little higher. "And let me tell you, I'm some stunned over that."

Jul walked around the corner and jabbed at another pile. The breeze polished the snow. "For your information, things *are* happening. Last night we—" He couldn't find the words to explain, and Darvvin didn't deserve to hear it, anyway. "We had a long talk last night before her aunt showed up. I have to be sure—"

"Be sure of what? You've been sure she's 'the one' for months now. Did you discover some deep, dark secret?" He heaved another mound on the pile at the side of the stairs.

"No. It's not that." He'd never really thought about what might happen if Julia knew the truth—if she found out about

Dar setting him up and the deer and the reason behind his move to the inn. Everyone had meant well, but none of it felt very honest.

Jul turned the shovel on its side and cut into a heap at the edge of the stairs. Darvvin joined him and they broke it down together. “Look, I’m sorry about the other day.”

“Which other day?” Dar leaned on his shovel. “And which part? The yelling, or the pushing, or pretending I don’t exist like at church?”

“I came to talk to you at church. You were the one who ignored me.”

“Fine then. You sorry for yelling at me or pushing?”

Jul's shovel slipped from his grasp. He dropped his arms to the side. “All of it. I should never have put my hands on you.”

Dar nodded. “And?”

“And I’m sorry for it. And I do want to work with you. Help you finish up as much as I can before Dawson starts. I have no excuse—”

“You don’t, but it’s too cold to drag this out, b’y.” Dar squeezed Jul’s hand. “I’m sorry too. It never should have come to that and I’m sorry I didn’t take you seriously. Seems like you overreact nine times outta ten, but the truth of it is … you’ve got good instincts, I’ll give you that.” He lowered his voice. “I feel like I have to tell you … he asked her out.”

“What?” Jul searched his friend’s face for any sign that he was just trying to get a reaction, but Dar looked as solemn as ever. “Who?”

“Shane. He asked Julia out. I’m sure I shouldn’t be telling you. She told Stel not to say anything.”

He didn't understand. After everything they'd been through over the weekend, how could that be true? "She said that was a meeting."

"Lunch that day *was* a meeting. But he asked her to dinner, too."

The iced air cut into him. Jul's eyes watered.

"She said no." Dar held his shoulder. "Sounds like she doesn't want him, but you've got to do more, faster. Something more than what you're doing, my friend."

✦✦✦

JULIA TEXTED AMANDA once she got inside. It was the middle of the night in Sydney, but things had to be said. She'd made a fool of herself and hoped her cousin would forgive her.

If she could forgive her aunt, anything was possible.

"I know it will take time," her aunt had told her before they left, "but I'm so grateful that we're starting to clear the air."

Julia felt that way too, wondering at the circumstances that had brought them together, even at the expense of her time with Jul.

"He's not going anywhere," she said to herself. The weather would likely keep work to a minimum for the day, leaving lots of time for him to tell her whatever he wanted to say. Then they could pick up where they left off and see where things went.

Her phone rang. "Hi there. Are you feeling better today?" No one spoke, but there were noises in the background. "Stel?"

A panting sound came through the speaker. “I meant to call Dar. Is he … there?” Her breath came in gasps, delaying her words.

“What’s wrong?”

“The baby … I’m in labour.”

“Hold on.” Julia grabbed her coat and ran out the back door. “Darvvin!” The men were working at the front of the house. Her worn runners slipped in the snow. “The baby’s coming! We have to get to Stel.”

Darvvin dropped his shovel and ran for his truck, but Jul caught him. “You’re not driving. My truck.”

“I’ll open the garage.” Julia pressed her phone into Darvvin’s hands. “I’ve got my keys.”

“I have mine too.” Julian slapped his pockets.

“No time. Mine’s warm.” Darvvin relinquished control to Jul and took the passenger seat.

Julia climbed in the back. She could only watch while they raced to the acreage.

“My love, talk to me.” Darvvin’s fingers were white around her phone. “How far apart are the contractions?”

“Not … a minute.” Stel gasped.

“Less? Oh, my God.” Darvvin looked at Jul.

“I’ll get you there, I swear.” He accelerated.

The town streets looked like a maze, piled white, unfamiliar.

“Martine’s coming …” Stel breathed.

“Where are you?” Darvvin shouted.

“Shower.”

They stopped at a red light. Darvvin clutched at Jul's sleeve. The tires slipped when they got moving but Jul kept control.

"Have to push …" Stel groaned.

"Hang on. We'll be there in just a minute."

Jul had both hands on the wheel as he navigated the slick hill. "We'll make it in time, I promise." Tires spun on the ice, reducing them to a crawl before they could turn onto Darvvin's road.

"Let me hear you breathe, love."

Pained cries came from the phone in Darvvin's hands, pained cries came from him.

They rounded the last turn to the acreage. Darvvin jumped out as the vehicle rolled to a stop at his house.

"He's going to fall." Julia watched him stumble when he ran up the stairs, but he caught himself. After multiple attempts at entering the code on the keypad lock, he got it right. He ran inside, leaving the door swinging wide behind him.

Silence and stillness came over them. She felt like she was in a haze.

Jul's voice broke through. "Where are the boys?"

They rushed inside. The melting snow from Darvvin's boots was the only evidence of activity.

"They must be in their rooms." A cry stopped Julia before she went any further.

Darvvin's voice came next. "I've got it, I've got the head. Nice and easy—"

"Oh God, he's delivering his own child." Julia clung to Jul's arm.

“Mama?” They heard Davey sob from his bedroom. “Mama, what happened?”

“I’ll get David.” Jul rushed down the hall.

“I’ll see if I can help Stel.” Lights beamed from the ensuite, giving Julia a pathway to follow. Darvvin knelt in the shower behind his wife. Only her head and shoulders were visible as she leaned away from him over the seat within.

“What do you need?” Julia called out.

Darvvin didn’t turn around. “Towels.”

A tower of terrycloth toppled from beneath the sink. Julia set the stack next to Darvvin, then backed away. She felt useless. “Whatever you need, we’re here for you.”

He grabbed the first one he could reach while he spoke to his wife. “Breathe, my love. Baby’s almost here.”

Stel pushed again and moaned.

“Yes … yes that’s it …”

Julia backed out of the bathroom. Her legs felt weak, but she had to get to Luke. She could hear him crying.

His bedroom door was opened a crack. Luke whimpered and reached over the side of his crib. When she walked in, he pulled back.

“Hi, honey,” she tried to stop the shake in her voice. “I came to say hello.”

He rubbed his eyes and looked at her again. “Shu-shu.”

“It’s okay. Everything is okay.” She lifted him out of the crib and wiped his face. His hair was damp on his forehead.

“I’ve got him,” Darvvin cried.

Luke tugged her hair.

Another strain sounded, then a yelp. The new babe tested its voice. "Your baby brother is here." Julia swallowed and kissed Luke on the cheek.

There was crying and rustling, then happy noises. The baby cried again. Luke rubbed his face on her shoulder.

"Let's go find Uncle Jul and your big brother."

In the hallway, they heard the baby and Darvvin clearly. "Good lungs on ya ... That was the cord ... we have a little girl. A little baby girl!"

Davey and Jul were on their way out of the boy's room when she got to them. "It's a girl," she said. "You've got a baby sister."

Jul put his arm around her. They held onto the boys and each other and listened.

"She's beautiful like her mama." Darvvin's voice cracked. "Here, let me hold you. I love you, Stel. Look at our little girl."

"You did it." Julia breathed the words into Jul's ear. "You got him here, just like you promised you would."

"They did it—I ... we ..." His words failed, squeezed away when he hugged her and the boys into his chest. "I can't believe this is happening." He kissed her forehead.

Julia felt like melting. The moment was almost too much to manage. In the other room, the newborn cried, and they heard Stel giggle. The boys kept looking between Julia and Jul, confused and quiet.

She rested her head against Julian's shoulder. "Everything is going to be fine now. Everyone is fine." She glanced up and her eyes flooded the instant she saw him.

Jul had lost all composure. His chin quivered and tears streamed down his face like rivers in a storm.

Davey dragged his palm over his uncle's cheek. "Why you crying Unca Jul? You want a brother too?"

Chapter Twenty-Nine

"HEALTHY AS ANYTHING! God above me, we're so blessed, we are." Dar's second, maybe third wind had kicked in. He drove Jul back to the inn to get his truck while Julia stayed at their house to watch the boys. "Can you believe it? A baby girl. Me, the father of two sons and a daughter." His voice wavered every time he talked about his little girl. "Sweet Bella Rose Matilda. Did you see how perfect she is? Spitting image of Stel, isn't she?"

"Totally." Jul couldn't see a resemblance to anything but a potato, but he let his friend believe what he wanted.

"She's a miracle. Those ears. Your little finger is wider than her ears are big. And her fingers and toes ... we counted them one by one ..." His voice faded, and he touched his fingertip to the corner of his eye. "Mum's so excited. I'll have to take the family out there next year. They have to meet my little girl." He slapped his knees. "See, you should come back to Brewer's Builders. I need someone I trust to help me. Split the work of running the company ..."

Jul let the random chatter continue. He'd never seen Dar quite so elated.

"Beautiful Bella. We made her, me and Stel together. She's our love—the living image of our love." Dar swallowed. "You have to experience this. You have to. There's nothing like being with the woman you love and bringing children into the world."

There was no way Jul could ignore how Darvvin's words sunk in. They reached all the way to that deep place, that empty spot that he'd always wanted to fill—that place he'd always been saving for Julia, even before he knew her.

Momentarily, everything became clear—only for an instant, but it was there. He belonged with Julia, and she belonged with him, and they were a part of the Brewers together. Life with her was the only thing that made sense—the answer to every problem he'd ever had or ever would have. She was the only answer.

Shane thought so, too, and he'd asked her out. Jul's pulse surged. "I'm so happy for you, Dar-man. Such a relief that everyone is happy and healthy and—" he choked.

"Good Lord, I'm blessed, and I don't even know why."

They ran out of things to say, each man in his own head until they made it into the driveway at the inn.

"I have to hit the store on my way back home. We're seriously lacking in newborn diapers, for one thing. Do you mind waiting on me at the house? I won't be long." Dar texted something on his phone, then smiled. "I'm so thankful you were there today, Jul. Couldn't have done it without you and Julia."

"I'd man hug you, but—"

Dar laughed and slapped him on the shoulder. He called out before Jul left him. "Make it happen b'y. This is for you too, you know? You and Julia. This is the very reason we were put on this earth."

✦✦✦

Warming up the truck. Be there soon.

Julia played babysitter to Davey and Luke. She'd fed them a snack, cleaned them up, and figured out the remotes for the TV. The three of them cuddled together and watched cartoons when the men left.

"Hello everyone." Stel came down the hall with a small bundle in her arms.

Davey ran to his mother before Julia could catch him.

"Stop, David. We have to be gentle."

The boy skidded into the wall and then followed his mother like a baby duck.

Stel arranged herself between her younger son and Julia. "She's all brand new to this world. We have to take care of her."

"You're supposed to be resting, aren't you?" She hadn't expected to see her friend or meet the baby.

"Martine gave us a clean bill of health. She was still awake after she ate, so we thought we'd come and say hello." Stel looked radiant, as tired as she was.

There was a higher wisdom, knowledge that seemed to emanate from Stel. Julia couldn't put her finger on what the difference was. Becoming a mother again had made her privy to a great secret. It could only be known by experiencing it—by checking off a Baby Girl Brewer-shaped box.

Stel set the child on her legs and pulled down the blanket, revealing the tiniest face Julia had ever seen. "This is Bella Rose Matilda."

Did Stel know? "My middle name is Bella."

Stel held her hand. "I saw it on your degree, and I love the name. When I saw her little face, it seemed to be a perfect fit. So it's Bella for you and Rose for my gram and Matilda for Dar's mother. She'll have a fit when she finds out about that. Not a fan of her name, but it's done now." Stel stroked her baby's hair. "The family's so excited. First girl in three generations for the Brewer side."

Julia couldn't speak. The baby was a miracle. There had been so many of those in the past few days. "Jul—" she cut herself short. The last thing a new mother needed was to hear about her romance.

"Jul what? Did something happen?" Stel urged her on. "Are you two ...?"

All signs pointed to the start of something big. They'd been dancing around it for months. "I think we're finally getting somewhere."

"Finally." Stel hugged Julia. "We've been waiting on you and him to get together for half the year. We'd almost lost hope. Dar's going to have to eat his words."

The woman was delirious. She had her timing mixed up.

"I'm so happy for you two. You belong together. Like a match made in heaven. And we get to keep you in our lives too."

Julia inhaled, trying to slow her heartbeat.

"Want to hold her?"

"I'm not sure I know how."

"Here." Stel curled the little girl's blankets over her and set her in Julia's arms. "You can do this. You're a natural. Maybe one day, you'll have one of your own."

Davey ran off when he heard the back door close. Jul carried him around the corner a few minutes later then stopped still when he saw her. His smile kicked her heart in high gear.

She had to get to the bottom of things and figure out what Stel was talking about.

✦✦✦

DAR DIDN'T TAKE long and as soon as the family settled, Jul and Julia headed back to the inn.

Jul fiddled with the heat vent and cleared his throat. "I wish you could sit closer. Console's in the way."

"I can still reach you." Julia rested her arm on it, palm up for him to hold.

It felt exactly right.

"Look at everything that's happened in the past twenty-four hours. My aunt and uncle and then today. I can't believe Darvvin delivered his own child."

"That's Dar and Stel for you. That was pretty much the only thing they hadn't done yet. DIY baby delivery." Dar had it all. "And now you have a baby named after you. How did Stel know your middle name was Bella? I didn't even know and I live there."

"She read it on my degree. It's on the wall over my desk."

He'd never noticed it.

"I can't believe that they called her Bella," she whispered. "My dad used to call me Jula-Belle when I was little."

"Jula-Belle," he repeated. "That's a wonderful name." But then her sniffles intensified, and he wished he'd never said anything. Jul held her hand a little tighter.

"I'm going to wake up and this has all been a dream." She tried to giggle. "Last night wasn't a dream, was it? Those moments before my aunt and uncle showed up?"

"No." If Julia had brought it up, it had to be alright. It had to be a direction she wanted to go with him. "Should we sit together for a while when we get home? Unwind?" A little relaxation would go a long way. He had to come clean. He had to move forward. The reality that she could have been out with Shane instead of with him was ever-present in the back of his mind.

"I think we need that, actually. It's been a challenging couple of days. Park in the garage again. It's cold."

They locked the truck away for the night and decided on wine instead of warm chocolate.

"I'm going to bring my things upstairs and text Eddie quickly. I'll be right down."

"It's really exciting for the family, isn't it?"

"What? Oh, the baby. Yes." He wasn't going to text about that at all, but there was no need to correct her.

She swept her hair over her shoulder as she walked away. "I'll get everything ready down here. Don't be long."

Jul took the stairs two at a time. It was too late for any response from Ed, but he wanted to tell his friend about Shane. He dropped his wallet and keys on the side table and took a second to admire their Halloween photo before going back downstairs.

All the lights were off in the main part of the house, but the doors were open to her suite. Again, firelight and coloured bulbs from her tree illuminated the room. The music played low and two glasses rested on a silver tray, each filled halfway with dark red wine.

Julia was coming out of her room. “I was expecting you, and you still surprised me.”

She’d brushed out her hair and left it free. It waved like harvest fields in a gentle breeze. The movement remained even when she stilled a few feet away from him.

Possibility seeded the air around them and carried between them on a song.

“You love this music, don’t you?”

“My parents used to listen to it so I guess it’s engrained in my life for all time. Helps me relax. Helps inspire me.” She closed her eyes. “This one is my favourite, though.” Corcovado played, the same one he’d learned for his birthday. “I used to imagine I was dancing to it on a beach or some seaside terrace whenever I heard it.”

“Used to?”

“Until you changed the words. Now it makes me think of that view from your place at Darvvin’s.” She put her arms over his shoulders. “Dance with me.”

“Trust me, you don’t want to see me dance.”

“I won’t look.”

Jul took a breath. “Of course.” He tried to let himself go.

“Sing those words you changed.” Julia pushed closer into him, mouth as near to his ear as she could reach.

"Sinatra would never forgive me."

Her head fell back when she laughed, the pressure of the moment released. "Let's sing them together."

He rested his chin on her head as they swayed in time. The verse came and their two voices said the new lyrics between breaths. Jul closed his eyes. He could almost believe it would change everything and once he opened them, time would have passed, and they'd belong to each other for real, for keeps. In seconds, it was over. They held onto each other while the intro for the next song took over. He couldn't just tip her back and kiss her. He still had to explain—

"Let's sit. It's been a big couple of days." Her hands slid down his shoulders, and she pulled him to the sofa.

"Julia ..."

"Is everything okay?"

It wasn't okay at all. They were together but things should have been further along, and it was all his fault they weren't.

"I just need—" they sat close. "I don't know."

She tightened her hold on his hand. "It's all good." Julia reached over him to the blanket on the arm of the couch. "Let's get comfortable and then you can tell me everything."

Overwhelm let impulse take over and Jul grasped her around the waist, sliding her onto his knees. She ended up cradled over him, one of his arms around her shoulders, the other over her legs. Julia's eyes opened wide, flickering between his. There was no doubt that he'd taken her completely off guard. "Is this okay? I just need to be close to you."

“I just wasn’t expecting it.“

“I know. It’s all because of me.” He dragged his hand through his hair. “I take all the blame. We shouldn’t be like this. Our lives shouldn’t be like this. We should have been together a long time ago.”

Her features were so soft, so loving. She kissed his hand. “I regret the years I didn’t know you, too. But who’s to say—maybe we needed to go through all our years alone to get to this point?”

“This should have happened months ago.” His entire chest moved when he swallowed. “When I first saw you.”

Her hand smoothed over his cheek and chin. “That wasn’t that long ago. Unless—explain.” Her back tensed up like she was ready to jump, only she couldn’t because his arm was still over her legs. “Stel said something about it taking half the year. I’ve only known you for two months.”

“I saw you at Wildon’s. In June.”

Julia frowned.

“And then around town. Everywhere. Like you were following me or I was following you. But I didn’t know anything about you and you never noticed me.” He looked towards the fire but didn’t see the flames. “I saw you at the Coffee Stop a couple of times, so I started to go there. I thought—I hoped you’d see me and we’d connect.”

Julia’s glossy lips were parted, her eyes wide.

“Then I started working here, but nothing was happening between us. I knew I needed to move in. There was too much pressure—”

“They knew this whole time?” Julia climbed off of him. “Darvvin knew? Stel knew?”

"Yes, but—"

"So Darvvin came to work here and dragged you in and then they moved you in here too? I thought they might be trying to set us up. I didn't realize that you were behind everything." She held her hands to the sides of her face. "I'm such an idiot."

"No." He went to her side, but she wouldn't let him touch her. "I didn't know how to get your attention without getting in front of you. I wanted to be sure that you were who I thought you were—"

"Make sure I'm not like your ex, hey? Was it some kind of screening process I had to pass with your friends before you'd accept me as quality girlfriend material?"

"No. That's not it at all—it's not what it sounds like." She didn't understand. He had to be perfectly clear.

"You know what it sounds like? Like I'm in some talent show, or Miss Julian contest." She rushed behind the couch, "It's like I had to pass the qualifying round before we can go to the next level."

He put his hands on her shoulders and tried to get in her line of sight. "It isn't like that at all. I've always wanted to get to know you. My gut instincts were right from the moment I saw you. It just took me some time to ..."

She pushed him away and went around the couch again. "I thought I'd found friends. I thought I'd found ..." She crushed her lip between her teeth. "I need some time. It's been a long few days and I'm drained. I need some space. Some sleep."

"Julia, no. We need to—"

"Just go. Right now, we both need some time."

Chapter Thirty

JUL MADE IT TO THE top of the stairs in a daze. He went to the wrong suite.

The last few days had been so mixed up that it was hard to believe any of it was real. When he got to his new room, he sat on the bed. His eyes landed on his suitcase.

There hadn't been a chance to empty it after he moved, so it would be easy enough to top it up. He'd left his pyjamas on the end of his bed that morning. He shoved them inside with the rest of his clothes. After a quick sweep of the bathroom counter, he had his toiletries packed up. He jammed his shaving kit along the edge of the case and pushed it shut. The zipper was a struggle—it caught on some clothing that wasn't quite contained within. He gave up the battle briefly to gather the rest of his belongings.

Jul set his guitar and garment bag at the door. There was no reason he couldn't be gone before Julia got up in the morning. She didn't want to talk to him, anyway. "I could leave right now."

Dar and Stel would be surprised to see him, and he would no doubt get a 'talking to', but the Brewers had bigger things to worry about with the newborn. It wouldn't be so bad, in the end. It would just be another new beginning. The year had been so full of them that he was almost used to the uncertainty.

But he couldn't get himself to move.

Jul fell on his knees beside the bed. "Please, help me." God could do anything, but why would He bother for someone as lost as Jul? He punched the mattress and prayed for an answer.

When he opened his eyes, the first thing he saw was his phone.

"Ed." He dialled, but there was no answer. He called again.

"Julian," Ed's dry voice came through the line after the third try. "I got the message, I did. Dar delivered a girl. Mum called me, then Dar called ... then mum again."

"Julia asked me to leave."

"What? What the hell?"

Jul rambled about all that had happened the past two days—about the snowstorm and her aunt and uncle's arrival, and how Shane had asked Julia out. "We were getting close, so close, then it all fell apart. She said she wanted me to leave ... to give her some time."

"You need to give *me* some time, b'y. I'll call you in the morning. Maybe."

"Ed, I need–"

"You need a smack in the head."

✦✦✦

VIOLINS PLAYED ON Julia's speaker, burning her ears like acid. She punched at her phone until it stopped, then cast the device to the edge of the ottoman.

"He left, just like that—walked away without a fight." She paced the room. "Just like everybody else."

The whine in her words was almost worse than the music.

A beep sounded, announcing a new text message. Julia shook her head. "He texted instead of talking to me? What does he want now?"

The message wasn't from Jul. It was from her aunt.

Jul is a wonderful man.

We look forward to getting to know him.

That wasn't going to happen.

She dropped her phone again.

"I need some fresh air."

It was a crisp night, but her wool coat would have to do. The other one was still behind the door in the kitchen. She had no intention of going out there.

"I don't need to see him right now." Or worse—not see him because he wasn't even looking for her.

She fastened the buttons and flipped up the collar. She wasn't going to be long anyway. Only long enough to reset her judgement, to clear her head. "To get some perspective."

Julia slipped on her old runners and stepped into the night.

✦✦✦

JUL HEARD A door close below him.

Julia was leaving.

He held his breath while he watched her go, exhaling once he was sure she was going towards the greenhouse instead of the garage. It didn't make sense, but he tried to ignore her. She wouldn't listen to reason and she could do whatever she wanted. He had no say over anything she did, and that was abundantly clear.

"She thinks you were putting one over on her? Imagine that." Ed mocked him.

"She thinks we all were—me, Dar, Stel." He kicked at the suitcase. "I'm almost packed. I should just go."

"But you 'love her', remember?"

"Don't say it like that." His best friend was ridiculing him.

"You can't even say it. You can't even say you love her after the whole circus you've put her an' yourself through."

It was on the tip of his tongue to say he'd been wrong, to say he liked her but didn't know what love was. The words got lost in his heartache. "I love her with everything I've got."

"Then you're full of shit."

"What?" He needed advice, not a smack in the face. "Calling you was a waste of time—"

"You're a waste of time! You either love her and you're gonna work for it, or this little fantasy of yours is nothin'." Ed grumbled. "Stunned arse—"

"Fantasy? I love—"

"Last time I checked, you don't just pack up and run when hard times hit if you really love someone. So, if you've got your bags packed an' ready to go, you've been lying to yourself an' everyone else this whole time, ya doorknob."

Conviction edged over him.

Ed's rant continued. "Listen to yourself, for god's sakes. Sounds like you didn't give her much to work with, and she still wants you. Even with that other guy poking around."

If only that were true. "Wanted me. Past tense."

"Oh my god, you're a baby." Ed groaned. "Alls I'm saying is to get your head out of your arse for one second and think of what that other guy would do if he was in your boots."

Jul's subconscious instantly provided imagery for the scene. Shane would run after her and pull her close. The air would be thick with aftershave, and he'd declare his undying love. He'd make Julia understand, no matter how long it took. She'd fall into him and press her perfect lips into his neck, his jaw, his mouth—

"Dammit." Jul kicked his suitcase repeatedly. The zipper burst, spilling his clothes all over the floor.

"Yeah, that's exactly what I thought. Get off yer arse, b'y. Make this happen. If it's love, like you say it is, you've got to."

✦✦✦

"THESE SHOES SUCK." They weren't great on a wet sidewalk, never mind the icy yard, but they would have to do. The wind had come up during the day and polished the fresh snow into a shiny, slippery crust. A chill bit at Julia's skin and she pulled her collar higher.

There was no way she could let Jul stay. As she walked over the frozen lumps of grass, she remembered she didn't have to. He was only supposed to live there until the baby was born. Bella had arrived. He could go back to Brewers at any time.

'Bella.'

It was stunning that they'd named their child after her. "Talk about going the extra mile to make a match."

The moon lit her way through the yard, revealing her path one step at a time. She marched towards the greenhouse at the far end of the land. Julia hugged herself against the breeze. No clouds meant cold air, and it surrounded her with a bite. She skidded down a short slope to the main lawn.

"I just have to accept it." Accept everything that had happened and let go of the wish for things that hadn't. "Focus on the good." She was practically an encyclopedia of positive buzzwords. "Without anything to back them up." But that wasn't true. There were good things—reconnection with her aunt and uncle, for one.

"Renos are nearly done. I can probably open earlier than I planned." She'd be lighting a bonfire under Darvvin, now that she knew the truth. Maybe he'd work that much faster since he didn't have to waste so much of his time playing matchmaker.

And there was the new name for the inn to get excited about.

"Jewels." She stopped in her tracks. It was the perfect name, but he'd thought of it. He'd be on her mind every time she read the word.

She dropped her head and turned around. Only two lights glowed from the house—the light in her room and the one in Jul's right above it. He appeared intermittently as he walked back and forth across the window.

Julia huffed and turned back to her original path. "Lots of good to come without him. That party ..."

Even though she'd declined his dinner invitation, Shane Harnes had left the door wide open should she want to get to know him better.

"Maybe I do."

Her heart denied it at once, paralyzing her in the middle of the frozen grass.

"Jul," she sputtered.

Julia shoved her hands deeper into her pockets. The breeze had blown most of the snow into the lilacs and trees on the west side and iced over the rest. Despite the grasses that poked through, there wasn't much grip. Her initial plan to walk a loop of the garden wasn't going to work. Drifts climbed the hedges and even if she had been wearing her boots, she wouldn't have tried to tackle them.

The tears on her face froze faster than she could dry them, and she knew she had to get back inside. There were no answers for her in the frozen yard. As she plotted her return path to the house, she heard a burst behind her—a brushing, then a thud.

Two large animals leaped past, bounding through the snow. They missed colliding with her, leaving only inches to spare.

Julia cried out as her reflexes twisted her away. Her left foot caught on the right, and there was no grip to be had on the slippery surface. She ended up face-first on the ground.

Her chest moved, but her lungs stayed empty. She wheezed until she could take a breath, then pushed herself up as she gulped in any air she could get. Her wrist was sore, and she'd hit her face, but worse than that was the throb in her ankle. She couldn't even flex it.

And she was about as far away as she could be from her door.

It was going to be a long crawl.

JUL RUBBED HIS neck and returned to the window. Deep blue movement caught his eye, and he tracked a pair of deer running towards the house. They lurched to the left, then detoured behind the garage.

"Where is she?" He couldn't see Julia, but there was no way she could have made it back inside in such a short time. He cupped his hand around his eyes at the window and saw a shadow on the ground at the back of the lawn. Julia was facedown in the snow.

"Got to go." He dropped his phone and ran down the stairs. Jul shoved his feet into the first pair of boots he could find and tugged a jacket over his arms as he ran out to her. The mounds of frozen ground slowed him down as he tried to balance. "Julia!"

Her chest shuddered as she sat in the snow.

He slipped when he tried to stop, landing hard on his left hip. "I'm just going to help you up, okay?"

"I can get there myself." Her eyes squeezed shut when she tried to pull her legs under her. A whimper sounded.

"Let me help you up." He got on one knee and reached for her arm, but stopped when she cried out. "Let's try the other side."

"I can do it." She sounded less sure than the first time around. "I ... just a minute. It's sprained."

"I'm sure you can do it by yourself, but we have to get you in where it's warm." Repositioning, he tried to get her onto her left knee. "One more time to get you on your feet. One, two, three." He dragged her up. "Okay?"

"Yes." She sounded weak.

"Use me as your crutch. We'll get there in no time."

She started to shake and Jul struggled to hold her up. They weren't making any ground. The snow was like quicksand.

"We have to get you inside. I'm going to carry you."

"No, I can do it," she said, clenching her teeth.

He'd carried bales heavier than she was, two at a time. Jul grabbed her by the hips. A second later, she was hanging over his shoulder.

JULIA'S WORLD TURNED upside down.

At first, she thought she'd fallen again. When she realized where she was, she lashed out, smacking any part of him she could reach. "Put me down." The anger took an edge off her pain.

"Take a deep breath, we—"

"You can't haul me around like a cardboard box." She pounded her fist into his back.

He staggered but caught himself.

"Put me down, Julian, or I'll—" She slammed her hand into him. "You can't carry me around like this." She emphasized every word with a strike.

"I have to get you to the house." His steps were clumsy. "Trust me."

"Trust you?" she shrieked. "You don't even trust yourself."

He stopped dead still, tightening his hands on her hip and thigh. His chest and shoulders heaved, and the steam from his breath shrouded his head when she looked up. She wondered if he'd drop her—let go of her and leave. Maybe he'd argue, tell her to calm down, deny it.

But he didn't do any of that. Jul slid her off his shoulder and into his arms in one smooth motion, cradling her like a baby. "You're right."

The lights from the house glared over them, and she saw the look in his eyes—the combination of care, concern, and affection ... all covered by a great sorrow. Her heart pulsed. She couldn't deny how he felt about her. Everything became clear, even in the mess of it all, but it was a mess—a total disaster.

Jul dropped his face close to hers. "Just let me help you. Get you safe. Then I'll go."

"I don't want you to go. I just want things to be ..." She hid her face in his coat as he carried her to the house. "I want it to be what I thought it was."

His steps steadied, and Jul made it over the rest of the slippery surface without issue. She knew he wouldn't let her fall. Her soul was sure of it.

In the kitchen, he kicked the stool out of the way and set her on the island. "Your nose." He gathered a handful of tissues and touched them to her face.

It stung.

"This might feel better." Jul dabbed a damp paper towel over her skin.

Bloody snot stained his jacket. "Your coat."

"Shh. It washes. I don't think your nose is broken. It's only a scratch." He knelt to look at it. "Not sure about this ankle, though." He eased the shoe off her foot, then peeled off the sock. "It's swollen already."

"I'm sure it's just a sprain."

"Let's get some ice on it." He hung his coat behind the door. "I'll set you up in your room, bring an ice pack and some ibuprofen."

Julia had her arms up, awaiting his, before she gave it any thought.

He carried her to her room and propped her foot on the ottoman.

"I'll make a doctor's appointment for the morning."

"Unless you want to go now?"

"Let me see what time I can get in." Moments later, she flashed the confirmation screen to him. "See? Nine tomorrow morning. That's not too bad."

He passed over a pair of pills and a glass of water. "It's not too good either. I swear, if it starts to turn black, or a bone pops out, we're going to emergency. If I have to take you kicking and screaming."

"Just like you did in the yard?"

He didn't reply. "I'll be back in a bit with the ice."

Chapter Thirty-One

JULIA WOKE TO A SNORE, but it wasn't hers. Jul had fallen asleep beside her on the sofa.

Her throat was dry. She reached for the water on the tray. The pressure on her foot made her cry out.

Jul stirred. "You okay?"

"Still sore." The heat pulsed up her leg. "And I need some water."

He passed the glass to her. "Do you suddenly want to go to emergency?"

She shook her head, eyes heavy. "No, but going to bed might be a good idea."

"Up we go, then."

"Jul, no—"

"You can't even rest your foot on the floor. How do you think you're going to get to your room?"

She reached over his shoulder and let him pick her up.

He made it all the way to her bedside before she had the nerve to say it. "Unfortunately, I need the bathroom."

He brought her to the ensuite. "Let me know when you're ready."

Julia shut the door hard, hoping he'd have gone up to his room by the time she finished.

He hadn't.

Jul carried her to her bed. "Where are your pyjamas?"

"I keep them under my pillow."

"Good trick." He crossed his arms over his chest. "I'll ah, wait outside your door. Let me know if you need anything."

"I think I'm good now."

"Just in case."

She was still shaking her head when the door closed behind him.

"Mortifying." Julia took a moment to breathe, unsure how she'd navigate undressing. Balancing her toes on the floor, she lifted her hips to slip down her jeans. It had definitely been the wrong day to wear skinnies. They clamped around the good ankle, never mind the one that had blown up like a balloon.

She looked up in disbelief. "Really?"

JUL HEARD HER talking to herself. He rapped on the door. "You okay?"

After a short delay, Julia answered. "Can you come in here?"

She perched on the edge of the bed, exactly where he'd left her, pants down to her ankles with a blanket draped over her hips.

"You can't get them off?"

"No." Her hair had fallen over her face. "I need—"

"It's okay." Jul knelt at her feet. The cuff was pressing into her skin. "I think you'd better take a deep breath. These aren't letting go without a fight." It was a struggle to peel the denim over her swollen ankle. "It's worse than it was. I can't even tell you have bones in here." Her foot was fully inflated.

"I can take you in now. It can't be that busy in the middle of the night."

"You said we'd go if it turned black. It hasn't."

It had turned dark purple, but he decided not to argue. She had fire in her eyes.

Jul reached beside her for her flannel pants. He set them over her feet and supported her as she took hold of the waistband to pull them up. "Can I get you anything?"

"A do-over of the evening?"

If only. He'd do things so differently if he had a second chance. "Here," Jul pulled back the covers, "get some rest."

She lay back cautiously. "The blankets are hurting my foot. Can we—"

"I'll prop them up." He used a pair of throw pillows from the sitting room to keep the comforter off her lower leg. "It's not going to be the best sleep you've ever had, but that should help." He put his hands in his pockets. "Anything else you need besides a doctor and some rest?"

"No. You need some rest too, you know. If you leave my phone close, I can always call—"

"It's too far to run down here if something happens." He glanced through her doorway. "I'll find a spot. Don't worry about me."

She pressed her lips tight for a moment before she spoke again. "The far closet—there's a quilt in there. Can you get it?"

It was neatly folded on a low shelf. He set it over her.

"No, put it on the other side of the bed."

It made no sense, but he did what she asked. "There. All set."

"Now lay down."

He crossed his arms. "That's not going to happen."

"It's not romantic or anything. I just don't want you to be immobilized tomorrow if you try to sleep in the chair."

"I'll be fine."

"Why are you so stubborn? What difference does it make?" She smacked the bed.

Sleeping close was supposed to be different, an occasion reserved for a special situation, a special someone. "She always tried to get me in bed."

Julia leaned on her elbows. "That girl you dated? That was the thing she wanted."

"That was all she wanted. And when she didn't get it from me, she found it somewhere else." He backed towards the door. "You don't need to be special to satisfy that 'want'. Any guy can do it."

"But you didn't."

"No. I always wanted things to be about more than that." He stepped out of the room. "I'll see you in the morning. Call me if you need me."

In the living room, he reshaped a throw pillow. The two-person sofa made him think of a dog bed. If he could figure out how to curl up small enough—

"This is stupid," she cried. "This whole thing is so stupid."

Jul leaned on the doorframe.

"You know that I'm not trying to get you in bed. It's a queen size. Lots of room for both of us. I'll be under the covers on my side. You'll be under the covers on yours. You can't sleep on the couch if that's what you were going to do.

You won't be able to walk tomorrow. And I know you won't leave me to go upstairs."

That was progress. "You don't think I'll leave?"

"No. I don't." She pulled three tissues from the box on the nightstand and wiped her eyes. "It's late. We're tired and we have to get up early. Please, just lay down. Let's forget all this extra garbage and get some sleep."

Jul switched off the living room lamp but left the tree aglow. When he reached the far side of Julia's bed, he took off his belt and loosened his collar. He set his watch on the nightstand and after he cracked his neck, Jul lay down. As his head hit the pillow, he pulled the blanket to his chin.

"There, now get some rest." Julia switched off the light. "Thank you. For everything."

"I'd do anything for you, Julia Matthews."

The bed moved when she sighed. In minutes, her breath was deep and even. The edge of her features appeared, glowing in the Christmas tree lights.

Jul watched her until his eyes wouldn't stay open a second more. He drifted into the haze between slumber and waking and just as sleep came over him, his brain reminded him of something that had been on his schedule for a week.

Julian had his meeting with Dawson the next morning at nine.

✦✦✦

"JUL?"

He had to blink multiple times to believe what he was seeing, then he remembered—he was in her bed. "How are you feeling?"

Julia's voice scratched when she spoke. "I must be better because all I can think about is how I must look like a mess and how bad it is that you can see me like this." She pushed herself up and carefully dropped her legs over the side of the bed. "I guess you've already cleaned up my bloody snot-nose, so there's no illusion of beauty left to maintain." She tried to stand but couldn't. "And I need the bathroom again, which is completely embarrassing. Do you mind helping me?"

"Of course."

She could hop, more or less by the time they reached the ensuite.

"Will you be a bit?" Jul asked. "I'll get cleaned up at the same time."

"Sure. Take your time."

He set her up with her phone on the counter before she shut the door, then waited in her living room. As soon as he heard the shower, he made a call. "Can I speak with Mr. Dawson, please? Julian Ariets calling."

The wait felt like forever before the man's voice boomed on the line. "Calling me an hour before our meeting isn't a good sign."

"A call I wouldn't have had to make if it wasn't serious." He switched ears. "Unfortunately, I've had a ... family emergency. I'm going to have to reschedule."

The line was quiet for so long that he wondered if Dawson had hung up. "You're cancelling?"

"No. I need to meet you later today." He hadn't looked at the file since Friday. "This afternoon will work. Or later this week."

"Listen, Ariets, I've got a contract on my desk with your name on it, waiting for you to put pen to paper. So nine then? Or is your reliability an issue?"

"That's not it, sir. I have something pressing to take care of." He squeezed his hand so tight that his knuckles cracked.

"More pressing than a meeting that's been scheduled for a week? Noted."

The guy didn't get it.

Warm memories from the weekend before flooded Jul's mind. Julia called it right—he was at a crossroads. He had to choose his path carefully.

There was no time to convince Dawson—and Jul realized he didn't want to. "Thank you for meeting with me last week and I'm sorry it won't work out between us after all."

"Excuse me?"

It was the principle of the thing. He had to take a stand for the future he wanted to build. "I won't work with a company that prioritizes business over family."

"Ariets?"

"Good day."

He ended the call with shaking hands.

The shower was still on. Jul wanted to see her, to ground himself in her eyes even though he wasn't sure if things would be okay. But there wasn't time. He picked up his belt and headed to the main part of the house.

"Julian?"

He jolted. Dar's shadow stood between him and the stairs.

His friend walked closer. A grin crept up the left side of his mouth.

"What are you doing here? Why aren't you at home? The baby—"

"Thought I'd just see what was left ... undone." His eyes landed on Jul's open shirt and the belt slung over his shoulder. "I guess it's pretty clear what's goin' on here. I wasn't thinking you'd go this far in a million years, but here you are—"

"It's not like that." His belt whacked his leg when he yanked it down. "Julia—"

"You shouldn't be sleeping around if it's not official, but maybe it doesn't even matter at your age. You're sure taking Eddie's advice to heart."

"It's not that—"

"Had to cut it short for your meeting, eh? Shame—"

"Darvvin would you stop for a minute?" Jul raised his hands. "She has a doctor's appointment." He had to qualify that statement, Dar would really get the wrong idea. "She fell in the yard last night and hurt her ankle. I have to take her this morning. And I really have to go. The appointment's at nine."

"She okay? When's your meeting?"

Jul looked for his watch. He'd forgotten it on her nightstand. "Nine. I just cancelled."

"I can drive her. Or one of the guys."

"No, I mean I backed out of the deal with Dawson." He'd cut ties, burned the bridge down to nothing. "I've got to go."

Dar grabbed his arm. "You quit Dawson? For Julia?"

"It's a family emergency and he wouldn't reschedule. What else was I supposed to do?"

Dar closed his eyes and started to laugh. “God above me. Family emergency.”

“I’ve got everything under control. I’m taking care of her. That’s what you do when you’re—”

“A tenant?” He shook his head. “Call it like it is. If it’s true you didn’t spend the night with her—and I sure haven’t seen any signs you two are gettin’ together—then she’s still just your landlady after all this time. And you gave up your chances with Dawson for nothing.”

“You need to stop right there.” Jul bent his belt in three and clamped it in his hand. “You, of all people, know that she’s always meant more to me than that. From that first day I saw her.”

“You’ve got it bad, my friend, so bad.” Dar smirked. “But I’ll give you this—you’ve definitely succeeded in what you were originally after.”

“And what’s that?”

“You wanted the relationship without having to ask her out, and you did it, b’y. Said you were in love and you didn’t even know her. Most people wouldn’t pass up the perks of love for the work, but congratulations my friend, you’ve done it.”

Jul pushed his finger into Darvvin’s chest. “I love her get it? I love her more than I love breathing. If I get nothing back, if she ignores me for the rest of my life, just seeing her safe and happy is more than worth it.”

Dar’s smile faded. He looked at Jul’s finger, then slowly raised his head.

Jul stared him down and took a jab. “I love her with all my heart.” Then he spun towards Julia’s suite. He needed to see her.

It was true, every word of it. If Darvvin didn’t understand, that was his problem. Julian would tell her—tell her everything. As soon as her appointment was done and he knew she was alright, they’d hash it out.

But as his vision cleared, he saw Julia there, clinging to the door frame.

She’d heard every single word.

IF IT WEREN’T for the clock ticking in the hall, Julia would have thought time had stopped. Her heart certainly had.

Darvvin was wide-eyed but forced a salute. “Good morning. I hear you took a spill in the yard—”

“Darvvin,” she and Jul shouted together.

“Now is not—” Jul started.

Julia finished, “not the time!”

Darvvin eased between them, hands high. “Now, I know a lot has happened in the last few days. I know there’s a lot of … of emotion here—”

Jul pushed past him. “I need to talk to you, Julia. We have to figure things out.”

“I have nothing to say.” She put her hand on the door.

“Then let me explain—”

Darvvin clapped his hands twice. “If everybody would just stay calm here—”

“You’re both something. I can’t believe I fell for any of it.” Julia slammed the door and locked it.

The knob rattled.

"Julia, please let me in. I have to explain."

"I don't want to hear it." But she did—more than anything.

'Love.'

She'd heard Jul say it repeatedly—the most significant statement a person could make.

Too bad he was telling his friend instead of her.

"It's all too much. It's unbelievable," Julia whispered as Jul banged the door behind her. But she had to believe it—she'd seen his love looking back at her too many times to deny it.

His eyes couldn't hide it, even if he tried. Love was there the night before when he carried her inside. She'd seen it on his birthday. It was even there that night she cried on his shoulder. Love infused that first touch of comfort from his arms. It was the secret his eyes tried to tell hers that first day in the café.

Julia pressed her hands on her face. She had to pull herself together. She had an appointment, and she had to get ready. But she also had to get to the bottom of things, once and for all.

He pounded on the wood again. "Just give me ten minutes. Please."

Julia bit the inside of her cheek and opened the door for him. She wished she could have swept ahead and arranged herself on the edge of the couch before he saw her. Her leg was too weak. She could only hobble to get out of his way.

He put his arm around her, supporting her while she walked.

"You're going to get soaked." The towel from her hair had fallen to her shoulders. It seeped onto his shirt.

"It doesn't matter. You need to sit down." He helped her to the sofa.

"Don't tell me what I need to do."

Jul took a seat in the chair.

They both held their breath.

It wasn't a surprise that he had nothing to say. Julia set him free. "I can figure things out on my own. You don't have to help me. You're not obligated to do anything for me." She crossed her arms.

He mirrored her. "Yeah? Well, I'm going to keep helping you. This is what I do, help people. Of all the people in the world I want to help, it's you."

"I'm fine, and you've done enough. More than enough." She gripped her fingers on her lap. "And you can go home now. Bella's here."

He stood. Tears rushed her eyes and she wished she'd never said it. If he walked out of her life, she wasn't sure what she would do.

But he didn't leave. Jul paced between her and the fireplace, one hand rubbing the back of his neck. "You overheard some things ... I have to explain."

She wanted to hear it, but she couldn't stop her mouth for long enough to listen. "You shouldn't have cancelled your meeting. Darvvin's interfering where he shouldn't be, but he's right. It was a poor decision to cancel. Your *landlady* agrees."

His arms slapped to his sides when he stopped. "You're not my landlady. Dar was just being—"

"You have eight minutes left."

Jul closed his eyes. "I'm sorry."

"Sorry?" There was no chance for a power pose while she sat crippled on the couch, but Julia did her best to sit tall. "Usually, declarations of love aren't followed with 'I'm sorry'."

"What?"

"You're sorry that you love me?"

"No." Jul sat beside her. "I'd never be sorry about that. I wish you hadn't heard me say it to Dar. You should have heard it from me to you. There should have been lights, music—"

"That was basically the day before yesterday. You had the chance then. Or when you got Darvvin to introduce us and start your 'girlfriend screening process'. Or when you moved in." She listed his missed opportunities. "Maybe you could have said it to me instead of driving away that first weekend. Or if you'd shown up after we changed on Halloween. Or knocked after your call on the night of your birthday."

His lips moved, but he didn't say a thing. Jul covered his eyes and leaned back.

"I've got to get ready. I'm sure I can figure out another way to get to my appointment." She wriggled to the far end of the sofa.

"It wasn't a screening process. You've got that all wrong."

"Sure it wasn't. You were all in on it."

He moved between her and the door. "You were right when you said I don't trust myself. I don't. I can't believe I got stuck in a situation like I was in with that other girl." His chest moved like Julia's heart ached. "Then I saw you and met you and I had to be sure I didn't mess up again. I should have trusted in you more than I didn't trust myself."

She bit her lip. "You should have."

Jul knelt and took her hands. "I don't know how to do this. If I did, we wouldn't be in this position. Would I do things differently if I had the chance? Absolutely. For one thing, I would have said hello months ago, way before it had to happen at Dar's place."

"Maybe you could have done your own dirty work instead of getting the Brewers to do it for you."

His head dropped.

Julia pulled her hands away and stood. "I've got to get ready." She hobbled towards her bedroom.

"You're the one who called Dar."

Julia paused when she got to her doorway. "Pardon me?"

"You think this is all some grand scheme, but you're forgetting a few key details—like the fact that you were the one who called him." He stepped towards her. "You hired him before you knew me. You let me move in—"

"To help Stel," she raised her voice, "but that was all a setup, too. I knew it from the start."

Jul walked closer. "You knew, but you let me move in?"

"I have to get dressed." She put her hand on the door and planned to close it in his face, but she had to listen when he spoke again.

"I couldn't even function around you at their place. You remember that, right?" He approached her carefully. "I had to get in front of you without an audience. I just wanted you to notice me. That's why I wanted to move in here."

“Notice you?” That was a laugh. “I couldn’t stop thinking about you from the second I saw you at the café.”

His shoulders fell forward when he exhaled. “Then you know exactly how I felt when I saw you in June.”

She wanted that to be true, but—

“On one hand, you’re accusing me of being some kind of master manipulator. On the other, I’m in trouble for not doing this right. All I can say is that I’m sorry. Please forgive me. I want to work this out with you if you’ll have me.”

“I don’t know how we can move forward with everything that’s happened. And everything that hasn’t.” Hindsight was easy for Jul—he was busy defending himself. “There’s so much we’ve missed. Your friends set us up and you move in and openly declare your love for me, but you’ve never even asked me out to dinner.”

Jul’s voice rumbled between them. “But I did.”

Goosebumps sparked over her arms. She bit her lip.

Jul put his arm around her and helped her to the bed. When she was seated, he took her hand. “What if we start fresh?”

“Again?”

“As often as it takes.” He sat beside her. “Hi. Hello. I’m Julian Ariets. I’m scared. I might be a disaster.”

She smoothed her lips one over the other and shook his hand. “I’m Julia Matthews. I’m scared too and I *am* a disaster.”

“No, you’re not. I’ve wanted to get to know you since the first second I saw you.” The blue in his eyes seemed to twinkle. “Would you go out for coffee with me?”

She felt a buzz in her chest, butterflies rushing through like the very first day she saw him. "I would—anywhere but the Coffee Stop."

"Deal." He smiled. "How about dinner? I hear Myrtles is good. We could go one night this weekend."

A dinner date with her dream guy? She couldn't refuse. "Dine-in, right?"

He hugged her and almost laughed. "Dine-in for sure."

She let herself sink into his embrace. "I've wanted to go out with you for a long time."

"Me too."

Julia closed her eyes. It seemed silly to ask, but since they were making plans—"We've been invited to my aunt's for dinner on Sunday ... if you're free."

He kissed her hand. "I'm free."

Free because he'd given up his job. "You shouldn't have cancelled your meeting today. It was too important to miss."

"You are too important to miss. More important than anything. I'm sorry it took so long." His thumbs brushed over the backs of her hands.

It sent all kinds of shivers through her, head to toe.

"I'm sorry about the mess I've made here. Don't blame Dar and Stel. They love you. They were just trying to help."

She believed him. "I love them too."

Jul kissed her hair and whispered in her ear. "Will you try to work this out with me?"

"That's all I've ever wanted." Since the first day she'd seen those eyes, it had been her hope. "You're the answer. You're the answer I didn't even know I needed."

His brows creased, then he seemed to understand. He kissed her hand. “I want to be here. I want to work towards a future ... with you.”

She hugged him close, sharing his comfort and strength.

They rocked together, heart to heart.

“Did you mean what you said to Darvvin? That you love me?” It was unnecessary to ask. She knew he did, but she wanted to hear it.

He looked her straight in the eyes. “I love you, Julia Matthews.”

She tipped close, touching her forehead to his. “I love you, too.”

Jul nuzzled her nose. There was no escape from staring into each other’s eyes, brown against blue. His lips pressed into hers, offering a perfect resting place. She pulled him in and let the wave flow through her. It was like running and taking a giant leap—jumping side by side. They linked together, completing the bond that she’d wanted for months—the connection he said he’d craved for even longer.

“Jul, my jewel.” She let herself fall into his gaze. “Promise me one thing.”

“What? Anything.”

“Promise me we won’t waste any more time.”

Chapter Thirty-Two

"THANKS CAIT." Julia smiled as the assistant manager set down two cans of paint.

"Can I help you out with that? You've got your hands full." The girl looked at the crutches propped against the counter.

"I've got it." Jul swept them up.

They paid and navigated their way out of Wildon's Hardware.

Jul pushed the door open for her. A man was trying to enter at the same time. He paused for a moment, then opened it a little wider. "Hello, Mr. Dawson."

"Ariets," the man grumbled and stepped out of the way to let them pass.

It wouldn't help to glare, but Julia didn't bother to smile. She hopped to the truck while Jul went ahead and opened the door. He helped her in, then set her crutches in the back seat along with their supplies.

"That's the guy who wouldn't reschedule that meeting?"

"That's him. And he's right there," he whispered.

Mr. Dawson was waiting on the driver's side of the truck.

When Jul got to him, the man lifted his head. She couldn't quite hear what they were saying. Jul had his hands on his hips and nodded a couple of times.

To her surprise, they shook hands.

Mr. Dawson walked away and Jul climbed in the truck.

"What was that all about?"

He turned to her and smiled. "I think I just got that contract."

THAT EVENING, AFTER dinner at the Brewer's home, they shared the story.

Jul was still shaking his head. "He apologized and said 'Family's more important than anything'. Then he asked if I'd meet him again and I said I could be there in an hour if he was serious. He still had the contract ready to sign," Jul explained.

"Or he had it printed again real quick." Darvvin laughed.

Jul didn't.

Julia squeezed his hand. "I'm so proud of you."

His smile almost made her feel like there wasn't a soul around them.

Darvvin broke the moment. "So three months working for him? What's happening after? Will you go into business with me? It's a match made in heaven."

"Let's go talk about that in the shop." Jul pushed his chair in.

Darvvin did the same.

Stel cuddled her newborn close. "We're going to visit in the living room. More comfortable there."

"We won't be long." Darvvin paused to kiss Stel and Bella before he left.

Julia held her breath, wondering if Jul would kiss her too. He leaned over, barely pausing before they connected.

“Unca Jul,” Davey cried and covered his eyes.

The big man blushed, touching his fingertips to his lips as he walked away.

It still felt weird—weird because they were with friends. If they’d been alone, it would be another story completely.

Stel grinned while they relocated to the living room. “So things are going well for you two then?”

That was an understatement. “They are.”

“Glad to hear it.” Her friend watched her for a moment. “You want to hold her?”

Julia set Bella on her legs. She stroked the baby’s petal-soft skin. “Sweet baby girl.”

“She’s a good one. We’re lucky to have her.”

“I’m lucky to know her.” Her phone beeped, announcing a text from Amanda. “I sent my cousin a picture of Miss Bella earlier. She says ‘Bella’s an absolute doll’. I’m sure you haven’t heard that before.”

“It’s always nice to hear. We’re blessed.” Stel leaned back. “Blessed with each other and our children. Blessed with our friends that feel like family.”

They did feel like family. Stel felt like a sister.

Julia swallowed. She never should have thought badly of Stel. The Brewers were the finest friends anyone could have and she loved having them in her life. She wouldn’t be with Jul if the couple hadn’t nudged them together. “I’m sorry I doubted your friendship.” Her voice cracked.

Stel put an arm over her shoulders. “Don’t worry. You had a lot going on. We all did. Too bad Jul didn’t spread things out a bit.”

“We did everything, all at once.” It wasn’t only her ankle keeping her off balance. Julia’s world had gone from single to serious in the blink of an eye. “But we’re figuring things out quickly. Figuring out each other. It feels like we’ve known each other for so much longer than we have.” She’d always felt like they were meant to be. “Time is sorting things.”

“It usually does.”

Luke toddled to Julia and reached for her. “Shu-shu.”

The women looked at each other.

“What’s that, my son?” Stel lifted him to her knee. “What did you say?”

“He said that before—the day Bella was born.” Julia took his hand. “I didn’t pick up on it … there was so much going on.”

Luke rubbed his face in Julia’s hair. “Shu-shu.”

“He’s trying to say your name,” Stel squealed. “You’re saying your first word.”

Davey was less impressed. “He said ‘hair’.”

Julia hugged Luke with one arm and Bella with the other. She belonged with Brewers, somehow, and they belonged with her.

And she and Jul belonged to each other.

✦✦✦

WHEN THEY GOT to the workshop, Dar pulled out a seat for himself and one for Jul. He got right to the point. “I know you love the work, especially smashing things, but what do you think about my idea? Partnering up once you’re done with Dawson. You take care of the projects, scheduling—the big-picture stuff. You could still work on-site when we need you. It's right up your alley. We could call it 'Brewer and Ariets', or 'AB Builders' or—"

"I wouldn't mess with your business name. Your reputation is too good to change it." Dawson was a dream fulfilled, but working with his best friend was the chance of a lifetime. "I'm going to say yes."

"We're partners?"

Jul reached for his friend's hand. "Partners."

Their handshake turned into an embrace.

"Look at everything happening for you now. Your company, our company, your love life. It's so good to see you and Julia together. Finally." Dar crossed his arms. "Took you long enough, but I guess it doesn't matter, does it? You've jumped right in."

"She doesn't want to waste any more time."

"Well, she wasn't the one wasting it, was she?" Dar raised his water bottle. "Cheers Jul. Imagine where you two will be this time next year."

The moment felt right. "You wanted me to tell you if there was ever a ring." Jul dug a cranberry velvet box out of his pocket. "You're the first to know, Dar-man."

"What's this?" He lifted the lid. The smile started on the left side of his mouth. "You're gonna do it."

Jul tapped his fingers on the workbench. "I've been wondering something else. Julia's been thinking of getting a resident manager for the inn. If you guys are okay with it, I'd like to live out here with her once we're ..."

"Married? I think that's the word you're looking for." Dar laughed.

His lips twitched into a smile. “Yeah. Somewhere to stay for a while. Just until we get our own place.”

Dar’s bottle thunked on the counter. “Did you see the Lang’s property’s for sale?”

“It’s sold. The deal was finalized this afternoon.”

“How do you know—” Dar lost his words and his chin dropped.

Jul breathed out a laugh. There was no way he could explain it without his voice breaking.

Dar figured it out before he had to. “You two kept that quiet.” He hugged his friend again. “We’re gonna be neighbours.”

“Julia doesn’t know and you can’t tell her. Please. We don’t get possession until February. I thought it would be a good Christmas gift—”

“For your wife.”

Jul nodded. “Don’t say a word to anyone else, either.”

“Who am I gonna tell?”

“Stel … your brother.”

Dar grinned. “I can’t promise I won’t tell Stel, but I swear we won’t tell Julia. And as for my brother, I bet you’ve told him yourself. Can’t believe you were getting relationship advice from him, of all people.”

Ed had helped him more than Dar would ever know. “We can’t waste any more time” He looked at his feet, then the ring, and then at his best friend. “It’s fast, hopefully not too fast. I guess she could always say no.”

Dar’s hands were solid on his shoulders. He put his face close and was as serious as he’d ever been. “She’s going to say yes.”

+++

BEFORE LONG, THE men returned to announce the news of their partnership. There were hugs all around, but the celebration was short-lived. The children were tired, and Stel was, too. Julia and Jul said goodnight.

She was getting pretty good at using the crutches, but it still took a bit of maneuvering to get over the snowy gravel in Dar's yard. Julia took advantage of holding onto Jul as he helped her step by step.

"I'm glad we came out for a visit tonight. It's good to see little Bella and the boys." She'd never forget hearing Luke try to say her name. "It was nice to escape from the inn. There's been too much chatter about Two Jewels today. It has a nice ring to it though, don't you think?"

"I love it." Jul changed direction just before they reached his truck. "I need to do something in the suite before we go. You okay with that?"

She wondered why he hadn't taken care of it when he was out there with Darvvin. "I'll wait here."

"No, you need to ..." he rubbed his neck. "I don't want you to get cold. And I'm sure the view from the patio is pretty tonight, what you can see of it, anyway."

"I can probably crawl up the stairs."

"You could probably just let me help you."

They left the crutches in the truck and Jul helped her climb upstairs. Julia hopped herself over to the patio doors when they entered. For a night only lit by the waning moon, she could still make out some of the landscape. "This is amazing. How can there be so many shades of blue?"

“See those dark mounds along the bushes? Those are deer.”

There had to be half a dozen lying in the snow. “I see them now.”

“It’s chilly in here. I’ll turn on the fire.” His hand seemed to get stuck in his pocket when he went for the switch.

“Are we going to be here long?”

“Long enough.”

Flames cast a golden highlight in the room. It was cozy—nearly romantic. “I still don’t know how you left this place.” She laughed softly. “Well, I guess now I do. Do you think you’d ever want to live out here again someday?”

He’d wandered away and didn’t answer.

“Jul?”

“Hm? What’s that?”

“I asked if you’d ever want to live out here again.”

“I’d love to.” He opened the fridge.

“You didn’t leave anything in there, did you?”

A dry cough came from his throat. “Ketchup. Malt vinegar.” He let the door fall shut. After opening and closing random drawers and cupboards, he pulled out a glass and set it under the tap.

“Has Dar turned on the water again? Remember, he shut it off when you left.”

Julian set the glass to the side and puffed air through his lips. “Right.” He pressed his palms into the counter.

Something was up. “Are you alright?”

JUL PUT HIS hand in his pocket. The velvet box felt larger than life. If he’d already asked her, things would feel so much better. If he already knew the answer was 'yes' and that damn box was empty, he could breathe easy.

As it was, he felt like he was going to pass out.

"Are you alright?" She asked a second time.

"Oh, yeah." What he really needed was a glass of water. There wasn't any in the kitchen, but downstairs in Darvvin's fridge, there was an entire case. One bottle would carry him through. "I'm going to get some water. Do you want one?"

He could see her frown in the low light. "No. I'll be fine until we get home."

"I'll only be a sec." He was going to do it, really he was. A drink and some fresh air would help. If his heart would stop racing and his hands would stop shaking, that would be good, too.

One foot hovered over the top stair. At once, it hit him. If he finished stepping down, it would be that much harder to climb back up. Jul smacked the half wall. "Enough."

The noise made Julia jump. She was bathed in gold from the fire and wore a curious twist on her lips. "Are you done?"

"No. I'm just getting started." If he kept his focus on her, he knew he would make it through. A moment later, Jul held her hands while he lowered himself to one knee. The ring box stuck in his pocket for an instant as he tried to take it out, but she didn't seem to notice. The tears fell all the same. "I know this is fast, but I am completely sure about this. I'm sure about us. I have been since that first day I saw you."

Her eyes were wet with love and tears.

He puffed air through his lips. “I love you.” Surely that had to be harder than his next words. He’d only ever have to say them once. “Julia Matthews, will you please marry me?”

She knelt with him. “Ah, Jul.”

He watched intently as she opened the box. Not a sound came as she ran her fingertip over the marquis-cut diamond. Her face revealed nothing.

“If you don’t like it as an engagement ring, we’ll find another. Or get one made, exactly how you want it. Whatever you like. This can be a placeholder.”

She put her finger to his lips. “It’s spectacular. I love it.” Julia kissed him. “You’d better put it on my finger.” She lifted her left hand.

Relief poured over him. He dropped his arms, carrying the ring with them. “But you didn’t answer my question.”

“Jul!” She laughed wildly. “Of course, I’ll marry you. I do. I will.” She pulled at his arm and then they fell together, him on his back and her over his chest.

“This isn’t how I pictured the moment.”

Julia giggled and cried and tried to hold her hand still.

He almost dropped the diamond on the floor. “My hands are shaking nearly as much as yours are.”

Together, they slid the ring into place. It settled on her finger like it was made exactly for her.

Julia kissed him again. “I love you. So much.” Then she sat up, tilting her hand side to side as the jewel glittered in the fire’s light.

He watched her glitter the same way.

Jul held her close, heart beating in time with hers. “I love you,” he whispered.

Julia scratched her fingers over his chin and looked into his eyes.

Brown eyes met blue, and she kissed him, gently nibbling his bottom lip from side to side.

Epilogue

"PARDON ME," AMANDA SWEPT her hair back and smiled at her parents, "I need to borrow the groom for a moment if you don't mind." She looped her arm in Julian's and started walking.

"Is everything alright?" Jul asked.

She led him to the butler's pantry and nudged him into the dark space without an answer.

Hands slipped into his and pulled him close. "Mr. Ariets, your wife wants you." Julia kissed him.

He breathed out a laugh. "Is that right? I've been wanting her myself."

They stared at each other.

"I love you, Julia."

She kissed his fingers. "That's funny. I was going to say the same thing."

Dar coughed from the entry. He had his hand over his eyes. "You decent? Your car's here. I lost Ed, but everyone else is waiting on you in the hall."

He led the way through the sea of guests to the front door. Jul's parents helped with his jacket. Julia's aunt and uncle draped a fur cape over her beaded gown.

"Congratulations on your new and beautiful life together." Dar took the floor, as he had all night. "God's blessing on you, Jul and Julia Ariets. May your love be a light for all around you and may your lives bless all whose lives you touch."

There were cheers when the bride and groom waved and blew kisses, and then Dar ushered them out the door without further delay. The crowd followed to the verandah, each person trying for a last glimpse as the newlyweds climbed into the silver limousine and drove away.

Dar pulled the head server aside. "Meghan, are you ready?"

"Yes, I'll make the announcement." She stood in the middle of the hall and clapped her hands. "May I have your attention? Evening tea and other refreshments have been served in the dining room. Please, enjoy."

The guests scattered around the house again in search of food, and drink, and conversation.

The celebration had nearly been perfect.

Stel lingered near her husband. "What an amazing day."

"It was a miracle that this worked out if I ever saw one."

"Theirs is a match made in heaven. Just like us." She held his hand. "And now they're off to start their life together."

Dar tipped her back in a dramatic embrace. "Too bad we can't sneak away and start the rest of our life together."

She giggled. "Soon—"

A snivel carried through the hall, a whiny, pathetic noise paired with a low bubble just below it. It was coming from behind the desk.

The couple went to investigate.

They found Eddie slumped on the floor, sobbing sloppily. He tore at his hair. Julia's lace garter was wrapped around his fingers.

“Oh dear, what happened?” Stel crouched by his side.

Dar followed.

“No one. I’ve got no one. I’m alone and she’s on break. I’m goin’ … I’m goin’ home alone and Jul sang that damn song … that goddam song—” his rambling stopped when a shudder wracked his shoulders.

Dar sighed. “One down—”

Stel smoothed her brother-in-law’s hair. “And this one to go.”

✦✦✦

Many Thanks

WRITING WAS THE ANSWER TO a prayer I had. Amen. It truly takes a village to achieve anything in life, a village of people that help you, cheer you on and sometimes remind you of who you've always been. I can't express exactly how much it has meant to have your support, but please know you've all changed my life in a marvellous way.

Thank you so much to Marc, my own romance story. And to our children, thanks for respecting your mother's 'write-y time' and for your energetic encouragement.

Kaylee, thank you for traveling all the way to Newfoundland with me to see where Dar and Stel came from. It was an experience I will cherish forever. Sorry I cried—but not as much as you expected, right?

Diana, you've kept me going through this whole process. Thank you so much for encouraging me, for your advice and expertise.

Sonia, remember when I was talking about the 'winds of change blowing'? I think this is what that was all about. I'll get you that hard copy.

Jen, will you be my agent? I can't think of anyone who would do a better job.

Denise and Lara, thank you for remembering my writing from way back when. Thank you for reading those early drafts and the continued encouragement while I attempted to make it better.

Debbie, thank you for reading the early versions, for being real and offering me fresh perspectives when I was stuck in my zone. I say that like I'm out of my zone, but we both know that's never going to happen.

Patti, we need to burn things again. I've got a stack of early drafts of 'Jewels' just ready for fire pit night. Thank you so much for encouraging me and reviewing the final product.

CB Czech, you helped me believe I wasn't wasting my time and gave me the push to 'get it out there'. Your notes were invaluable. This work exists because you encouraged me.

Eldyka Simpson, thank you for your home birth expertise.

Colin White, I'll never forget your last words to me. I treasure them. Thank you.

Sarah Kades Graham, you appeared in my life exactly when I needed you. You opened doors for me that I didn't even know existed. I am extremely grateful.

Jonas Saul, my writing evolved because of you.

Moira Stelmack and Katie O'Connor, thanks for sharing your expertise, even if you didn't know you were doing it.

Deanna and family, your input added some beautiful layers to this story and to those yet to be finished.

Friends and family, thank you for listening to me, thank you for reading.

You can do anything you set your mind to, but it's better with a village.

Next in the *Juniper Creek Series*–

Golden

Ed's the best man, the best friend and supposedly, the best brother. But if he's really the best, why has everyone only been hearing the worst about him? His lifestyle was unsustainable, and he knows it, but it's hard to keep believing things can be different when no one else is there to believe with you.

And then there's Meghan, recently graduated and determined to land her dream job—manager at Two Jewels Bed and Breakfast. She fell into the opportunity and fell for Ed at the same time. Sure it's her dream, but what holds more weight—landing the perfect job, or finding the love of your life?

Please find me at
www.traceyretallack.com
for more information on upcoming events,
stories, and exclusive content.
I'd love to hear from you!

About the Author

There is a mystique in how a chance encounter can result in lasting love. Tracey Retallack spends way too much of her time pondering that mystery, and channeling her daydreams into works of art and fiction.

When she isn't writing about the lives of people she's invented and the fictional town that they live in, Tracey is an artist and designer. Her most profound and adored creation is her family. She is currently living out her personal romance in Alberta, Canada.

Manufactured by Amazon.ca
Bolton, ON

44017666R00236